Emerge

—⟋—

EVOLVE SERIES, BOOK 1

A NOVEL BY

S.E.HALL

Prologue

LIL' LANEY

I simply cannot hang out with the girls at recess. No one should expect me to, right? At the ripe old age of ten, I've already figured out one should be interested in far more than boys and gossip—the only two things they ever seemed to talk about. Besides, they don't want anything to do with me anymore. Michelle, the loud one, has made it clear that her mother thinks "it's a shame I have no female influence," so surely my dad will completely understand the call from Principal Mills...again.

Principal Mills doesn't really ever get mad at me. He's a lot like my dad, easygoing and a bit of a softie, so it's easy to sit with him in his small, cramped office until Dad gets here. I'm not too concerned about getting in trouble; I never get in any real trouble. I've heard them talk many times after sending me out to the hall. They think I'm "angry and acting out."

They're wrong.

I'm not angry and I don't need their pity. They should pity her. She's the one who gave up. Well, she gave us up, anyway. Who knows what her greener grass was exactly.

Soon enough my dad strides in, casual as always, and all too comfortably takes a seat. He's here at least once a month, after all. They shake hands like they're poker buddies or something. I'm not even sure Dad calls him Principal Mills, or even Mr. Mills, anymore. I think he just calls him Paul. They talk for the first ten minutes about this year's high school hopefuls. This town lives for high school football and baseball, depending on the season. Hopefully they forget my dilemma altogether.

No such luck.

"Wanna tell me what happened, slugger?"

I put on my best puppy dog face. "Daddy, 'member what you said about not starting a fight, but I could damn sure finish one?"

The fine Principal tries to hide a chuckle and my dad reminds me to watch my mouth.

"Well…Andy Collins shoved me first, 'cause he's a sore loser, so…I finished it. I whooped him in Horse and then I whooped him for shoving me." That should clear all this up, right?

"Now, Laney, one shove only warrants one shove back. If I got a call, you musta tore the boy up. Why didn't you just go tell a teacher?"

Is he serious right now? I'm not a snitch.

"Daddy, please. I didn't tear him up that bad…I didn't have to."

"And why is that?" He cocks one eyebrow curiously.

Principal Mills answers for me. "Cause Evan Allen did it for her."

It didn't take long to find Mr. Allen. Turns out the Allen family had recently moved in right down the street. Dad wanted to let the man know that he thought what his son had done was noble and sure hoped Evan wasn't in any trouble. Confirming he wasn't, it'd only seemed right to invite the boy fishing with us.

At least, that's how Dad explains it to me. It doesn't stop me from pouting the whole ride to the pond and trying to ignore the intruder in the back seat with me.

"Thanks for inviting me, Mr. Walker. I love fishing." Sure he does; what a butt kisser.

"My pleasure, Evan, we're happy to have ya along. Aren't we, Laney?"

"Of course, Daddy." I smile sweetly before continuing. "Say, Evan, you know how to bait your own hook, right?" What? I'm genuinely concerned. I don't want to end up doing everything for the kid.

Evan just looks at me from the corner of his eye, not answering.

"Dad, did you bring him a life jacket? We wouldn't want him to fall in and drown if he hooks a big one."

Dad doesn't answer me, either. They both look uncomfortable; I'm not the least bit perturbed. There's more where that came from, boys! I can do this all day and it's well-deserved, as far as I'm concerned. How dare Dad invite this boy into our time together? My time with Dad is sacred. We don't need company.

"Hey, Evan..." I drawl, kicking the smartass act up a notch as we climb out of the truck and grab our gear, "don't get used to this. One rescue, one trip. Got it?"

Dad acts like he doesn't hear me and walks ahead to the water. He thinks his new little hero can hold his own with me. We'll see.

"Rescue, huh? That's what you think that was?"

So... Evan can answer. "Whatever, you know what I mean. I don't care what anyone thinks of me. My dad and I are just fine without them. I don't need new friends any more than I needed saving. I can take care of myself just fine."

"Oh, I could see that, tiger. That's not why I did it."

Tiger? Could he not remember my name? Typical boy. "Why did you then?"

He thinks for a minute, kicking the dirt with his toe, and then shrugs. "I'll let you know as soon as I figure it out."

I never heard what he came up with. Turns out we had plenty of other things to talk about.

Chapter 1

8 YEARS LATER

-Laney-

"Walker, you're up!" Coach Logson yells at me.

Here we go again, hero or zero time. Since it's my senior year, and I've played softball since I can remember, I ought to be used to the pressure, but those familiar butterflies in my stomach start to stir.

Coming off the bench cold in the last inning sucks. It can only lead to disaster or heroism, often making DH the worst position on the team. So, armed with my fifty--fifty chance, I grab my helmet and bat and approach the warm-up circle.

Taking my practice swings, timing with the pitcher, I really should be too focused to hear my father's voice above the crowd and my own thoughts.

"Fall down swinging, slugger!" he shouts in that "ball is life" voice of his.

My dad was an all-star pitcher and hometown hero in his day, so he knows the game inside and out and has a true love and respect of it. He's rarely missed an inning of my many years playing and I'm always pleased when my performance delivers and makes him proud.

More distracting than his voice, however, is the glance I catch of my other fan that never misses a game, Evan.

Evan Allen, my best friend and rock, is sitting on the top bleacher as always, sporting his navy #14 t-shirt that proclaims him a Walker fan. I sneak a longer peek at him out of the corner of my helmet and see that he has his fingers crossed on both hands, left leg twitching up and down. Sometimes I think he gets more nervous for me than I do.

He knows I'm looking, much like I can always sense his gaze upon me, and turns slightly to wink. "You got this," he mouths with a firm nod.

Focused on me, he doesn't notice the pack of she-wolves sauntering up the stands. Giggling and prancing, or whatever it is they do, they take the bleacher in front of him, almost blocking his view. I'm sure my helmet doesn't hide the eye roll I give, but I don't care. I turn my focus back to the game.

Kaitlyn Michaels, our right fielder and pretty much the only female friend I have, pops up and the ball is easily caught, the second out of the inning. It's go time and I step up to the plate. My father again shouts to swing for the fence. He, too, gets annoyed when I get pulled in cold at the end, so he's basically telling me to ignore my sign and swing for it.

My first pitch is outside, and although Coach Dad has always advised me to lay off those, I of course swing…and miss. Banging my bat across the plate, I ready myself for the next pitch. This one comes in low and I lay off; one thing I've always had is a good eye. I take a deep breath. I can do this. Swinging late, I get a piece of the pitcher's third attempt.

"One-two." The ump calls the count…right before I swing again and whiff.

That's the thing about my dad's "no guts no glory"

theory: if you connect, it's gone, you win and you're the MVP. But if you miss…it feels like this.

I had struck out, ending the game in their favor. Being the last out of a game is the worst feeling ever. I'd almost rather not get in the game at all.

After feigning interest in the Coach's post-game speech—not that I don't respect him and my team, but I'm kinda over it right now—I start on my trek to the locker room…only to have Dad step in my path.

"Good swing, kid. You ever get a piece of those outsiders you can't lay off, it'll be gone," he says, scrubbing my head.

I give him a half smile and shoulder shrug. What else can I do? I wonder how many people my dad made feel exactly like this during his time on the mound.

"I'll see ya at home," he says as he walks to his truck.

I make quick business of showering and gathering my stuff, offer a half-hearted "good game" nod to the few teammates still lingering among the lockers, and begin the walk of shame to my truck.

The field lights give the parking lot just enough light for an eerie glow and I see him immediately. I knew he'd be somewhere close by; he always is. Sometimes still surrounded by the wolf pack by the time I'm ready, sometimes right outside the door…but always close by. To this day, I don't take it for granted and it never ceases to amaze me how I feel a unique sense of appreciation every single time.

Tonight he's by himself and has chosen to lean against the hood of my truck. With his arms folded across his chest and one ankle crossed over the other, there really isn't a more comforting sight than my Evan. At just over six feet tall with a lean but solidly muscular build, shaggy brown hair that needs no product to look fixed, crystal blue eyes, and cocky smile, Evan Allen need only breathe to cause a stirring in any girl fortunate enough to cross his path. Throw in his football star status, navy blue letter jacket, and slightly shy demeanor and you've got every high school girl's fantasy.

"Hey," is all I say as I approach him, slinging my bag into the back of my truck.

Yes, I drive a truck, and play softball…not every high school guy's fantasy. Not that I care.

"Hey yourself, bootyful," he says with a smirk, obviously quite proud of the newest addition to his ever-growing list of nicknames for me.

I secretly love it and am never disappointed in what he comes up with, silly boy.

Looking around, I don't see his jacked-up beast of a truck, which is very hard to miss, so I ask him if he needs a ride. He nods and puts out his hand for my keys…as if! "My truck, I'm driving," I tell him, even though it should go without saying.

"Not a chance, woman. You're the worst driver I know, especially when you're mad, and I'd just as soon get home alive. Hand 'em over."

"I'm not mad," I huff, "I'm disappointed in myself…as usual." I mumble the last part.

"Don't talk about my girl that way, and don't make me manhandle you for those keys." He lunges for me, which I narrowly escape.

Smiling now, despite my mood, I concede and hand him the keys. I simply can't resist the charms that are so completely Evan; those flirty blue eyes framed by dark, thick lashes, and his crooked little grin as he spouts off those pet names would test any girl's resolve. Not to mention, and I never will, but I really am a bad driver. Then again, Evan taught me how to drive, and I take satisfaction in knowing I can use that against him if he gets too cocky about my surrender of the keys.

Driving is one thing, but there's no way I'm conceding

control of the radio; he knows music is my escape. I know he's going to try and talk about my epic fail, so hopefully he'll take the hint that it's the last thing I want to do.

I turn my gaze out my window, thinking about the game, about my dad's disappointment, but also about nothing at all, when his willpower finally gives out.

"Wanna talk about it?" he asks sweetly.

I turn to him, roll my eyes, and return my fascination with anything outside my window. The drive to our neighborhood includes a beautiful expanse of land, still untouched by society, nothing but wide open field and dark sky filled with stars. I try to pick out the brightest one, the wishing star, but Evan's husky voice diverts me.

"It's not worth beating yourself up about. It was one at-bat, not the end of the world. And yes, he still loves you."

I hate it when he knows exactly what I'm thinking…or do I?

"Easy for you to say. Every time you walk on the field, you make the whole damn town proud, let alone your dad. And every at-bat I screw up, well, that's exactly what it is: one more screw up. I'll probably have to work through college just to pay them to let me get splinters in my ass." I say it with a little more bark than he deserves, and I feel somewhat guilty, but sometimes I don't think he understands.

His scholarship offers have been rolling in for months; mine haven't. My dad and I live paycheck to paycheck, he can't afford college for me, and I've already been too much of a burden on one parent. A good scholarship is vital to my future.

"Ah, Laney, you're way too hard on yourself."

Maybe he's right, but thankfully we're home, so I don't have to decide right now.

We only live three houses apart, so Evan parks my truck in my driveway and turns in his seat to look at me, pulling a piece of paper out of his back pocket, his blue gaze a new shade of serious. "I thought you were gonna tell me if this didn't stop?" he asks, handing me the note. I don't have to open it really, they're all the same, but I do anyway. This one says: "Great game tonight, Laney. You're amazing."

Who is this freak? Why not just walk up to me and say, "Hey, I like you" or "Hey, wanna grab a burger?" Surely it would be less trouble than sneaking around, leaving creepy notes and presents. Maybe we could have had a normal friendship before it got weird.

At first, I'd just thought it was a cute secret admirer, especially since we were so young when it started, but now we're adults and it's creepy. Evan begs me all the time to tell my dad, but there are some things you just don't tell the single father of an only daughter; he would stage a manhunt. One promise I've always made to Evan, that I will keep, is if there's ever a threatening tone to the notes or a personal encounter, I'll report it immediately.

I sigh, not really wanting to talk about this now. "It's been a while since the last one so there was nothing to tell you. Besides, you found it, not me. I don't suppose you saw anything?"

He just gives me that "really, Laney?" look. Of course he hadn't seen anyone; they'd still be lying in the parking lot, beaten to a pulp, if he had. "All right, well, make sure you stay alert, Laney. I can't always be there and I worry about you."

"I know, Ev, I will."

We climb out of the truck and he grabs my stuff out of the back for me, tossing my keys with a "Heads up!" After we hug, the way we always say goodbye, he heads to his house, walking slowly, of course, always making sure I get inside okay. He calls over his shoulder on the breeze, "Night!" to which I smile and give a small wave, knowing I'll talk to him again at least once before going to sleep.

I'm barely out of the shower when my text dings. I know it's Evan before even looking.

Evan: You okay?

His thoughtfulness sparks a grin despite my slightly dismal mood.

Laney: Of course, always am eventually. Hot shower helped.

Evan: So this wknd, let's do something.

Why he has to clarify this, I'm not sure. I can't remember the last weekend night I didn't spend with Evan, but I'll play along.

Laney: K...?

Evan: I meant let's do something different.

Laney: Like?

Evan: Idk, maybe a nice dinner out?

Laney: Evan, are you asking me on a date?

Of course he's not, Evan and I aren't like that, but I love to tease him.

Evan: Maybe.

Laney: Maybe you should slide me a note tomorrow and I can check the box yes or no.

Evan: Huh?

Laney: Come here please.

I'm leaning out my open window when he saunters up. He's changed into black basketball shorts and a grey t-shirt, no shoes. He runs one hand through his hair as he walks up to me, a sure sign he's nervous. Why?

"Hello again, Mr. Allen. You could have stopped to put

on shoes." I nod to his feet and laugh.

"Nah, I'm good."

"I guess you're wondering why I've called this meeting." I have to really try to keep a serious face, but he's smiling.

"Yes, Ma'am."

"Well, should a young man wish to take a young lady to dinner, he should probably ask her in person. There are certain things still not textably acceptable."

He laughs; I love that sound. He really is the most adorable guy alive. No wonder the girls at school make fools of themselves over him.

"I mean, I know it's not a date date, but still…humor me."

"Laney Jo Walker, I would very much like to take you out for a nice dinner this weekend. I would like to open doors and bring you flowers. You can call it, or not call it, whatever you want."

Hand through hair again; why is he anxious? We've eaten together more times than I can count, and usually whichever of us has money right then pays, so what's the big deal?

He looks past my shoulder. "Sound good?"

"I accept. It sounds very nice." I cock my head to the side, forcing him to meet my eyes, and smile. "But how nice are we talking? You know I'm not wearing a dress, right?"

"The crazy thought never crossed my mind, sunshine. Wear whatever you want."

"K, then I'll see you in the morning. Am I riding with you?"

"Yes, Ma'am." And with that, he winks and walks back to his house.

Despite my clammy, fidgeting hands and perpetual cotton-mouth, dinner is amazing; even better than I expected. Vicenza's is a new Italian restaurant one town over with candlelight, soft music, and all those other "date restaurant" things. It is the nicest place I've ever been to and the food is delicious. I'm always grateful when he gets me to try new things and I can't help but reminisce.

Evan's 11th birthday party was the first time I'd ever ice skated. I only fell on top of him like five times before I got the hang of it, which I counted as a success.

The first time I jumped off the bluff at Miller's Landing, it was because Evan had jumped with me, hand in hand. There has never been an encore and we pinky swore not to tell our parents.

My first tryout for a team my dad didn't coach, in ninth grade, Evan gave me the pep talk to do so. He'd left a Good Luck card in my locker that day and rode with my dad to pick me up after tryouts.

He clears his throat to bring me back to the present. One glance at him tells me he has something big to say. "Laney, I'm signing. I'm going to play ball at UGA." The University of Georgia, our dream.

I jump out of my chair and round the table to hug him. "Congratulations, Evan! I'm so proud of you!"

He pulls me into his lap and kisses my forehead. "Thanks, boo! You heard from them yet?" Sweet Evan, his eyes optimistically hopeful, like perhaps I just forgot to tell him, because he just knows they should have called for me. He believes in me completely.

But I haven't. As of right now, my options look like Tech or Southern. I don't understand; my visit in the fall to the Bulldog campus went great. The coach talked as though he'd been watching me for a while and my showcase for him was spot-on. I'd timed his pitchers instantly and hit their change-ups the first time.

"I haven't," I say with as much cover over the sadness as I can muster. I really want to go to school with Evan. I'd tried for UGA first in hopes of doing just that. Everyone had known forever that UGA would want Evan and we'd planned to go together.

"You will, Laney, I know it." His confidence makes me want to hold out hope, but deep down I'm a realist.

"I'm sure you're right," I agree, smiling at him and moving back to my seat. "Let's just enjoy our night."

The rest of the evening is wonderful, with no more talk of our impending separation. If he's honest with himself, he knows it's coming, as do I, but no amount of misery will change it, so instead we carry on in cheerful denial.

Chapter 2

SOCIALISM

-Laney-

Why is my phone ringing at 8:00 am on a Saturday? I'm the polar opposite of a morning person, which anyone close to me knows, so I ignore it; it's obviously a wrong number. When it immediately rings again, I pull my head out from under my pillow with a grunt and hotly answer.

"Hello?"

"Hey, Walker! Whatcha doin'?"

Has Kaitlyn's voice ever sounded more annoying? "Not sleeping, if that's what you're thinking," I snarl with no attempt to hide the sarcasm.

"Well get up, cause Parker's having a bonfire tonight and we're going!"

Big deal.

Parker Jones has bonfires all the time, none of which I have graced, even though he's one of my good friends. What's the point? I can hang out with the best person in this town, Evan,

17

anytime I want, without drunken, obnoxious onlookers. I yawn loudly, already bored. "Not only am I not going, but I'm guessing it doesn't start at 9:00 am, so why are you calling now?"

"Laney, when was the last time you went out, like out? I'm gonna need all day to get you party presentable, so get up and I'll be there at eleven." Such a girl; good thing she doesn't bat like one.

Every bit as stubborn as Kaitlyn, I reiterate that I'm not going and sincerely doubt she will find Mr. Right in a field full of drunken idiots stumbling around a bonfire.

"It's our senior year, Laney. You have to make it to one social event before your high school career is over. Besides, it'd be unsafe for me to go by myself."

Damn her! This point actually puts a dent in my armor and I inwardly cringe, knowing I'm now committed.

"Fine, I'll go to look out for you, but we leave when I say and I'm driving. Plus, don't even think about showing up here before 6ish. I don't need time to get ready. Really, neither do you, diva. Not only will it be dark, but everyone there will have on beer goggles."

Surely she sees the sense in my reasoning, but she doesn't comment on it, only squealing as I hang up.

Having finished that nightmare of a conversation, I slam the phone on my nightstand and attempt to go back to sleep, but Evan struts into my room about fifteen minutes later, all bright-eyed and bushy-tailed. We really need to review the open door policy…I am a sleeper inner!

"Morning, beautiful. Sweet dreams?" he asks amorously.

With my messy bedhead hidden underneath the pillow, I can't help but peek out to run my covert, lazy gaze over him. Okay, he's forgiven. He can't help it if he's a morning person, ever evidenced by his still damp hair and the fact his baby face is freshly shaven. I can smell his aftershave, a lot like fresh, clean cotton with a hint of musk, from where he leans against my dresser.

I can't let him totally off the hook. "Evannnnnn," I whine, "we are not farmers. Why are you here so early?" I sit up slightly, resting against the headboard and rubbing the sleep from my eyes. My comforter falls down and the draft causes goosebumps to rise along my skin, tightening it. It's not the only thing that tightens and I glance down to my now hard nipples and grimace at the fact that I'm wearing a white sleep tank.

I look up at Evan, blushing what I can only guess is crimson, and realize he's noticed my physical aversion to chilly mornings. He immediately diverts his focus and clears his throat.

"I came to ask if you want to go fishing with me today. It's beautiful out, and Dad says they're bitin' down at Miller's Landing. You in?"

He's still not looking directly at me, but rather taking in the team softball poster on my wall like it's the most interesting thing in the world, even though I've long since pulled the comforter back up under my chin.

"That actually sounds wonderful," I start, his mouth immediately turning up and his eyes beginning to twinkle, "but Kaitlyn called me at obscene o'clock and asked me to go to Parker's shindig tonight."

His mouth actually drops open before he can stop it, his eyes bulging. "You're going to Jones'? You never go to parties!" he says, half-accusatory.

"I didn't say I wanted to go, but she's a good friend and she didn't want to go alone. She played the 'safety in numbers' card," I explain.

I see his lil" smirk and dimples; he really is captivating. Seconds before he finally makes direct eye contact, he says, "Cards, huh? Well, I call. I'll pick you girls up here at eight."

Smug in what he believes is his clever victory, he turns and leaves my room with a little extra cock to his walk. I'm actually thrilled he's taking us because I'm always the most secure when Evan's around, but I dare not burst his bubble.

What have I gotten myself into now? I'm currently being brushed and plucked, courtesy of Kaitlyn, like a pedigreed poodle about to take Best in Show. After a tortuous hour, she's finally decided I'm bonfire worthy and releases me from the cloud of sprays, powders, and other girlie majiggies she so loves.

I have four forms of myself perfected: uniform covered in dirt and sweaty, just woke up with sleep in the corners of my eyes, fished all day ponytail and smelly, and lastly, going to school ready. Tonight, my dark blonde hair hangs just past my shoulders with a slight curl. The neckline on my soft green shirt is a little low and my jeans a little tight, but Kaitlyn conceded to light makeup so I caved on the outfit. Plus, she let me wear my boots! This Laney needs a second opinion and I know the perfect polling subject and exactly where to find him…to the couch I go!

"Dad, how do I look?"

My father does a long, anguished appraisal. "Not much like my slugger, I'd say, but real pretty, honey. Real pretty."

Is he still breathing? That whole throbbing vein in forehead thing can't possibly be good for him.

"Daddy…don't worry. I'll be home before you know it. It's not really my or Evan's thing."

"Well hell, slugger, why didn't you tell me Evan was going before I looked at ya? Have fun then," he says as he turns back to the baseball game on TV, vein in his forehead no longer visible.

I love how he trusts Evan, but not if it's more than he trusts me! Oh well, he's letting me go without a hassle.

Disaster averted, I head back upstairs where Kaitlyn is finishing up her own final touches and grab my phone to let Evan know it looks like we're ready.

Laney: Hey, ready when u r

Evan: Born ready, just walked in.

Chapter 3

EYE OPENER

-Laney-

Evan seems off the whole ride to the party. Kaitlyn is chattering from the backseat and I'm chiming in an "uh huh" here and there and the occasional "oh really," but Evan hasn't spoken.

When I came downstairs, I thought I looked pretty tame, maybe even good. Hell, half his groupies wear more suggestive outfits to school, but the look on his face was one I didn't recognize. Never before tonight did I notice how his Adam's apple bobs when he swallows. And the tugging on his collar is definitely a new move. He seemed to want to say something, like "who are you?", but never did, just guiding me to his truck silently. Was it disgust? Disappointment? I never should've let Kaitlyn dress me.

Second guessing myself, it seems to take forever to reach Parker's. As we pull through the gate, I can see a makeshift hayride up ahead, perfect farm party transportation as many of the vehicles tonight won't make it out to his back pasture. I'm quite familiar with the Jones' farm; our families have been friends since before Parker and I were born. In fact, our fathers used to be fishing partners, so we were raised together. I'm quite comfortable with my actual locale, and thank goodness, since Evan's weird vibe is throwing me off a bit.

Evan lets us out, but not before he breaks his vow of silence to ask me to wait up for him to park. I stay put and wait while Kaitlyn runs ahead to the hayride, jumping in with the other waiting passengers. I glance ahead of her and do a quick inventory…everyone waiting is pretty cool, with the exception of Madison and Michelle. Ugh.

Not only are they captain and co-captain of the cheer team at school, they are also the self-nominated President and Vice President of the Evan Allen Fan Club. I lovingly refer to them as "MM." Not only does it fit their names, but also "Malnourished Morons." I've never told Evan any of their backhanded comments; he seems to see their ugliness fine by himself.

"Laney Jo? No freakin' way!"

Thanks, Parker, for not drawing attention to me.

He runs over, picking me up around the waist and twirling me in a classic Parker bear hug; he's not a small boy. "How's my girl?"

Starting offensive and defensive lineman, Parker is a gentle giant. He's also a great ear and amazing friend; I'm feeling better and better about coming tonight.

"Hey, brother," I say with a kiss on his cheek. "Thought I'd make an appearance."

"I am so pumped you're here! I can't believe it!"

Neither can I, Parker. Neither can I.

"I am sooooo getting you drunk tonight, Laney!" Parker gushes. I secretly know he's all talk. He'd never put me in harm's way, nor would he ever allow anyone else to do so, either.

"Not a chance in hell, Jones. I got her."

There's Evan with that perfect timing again. There was zero chance I was getting drunk tonight, but I'm glad to have the back up. Not to mention, Evan's now spoken twice!

"Damn, Evan, lighten up, dude. Laney needs to have some fun," Parker argues.

Evan says nothing back, he simply puts his hand at the small of my back and leads me to the wagon. I'm not sure what's going on with him tonight, but I hope it ends soon. Evan's very seldom in a bad mood, and I never don't know why, or how to fix it. I'm so getting to the bottom of this.

The wagon takes off, and as we get lower and lower in the valley, I get more anxious for the actual bonfire; I always get cold easily. Sitting beside me, Evan takes off his letter jacket and drapes it around my shoulders. Even more than the warmth, I enjoy the manly scent that is signature Evan and flush. Oh my God, did I just inhale out loud? Judging from Evan's low chuckle, I did. Nice.

More than Evan's weird mood, what is going on with me tonight? I'm at a party, I'm dressed like a Kaitlyn-bot, and now I'm audibly sniffing my best friend's jacket? MM should be handing me a membership application any minute now. I do a count in my head; nope, not premenstrual...

Not a second too soon, we arrive at the back pasture and the ride stops. Evan unloads ahead of me and he turns, putting his arms out, ready to catch me. He gives me a smile that causes my breath to catch and says, "Come on, let's live a lil'."

So I do what any girl who has a gorgeous, all-American boy waiting with his arms out would do...I jump.

This party is actually pretty fun and I like almost everyone here. Kaitlyn has obviously nominated herself the non-designated driver. She's chugging drinks down and flirting with every guy here, including Evan. I'm happy just sitting on my bale by the fire actually giggling a bit at her, when Matt Davis quickly slides in the empty spot Evan left in search of some non-barley based drinks for us.

"Hey, Laney. To what do we owe the honor?" Matt slurs.

"You don't owe me anything, but I'm flattered you consider it an honor," I retort with a snap in my voice. I'm not oblivious to the fact that Matt has always had a "thing" for me, one I do not reciprocate. I've often wondered if he's the culprit behind the creepy notes, but he's had an alibi on too many occurrences.

"You want a drink?"

"No thanks, Matt. How are you getting home tonight?" He's not a completely bad guy and I for sure don't want to see him hurt.

"I don't know. Wanna gimme a ride?"

"I didn't drive tonight."

"That's okay; you can still give me a ride."

Oh, isn't he clever? His drunken innuendo doesn't warrant a response and it's not the right time for Evan to walk up, I assure you. Matt's legs are dangling in the air before I even register it completely, as he's lifted by his shirt collar in one of Evan's huge hands. "You've got five seconds to apologize to the lady," Evan growls.

"Geez, sorry, Laney, I was just kidding," Matt musters insincerely.

I don't tell him it's okay, because it's not, but I do say, "Put him down, Ev. So not worth it."

"You sure, Laney? Your call."

"Yes, I'm sure, Brutus. Put him down and let's take a walk?" I don't have to ask him twice. Matt's flat on his ass and Evan's at my side in a flash. Walking away for a little breather, I latch my arm through his. "What's up with you?" I nudge him.

He shrugs. What's this? Evan never broods. He's my rock, my Mr. Grain of Salt.

"Evan, it was no big deal. Just a drunk comment by a boy scorned. Why are you stressing over it?"

"I can't stand the way he talks to you. Not to mention, he's always staring at you and talking about you; he's obsessed. I don't like it one damn bit. I'm on to him. If I find out he's the one stalking you…" He runs his hand through his hair and blows out a breath. "I'll kill him."

The silence seems to go on forever, but Evan needs a minute to calm down and I don't dare chance saying the wrong thing right now.

"And the first guy brave enough to hit on you, and that's how he goes about it?"

"What does that mean? Brave enough to hit on me?"

"You really have no idea, do you?"

I just stare at him, my expression reminiscent of my "trying to solve quadratic equations" face.

He sighs and casts his eyes down. "Laney, you're that girl. The one guys make up in their head when they put all the best parts together to make one perfect girl. The man who gets you to actually pay attention, well, he'll be the luckiest guy on the planet, and he'll know it. All that, and the fact that you never date, is pretty damn intimidating."

There's a flutter in my chest; does he mean I'm the perfect girl made in his head? Is he intimidated by me?

He moves closer now. I can feel the heat coming off his body. Yes, Evan, find the courage. And then his hand is cupping my cheek and I instinctively lean in to it, a little gasp of air escaping my lips.

I've never imagined this with Evan. It's never occurred to me to even dare hope what he felt for me was more than a protective best friend. Good thing, I would have done the fantasy no justice. His thumb brushes my bottom lip and I realize…I could be swinging a bat, casting a reel, and driving a truck all at the same time, but I'm still 100% woman.

I think I speak out loud. "Are you intimidated, Evan?"

He leans over, touching his forehead to mine as he takes a deep breath. His nose brushes along mine, his whisper on my lips. "Not anymore, I'm done with that, and I'm done not kissing you. All you have to do is say no, precious girl. But please, please…just say yes."

As I whisper "yes," his mouth takes mine. His lips are soft and gentle, sending a sizzle throughout me. His hand glides from my cheek to the hair behind my ear, stroking it slowly, over and over again. He breaks contact to lean back slightly, meeting my eyes, and a whiny protest from the loss escapes me. I'm positive he sees a confusing mixture of happiness, shock, and…lust?

"Again?" he asks me in a low grumble. I leave the question unanswered, putting one hand firmly on the back of his neck, the other over his heart, feeling that hard chest and rapid beat under my palm, and pull him hard against my lips. He groans and steps in so his body is flush against mine as I open to allow him free reign of my mouth. Our tongues tangle together, knowing each other just as Evan and I do.

My mind is racing as quickly as my pulse, but instinct takes over as my hands move all over him. His solid arms, firm shoulders, strong back…tight ass. I can't feel enough of him in this moment and lose myself to the desire consuming me. His sweet murmurs along my neck, jaw, in my ear spur me on, almost to the point of no return, until loud squeals from the party rip through our haze.

All at once, I remember where we are and that anyone could walk up on us. It also shames me that I was careless enough to leave Kaitlyn alone this whole time while I fondle my best friend in a field, so I regretfully pull back. Evan's eyes take a while to slowly open and find mine, but in them I see everything

I need to, overpowering any inkling I might have had about regret or embarrassment. In those blue pools, there's no second guessing—these are not the eyes of my "friend." I know my Evan, and he liked it. I really liked it, beyond my wildest dreams that I never had.

"Come on," I say almost painfully, "we have to get back and check on Kaitlyn."

His shoulders slump and he rolls his eyes, but finally grabs my hand and interlaces our fingers. We've held hands a million times, but never like this. It feels good, I feel secure, but most of all—I start to believe what people have said here and there in recent years...I feel beautiful. Evan tugs on my hand slightly, slowing me up some, and turns me to him. "Laney," he barely whispers, "can you do one thing for me?"

He could say climb Mt. Everest right now and I'd agree. The look on his face is so sexy and now that I know how that mouth feels...wait, what was the question?

"Yesss?" Am I flirting?

"Can we pretend you're really mine, just mine, Evan Mitchell Allen's, at least for tonight?"

I think of the gentle hand on my cheek, the soft then rougher kiss, the protection from Matt, the #14 on his back every week, the Disney movie marathons, and I say, without a doubt in my mind, "With pleasure."

The smile that spreads across his face and the fist pump I doubt he realizes he's just thrown assure me I should feel as good about my answer as I do. At least for tonight... Is that all I want? All he wants? I refuse to overanalyze right now; this is new, overwhelming, and exhilarating...I'm just gonna ride this wave without worrying; there's a first time for everything.

I'm not sure which of us sets the pace for the walk back, but neither speeds it up. Once back, still hand in hand, I immediately notice that Kaitlyn is slow dancing with Matt, so she's definitely way past drunk, or maybe he used a better line on her. Whatever. As long as I can see his hands, I'll let her enjoy herself. Evan nudges me, so I look up.

"Dance with me?" Evan asks with an eyebrow raised and sexy plea in his eyes.

It's "Big Green Tractor" by Jason Aldean in the background; we both love this song. I nod.

Evan sings the song softly in my ear as we dance. He has no idea what a good singer he is, and apparently my body just received the memo tonight as well. All the times we've cruised around together, singing at the top of our lungs, or played iPods while we fished...it did not have this effect on me. Why oh why could this not be the longest song ever written???

When the song ends, Evan guides us to settle in on staggered bales. Evan sits behind me and I lean back between his legs. He's pressed against my back and his hands rest on my shoulders, hanging over slightly. His pinky moves up and down the outside of my arm, lightly, but I feel it.

Oh, do I feel it.

Turning my head to look back at him, I give him a smile. His own reflects back to me as much happiness as I'm feeling. It always feels good being around Evan, but something has shifted and now it feels even better. Consumed by these new stirrings and the cover of the night sky, I'm emboldened. I place my hand on his thigh and pull his leg in until it's tight against me, hearing his sharp intake of breath. His body stiffens for a moment and then relaxes with his exhale.

"How long are we staying?" I ask quietly.

"We can leave whenever you're ready. I'm only here because you are." He tucks my hair behind one ear as he says it and I've never felt more feminine in my life.

"I'll be right back," I say as I get up to go wrangle Kaitlyn home.

I secure a ride for Matt, who again apologizes for his

earlier behavior, probably because he and Kaitlyn think it'd be a great idea for her to ride with them; which I respond to with a laughing "hell no."

Holding Kaitlyn up as we wait for Evan to bring the truck proves to be a challenge and I wonder how I'll get her past my dad. Her rancid breath is really testing the duties of friendship right now…and if she pukes in Evan's truck, Lord help her.

"Laney, did you have fun?!" Kaitlyn shrieks from the backseat when we're finally loaded.

"I actually had one of the best nights of my life. Thanks for making me go," I tell her, casting a sidelong glance at Evan. So worth it; the smile on his face as he reaches for my hand is one I will never forget.

"Me too, beautiful. Me too."

Chapter 4

HIT OR MISS

-Evan-

This is a huge risk, but it's one I'm willing to take. Ever since I finally kissed Laney Jo Walker, fantasy and reality collided, and my two worlds will never be separate again. I've dreamed of kissing her since I was ten years old. I knew I'd never be the same when and if it ever happened. I'm not.

Girls seem to throw themselves at you when you play ball, and temptation has gotten the better of me a time or two, but it's never taken more than a couple days for the comparisons to mount up and my total focus to return to her, even if she's oblivious to how I feel. She's finally coming around and I have to push forward and never let her backtrack.

Now that I know those lips really are as sweet as honey and those hands are small but seeking, I can think of nothing else. And that little noise she makes in her throat when I touch her…my new weakness.

So here I am, sitting at the baseball field, about to ask Laney to prom. She's blown off every dance in history, but I can't think of any better way to end our senior year, our long journey from youth to adult that we made together, than with her in my arms. I've thought long and hard about how to ask her; this plan speaks her language. Her sweet little voice interrupts my thoughts.

"Evan, not to sound ungrateful, but you picked me up from the softball field to surprise me with the baseball field?"

She's so ornery.

"Lovebug, don't say anything until I'm done, okay?"

She says nothing and cocks an eyebrow.

"Prom tickets went on sale today, and I know you hate that kind of thing, but I'd be the luckiest man alive to take you. So…I have a proposition for ya."

Still nothing. I see the wheels turning, though. I was counting on that.

"Now, I know you'd never back down from a bet with me," I say, recalling that a lost bet resulted in her eating a worm when we were eleven, "and I also know you'd never welch on one, so let's leave it up to fate. If I can strike you out, you go to prom with me. You hit off me, I'll drop it."

Still nothing.

And still…

"Okay, I'm done, say something."

"You're on."

Almost all in one motion, she jumps out, grabs her bag, tightens her ponytail, and then heads to the field like a little wildcat. Adorable.

"Okay." She smirks and taps her bat against the plate, popping out her butt further than usual in an attempt to distract me. "Show me whatcha got."

I love when Laney's like this, self-confident and playful, but I'm still gonna strike her ass out. Knowingly, I put the first pitch on the outside of the plate and she reaches, cutting through air; she can't lay off those. She mumbles what I think is "bastard" and I chuckle, reaching down for another ball.

Her bat never leaves her shoulder with the next pitch and I ask her, arms out to my sides, "You gonna swing or stand there and look pretty?"

"That was low. Ball one."

"Ha!" I raise my brows at her. "You think I'm gonna let you call? That was perfect and you know it. Swing the bat, picky pants."

A full count, thanks to her continued one-sided umping, and a clenched jaw later, I see my dreams dwindling before my very eyes. Her dad taught me how to pitch and her how to bat…probably should have thought that one out a little better. As the last pitch leaves my hand, sweat that I refused to wipe now dripping from my hairline, I know she's got it. I've been in tune to her body language for years, and I've watched her go yard as many times as strike out…and as the ball sails by me and out of the park, there's actual pain in my chest.

I start to load everything up as Laney rounds the bases. Oh yeah, there's no way she wouldn't run 'em. I can't even talk as I turn out the field lights and follow her to my truck.

She turns and gives me a grin over her shoulder. "No pouting."

The drive home is dead silent and I ache. None too soon, we're there. Just as I begin to drum up the voice to say goodnight, she turns in her open door and says, in the voice of an angel, "Go with a tie the color of your eyes; it's my favorite."

Ornery.

Chapter 5

BEDFELLOWS

-Laney-

The last few weeks have flown by; softball season ended and I survived dress shopping with Kaitlyn. Things are wonderful with Evan and me. We've always spent every lunch and tons of time together, but lately the hordes of girls at his locker have died down and he walks me to every class, now with his hand on my back or tangled in mine.

Apparently today is another new chapter, because as I'm getting my books out of my locker at the end of the day, I feel his arms slip around my waist. His breath tickles my neck as he leans. "My girl ready for the weekend?"

We appear to do PDAs now and surprisingly, I'm just fine with that, so I turn in his arms, sliding mine around his neck. "Ready when you are."

I blush at my own boldness, but I just can't resist. Evan makes me feel safe to be whoever I want, anytime, and that person is evolving. That inner woman is starting to think that sometimes, if you feel like kissing, you should pucker up like it's your last. Every once in a while, getting whisked away in a moment feels nice; real nice.

"I missed you all day," he growls and I give him a little kiss on the end of his nose.

My fingers slip between his as I pull him to the parking lot; I am so ready to be home.

"I can run by and grab a movie; meetcha at home?" he offers.

"We could go to a movie if you want." Was that just my voice? I hate going to the movies. No one ever laughs or shuts up at the right time, and I'm confident the theater doubles as an underground morgue since I can always see my breath, even if Kaitlyn and Evan swear the temp is fine.

"I'd really like you all to myself tonight. Please?"

Oh Lord, Evan, save the hurt puppy face, you and I both know that I hate the movies. I'm totally down for the "let's reward Laney for making a sacrifice" plan, though, so I wink to let him know he's "won."

"Text me in a bit, and get something we'll both like," I say with an air kiss as I drive away happily.

A bit, as it turns out, is twenty-five minutes. I've just changed into comfy clothes, gray yoga pants and white sports tank, when my phone dings.

Evan: Still ready when I am?

Laney: Always. My house or yours tonight?

No text back. Knock on door.

"I choose here." He beams as I open the door. Decked out in a backwards ball cap, tight blue t-shirt, and gray gym shorts, he is the sexiest, sportiest thing ever. That cocky smile he's wearing as he taps the end of my nose does crazy things to my insides.

"Okay, silly boy, go make sure the movie room has blankets and pillows. I'll bring up popcorn and drinks."

Half an hour later, I'm all but one eye under the covers, curled into his body with my face buried into his chest. I'm pretty sure I'm drawing blood from his arm but I can't help it. Who dreams up this scary crap? Better yet, why does the girl always ignore the creepy old townsman who tells her people died in her new house? Why does she insist on staying home alone and opening every damn door she can find?

I stay huddled under the covers, Evan holding me tightly with one arm around my back and the other on my leg, in a little anti-zombie haven…good stuff. He wouldn't have to do this if he ever picked a comedy or drama, but I'm starting to understand his cinematic ulterior motives. I really have been walking around clueless for years, cause that's how long he's been choosing scary movies.

We haven't really talked about how we went from what we were to what we are now. Much like everything else with us, it just was.

When we start the second movie, sans blood, guts, and the undead, I decide to stretch out, draped all over the couch. Evan makes for the floor to lean back, but I reach down and take his hand. I silently guide him to lie behind me and share the covers. His arm slinks around my waist and I feel him breathing against the back of my neck. In our years of constant companionship, I've lain on a couch with Evan many times before, but not like this.

The next thing I know, I'm being woken up to the light and my dad telling Evan his parents probably want him home.

"Sorry, Mr. Walker, we fell asleep watching the movie." His sleepy voice is yummy.

"I know, bud, I just don't want your parents to worry. Laney, go get in your bed, kiddo."

"Yeah, Dad, let me just walk him out."

At the door, Evan leans in to give me a hug and sweet kiss on my cheek as we say our goodnight. There's no way he could have missed my shiver.

Just as my eyes are closing, I get a text.

Evan: I had a great time tonight, another best

Laney: Really? We've done movie night for years Babe

Babe? Yup, I'm leaving it—send.

Evan: But not with me up against your body, holding u, falling asleep with u

Long delay as I talk myself out of talking myself out of it. I am 18 and it's Evan. I'm finally getting a glimpse of being a girl noticing a boy, and the bravery it suddenly instills in me.

Laney: Can you sneak back out?

Evan: Yes. Why?

Laney: I want to fall asleep with you again.

Evan: Now?

Laney: Now.

Four minutes exactly until his gorgeous face appears at my window.

"Did you lock your door?" he whispers when he's finally through the window and inside my room. "I don't want your dad to kill me!"

"Yes, and I set my phone alarm for seven. You're safe."

"We haven't done this since were like what, thirteen?"

"I loved that cat, Evan! I couldn't possibly have slept alone the night he died!"

"I know, angel, totally understandable."

I hope he doesn't think he hid that patronizing smirk. Truth is, he'd made that night bearable and risked getting in a ton of trouble to comfort me, so I'd finally reward him...right about now seems good.

I scoot to the side of the bed, and in my best seductress move, pull him to me by his belt loop. His gaze never leaves mine; we speak without words. My heart is slamming against the walls of my chest as I run my hands up his chest. He lets me raise his shirt above his head and toss it to the floor. God, he's amazing. His pecs are so well-defined and his abs are lined in a perfect six pack that v down into his waistband.

There's no way this is the same body he's been bringing to family picnics and swims all these years! I mean really, how bad was this damn fog I'd been living in? The thought of running my hands, mouth, and tongue all over him doesn't quite shock me this time. I get more comfortable with my reactions to him every day, but I'm still nervous as hell right now. You're probably supposed to ease yourself from foggy tomboy hermit to jezebel, but I'm ignoring that inner voice right now.

I start to unbuckle his belt, stopping to look up at him and make sure this is okay. He nods slightly and runs a hand down my face. I slide it through the loops, adding it to his shirt. My hands are trembling as his hand joins mine to guide me as I unbutton his pants and pull down his zipper.

The air hisses between his teeth and I feel his body tense, but he helps me move his jeans to the floor, our gazes still locked as he steps out of them. He is now standing before me, lit only by the moonlight through my window, in just his navy boxer briefs. I can clearly see the effect this is having on him, and I have to force myself to hold his gaze rather than let my eyes wander.

I really hope he doesn't think less of me right now, but I can't seem to help myself. He's awakened something in me and I feel a little forward, but yeah...not quite seeing disapproval in his eyes, more the exact opposite, so I'm thinking we're good.

I lie down, folding back the covers, and say, "Hold me,

Evan."

He gently slips under the covers with me, sliding up against my back. I lift my head up and pull up my hair so he can slip one arm under. The other arm goes around my waist and pulls me tighter against him. I don't even try to stifle my satisfied sigh and I feel him twitch against me in response.

"Night, Evan." My voice comes out shaky.

He kisses my hair. "Night, my Laney."

Chapter 6

AMAZED

-Laney-

Prom night is finally here and it's one of those moments it'd be nice to have my mom. My dad is amazing, the best man I know, and I'm sure he'll cry at my wedding if I ever have one, but what I wouldn't give to have her helping me right now.

I wonder where she is at this exact moment? Did she think of events like this that she'd miss before making her departure? I'd feel better knowing she overlooked some things instead of simply not caring. Shaking the thoughts and threatening tears away, I go to assess myself in the full-length mirror. Apparently we have one of those handy.

Upon initial review, I'm actually quite pleased. I clean up nice. I've chosen a light blue gown, just like I told Evan I would. The dress is strapless with a sweetheart neckline, the edges of that lined with the slight twinkle of tiny beads. The corseted waist flares out to a "flirty" skirt, so said the saleslady, and stops just below the knee. The dress tightens around my bottom and has a revealing, low-cut back. Thank you, Coach, for the pushing that enabled my body to actually pull this off. And no, my father has not seen it yet.

The blue compliments my tan skin and blonde hair, which is pulled into a loose twist with a few tendrils left around my ears and embellished with sporadic beaded pins that match the twinkle of my neckline, as do my new stud earrings. The silver glitter heels Kaitlyn loaned me put me at 5'9", no problem with Evan's tall frame, and I've put in plenty of practice sessions to make sure I can walk in them. I've gone with a very light and natural look on the makeup, the only kind I really know how to do, but it's enough that I try not to cry as I imagine my mom behind me, catching my eye in the mirror.

"You're so beautiful, sweetheart," I imagine her saying.

"I get it from you, Mom," I'd respond.

She was beautiful, I remember. Oh, enough of this...tonight will be great.

Walking down, my breath catches with the sight of him. His deep blue gaze slowly comes up to meet mine. I feel dizzy and send up a silent prayer that I don't fall the rest of the way down the stairs.

How do girls go to these dances all the time? I'm a nervous wreck right now.

He looks like Prince Eric, Prince Phillip, and whoever the supposed sexiest man alive is all in one. He's used a little something to tame his hair and it sticks up just so in the front. His dark tux fits him perfectly, showing off his sculpted shoulders and arms. The blue tie not only matches my dress, but makes his eyes absolutely glow.

"Hi," I say softly as I come to stand in front of him.

He leans down to whisper in my ear. "Laney, my love, you are absolutely breathtaking."

I shiver a bit and barely get out a "thank you, handsome.

And thank you for the flowers this morning. I'm sure you'll see to it that I have an amazing night."

He looks at me, confused, and it dawns on me. "You didn't send them, did you?"

He shakes his head slowly, realizing the same moment I do what this means. "Go bring me the card and envelope," he whispers.

He knows not to let my dad hear. He would flip and not let me out of this house. I discreetly grab the card and slip it in the pocket of Evan's tux. I know he'll read it later and let me know if it's any different than all the others; right now we're focused on our night together.

Our moment of tension is short-lived as my father clears his throat behind us. "I thought I'd take a few pictures now."

I'm shocked he'd want photographic evidence he let me wear this dress, about which he hasn't said a word... Good Daddy.

Evan's parents soon wander over, his mom armed with a camera as well. Almost an hour later, when Evan and I have conquered every pose his mother could come up with, including some where Evan's head is actually slumped on my shoulder in frustration, we're finally on our way to Senior Prom.

The gym has been completely transformed, and Evan and I both agree it looks great. Several of our classmates are already dancing amongst blue and white balloons, our school colors, when we arrive, but we opt to find a table. They're covered in navy blue cloths and littered with white rose petals and we choose the one already occupied by Kaitlyn and her date, Matt Davis. Yup.

"Laney, hot mama!" my friend says, Kaitlynese for "you look good," as she stands to hug me.

"You look gorgeous, Kait," I tell her. She does wonders for her hot pink dress, shorter in length than mine and so Kaitlyn.

"You look great, Matt," I turn and tell him, sincerely.

"Thanks, Laney, you too," he says quickly and somewhat awkwardly. "And look at you, pretty boy," he adds, reaching to shake Evan's hand.

"Thanks, man," Evan replies, only just politely. "You look really pretty, Kaitlyn."

Kaitlyn blushes. Only Evan can make a girl as brazen as Kaitlyn blush.

"Thanks, Evan, you look great. Can I have a dance later?" she asks, eyelashes fluttering a mile a minute.

Evan looks over to me and raises his eyebrows in question. I bite my bottom lip to hold in a laugh while I give him a quick nod. I love that my two best friends get along and certainly don't care if they share a dance, but no one better assume I'll dance with Matt during that time. So not happening.

"Of course," Evan smiles at her sweetly, "a dance later would be great."

"Oh, and guess what?" Her high pitched squeal may actually be louder than the music. "We're gonna be college partners!" She holds up her palm to high-five Evan.

Oh damn, that stings a little. Don't cry at your prom, Laney, hold your shit together.

"You got into UGA?" My voice wobbles and my smile is forced as I ask her.

"Hell yes! How 'bout that? Isn't it awesome?"

It is awesome. It's the most awesome thing I can think of happening right now, but it's not happening to me. It's happening to Kaitlyn. And Evan. Together. Without me.

"That's wonderful, Kaitlyn, congratulations." I hug her

quickly; it's all I can give right now.

"Dance with me?" Evan murmurs against my neck from behind.

Grateful for the distraction, I turn and grab his hand.

"Amazed" by Lonestar starts, and I'm not surprised to hear Evan's low, sultry voice singing along in my ear. I have one of my arms around his neck, my other hand held in his and pressed against his chest between our bodies. His strong arm around my back holds me close to him; he's exactly the support I need right now.

"This is your song, Laney. I will always be with you," he whispers in the closing notes.

He just sang to me that he wants to spend the rest of his life with me, that it just keeps getting better. God how I wish it was true, but it's not looking like that's gonna happen.

The song ends too soon, and we walk back to our table hand in hand. Evan pulls out my chair for me and then takes his own.

"You okay?" he leans over and asks softly in my ear. I give him a quick smile and nod, grabbing his hand in mine.

"So are you guys like, officially a couple now or what?" Kaitlyn asks abruptly.

I glance at Evan and the blush that creeps up his cheeks matches my own, I'm sure. He picks up my hand and kisses the back of it gently.

"We're anything Laney wants us to be," he answers, his gaze locked on mine.

Heat sweeps through me, toes to scalp, and I can barely form a thought. Do I want to be a "couple" with Evan? Yes, I do. I guess we've kinda always been, just without the blatant physicality, which clearly sways my vote. So, it would seem I need to establish my exact intentions with him. Do I have to go ask his father first?

With so many after parties and invites, I wasn't sure of our plans as we made our way to the car. His mother had been thoughtful enough to make him take her Camry, sparing me the climb into his truck in my dress. Bless Mrs. Allen, she's always looking out for me.

"Where are we going now?" I ask as we leave the lot.

"Well, I figured we'd run back home and change first. I know your skin's crawling; you've been in a dress for almost three hours." He laughs.

It's nice that he truly knows me. It saves a lot of having to explain myself. He's like the perfect song, all said for me.

I reach over and take his hand, lifting it to softly kiss his knuckles. He looks over at me and flashes one of his signature smiles. I can tell he's happy and the feeling's mutual. I settle our joined hands on my thigh. "Tonight was magical, Evan. Thank you for taking me."

"Ah, Laney, I should be thanking you. Tonight was perfect. You're perfect."

We sit in the driveway for several minutes, just staring into each other's eyes, the fingers of our interlaced hands teasing and stroking. I lean in first, overcome with how he makes me feel, how I feel about him. An inch from his lips I stop, letting his hot, fast breath wash over my face…I love the effect I seem to have on him.

"I'll race you back here," I tease and leap out for my head start.

Chapter 7

THREE LITTLE WORDS

-Evan-

I'm running around like a crazy person, trying to change my clothes and grab all the stuff I packed for tonight. I don't want Laney to beat me back to the car. I want to be waiting to open the door for her.

God, she looked beautiful tonight; I hope I told her enough. I've waited half my life to take my princess to the ball, and it's been perfect. I want tonight to last forever, for everything to be that of her dreams. I just pray she'll love what I have planned.

We're about to start a new and very different chapter of our lives with college, and the same school plan is looking less hopeful every day. So tonight, I want to take her back to the beginning of Laney and Evan, the beginning of us. I want to remind her that we're ingrained in one another and always will be.

I'm taking her fishing.

She beats me back to the car, but since we're changed now, I tell her we'll take my truck, so I do get to open the door for her. "Where are we going?" she asks as she gets settled in her seat.

"You'll see." I wink and close her door, walking around to my side, whistling.

It doesn't take long before she figures out where we're headed; we've driven this route a hundred times.

Climbing out, I say, "Wait for me to come around. We're still in 'I open the door' date mode, woman."

She smiles and stays still, but starts in on me as I open her door. "Evan Mitchell Allen, does your dad know we have his boat out at night?" Her hands are planted firmly on her hips. She's traded the dress in for worn jeans and boots, and her hair's back in a ponytail; gorgeous.

"Yes, Ma'am." I take her hand and lead her down to where the boat is banked, helping her in. "Wait here, I'll run back up and grab our stuff."

I turn back once, taking her in, sitting there sweetly with her hands in her lap, the slight ripples in the moonlight water the backdrop. I speed up my steps, wanting to get back to her.

Once I'm boarded, I turn around and hold out the lifejacket to her. "I wouldn't want you to fall in and drown if you hook a big one." I give her a devious wink.

Her eyes shoot up and she makes to shoot off a smart retort, but then I see the realization take over and her face calms. She's on to me, but says nothing.

"Say, Laney..." I've started slowly trolling us towards our favorite cove and glance over my shoulder, "you do know how to bait your own hook, right?"

She doesn't answer, so I turn all the way around to face her, half-expecting her to smack me, but what I see is unnerving...Laney's got silent tears falling down her cheeks.

I scoot quickly toward her, stopping on my knees in front of her. "What is it, baby girl?" I brush the tears away with

SE Hall

my fingers.

She's barely even whispering. "It's just...you're just..." She stops, more tears falling.

"Tell me."

"This. Us...since...well, since ever. And after this summer, who knows."

I can hardly hear her now, but I'm hanging on every word for dear life.

"I don't know how...I don't want..." And then she looks up, right into my soul, as she finishes. "I don't want to be without you."

I've done it. I know exactly how to reach my girl. I've made her realize what we are, that we have always been together and always should be.

All of the air leaves my lungs in slow relief, years of want and wonder weighing on me gone in an instant. I move slowly up to take her in my arms. "You never have to be without me, Laney, never. All I want is you; all I've ever wanted is you." I cup her face in my hands and take a deep breath. I'm shaking; I've waited so long.

"Laney, I love you."

She lifts her head and looks dreamily into my eyes, a sweet smile pulling at her mouth. "I love you, too, Evan."

It's the best thing I've ever heard and my heart swells in my chest. I love her more than any man has ever loved a woman, I'm sure of it. I've loved her since the first time her little tomboy ass smarted off to me, when she was all dirt and elbows. And now, she's a goddess.

I kiss her then, telling her in it everything I want to say. She opens her mouth and lets me in, brushing her tongue slowly along the length of mine. Her lips are soft and sweet, a taste all her own that I'll crave until my dying day.

When she runs her hands up my arms, into my hair, I

48

growl into her mouth. I can't stop it. God, what this girl does to me; and she doesn't want to be without me!

Best. Night. Ever.

When she pulls back slightly, despite every instinct in my body, I let her. I can't push her; I've already led her into a dark cove on prom night. Good Lord, she's probably wigging out right now! Okay, damage control.

"You ready to head home?" Please say no. Please say no.

"Did you bring a blanket?"

"Yes."

"Hot cocoa?"

"Yes."

"Then I'm good."

God, I love my girl.

Chapter 8

LET'S GET REAL

-Laney-

Evan and I graduated high school side by side, so excited about the future, together, but…well, I guess things really do get more difficult the older you get. College no longer sounds like "the time of my life" anymore. We finally had to face reality. My letter from the University of Georgia didn't come.

I'll be going to Southern, less than an hour from home, but I'll live there in the dorm, which is co-ed and scary as hell. Evan is, of course, headed to Athens, about five hours from home; five hours from me.

The "new adventures" Kait keeps gushing about seem more like huge, cold hands wrapped around my throat. I don't want to be apart from my dad, Evan, or Kaitlyn. I don't want things to change.

Oh, grow up, Laney! Yes, I've resorted to mentally chastising my own pity parties.

"Ladybug, you hear me?"

"Huh?"

"Where you at, pretty girl?"

I completely zoned out and missed everything Evan just said. "Sorry, you know I have to worry about things months before they happen."

"What's got you worried?" he asks, frowning.

"Things to come, change, my dad being all alone…"

I sigh. Should I go on? "I don't want us to grow apart, Evan. I'm going to miss you so much."

And cue the waterworks…again. When did I turn into such a girl? Oh that's right, when he started making me feel like one.

"Oh, please don't cry. It kills me." He wraps his arms around me, pulling me closer to his side. He smells like my Evan, he feels like home. "I don't have to go, Laney. I swear. I'll back out right now. I don't ever want to be the reason you cry, baby." His usual vibrant blue eyes are stormy as he places a tender, lingering kiss upon my lips.

I know he means it, too. He's suggested different plans and beats himself up daily that we won't be together; life sounded perfect when we assumed I'd be going to UGA. He could red shirt at Southern, I could work and just pay to go with him, without ball, maybe walk on next season…we've talked about lots of options, but decided it just didn't make sense to add the strain when classes limit our time together anyway. Not sure there's a lesser evil, but we think we've picked it. I've had to reassure him several times that I'll be safe. Whatever spineless guy has a crush on me here won't stalk me to college, surely.

I breathe his scent in deep, letting it balm my shaky soul, and try to slow my tears. I'll never be the girl who makes him give up his future for me.

"God no, Evan, don't even talk like that. We've been through this, and I shouldn't have brought it up again. You're gonna go and be great, and we'll see each other every chance we get."

I have more to tell him, something I've decided and thought a lot about. If it's plaguing me now, imagine how it will be when he's actually away from me. I refuse to turn into the nagging, insecure, jealous pain in his ass...I'd rather let him fly and remember the girl I am now.

"Evan, let's be real for a sec. I gotta get this out."

He looks at me like he knows I'm about to drop a bomb. Good call.

"Let's not turn into a cliché, let's be open about it. We both know you'll be the hot new football star and girls will throw themselves at you. The temptation will be a constant pressure dragging you down. One night, at a frat party, maybe you'll get too drunk and sleep with one of them. Everyone around you will be getting laid constantly. I don't expect you to be superhuman." I'm being too harsh, I know it, but dammit, I want worst case scenario hashed out. I DO NOT want this to ever be my reality, sneaking up on me like I'm a naïve idiot who lives in Never Never Land. I inhale a slow, calming breath and reach out my shaky hands to embrace his. "You'll regret it and debate whether or not to tell me. I'll find out anyway, blah, blah, blah. I wouldn't forgive it, Evan, and not only would we be over, so would our friendship. Let's just start college as best friends, with no unrealistic commitments or expectations, and see what happens. I'd rather our eyes be open and not hurt each other. That's not who we are; we don't hurt each other."

Evan pulls back from me, jaw clenched tight. I can't quite read his face, but it's obvious I've hurt him. That's exactly what I'm trying to avoid, a huge hurt we could never fix. He opens his mouth, but then snaps it shut, open, closed.

"Evan, I know I'm kinda being a bitch. And yes, I'm assuming the worst of you and putting words in your mouth, or girls in your bed, so to say, but I can't sit back and wait to live out an episode of *Gossip Girl*. It would literally kill me."

I try to move closer to him, but he backs away from me, without a word, and walks away.

"Evan?" my shaky voice squeaks out through the silence.

Nothing; he just keeps walking.

Chapter 9

SPEECHLESS

-Evan-

Did that just happen? Is this real life? Of course it is, only life could pull off such sick irony.

I've worked my whole life to keep my nose clean, get good grades, and push myself to be the best football player I can be. And right when all that hard work starts to pay off, it jeopardizes the only thing in life I've worked harder for...Laney Jo Walker.

Does she honestly believe I'd cheat on her at college? And why would she give me a free pass? Is this so she doesn't have to stay committed to me? Of course it isn't, she's never even kissed another guy! What the hell is she thinking then? Why is she doing this? How do I fix it?

This is because of her mom, it has to be. Laney doesn't trust easily. She doesn't put herself in any position where she sees a chance of real hurt. That's why we're here right now.

I just walked away from her. I never do that, but I

honestly had no idea what to say, or what not to say.

Shouldn't I be pissed that she thinks I'll go all manwhore? When do I ever assume the worst of her? Never.

I have literally never been so absolutely at a loss in my whole life. Clearly it's time to call in back up…so I go find him.

"Dad, can I talk to you?

"Sure son, what's on your mind?"

Turn off the TV, Dad, this is a biggie. "Um, well, it's about Laney, and me, and…damn, Dad, I just don't even know." There we go, got his attention now; TV off.

"Evan, start at the beginning, son, and when you get to the part where you're ready for my advice…stop."

My dad really is the most uncomplicated genius alive.

"Well, Laney thinks that since we'll be at different colleges, we should break up. She thinks I'll be tempted with parties and girls and do something to hurt us forever, so she basically wants to let me off the hook now."

I guess I kinda get it and she's right about the girls. I mean, they're the same way in high school, but I barely even cared when she wasn't mine. There's no way I'll care about any floozies when I finally have her to lose.

"How could she have no faith in me, Dad? I'm not some big player. What do I do?" Come on, Dad, spit out a cure-all, please.

"Geez, son, you set out to stump a man, you really go all out." My dad chuckles, scratching his cheek. "Bottom line is, that sweet lil' Laney is a realist. She was forced to put up a guard. She's got the oldest soul I've seen, always has, and she's brave enough to put all her fears out on the table. Gotta respect the hell outta that, cause a woman who actually tells ya what you're doing wrong, hell, before you've even done it; rare breed there." He laughs a bit, probably because he never has a clue what my mom is mad at him about.

My dad's right, Laney is something very special. I guess I should appreciate the fact that she's being honest with me and telling me how she feels, because it gives me a chance to fix it.

"Son, you know she's right about the girls. You're a good looking young man, a new athlete on campus. They'll be sniffing around you every chance they get. How's she know you'll be able to handle that? Better yet, do you know you'll be able to handle that? You could worry the same thing about her, you know. First time living out from under her dad's roof, first time you guys have been apart, and boys will notice her, son. Maybe you ought to cool off and see where things go? That out of sight out of mind stuff can get tricky."

"Dad, guys notice her now. Girls notice me now. She will never be out of my mind. I want Laney, only Laney."

"Yeah, I know. Now go tell her."

Chapter 10

BACKBURNER

-Laney-

I may be almost nineteen years old and about to start college, but *The Fox and the Hound* is a classic, and this really is therapeutic; anything Disney is, really. I can't even begin to count how many times I've made Evan sit through this movie; basically anytime he'd screwed up and I felt he needed a reminder of friendship. Right now I'm watching to remind myself. Oh, here it comes...

"Copper, you're my best friend."

"And you're mine too, Tod."

"And we'll always be friends forever. Won't we?"

"Yeah, forever."

Wait for it, wait for it...and there's the tears. I can't fight with Evan.

In a few weeks he'll be gone. There's no way I'm spending our dwindling time together fighting. Time right now is precious. He is precious. I'm not too proud to extend the branch first, but I'm snuggly, so a text will have to do.

Laney: Hey Tod

Oh, I know he got it, the text and the reference. Is he really ignoring—

Evan: Hey Copper

Laney: You're my best friend

Evan: And you are mine, and so much more, forever

Laney: Where are you?

Evan: Sitting under your window

Laney: Creeper

Evan: Guilty

Laney: Movie?

Evan: Open up

The window isn't locked and he knows it. He chastises me for it constantly, but I'm actually proud he held out for once and let me come to him. I want things to be okay so badly. I hate fighting with him and feeling insecure, but I couldn't live through him cheating on me. Cheating is more than betrayal. It's letting a selfish, physical need take over with blatant disregard for the other person's feelings, as if they're of no value. If Evan ever treated me with that type of disrespect, it would change us forever. It would hurt way more than this.

Do I want to think of him with another girl? Hell no. But thinking of him not caring if he hurts me, even for the few minutes it takes to get to the goal line hurts much worse. If we're not "together," not only is he not physically cheating, he's not emotionally cheating…the ultimate deal breaker for me.

I scoot over and make room for him, pulling down the covers. "Evan, I don't want to fight with you. I don't want to hurt you. I don't want you to hurt me. Please say we're okay."

I feel him sigh, reaching out his arm so I can snuggle in against him. He's so warm and solid; this is the best spot in the whole world.

"This is all because I broke a promise to you. I've never broken a promise to you and this is why; look at us. I'm supposed to be with you, I said I would be." He looks so sad and broken. "Laneybaby, I'm so sorry I walked away. I just had to make sense of what you said and how it made me feel. All I heard was that you don't trust me, but I realize you were saying that you do trust me, enough to tell me your fears. Maybe you were a little harsh." He smiles slightly, but not a real smile. He props up on one elbow, looking down at me lovingly, desperately. "I get what you're saying, Laney, I do. There'll be girls and parties, but there'll be boys and parties where you are, too. All I can tell you, with all my heart, is that there is only one you. I'd never risk this; us."

God, he's amazing. I know he believes everything he just said, and I know he'd die before he consciously hurt me, but girls can be persuasive and so damn manipulative. Alcohol and college are the matches to their gasoline.

"Not everyone leaves for good, Laney. Not your dad and not me. Life doesn't overwhelm us all. It throws snags, but we'll deal, together, like we always have."

He's right, he's not a runner. Maybe I'm overreacting and imagining the worst.

"You know what, Ev, can we just forget I said anything? We've still got weeks left before it's even an issue, and maybe all the girls there will be really ugly."

He laughs and places a kiss on my forehead. "We'll curb it for now, cause I've got time left to show you I belong to only you. Prepare to be wooed and subdued," he says with my smile, half love and respect of a best friend, the other half love and sultriness of my man and forever; the smile only for me.

"Woman, you went a lil" crazy, so you know I'm picking the movie, right?"

"As long as it's in this room, pick away." Like he'd leave this room right now, surely he's not dying to tell my dad how he missed using the front door. Oh yeah, Evan, you da man. Pick the movie, Mister All Powerful, cause you win.

I don't even ask—he chooses *Robin Hood*. He thinks it's the "manliest" of my collection. I try to hold my eyes open, memorizing how often he breathes, the sound when he blinks, the exact speed he rubs my arm…but soon I am asleep.

Chapter 11

EXPLORATION

-Laney-

Summer is bliss as Evan and I spend every second we can together. We fish a lot, lay out by the lake, and look up at the stars. Our slumber parties are a nightly occurrence. Tonight when he shows up, I have big plans of my own. His text pulls me out of mentally writing *Make Your Move for Dummies*.

Evan: Hey Sugar Bear. Leaving gym, home 2 shower, then b there. Maybe 1 hr.

Laney: Hurry…safely.

Evan: Why, what's up?

Laney: Lil' chilly in this outfit. Need snuggled.

Look at me, all suggestive vixen. I can't very well send him to the University of Orgy without some clue of what he's missing.

My phone starts ringing, "Ho Hey" by The Lumineers. It's our matching ringtone that Evan picked out. It only plays when we call each other.

"Hello?"

"Woman, you can't be telling me stuff like that over text when I've gotta drive to you. You trying to kill me?" He's actually groaning out his words.

Hearing him so worked up sends goosebumps across my skin. "Oh, I'm sorry, my bad. I didn't think of that." Lie. I'm kinda good at this game.

"What are you doing right now? Where's my Laney?" His soft chuckle sends warmth throughout me.

"She's right here, under her covers, all chilly and lonely." That was my best innocently sexy voice, which I didn't even know I possessed.

"I'm hanging up now, baby. I'm gonna run off the road. See you in just a bit."

Oh Lord, now I actually have to face the music. I'm sooo scandalous! 'Bout time!

I jump out of bed and quickly brush my teeth, spray on some body mist, and brush out my hair. I take one last look at my new ensemble: boy-cut pink sleep shorts and a matching cami. I almost put it back at the store, losing my nerve, but I've got a point to make.

"Hey, sleepyhead."

I rub my eyes, waiting for them to readjust to the dim light. I must have dozed off waiting for him, but his sweet, throaty words in my ear, his arms around me, and his body pressed against mine from behind is a welcome wake-up call.

I roll over to look at him, shaggy brown hair still wet from his shower and latent heat in his blue eyes. "Hey, sorry, I fell asleep."

"Don't be sorry, I love sleepy Laney. I missed you." He rubs his nose along mine; I love it when he does that. How will I live without this? No, stop that.

"I missed you, too."

"Mmmm, good. Gimme some sugar."

I smirk and lean in, placing a silky kiss on his lips. He groans, running his long fingers through my hair and sucking my bottom lip eagerly.

"By the way, loving the new pajamas, baby girl." His hands explore timidly, feathering across arms and back, slipping lower with each sweep. "Ah Laney, damn," he grumbles as I pull away and place wet, open-mouthed kisses along his neck.

That voice of his, so sensual, does things to me and I know he feels my nipples harden against his chest. I run my hands under his t-shirt and over his rock hard abs, slowly making my way up his chest. God, he has a nice body. Touching it burns me from the inside out. My hand tugs on the hem of his shirt.

"Off, now," I breathe out.

He moves to pull it off from behind his neck. Such a provocative move. I'll have to work on my girl equivalent. He's looking at me through heavy lids and smoky, carnal eyes; ones I've never seen, but like. I know he's dying to touch me, but would never do so on his own. I have to give him the okay.

"Evan?"

"Hmmm?"

"Touch me."

He sucks in a deep, ragged breath, his nostrils flaring just before the corner of his mouth turns up in a sexy, one-sided grin. It's the most arousing expression I've ever seen and it does crazy things to my lady parts. My thighs clench together. I'm surprised and eager to learn more about our bodies tonight.

"Laney, you'd tell me if someone gave you some weird pill right?"

Oh my God, he thinks I've been roofied? My brows scrunch at his crazy question.

"Kidding! I just…you're just acting different." His expression is confusing. Is he lusting or actually worried I may need my stomach pumped?

"You don't like it?" Oh God, I'm not seductive, I'm silly… I'm not good at this. My cheeks burn and I pull back in embarrassment.

"Oh, I like it." He tugs me back against his chest, my body melting to his whisper along my neck.

"Yeah?"

"Yeah. You're the sexiest girl in the world, Laney."

"Then hush and show me."

His fingers delicately trace my neck, rubbing down to my shoulder, while the other hand grips my hip. His pinky sneaks between my cami and skin, sending a delicious zing of goosebumps in its wake.

"Oh yeah, love the outfit." His kiss grows deeper, devouring my whole mouth. His tongue caresses everywhere before sucking mine, nipping my lip. It's a kiss unlike any we've shared. He moves a strap down and begins to kiss along my shoulder, to my neck, and back again. His other hand has moved under the cami completely and rests right below my breast. The willpower on this boy!

"It's okay, Evan," my voice cracks through my heated panting.

"What's that, baby?" His breath scorches my skin.

"More," I sigh.

He runs his nose along my shoulder and moves his hand up slowly to cup my bare breast. I feel him tremble, so I run one foot up his leg and wrap around his hip, embracing him. We have now officially entered new territory; this is the farthest we've ever gone. Thank God I didn't sprinkle breadcrumbs, cause I never want to find my way back.

Chapter 12

SAVOR

-Evan-

Sweet mother of—I've clearly died and gone to heaven. I've never experienced anything as wonderful in my life as Laney, bare skin, flushed and wanting. Her lil' pink outfit, hard nipples, and sexy whispers are more than any man can take. Her perfect breast in my hand is the hottest thing I've ever touched, and that leg wrapped around me...Lord help me. My sweet lil' Laney is a hot seductress and she's all mine, untouched by anyone but me, ever.

I have to have more or I'm gonna explode, so I move to take her shirt off slowly, giving her time to stop me if she wants. My girl leans up to help and looks at me with those innocent, big brown eyes, a slight blush on her cheeks. She's the most beautiful thing I've ever seen and I love her. I love her so much I can barely breathe. It's like staring at the sun and trying not to turn away.

Leaning down, I brush my lips across one nipple, light pink and perfect, hardened to a tight peak all for me. My touch; I

do this to her. She moves her hands into my hair roughly and pulls my face tighter to her, arching her back, pushing herself further into my mouth. She moans long and soft as I suck on her harder, kneading her other breast with my hand, a perfect fit. Her other leg goes around my hip and she grips tight, bless those softball muscles, and then she starts to grind. My Laney…starts to grind.

Oh God…think of something else…do not lose it and end this now. The heat of her seers through the thin layers of our pajamas as I slowly start to move my hand down along her toned, flat stomach. I feel the quivering, so I pull from her nipple and ask, "You okay, baby? Too much?"

She lays before me, pink cheeked. Her long blonde hair is spread around her; she looks like a dream. Topless, breathing hard with her eyes closed. The sight unnerves me.

"Look at me, Laney."

She slowly opens her eyes and connects with mine.

There she is…

"Tell me what you want."

"Touch me, Evan. Please, now." No sweeter words have ever been spoken.

Give. Me. Strength.

I slide my hand beneath her shorts, kissing her neck, sucking her ear, breathing in her scent. I'm dizzy and physically anguished I'm so hard, but this is about Laney, emerging, just for me.

That first touch, her first touch, all mine. My hand gently slides down beneath her panties, feathering light touches against her untouched treasure.

"Oh God, Evan," she moans and digs her fingers into my hair, kissing me with a desperate need I've never seen from her.

"You're so perfect," I whisper on her lips.

"Mmmmm, we're always perfect together," she purrs.

Damn, my little beginner is good with the pillow talk. I continue with the gentle caresses, slow and savoring, but she tells me with her grip and moans; my lil' tiger wants more. I give it to her and watch in awe as she soon comes apart on my hand. Her breathing calms slowly and she finally opens her eyes, giving me the sweetest smile.

"That was amazing," she hums out lazily.

I've never seen anything more so, and will replay it in my mind for the rest of my life. "Laney, was that your first orgasm?" I know without a doubt it's the first at someone else's hand, but I've often wondered if my girl pleasures herself. I suspect not.

"Yes, and I must say…I'm a fan."

I knew it. I laugh softly, she's so cute. "They get better, baby. I can't wait to show you it all."

"How do you know it all?" she asks me with a slight narrowing of her eyes.

I don't know it all, technically, and I don't want to go into exacts, so I answer evasively, yet honestly. "I don't, but I can't wait to learn with you. I want to give you everything. Every experience I want you to have with me, always."

Truly, I will kill any other man who ever touches her. Laney Jo is mine, forever.

"Me too, babe, you and me," she says, leaning to kiss me softly. "Can I touch you now?"

"Sweetheart, you can do anything you want. And for future reference, you never have to ask."

She laughs out loud and slowly moves her hand below my waistband. The trail of her fingers leaves my skin on fire, and when she runs one fingertip all the way down my cock, I grind my teeth. She pulls down my pants and just stares…and stares.

"Umm, sugar, you okay? Feeling a little exposed."

She blushes and bites her bottom lip. "Sorry, I just, um, it's just…"

I can't help but laugh a little; I know she's never seen one before. "Don't be afraid to tell me what you're thinking, sweet girl."

She takes a deep breath. "It's…beautiful. I mean, I guess, I mean, I think it is… And big. Like, how does…um…"

Oh yeah. Damn, my girl is adorable. She's my innocently curious vixen and I get to share every first with her. I get to be her only. I get to show her exactly what happens and how things feel when a man loves a woman with everything he is.

"Come here, cutie." I pull her in for a kiss, rubbing my hands up and down her arms to relax her. "Laney, I'm fine. Don't worry about me, baby."

"Oh, no you don't, mister! I wanna play, and you're gonna teach me," she says with her stubborn lil' sass. But then she turns sultry and takes my hand with hers down to my aching erection. "Show me what to do, Evan. Show me what you like."

Yes, Ma'am.

Chapter 13

DISTANCE

-Laney-

The rest of the summer flew by in a blissful yet shadowed haze, Evan and I exploring our relationship even as the looming end to it drew near, eventually leaving me alone to settle into Operation: Laney's a Big Girl.

I miss him.

It's only been two weeks, but the texts and calls every day don't begin to fill the void. I need to see him, hold him, smell him… I'm miserable without him.

Our last day together haunts me. In the end, I won the argument, an empty victory: we would not be starting college as a "couple."

"It's nothing but space, Laney," he said, dropping a kiss on my forehead. "It means nothing. I'm still yours. I'll always be yours." Holding me tight, kissing me tenderly, he tried not to tear up.

God, he felt so right against me. Could I just crawl inside

and go with him? How do I possibly meet each day without Evan?

"It's not goodbye, my love, it's just see ya later. Remember that, okay?" His hands held my face, forcing me to look into his beautiful blue eyes; the eyes that twinkle with my smiles and cloud with my frowns. Eyes that have watched over me for so many years.

When I close my eyes at night, our farewell plays on a reel in my mind that I can't escape. We kissed goodbye a hundred times. We held each other with desperation, tears streaming down my face, and finally we headed down our own paths. Just like that, as quickly as our love came out in the open, it crawled back in the shadows; the shortest fairytale ever written.

Also haunting me…the last letter from my "admirer." It was waiting in my lobby mailbox my first day, postmarked Savannah, GA, mailed three days prior. A congratulations card with a personal message: "Good luck at college, Laney Jo! Be as great as I know you are!" I'm trying to remain positive. It was mailed, which means he's not here.

My classes seem good and softball weight training starts next week. The girls on the team I've met so far seem nice, and I'm chalking up my lack of enthusiasm to a new team and new girls. Most days I rely solely on my massive iTunes account and earbuds to offer solace.

My roommate's name is Bennett, and so far she seems like a very cool girl. She reminds me a lot of Kaitlyn, which helps; so far we get along great. Bennett is a drama major and I'm already quite sure it was the perfect choice for her. Everything is "worth talking about" to her, and almost anything, including the wind, a chair, you name it…can elicit "a feeling." She's quickly turning into my saving grace; her flamboyance and whimsical charm often distract me from feeling completely alone.

"What are your plans this weekend, girl?" She's sprawled across her bed, which I have nicknamed Crayon Box because it is the size of one and encompasses every color I know, and some I don't.

"Nothing great. Evan's got speed camp, so I won't be seeing him, yet again. Why, what's up?" I've told her a bit about Evan, as much as I'm willing to tell someone I've known for two weeks.

"Welllll," the drama major drags out for effect, "I think we should do the Hall Crawl Friday night."

"What's the Hall Crawl?" I'm not expecting to even halfway like the answer.

"It's like a meet and greet through the whole dorm. The boys' rooms are open, and they serve snacks, drinks, play music, whatever. All the girls start to their left of their own room, and when they announce over the intercom, you go to the next room till you've made it through the whole dorm!"

"K…couple questions, in order of importance of course. Do we actually have to crawl?"

"No, silly goosehead, that's just a cute name."

Okay, I feel minimally better. "Well, that's a bonus. Do they hand out rape whistles?"

"Laney, all doors have to stay open, and roommates go in pairs. It's a tradition, and they wouldn't still have it if anything had ever happened. You worry too much."

"Are you still gonna do it if I don't?"

"I don't know if I can do it alone. I think it's a rule to go in pairs. But if I can, absolutely."

I knew that was coming, and there's no way I'm letting her to go by herself, nor do I want to be the reason she can't do it… "Okay, Friday night? What time?"

"Starts at seven."

"You owe me big, Bennett." Yup, she's a lot like Kaitlyn.

"Hey," he answers huskily. Hearing his voice settles me. I close my eyes to center on this sense. I need what I can have of him to infiltrate me, to bathe me in comfort.

"Hey, you, whatcha doing?" Getting it out takes effort, my throat is constricted.

"Just leaving practice, gonna swing by and get something to eat. You?"

"Nothing, just missing you. I was thinking today how we've never gone this long without seeing each other before."

"I know, I feel it, too. Soon though, I promise. I'll make it to you soon."

I shudder at the crack in his voice. His pain is my pain. "Maybe I could make it to you?"

"Well, you know I have speed camp this weekend. I mean, I'm done mid-Sunday, but that doesn't allow for the drive. I can't miss class Monday." His sigh breaks my heart even further.

"It's okay, we'll figure out something soon. So, have you seen Kaitlyn around?" I attempt cheerfulness. I know he's as frustrated as I am, so I force a subject change.

"I actually haven't yet. Tell her to text me so we can meet up and say hey."

"Will do, I need to call and catch up with her anyway, maybe invite her down for the weekend. You think she knows how to hall crawl?"

"What the hell is Hall Crawl?"

Oh good, I'm not the only one who didn't know. "Well, before you panic, there's no actual crawling. Apparently it's like open house night, where all the girls follow a pattern and go meet all the guys. They keep their doors open and serve snacks and drinks." It sounds even more pathetic when said out loud.

"And you're doing it?"

"Looks like it. I don't want Bennett to do it alone, which she will if I refuse. Anyway, they've been doing it for years, so I guess it will be okay."

"I don't like it, Laney. The thought of you going to visit every guy's room in the dorm doesn't give me the warm fuzzies." He sounds mad.

"Okay, why exactly do you feel that way? I've already thought about the danger aspect. The resident advisors are in the building." I understand his concern—I had it initially—but it's been covered.

"It's not just that, shortcake. I don't know. I just don't want you in other guys' rooms. Would you like me in other girls' rooms?"

No, no, I would not, but I choose not to think about things I can't control. It's just easier that way.

"Ev, it's like an open house, a planned event. It's not me just going to a specific dude's room just because."

Am I rationalizing right now? This damn crawl brawl or whatever is not worth fighting with him about. I couldn't care less about it, but I care about our boundaries. This is exactly why dating whole colleges apart wouldn't have worked.

"Laney, I don't want to fight. I'm tired, I'm hungry, and I miss you so bad. Maybe I'm being crazy. Let me think and I'll call you back."

"Okay."

I need an objective opinion on this, but my options are few. I can't ask Kaitlyn, she could never be objective about a "meet guys" situation. I can't ask Bennett, she wants a partner in crime, and if I ask my dad, he'll be here packing my stuff within the hour.

Any chance this answer will come up on a Google search? Maybe I could ask Jeeves? Siri? That chick knows everything.

After about an hour of miserably self-analyzing, "Ho Hey" saves me. He's calling me back.

"Evan." It's more an exhale than a word.

"I'm sorry, precious girl. Forgive me?"

"Nothing to forgive. I understand you're looking out for me. I'm not gonna go."

"No, Laney, go. I was being jealous and dumb. I don't get to do that, I know. Get out and meet some people." The silence stretches on for what seems like minutes. His heavy breath comes across the line, the torture audible. "It's great of you to look out for your roommate. I broke my promise to you. I'm not with you. I can't expect you to sit and do nothing all the time."

"You didn't break a promise, Evan. You are where I am, all the time. Every song, every thought, every day...you're here." The agony in my voice impossible to hide. "Did you know this would be so hard?"

"Not even close; I couldn't have imagined. God, this sucks. I miss you so damn bad I ache, Laney." He chokes up a bit. "But you need to get out and live. Go to the crawl. I'm so proud of you, taking on the world."

"Thank you for calling me back and for always having my back. You're so easy to fight with." I laugh softly. "I'll sleep on it and see."

He sighs. We both do that a lot lately. "Did I mention how much I miss you?"

"Me too, every minute. I'd kill for a Disney marathon in your arms right now." I can't help tearing up a little.

"We could fall asleep watching one together. I packed mine for when you visit." His laugh is fake. "What's your heart desire tonight, princess?"

"You, here with me."

"Awww, baby. Damn. You're killing me."

"I'm sorry, I know, I know, just slipped out. Okay, I pick *The Lion King*, sound good?"

"Sounds great," he mumbles, trying to hide his sigh. And that's what we did; we did us.

When I wake up the next morning, my call had ended but there was a text waiting.

Evan: Good night and sweet dreams my love, near or far I love falling asleep with you.

Chapter 14

GOTTA CRAWL BEFORE YA WALK

-Laney-

Classes weren't too brutal today and practice was short and sweet. Dragging myself into my room, I throw everything at the end of my bed and crash into it face first. I thought I was still undecided on the whole Hall Crawl thing; I should've known my mind was made up for me. Bennett's enthusiasm can barely be contained in our room and she makes me miss Kaitlyn. I've got to call her soon. We haven't talked since school started.

"Get up, girly swirly, we have to get ready! Are you excited? I'm so excited! What a creative way to bring people together!"

Oh God, Bennett is so close to being an obnoxious socialite, but then she throws in the "deeper" meaning at the end. Love her, though, already.

I grumble into the bathroom to shower as she puts her beautiful dark red mane into foam rollers. Amazingly, I've adapted to being in the bathroom at the same time as her. Good thing, or else I'd never get to use it.

"You gonna let me make you up tonight, Laney?"

"No. I don't need to impress anybody. I'm warnin' ya, B, this is gonna be very low key for me. Oh! I almost forgot, I wanna come up with a word or sign so that if either of us is uncomfortable, it means we're getting the hell out of Dodge."

"Laney, my personal bodyguard." She giggles. "You think of everything! Okay, so how about if we say, 'these shoes are killing me, I have to go change.' Or we could sneeze three times in a row?"

"Um, I'm not sure I know how to fake sneeze and I'm wearing flip flops, but sure, sounds good. Will you hand me a towel?"

She tosses me one and urges me to hurry. We have like, two hours, and she's about to learn firsthand that it doesn't take me that long to get ready. In fact, I throw on jeans, a nice top, and flip flops, dry and straighten my hair, add a little bit of mascara and lip gloss and voila! I'm ready, so I have time to call Kaitlyn.

We talk for a bit, catch each other up about our classes and our teams, but something's off. It just doesn't feel like talking to the same Kaitlyn. What a difference a few weeks have made.

"So, do you ever see Evan?"

"Ya, I saw him at a party the other night. He said we should hang, but we've both been busy lately. What about you, have you seen him?"

"No, not in weeks now." I don't add how much it feels like I've lost one of my limbs.

"Ohhh, Laney, you okay? Maybe he and I could do a road trip to you."

"Yeah, let's plan it soon. I mean, college is supposed to be awesome, right? I'm so not feeling that way."

Bennett walks in the room looking glamorous; she really

can't help it. Her little green dress accentuates her perfect figure (I'm guessing size two), auburn locks, and green eyes. She's one of the most naturally beautiful girls I've ever seen. She's real life Ariel.

"You ready?" she mouths.

"Listen, Kait, I gotta go to some open dorm crawling thing. I'll talk to you soon, okay?"

"I thought you said college wasn't awesome? That sounds pretty awesome." She laughs. "Have some fun for me!"

"Love you, Kait, talk soon." I feel a little jealous as I hang up; she sounded happy and excited about life. I sounded like a depressive flop. She could literally go search Evan out and be near him in ten minutes if she tried hard enough. I haven't been close to him in what seems like forever.

Bennett looks ready to crawl out of her skin, hands on hips and top tapping, so I paste on a smile.

"Yup—let's go," I choke out, forcing my feet to move.

We head down to the student lobby to get checked in and some Elle Woods wannabe slaps a nametag on my chest. "Um, you spelled my name wrong. It's L-a-n-e-y."

"Oh well, close enough!" she chirps back at me.

Yeah, she's really good at her job. Meet and greet people with the wrong name?

"Come on, Laney." Bennett laughs and speaks too loudly as she pulls me along. "Let's have some f-u-n."

Couldn't have come up with a better one myself.

The first room is occupied by Dumb and Dumber. I'm not a fan of the movie, either. They offer us beers and their snack is cheese in a can, no crackers. I sneeze like, five times in a row and pull Bennett out; I have absolutely no tolerance tonight. As we walk down the hall, reviewing those ten minutes we're never getting back, the RA announces it's "switch" time. Way ahead of ya!

Room two belongs to what's-his-name, a soccer player, and his roommate, who simply gives us a "sup" head nod. They, too, serve beer and no snack. Not that I'm hungry or thirsty, or even trying to feign interest in this whole extravaganza, but were the boys not told to even try? For God's sake—if you know the parade starts tonight, at least kick your streaked underwear under the bed and switch the trash! How 90% of girls my age aren't virgins is beyond me. The thought makes me miss perfect Evan, so I walk just outside the door, still with Bennett in view, and text him.

Laney: As if you didn't b4, you're looking even more like a Prince now

Evan: Why is that?

Laney: 2 rooms into this and I've been offered cheese in a can and spotted streaked underwear. You should be outside of your mind with jealousy.

Evan: Lol. So basically I'm a God, you finally realize it and r now ruined for all other men?

Laney: That was already the case b4 tonight.

Evan: I love it when you say things like that. I miss you.

Laney: Miss you too. Gotta go to hell #3, ttyl.

The RA again announces switch. Putting my phone away, Bennett appears and we head off down the yellow brick road. It won't even slightly surprise me if the next two are representing the Lollipop Guild.

Try three isn't a complete loss. Zach and Drew actually remind me a bit of Parker and Matt back home. Zach is a big, football-playing junior who seems nice enough. If I had to put money on it, I'd say he's 6'4" and 240, but his size isn't intimidating, the big brother vibe oozes off him. Drew is a huge flirt, but you can tell he's harmless.

They have wine coolers "for the ladies" and a sweet but pathetic attempt at a spread of finger foods. I take a seat to talk with Zach comfortably; it's like talking to Parker. He's quite funny and even finds a marker and fixes my nametag when I tell him that story.

"Hey, blondie," Drew says from the couch, where he's sitting with Bennett, "what's your story?"

So many options on what to do with this... "What, you mean besides the color of my hair? I mean, what more is there really?" I bat my eyelashes at him, cocking one shoulder up to my chin.

"Ya, like you got a boyfriend? Where you from? Whatever."

"Um, actually, Bennett, my shoes are killing me. Let's go so I can change them."

"Smooth, uncomfortable flip flops?" Zach smirks, his green eyes teasing me.

I look at him quizzically—he's on to my BS excuse to leave.

"I have sisters." He flashes me a beautiful smile, straight white teeth and a dimple. "It was very cool meeting you Laney with an e-y. Nice to meet you, too, Bennett. You girls have a nice night."

Zach doesn't seem bad at all. I could see being friends with him.

I'm past ready to "crawl" back to my bed with book, but B keeps begging me into another room, and another one. Bennett, of course, is enthralled with everyone she meets. "It's about meeting new people, Laney, everyone is different and special." I secretly think she's just looking for material for her poems.

Next up, Room 114.

"Hello, ladies, come on in, please."

We're greeted by a guy who even I notice is attractive, which doesn't even come close to what Bennett thinks, judging from her absolute and very uncharacteristic silence. I mean yeah, he's got a preppy-meets-Adam Levine vibe going, but we're not making me the spokesperson for damn sure.

Plan B. I guess we are. Bennett is literally a statue. "Hi, I'm Laney, and this Chatty Cathy is my roommate, Bennett." I shake his hand and then drag B in further.

"Nice to meet you both. I'm Tate Kendrick, and those two in front of *Call of Duty* are Sawyer, my roommate, and Dane, my little brother." His voice drops to a whisper, "the blonde is Whitley, the shadow."

Looking over I see two guys engrossed in a video game, and sure enough, a blonde girl sitting on the couch, watching them. It doesn't appear that either of them acknowledge her existence, but there she sits. I wonder which one she likes, both maybe? Hell, at least she does it openly.

She's pretty with huge breasts that she clearly wants noticed, judging by her shirt. She purses her huge, blood red lips, catching my eye and giving me the once over.

"Make yourselves at home. I've got beer, vodka, soda, water..." Tate offers kindly.

"So you live three to this room?" I ask.

"No, Dane doesn't technically live here, but I don't think he knows it. Right, bro?"

"What's that?" Dane has finally realized they have new company and breaks away to come over to us in the kitchenette area. Well, it's more like space for a small table, mini fridge and a strip of countertop that folds up and down; UGA's got nothin' on Southern dorm rooms. Whitley is right behind him...guess that answers my question on which one she's after.

"I was telling Laney and Bennett here that you can't

stand to be away from your big bro."

Dane turns to us, and Good Lord…I hope their parents are breeding professionally because they'd make a fortune! If big brother is hot, then little brother is illegal, immortal, and too damn pretty not to be a girl. This guy seriously belongs at the top of "World's Sexiest Reasons to Drop Your Panties."

WTF? Where did that come from? It may be the dirtiest thought I've ever had and I feel vulgar that it crossed my mind. But seriously, you'd have to be deaf, dumb, and blind not to notice this guy…or a lesbian.

Nope, pretty sure a lesbian would at least do a double-take.

"Hey, I'm Dane. Nice to meet you both." He's looking at me when he says it; right at me.

"Laney…Walker, nice to meet you, Dane. This is Bennett." I nudge her with my shoulder.

"B-B-Bennett Cole. Freshman. Drama. Single. Room 128."

The boys both laugh while I cook her with my eyes. Seriously, blabber out bio and MY room number much?

"Really?" Whitley says in the nastiest voice I've ever heard. I don't say anything, but this girl is pushing it. I won't let her dog on Bennett again.

"Okay, well now you know Bennett," I laugh. Awkward. What do I do? "Um, can I use your bathroom?"

"Sure, door's right there." Tate points.

"I'll show her." Ah, roommate Sawyer speaketh.

"Bennett, would you come with me, please?" It's not really a request, as I'm dragging her zombie ass by the arm. Yes, boys, girls always have to go to the bathroom in pairs, that's all; I'm not about to kill her.

"It's right here. Laney, Bennett, I'm Sawyer Beckett.

Sorry, didn't mean to be rude, I just had to finish that game."

Sawyer's a big ole badass-looking dude and I don't mean big like a teddy bear and I don't mean badass like could hold his own. He's all out intimidating as hell...until he smiles, which he just did or I'd be running from the room. His hair is dark brown, what he has, anyway, and cut pretty close to his head. I can't tell right away if his eyes are really dark, deep blue or what, but that's my guess. He has an eyebrow ring and the biggest muscles I've ever seen. Again, not talking Evan muscular, more like competition muscles.

"No problem, nice to meet you. We'll be out in a minute," I say as nonchalantly as possible while I shove Bennett in and lock the door.

"Okay, you have three minutes to snap out of it or we're leaving. You're the one who wanted to do this thing, Bennett. What the hell is wrong with you?"

"I don't know. I'm so sorry, Laney. I swear to God, this has never happened to me, ever. That Tate, he literally just short-circuited my brain."

"Do you want to leave?"

"NO! I want to stay, and lick him...well, maybe not really, but I want to stay. Please help me; cover the odd for me. Please kick in and be my wing girl! I know you can do it, for meeeee?"

If I'm her only hope for wing girl, she's obviously desperate, so pity for that alone takes over. Debating internally for a minute, I give her a confident nod. "Yup, I got this. I'm Laney Walker, all grown up and all alone. Well, except for you, B, but you're not really here right now. I got your back; let's go!"

I have no idea what I'm saying, but even I'm getting sick of feeling sorry for myself and acting all "sheltered bitch" with everyone, so what the hell. Bennett needs me! And for different reasons altogether, I need her. She's upbeat, jovial, loving life...the way I was when I was little, before I second guessed everyone's motives and intentions. I remember it being fun. I know how to hang out with people; I'm not a leper or shut-in…and these people seem cool, right?

I walk out of the bathroom determined; I'll be damned if I give these guys any reason to suspect I'm not a pro at this. The boys appear to be bartending and Stars of Track & Field is playing. Heck ya—I love this song. Sawyer's glance screams "You two freaky chicks gonna make it?!"

"Hey, guys, sorry. Soooo love this song." Oh hell, I am so bad at this.

"Oh yeah, what's it called?" Dane smirks.

"'End of All Time.'" I shoot him a know-it-all grin.

Don't even try it, boy, music is my thing.

"Very nice." He winks. He's a winker. I know someone else who does that, smiling to myself at the thought.

"This is a great song. I'm Whitley Thompson, by the way," she puts her hand out to me, long red nails coming at me like daggers.

"Nice to meet you. I'm Laney."

"Are you a freshman here, Laney?" The way she just sneered freshman and my name lets me know she's not trying to be friendly. So why even introduce yourself? I so don't do catty, and am unclear exactly what the hell her instant problem with me is, but I'll sure solve it for her if need be.

"Sure am."

"Well, welcome. I'm a junior, captain of the Lovely Larks." What the heck is a Lovely Lark? She must read my expression because she continues. "It's the award-winning girls' a cappella performance group."

That is pretty cool. "That's awesome. I actually watched *The Sing Off* and *Pitch Perfect* and really liked them both."

"Really, are you a singer?"

She doesn't care, why is she asking? Why am I still tolerating this conversation? "Oh, God no, I'm a terrible singer." I laugh. "I'm on the softball team here."

"Ohhhhh, you're a softball player?" So snide…and I'm officially done.

"I am, wanna see my bat?" I step closer to her, dead calm in my eyes.

Dane doubles over laughing and Sawyer spews beer all over the place while Whitley turns the color of her lipstick.

She opens her mouth to say something else, but Bennett cuts in. "Come on, Laney, let's go."

I move to go with her, but Dane speaks up. "Oh no, you guys aren't leaving, she is. Take off, Whitley. Now."

Whitley's mouth falls open but Dane's cold stare silences her and she moves to the door. He walks her to it with no words spoken between them. He turns around to us, slightly red-faced, and offers a weak smile.

The tension in the room is thick, so I try to break it. "I'm really sorry about that. I wouldn't really take a bat to her. I could always just tie her up and force her to listen to me sing."

Dane's head falls back and he laughs with his whole body, Tate and Sawyer joining him.

"Damn, Laney, you're my new favorite person," Sawyer chuckles.

"Well, I'm glad I'm somebody's favorite. I'm sure as hell not Whitley's…and I'm all torn up about it," I say, sticking out my bottom lip in my best fake pout. "Enough about me, though." I change the subject. "So, boys, wanna tell us about yourselves? I mean, maybe not as much as Bennett chose to share." This gets laughs all around, even Bennett. I'm seriously doing a really good job running this show. Bennett needs to make me a wing girl badge or something.

"Shut up, bitch. I was nervous."

And now I know we're really friends.

"What were you nervous about, Bennett?" Tate flashes a beaming smile. He knows the answer. "Very cool name, by the way."

Bennett blushes, and she's a redhead, so it's noticeable. "I guess I'm keyed up from all of this tonight; feels a little like speed dating."

"Good call! It does feel like that," he agrees with her.

"Do you agree, Laney?" Dane asks.

I look at him and wish I hadn't. Evan is athletic, manly and gorgeous, whereas Dane is…beautiful. He, too, has brown hair, but it purposefully has a trendy cut and style to it. I doubt he's ever shoved it in a backwards ball cap like my sweet Evan. His eyes are big and brown and he smiles all the way through them. His skin is dark, like he's tan all year round, and he carries himself with a kind but yeah, I know you're looking air.

He's not as tall as Evan, not as broad, but he's built and muscular. His dark designer jeans and red polo fit him just right. Around his neck hangs a small silver cross on leather and I can see a tattoo on the inside of his bicep. It looks like a verse from here. This boy really should be in print or on a movie screen, and I can just appreciate the view like one would a movie star, right? Right.

Breaking away from my examination, I'm able to answer him. "I don't know anything about speed dating, but this night has not felt speedy."

WAIT, I got it! The movie *Sweet Home Alabama*; Evan is like Jake and Dane like Andrew…nailed that analogy! I can't wait to tell Bennett later. Not that I'm comparing, just proud of my cleverness. Crap, pretty sure I'm being asked another question…

"You haven't had fun?" He smiles coyly, looking right in my eyes again. Geez, this is new. I don't notice guys, or their tattoos, or necklaces. And why do I suddenly feel so guilty?

"Fun wouldn't be the right word. This by far is the least painful room of the night, though, so congratulations."

He laughs at me; so does Bennett. She hasn't moved from Tate's side, and blatant staring doesn't seem to be above her, either. Oh, and he notices; he leans in every time he talks to her.

"So, somebody besides Bennett wanna tell us about themselves?"

"How about you?" Dane can challenge with just his eyes I'm quickly learning.

"No, no…someone else can go first. I'm super uninteresting."

"I doubt that."

"Oh, for heaven's sake, I'm not gonna have to suggest Truth or Dare, am I?" I roll my eyes at them all. "And hurry, it's gotta be close to switch soon." We've definitely been in here the longest of the night.

"That was the last switch of the night." Dane winks again.

"Oh, okay, then I'm jammies and bed bound. Come on, Bennett. Nice to meet you guys!" I start to walk to the door but turn back. Why is Bennett not following me?

"Hold up now, y'all don't have to run off! I, personally, could go for a game or something. Damn, it's like ten on a Friday," Sawyer chimes in with a frown.

"Yeah, Laney, come on, it'll be fun!" Bennett squeals.

Oh, that lil' enamored redhead! "Um…" Do I look as uncomfortable as I feel? I was being a smartass about Truth or Dare; I don't actually need to know anything about anyone. I just thought Bennett would want Tate's stats. Forget this wing girl crap.

Dane walks over to me and leans one hip on the counter. "Laney, why don't you go put on those jammies." He grins. "And come back. I'll order a pizza."

His nearness doesn't go unnoticed and I cringe at my body's betrayal. "I'm not wearing pajamas in front of boys I just met!"

"Um, Laney," Bennett butts in sheepishly, "I've seen your pjs; they're fine."

Dane raises an eyebrow at me.

We just met these guys. It's late and the official crawl is over so now it would be me in a guy's room just for the hell of it; Evan's concerns echo in my head.

"Nah, I'm getting tired. I need my room, Bennett. I'd feel a lot better if you'd come with me."

"Perfect, game and pizza in our room, guys!" Alrighty, Bennett totally missed the plot. Ugh.

"Laney, what do you want on your pizza?" There's a god-like boy who's practically a stranger yelling through my bathroom door. This night has gone way off track, but this is Bennett's room, too, and she's really in to Tate, and thou shalt not cockblock.

"Anything...except peppers. Or onions. Oh, and no anchovies!"

"So...pepperoni?" So smug, that Dane.

"Sure." This is my room. I'm coming out in my pajamas.

"What the fuck are those?" Sawyer's face looks pained, like my sleepwear is actually the biggest disappointment he's ever had.

"You kiss anyone with that mouth, Sawyer?" He gives me the same weird look I always get when I say it, but yeah, I'd had to change the phrase.

"Sorry! But seriously, Laney. Hot girl says she's putting

on pajamas, I'm thinking she's gonna show me her secrets, like sweet Victoria. So what are you wearing?"

"I'm wearing my pajamas, and I don't have any secrets." I don't. Well, I might…haven't decided if I'm telling Evan anything more about tonight or not yet.

"Oh, I bet you do," he says with a leer.

Dane's leaning back against the counter, arms crossed over his chest, smiling right at me. It's a familiar pose that tugs at my heart, all the while I wonder why I consciously take note of where he is in the room. When I catch his gaze, he crooks his finger at me to join him.

I walk closer to him, but not too close. "Yeah?"

"Laney, I've known you a minute, but I can tell you're uncomfortable. I can make all this go away right now if you want. I'll take my boys back to their room, and I'll even leave you some pizza here. Just say the word."

Dane's giving me an out, I should definitely take the out… I turn to look at Bennett. She's sitting on the couch with Tate, Sawyer leaning over them. They're writing and laughing and eating…I look back to Dane.

"Can I be honest with you?" I ask sheepishly, but for some reason, I get the distinct feeling I can.

"No, lie straight to my face. I love it when people do that," he simpers. "Yes, tell me."

"I don't feel unsafe or anything, but this is weird. Two girls invite three guys they just met into their dorm room? Well, one girl, at least; not sure I invited anyone." I smile to alleviate any harshness. "I just don't know about all this. No sense in going all out the first social event, right?" I chew my bottom lip a little.

"I get it, and I'm not surprised you get it, frankly."

"What do you mean?"

"Well, not many girls don't want us in their rooms. Take

your roommate, for example, she's not thinking about getting us to leave. In fact, she's in cahoots with Sawyer, whether she's realized it yet or not."

"Uh, huh?" Still lost.

"Laney, they're over there getting 21 Questions ready to play. They both want to play some BS game; Sawyer so he can get to know you and Bennett so she can get to know Tate. They'll base it on shots so that everyone gets loose-lipped and tells their real story. This is college, Laney, guys and girls feeling their way through the masses until they find their someone. Using games and booze masks the fact they're too scared and insecure to just ask questions openly. It's just everyone playing the same game, Laney. But if you don't like this, or feel too uncomfortable, I'll fix it."

He's right. Well, about Bennett, anyway; who knows about Sawyer. Bennett's just a girl who likes this new boy and really just wants to get to know him. The game and shots give her an outlet to do that. Man, Dane's got it all figured out and he puts it right out there. I like and respect that. If he's running a game to fool me, he deserves an Oscar; I'm picking up no deceit.

"Okay, Mister Meaning of Life, I have a few stipulations."

"Shoot."

"No boys sleep here. At some point, you drag them out. If Bennett gets too drunk, you take my hint to end things." I tick off my rules on my fingers. "No one gets naked, no one has sex. No one invites anyone else over. No one tags this on Facebook, no one tweets…oh, and no one steals my pizza. Sound good?" I quirk an eyebrow and cross my arms over my chest.

He smiles and laughs. "Yeah, Laney, that sounds good. Now relax and quit worrying. Can you do that?"

It seemed like a rhetorical question so I don't answer him.

"No harm will come to you whenever I'm around, I

swear it. Welcome to college, Laney; welcome to life."

"Game on!" Sawyer yells from the living area.

So apparently the game is 21 Questions, and not as trite as Truth or Dare. Sure. Bennett has claimed the spot right beside Tate on the couch, and I do mean right beside him. Sawyer grabs the chair and Dane and I sit on the floor on opposite sides of the coffee table. We all had to put four questions in the cup, which is only 20 questions, but no one seemed to care. If you refuse to or can't answer a question, you do a shot. I've never done a shot, but I'm pretty smart, so I'm not too worried.

"Okay, ladies first, one of you draw and we'll go clockwise."

Bennett's hand is in the cup before Sawyer finishes his directions. "How old were you when you lost your virginity?" She blushes when she finishes reading.

I choke a bit on my sip of Dew. Clearly I didn't know the kind of questions to expect! Looks like my GPA won't be saving me from shots tonight. Shit.

"Um." She looks to the ceiling and taps her chin. Well, shit, she's going to answer, and she appears to have to think about it! "Fifteen."

I subtly tap my chest so I don't choke on my bite of pizza and stare at the ground.

"Sixteen." Not Sawyer's question, but he shares with the class.

"Fourteen! Mitzi Shawn, beat ya both!" Tate adds while giving Sawyer a fist bump.

Neither Dane nor I say a word. It wasn't my question, so I'm pretty sure it doesn't apply, but I will drink the whole damn bottle before I answer with "not applicable."

"OK, my turn." Tate draws his slip. "When's the last time you got laid and by who?" WTF! PLEASE let me draw one of my own questions. "Well, it was about three weeks ago, but I don't kiss and tell, except about Mitzi," he laughs, "so I'll do the shot." And he does.

Dane's turn is next, and I already feel sorry for him; Lord knows what it will say.

"What are your three favorite Disney movies?" He looks at me and a genuine smile lights up his face, it takes up the whole room. "Hmmm, I wonder whose question this is? Could it be, could it be…the little cutie in the princess pajamas?" He winks at me. "Let's see…I'm gonna go with *Toy Story*…" Classic boy pick. "*Monsters, Inc…*" Great choice. "And… oh, of course, *The Fox and the Hound.*"

"Oh my God, dude, you're a fag." Sawyer throws a wadded up napkin at him.

Dane just shrugs his shoulders and sneaks a peek at me. I'm just staring at him. I really liked his answer.

My turn. I could possibly throw up right now… "What would be your ideal date?"

"Oh yay, I was hoping you'd draw that!" Bennett squeals and claps.

I think of Evan, all the times we went to eat, to prom, fishing…were those ideal? I have no idea, but they were to me because Evan was there. Would I enjoy those things without him? Probably not, but he's gone and I haven't enjoyed much lately. I don't even really like softball anymore. I feel tears welling up…strangers, people examining me, it's all too much.

"I'll take the shot," I say and do just that. It burns, just like the backs of my eyes. I look up and Dane has me locked in his gaze, but he doesn't say a word.

Sawyer also draws one of mine. "What makes you happiest? Laney, did you ask one dirty question?" He gives me a teasing scowl.

"That could be a dirty question, depending on your answer!" I stick my tongue out at him, earning a laugh from everyone.

"Pussy, beer, and sports make me happiest, probably in that order." Sawyer is a pig, but in a "he'll grow on ya" kind of way.

After a few more rounds, I know way too much about everyone. I downed two shots and revealed nothing important or embarrassing, as Dane and Bennett went easy on the questions, too.

Finally Dane stands. "Guys, it's getting late. Let's go so these ladies can get to bed."

"You don't have to leave yet, right, Laney?" Bennett pleads at me with her eyes.

I say nothing because I'm tired.

"Tate, come on, man. Sawyer, get your ass up and say goodnight."

Tate leans over to whisper in Bennett's ear when she sees him to the door and Sawyer shuffles out, mumbling, after giving me an awkward hug.

Dane stops and turns to me. "Night, Disney, hope tonight was okay for you."

A nickname? Already? Not sure he's earned that privilege yet, but it's such a good one that I let it slide.

"Yeah, no worries. It was fun." I shrug.

"You're lying to me. Half of the questions horrified you." He laughs.

"Nah, some of them were funny. It was...different, good different."

"Well then, I'm glad. Sweet dreams."

I go to bed without calling Evan, not even a text, because I feel guilty, although I'm not sure why. He does the same, apparently, and that makes it hard to fall asleep.

Chapter 15

A PICTURE'S WORTH A THOUSAND WORDS

-Laney-

It's raining when I wake up, a perfect Saturday. There's coffee made and Bennett's gone. A note says she'll be home later tonight; she's off working on her play. I move slowly, picking up the room and bagging up my laundry, and then take a shower. I try to call Evan. It goes to voicemail, so I call home.

It's so good to talk to Dad. I tell him all about my classes and Bennett. He, of course, asks about the team and the coach. I keep my tone enthusiastic before finally telling him I love him and will see him soon.

Completely out of things to do now, I decide to go get in some swings in the indoor practice arena. I'm not really motivated about ball, but I literally have nothing else to do and at least it's something I "know."

I was always content at home, but now it feels like I'm disconnected from myself. Nothing seems really right or really

95

wrong, but I know I'm just going through the motions. I miss home. I miss Evan and all that was constant, safe, and familiar.

But then there's this other little voice in the background that hates that everyone around me seems comfortable, making the most of college, friends, parties, whatever…I'm stuck in the middle, of out of my zone but afraid to explore the other side.

I swing until I'm drenched in sweat and my arms are rubbery and then head back to the dorm. Two hours and another shower later, Bennett still isn't home. I still have no homework and my call to Evan goes to voicemail again. Okay, now it's bugging me. Evan's never missed two of my calls in a row, but I simply cannot bring myself to send a text, too. Don't be that girl, Laney. I should be happy that he obviously has more to keep him busy than I do; above all, I do want him happy.

Not sure how or why, but I find myself knocking on the door of room 114.

Tate answers and smiles warmly. "Hey, Laney, what's up? Come on in." He moves aside for me to enter, but I remain in the hall. Baby steps and all.

"No, I'm good, um, just seeing what was going on?" I can't force my gaze up off the floor and am already regretting my bold decision to come down here.

"Nobody's here but me, but the boys should be back any minute. You wanna wait?"

"No, that's okay. Just tell them all I came by to say hi, okay?"

"You sure you don't wanna wait?"

I turn to start back towards my room, and low and behold, Dane's striding towards me carrying a guitar. Of course he's carrying a guitar, that's quintessential for the evil boy tempter, right?

"Well hello there, Disney, looking for anyone in particular?" One eyebrow cocks, accompanied by that all-consuming grin. His hair is messy and his jeans hang low; he's a tempter all right.

Why are you here, Laney? You're mad Evan hasn't answered? Is this his payback? Go do all the things you prophesized he would do when you were apart? Nice, Laney.

"I just came by to see what was up. I'm bored out of my mind. Bennett's out and you guys are the only people I know." Not sure why I'm rambling. Not sure why I'm standing here.

"As flattering as that is, I'll take it." He's smiling, so he's not insulted. It sounded better in my head. "Come on in."

Without Bennett backup, I'm not going in their room...so why had I come? "I'm good, I just...well, anything fun going on tonight? Bennett will be home soon, I'm sure she'd love to do something."

"No set plans here, you got anything?" He looks to Tate, who is texting away.

"Bennett's home in about an hour, says she's down for whatever." Guess we know who he was texting.

"Perfect." Dane glances at me. "So Disney, you're brave enough to saunter down here; you brave enough to set the agenda?"

Am I? Yes, I am. Too bad I have no clue what would be fun. Not only have I not spotted a pond nearby, but these boys don't strike me as fishermen. Something tells me a movie marathon won't fly either, and I could use a change. "Social coordinator isn't my forte, so feel free to override me." I glance at his guitar. "How about Chinese takeout and music trivia?"

"For shots?" Tate asks hopefully.

"Of course," I spout definitively. There's no way I'm losing at music trivia.

"Okay, hostess with the mostest, your room, hour and a half?" Dane's face lights up.

"Sounds good, bring your guitar." We're gonna see what

he's got.

Feeling guilty, at a loss as to why exactly, I text Evan when I'm back in my room.

Laney: Tried calling you x2, got voicemail. Evrythng okay? Bout to hang in room w/ frnds, miss you.

Bennett bursts in shortly after, practically foaming at the mouth. In spurts, while getting ready like a banshee, she declares her undying love for me setting this up tonight. I can't help but smile to myself. I'm actually looking forward to it, too.

The 114 lads arrive right on time, minus Sawyer, and I let them in...while holding a crab rangoon. I couldn't wait. They both offer to pay me back for the food, which I dismiss, and we all settle in comfortably.

"Thanks for the invite, Laney," Tate says and throws a casual arm across my shoulder. "I was kinda surprised, you seem kinda shy."

"You're welcome. It's nice to have something to do." I don't address the shy comment; I don't know what to say. "Sawyer knows he was invited, too, right?"

Dane coughs and shoots Tate a look, which I sure hope he doesn't think was subtle. Tate awkwardly answers. "He had to work tonight."

"Oh, where does he work?" Neither answer me before my cell phone dings and I race to it, elated. It's not from Evan though, rather Kaitlyn.

Kaitlyn: Thought you'd get a kick out of your crazy boy

The picture that follows gives me a kick square in the gut. Why would she send this to me? She's got to be drunk, thinking this would be funny. It's anything but. The sting moves throughout my body, starting at my toes and working up, tears threatening to spill. My sweet, classy Evan appears to be taking a shot from between the smashed boobs of a well-endowed blonde. Her barely there tank top is pulled down to "hold" his drink and his face is all up in that. His hands are braced on both her hips, just below the edges of a skirt riding ridiculously high as she lies back on a table.

How thoughtful of my friend Kaitlyn to capture this moment for me. Gritting my teeth, I try to remind myself that Evan can do whatever he wants; we'd discussed this at length. I have no right to be upset or jealous. The "spread your wings and fly" plan was mine. I just never thought he'd fly so far so fast. And I didn't think I'd have to see it.

Shaking my head as though that's going to erase the image, I snap loudly at everyone. "Let's play some trivia!"

Turns out Dane is a really good guitarist and has a broad range of musical knowledge. I don't stump him via iPod and he doesn't trip me up via his strings. Bennett and Tate are barely even playing, and are either shameless, or have forgotten Dane and I are in the room. Despite the brick in my gut and the many times I find my mind wandering back to the picture, I'm actually having a pretty good time. Dane is great company, keeping me laughing and guessing. His talent and obvious passion for music is infectious, and his competitive streak, matched only by mine, is hilarious.

"Okay, Maestro, let's see if there's a song you can't play," I tease him.

He waits calmly, no remark.

Think, Laney, a song where you feel the guitar... "How about 'The Cave' by Mumford and Sons?"

I think I've got him, but he jumps right into it. He plays flawlessly, even singing along. It's amazing, beautiful, and I can't deny how it captivates me. He winks when he's done and holds my eyes, waiting for me to speak.

"That was amazing, Dane." I clear my throat to continue in more than a raspy whisper. "You're very good, and I, sir, am impressed. Let me guess, you're in a band?"

"Nope, no band."

"And no college?"

"No college."

"So what do you do?"

He laughs softly. "Nothing important."

"Bullshit, Dane, you—" Tate starts but Dane cuts him off fiercely.

"I answered her, bro."

I don't pry further and the night, which really was fun, soon comes to a close.

Chapter 16

NIGHTMARE

-Evan-

When the team sets out to initiate the freshmen, they're not playing around. Last night was so insane I barely remember most of it. Looking around slowly, I shield my eyes from the light creeping through the blinds. It takes a minute to realize I'd actually made it to my own room somehow.

Groggily sitting up, despite the cracked-out drummer in my head, I try to remember how I got home. After about the fourth or fifth tequila shot via the chest of a Bulldog Babe, everything gets a little fuzzy. I've never been a big drinker, but when the upperclassmen on your college football team summon you to an initiation party, you go. I just hope I didn't make too big of a fool of myself.

I amble up to go use the bathroom and stop cold.

No, no, no…please say I'm still drunk and this isn't happening.

Kaitlyn Michaels, Laney's best friend, is standing just

across the room in panties and my t-shirt. I look down at myself quickly—only underwear. Oh fucking hell, this has to be a nightmare. Why is she here? What happened? This couldn't be worse. Laney will never buy the drunk excuse or forgive me. I'm pretty sure screwing friends wasn't part of our deal.

I swallow down the bile, slowly looking up, gagging again when I meet Kaitlyn's too-bright smile. She looks way too fucking happy and my gut coils. I might really throw up if this shit doesn't start making sense real quick. Did I sleep with Kaitlyn? Surely not, you couldn't get me that drunk, right?

She must see the question in my face because she clears her throat, beckoning my eyes to meet hers once again. "Relax, Evan, nothing happened. I'm an old friend; I just made sure you got home safe."

Trying to wake up, I shake my head. "Then why are we in our underwear? And why are you still here?"

"I wasn't gonna sleep in tight party clothes and you took your own stuff off. And thank you, but I didn't think you'd want me driving back alone that late, so I crashed. You're welcome, by the way," she huffs and crosses her arms across her chest.

Oh, now she's acting pissed and offended. Is she insane??? Laney will kill us both! This would be the worst betrayal possible—me and Kaitlyn. God help us if she ever finds out. We'll both lose her forever. Yes, Kaitlyn got me home safe and I appreciate that, but shit—call me a cab, don't spend the night in my room! I'd rather die in a ditch than lose Laney.

"Don't get mad, Kaitlyn. I'm not trying to be mean, this is just weird and a lot to take in. I really do appreciate you looking out for me. And I'm glad nothing happened." I go to grab water, my throat dry and tight. I turn back to Kaitlyn, full desperation in my voice. "I don't think we should mention this to Laney. We didn't really do anything wrong, but it'd be hard for her to understand. Right?"

"Of course, Evan," she snips as she gathers her things. "I won't tell Laney. I don't see why not, though, aren't you guys just friends now? That's what I was being, a good friend."

"You're right, you were. Thanks, I mean it." I pause to see what else she's going to say, but after too long an awkward silence, I speak up. "So, I'm gonna go take a shower. Thanks again. Guess I'll see ya around?"

She smiles and walks to the door, but there's still a defensive air coming off her. "Yeah, Evan, I'll see ya around."

I stay in the shower for way too long, trying to assess the situation. Nothing happened. Kaitlyn was just being a good friend. We agreed not to tell Laney and upset her over nothing. It's all gonna be okay.

Yup, everything will be fine.

Chapter 17

HOME BITTERSWEET HOME

-Laney-

Leaving ball on Monday, my phone rings and I know it's Evan before I answer.

"Well hello, stranger."

"Baby girl, how are you? I missed you."

I tell him I'm good and I've missed him, too. He explains how he lost his phone and just got a new one today. All I want to do is ask him about the picture I saw. I want to tell him how bad it hurt me, how disgusting it was, but I don't. Evan needs to enjoy college, be free, and have fun...whatever that means to him.

That doesn't mean I can't test the water, though, and see if he'll tell me on his own. "So, how was your weekend?"

"Okay, I guess, had speed camp mostly, hung out for a while Saturday night, nothing much. What'd you do?"

Nope, he's not going to tell me. The irony is not wasted

on me. What took us years to build, a strong foundation that withstood any element, has just suffered its first crack. It took a fraction of the time.

"I did the Hall Crawl Friday night; it pretty much sucked. Saturday I swung a while then hung out and Sunday I did laundry." All true.

We make plans to meet at home for the long Labor Day weekend coming up. I may be upset over the picture, but there's no way I'm passing up a chance to see him. He's still my best friend in the whole world, and I miss him.

Bennett calls during my drive home Friday night begging me to come back a day early and go out with her. Apparently something called "The K" will be "kickin'" because of the long weekend. Tate can't make it, but she "reaaallllyyyy" wants to go. She's working on our fake IDs right now.

I told her I'd see. I'm not sure when Evan's heading back, and I'm not leaving one minute before he does. Also, I have yet to go to a college party, and I've never heard of "The K," so I'm a bit hesitant. I tell her I'd call her the next day or so.

I get home before Evan since I have a way shorter drive, so I have lots of time to get settled in and catch up with my Dad. He's such a good man. I've never understood why he never dated after my mother took off. Once I asked him if he was lonely and he had a simple answer: "Now how could I be lonely when I have you? I already have the most beautiful, wonderful girl in the world."

He loved my mother with all he was. He tried to ignore for so long how she'd simply "checked out" on us long before she actually left, but I'd known for a while that she wasn't in the room even when she was sitting right beside me. I couldn't believe she'd actually left. I didn't know moms actually did that, but she did. We haven't heard from her since, and we've never left that house, so she simply doesn't want to talk to us, 'cause we damn sure aren't hard to find.

Since that day, it's been just me and Dad; every meal, every holiday, just us. His parents are both gone and I have no idea about her parents; they, too, are ghosts. He got me into playing ball, something he knew well and could relate to me with. He taught me how to fish, how to cook simple things, and how to be strong and self-sufficient. I may have been burned by my mother, but between my father, Evan, and even Parker, I'm set. I struck gold with the men in my life.

After we ate the spaghetti I made, he headed off for guitar night, a.k.a. old men sitting in a shed drinking beer. One may pick up a guitar and strum at some point, ergo "guitar night." He didn't need to skip it just because I was home, Evan will be here soon.

While I wait, I make up a meatloaf and a pot of chili for Dad. He can freeze them both and they'll last him at least a week of good eating. Then I wash all his bedding and clean the bathrooms, things he would never think of. I've gotta take care of my Daddy.

Finally, around ten, Evan appears at my door. I jump into his arms, wrapping my arms around him and smashing my face into his neck, ugly snapshots forgotten. God, I missed him so much.

He catches me and laughs, running his hands up and down my back. "I missed you, too, princess." He kisses my hair and sighs.

I pull him to the couch; I just want to hold him. We stay there for hours, as though my cheek can't leave his chest and his hands never leave some part of me. It would be so much harder to leave him this time, now that I know how bad it can actually be and what he does while he's gone. I wonder if he feels it, too.

Chapter 18

REMEDY

-Evan-

It feels so damn good to have her back in my arms. I've missed her more than I thought possible. She's always been the part of every day that I get up for, that I look forward to. Life just doesn't mean as much without her in it.

I knew it'd be hard; we've been together so long, the two sides of one coin. But there's no way I could have possibly foreseen the exact magnitude of emptiness I'd feel. She looks the same, but there's something different about her; a sadness in her eyes, a different air about her. I pray she hasn't been half as miserable as me; I'd never want that for her. I always pray she's accidentally woken up with a guy in her room...of course she hasn't, my sweet girl...God, I'm a dick. The guilt is consuming me but I can't tell her. I can't risk losing her altogether.

College is okay so far. The football team is great. My roommate and new friends are cool, there's always something to do, but she never leaves my mind. It's always there—what's she doing, who's she with, does she miss me, when can I see her again. It always finds a way into my thoughts.

When I lost my phone, I went nuts making up scenarios in my mind. Last I knew, she was at that damn dorm tour thing, and then my phone was gone. Was she at a party doing shots, letting guys doing shots off her, like I was? The whole "do as I say, not as I do" shit is driving me insane.

I should have stepped outside the party and called her from Kaitlyn's phone. I should have gone home. I should have never gone. I should have followed her to Southern. All those years, I'd never outright lied to Laney, and now I have. Omission is lying. I know it and so does she. There's so much I can't bring myself to tell her and the bigger the pile of secrets gets, the worse I feel.

Just a few months ago, we knew everything about each other. Nothing and nobody came between us. She was the first person I talked to each morning and the last sweet voice I heard before I went to sleep. When I planned my day, I knew she'd be in it. Everything now is tainted.

Laney had been exactly right about the challenges we would face; college girls are maniacs. And don't forget the Bulldog Babes. They're the cheer squad, and part of their "job" is taking care of the football team. Our laundry, our homework, cleaning our room, cleaning our pipes…you name it. I'm a freshman, so I get less attention, basically whatever time Courtney, the redhead assigned to me, has left after taking care of one of the senior linemen. I avoid her like the plague.

I'd thought I knew about temptation and women—hell, I was something in high school—no comparison.

And Laney was THERE in high school. I could always see her, go to her, be around her; everything in the background was white noise. I'm not a sexual deviant. I don't need to get laid, per se, but I need companionship.

Damn, I'm falling apart.

And what kills me the most—Laney is at college, too,

with the exact same things going on around her. Any guy with a brain will always notice her first in a room, it's inevitable. She's breathtakingly beautiful. Faces like that don't come along very often and her body doesn't quit. She's the real deal. Even before she speaks, you know she's got something; it shines off her in beams. And the more she resists, which I know she will, the more of a challenge she becomes, and everyone knows how guys feel about a challenge. Yeah, I worry about her; I worry about us. Official or not, she's mine. We're us. Always.

Not tonight, though. Tonight I just want to hold her. I just want to be me and Laney. I want our heartbeats to sync. I want the smell of her hair to course through my body and bring me peace.

She moves to get up and I pull her back down.

Please don't leave me, not yet. I just got you back.

"I'm just going to get a pillow and blanket. I'll be right back."

"I can go home if you want to go to bed, pretty."

"You're not going anywhere. You're sleeping with me; under this roof or outside, I don't care. The couch is plenty respectful."

Sounds good to me. I'd sleep in a lion's den right now if it meant her warmth beside me.

She comes back and snuggles into me; you couldn't fit a piece of paper between us. Her soft hair and sweet face lay against my chest. Her legs are wrapped up in mine and I can feel her little breaths against my neck as I rub her back and kiss the top of her head again and again. I know she's still awake, but neither of us speak. It's as if sound would pop the bubble around us, but I can't hold it in any longer.

"Laney, I love you."

She raises her hand to my cheek and gazes at me. Her eyes are glassy and I can see the tears she won't let fall. "I know you do, Evan. I love you, too. I always will. You're my best friend."

I'd kiss her right now, but there's no way I'd stop at that, so instead I pull her into my chest and whisper, "We'll figure it out, love, I promise." Please don't let me break this promise, too.

I hear her dad come in; he pauses but doesn't say a word. I stay all night here with Laney and finally get a good night's sleep.

Chapter 19

DOUBLE-EDGED SWORD

-Laney-

The next day, Evan and I walk hand in hand across Parker's field for a picnic. I know his family wouldn't mind, as if they'd ever even know, we're a good hundred acres from the house. I need some alone time with Evan and we need to talk, but the alone time first.

The sun is warm on our skin and the slight breeze is perfect. Evan carries the picnic basket I've packed while I cling to "my blanket," which I dug out from behind his truck seat. I've sat under this navy blue blanket at more of Evan's chilly football games that I can count, watching him do his thing. I smile a bit, despite the sadness that comes with the memories; this old blanket is about the only thing left that's still in the place it belongs. I turn my gaze to Evan, forcing the melancholy thoughts away, refusing to waste even one minute of the time I actually have with him.

He looks so handsome today; his silky brown hair is

messy from the wind and his sculpted body is showcased in a tight gray shirt and faded jeans. He takes the blanket from me and spreads it out, sitting first. "Come here to me, sweet girl." He stretches his hand out to help me settle down beside him. His gentle respect for me never gets old.

Lying back on the blanket, looking into his eyes, our hands joined between our bodies, I know that I will always be connected to Evan. Without having to say the words, we both know the other is hurting. Now that we're together, we can't wait another minute to show our love; to heal what we can for one another.

Evan rolls over on his side to face me, tucking my hair behind my ear. My heart and soul respond, all of me relaxing. He moves over my body and kisses me passionately, whispering sweet words, but in it I can feel the heartache. He runs his hand up and down my body, like he's memorizing every part. "I need to feel close to you, Laney," he says, his voice deep.

This boy. This amazing boy loves me platonically, romantically, physically, spiritually. Nothing he does is ever to hurt me. His eyes don't lie and he can't hide from me when I look into them. The pain I see there tugs at my heart. Can I fix the miles between us? No. Can I speed up time until being together again is an option? No. Can I ease his spirit right now? Absolutely. Running my finger along his jaw, soaking up his masculine beauty, I whisper, "My sweet Evan, I've missed you."

He pulls one strap of my top down my shoulder, kisses along its path, and then flicks his gaze to mine. Soothing him that this is okay with me, I reach up and pull the other strap down for him, revealing my breasts to his lust-filled eyes. He leans down to run his tongue excruciatingly slowly over my nipples, tracing them, learning them. Arching into his mouth, I gasp his name and a low rumble escapes from deep in his chest.

He makes me feel so good, so cherished. His hand moves up my thigh to the zipper on my pants, and I can feel the slight tremble and he sneaks his hand inside, teasing just along the edge of my panties.

"Ah, Laney, sweet Laney," he moans as he rubs against me.

I can feel how much he wants me. My hands refuse to slow down, taking in his back, his shoulders, his neck. His body is tense as I wrap my legs around his hips and push him into me harder with my heels.

Panting, he pulls back, reading my expression. "I need to touch you, angel."

Of course this is going to confuse us even more, make the distance more harsh, but I'll be damned if I can stop myself now. My chest heaves with my rapid breaths, my body writhing as I pull him even closer to me. "Do something before I go crazy," I pout achingly.

His chuckle is light as his hand finds the spot where I need him most, pulling my panties to the side. One of his long fingers runs tentatively down my center and a tremor shoots through me. His mouth moves along my throat in open, wet caresses. "Being with you, Laney, nothing compares. Nothing ever will, my love."

I grab him around the neck and pull his mouth to mine, kissing him with an uncontrolled fervor. His fingers move soft and slow, exploring me. That wicked tongue of his skims the shell of my ear, sending tremors to my core where his hand plays.

"You good, baby girl?" he breathes out.

"Never been better; don't stop."

He continues his mastery of my body, his thumb pressing the perfect spot, until I begin to shudder uncontrollably, devouring every inch of his mouth with my burning tongue. Within seconds, an ungodly moan rips from me as he takes me to heights I didn't know existed.

I finally break our kiss to catch my breath, the mad fluttering in my thighs taking a minute to settle. Once my heartbeat returns to normal, I gently push him onto his back. "Let me love you."

Pushing up his t-shirt, I kiss along his stomach and abs, licking every distinct line. His muscles tighten and ripple with every touch of my mouth, his breathing deep and anguished. When I've tasted every inch of his torso, I bestow sweet kisses down to the waist of his jeans. With my eyes locked boldly on his, I unbutton his pants. He lifts his hips to help me pull them, and his tight gray briefs, down.

Tossing them aside without a care in the world, I stare down at his bulging erection. His hand strokes my hair and I feel his eyes on me. Studying me? Memorizing this to replay in his dreams while we're apart? Knowing he's watching, I seductively nip my way back up the inside of his thigh, basking in the sounds he makes. His hands tighten on my hips as he groans out my name, spurring me on. I have no idea where I got my moves, it's coming so naturally. I want to make him feel good and just go with my instincts, next running my tongue the length of his hardness.

"Oh God, Laney, yes." His fingers dig into my scalp, moving my veil of hair back from my face. "I have to see you," he says, his voice throaty and virile.

I move my mouth down over him, exploring with my tongue. When I've tested and teased him enough, I take in as much of him as I can. Obviously no expert, my reflex tells me when I've gone far enough and I immediately tell myself to breathe through my nose and relax.

This feels...erotic. Having him in my mouth, feeling him twitch in excitement, feels as good to me as I hope it does to him. One hand on his thigh to brace myself, I feel his muscles flex and I run my nails roughly up and down. Wrapping a hand around the rest of his long, thick length that I can't love with my mouth, his hand joins mine. He shows me exactly what he wants; fast and hard.

"Oh sweet damn, Laney, that is so good." His voice

trembles just like his body. I look up at him and he's staring back down at me with genuine love, silently telling me what this, between us, means. His hand runs through my hair. "Lil' bit harder, baby."

His suggestive words empower me and I show him what he does to me. I put as much love and want into my sensual discovery of him as possible. Soon he growls out, "I'm close, Laney, ah…p-pull back, baby."

But I don't move away. I take all he has to give me.

He's even sexy when he pulls up his jeans and crouches down, pulling me back with him to the blanket. One hand draws lazy swirls on my belly as his erratic breathing settles. "You're so amazing," he whispers as I lay my head on his chest.

"So are you, Ev. I really needed today." I sigh.

"The thought of being apart again is killing me, Laney. I don't know if I can do this."

Hot tears begin to fall; I know too well what he means. We just loved each other. It felt so right, but very soon this euphoria will be gone and ice cold misery will replace it. We both already feel it coming and it's been mere minutes. Why is life so tough?

"I'm having a really hard time too, Evan," I choke out. "It's like I'm damned if I do and damned if I don't. I'm lonely and miss you terribly, but that wouldn't change if you were mine. You'd still be so far away and then I'd just have to add guilt if I had fun without you. I suspect you're dealing with the same thing?" I peer up at him questioningly.

"I know exactly how you feel, precious girl." He kisses the top of my head. "We've never been more than a stone's throw apart. It's going to be different and it sucks."

"It's not just that. I've met a few fun people, most are guys, and I feel like I'm doing something wrong. Then I wonder what you're doing and it eats away at me, Evan." I plead to him silently, tell me the answer, Evan.

We snuggle and talk and he opens up more; he felt the same way—worried and insecure about what I'm doing all the time. His social life is apparently a lot wilder than mine, and he's forthcoming that I'd been scarily accurate about the temptations he faced. He doesn't, however, admit anything specific, like what I saw in the picture. I say nothing. There's absolutely no point. Sure, I can make him feel guilty or get mad, but enough with the merry-go-round.

"It's not that I want them, Laney. I want you, but I can't have you…and sometimes the thought crosses my mind that it'd feel good to fill the void. Not sex, just someone to hug or spend time with, but the thought of another man touching you makes me want to kill someone, so then I'm a hypocrite…a lonely, depressed hypocrite. Do you know what I'm trying to say?"

"Yes, I do. Evan, I want you to be happy. I want you to do whatever you want, whatever gets you by. Well, I mean, be careful." I blush and let out a sarcastic snort. "Know that I don't hold you to anything. We agreed. Just be happy."

It feels like my heart is splitting in two and half of it will be heading back to Athens, but it's also suddenly easier to take a deep breath. The thought of Evan with other girls makes me sick, but I know that isn't his reasoning. That's a surface issue to the deep emotional havoc, so I don't outright ask him not to sleep with anyone. The thought of him sitting in the corners of rooms, sad and lonely, makes me so much sicker.

My entire drive back to school is done with tears clouding my vision, a gripping pain in my chest, and half my soul missing.

Chapter 20

KICKIN' IT

-Laney-

Bennett is thrilled I'm back early—there's no school tomorrow and she's immediately harping on me to go out with her. Has she even noticed I look like hell? That perhaps something's wrong with me?

Screw this. I'll call Zach, who has become a great friend. We've gotten together a couple times at the nearby coffee shop. He's a whiz at algebra and I'd be failing without him.

My first impression of him from the Hall Crawl was dead on. He gets cooler every time I'm around him. If he'd have come from back home, he no doubt would've been friends with Parker and Evan. A Kinesiology major, he wants to coach football later, and loves to play.

I couldn't imagine why he didn't have a girlfriend, but one day he'd told me some about his past, his heartbreak. His high school sweetheart had done a number on him. He found out she cheated on him several times after a picture on the Facebook page of someone who tagged someone who…however that works. That led to him questioning her and her breaking down into a fess-all. I got the picture (no pun intended). He'd been at arm's length from anything serious ever since. It may have left him love shy, but it hadn't made him one bit a bitter person. He was as sweet as sugar.

Sometimes I talk with him about Evan and he gives me much-appreciated advice, a guy point of view minus any "I really want to get in your pants" ulterior motives. His heartbreaking relationship had also been long-distance, so he understands exactly how I feel.

He answers right away and assures me Drew is out (his roommate definitely hasn't grown on me like he has), so I head to his room. The minute he opens the door, he knows something is wrong—thank you, friend! He pulls me in for a hug, rubbing my back, and leads me to sit with him on the couch.

I tell him everything in between hiccups and sobs and he doesn't interrupt, doesn't interject with opinion; he just listens. When I take a break, he finally speaks. "Want to know what I think?" I nod into his shoulder. "I think you two have an amazing relationship, even if it doesn't have a name or a box to fit into right now. It's no doubt a relationship, and one of the most forgiving, open, and loving ones of all time. What's that girly poem chicks are always quoting; something about if you love it, set it free?"

"Free, like do you think he'll sleep with a bunch of girls? That makes me want to puke." It does—my throat starts sweating.

"I don't, Laney. I mean, he might, but he sounds different. Believe it or not, some guys do make it through college without a STD. Do you see me sleeping around?"

And just like that, he makes it all better. What he said, that's exactly what Evan and I have, and that's exactly what we're doing—setting each other free to see if we'll find our way back one day. And Zach does seem fine not whoring, and there aren't girls coming out of Sawyer and Tate's room all the time either, although I'm sure that's more Tate's influence than Sawyer's. But it's another example that not all college guys are bound and determined to sleep with everyone available. Damn, Zach's better therapy than the actual therapist I used to have. His answer kicked her lame rumblings' ass.

"So, Miss Laney, what should we do now?"

"Well, Red over in my room would like to go to The K tonight, which I'm assuming is a bad idea. But it's not really college without a brush with public intox, though, right?"

"How are you gonna get into The K, Laney? You're only 18, right?" He raises his eyebrows in playful question.

I stick my tongue out at him. "I'll be 19 in a few weeks."

"Still not old enough." He grins.

"Apparently Bennett has connections in the world of fake IDs."

"Do you want to go to a club, Laney? I mean, I think The K is awesome, but I'm not sure if you'd like it."

"Honestly, I'm sick of being down, and whatever I've been doing isn't working! I just hurt the person most important to me, so maybe I oughta give something new a try."

"I'll go with you then." Not a question, but not really a command either; just right.

We agree to meet up at my room at eight and I head back to brave Bennett. She's lying on her bed when I get there, and sits up when I enter.

"Laney, can we talk?

"Yup, what's up?"

"Laney, I noticed you were upset today, but I'd rather focus on fixing it for you rather than dwelling on it. That's what I do. I breathe the life back into things. It's my specialty." Okay, so I kinda smile at that. "I want to get you out, show you some fun.

Come out of your cave, Laney, play with others!"

"Well, since I'm now completely alone, I guess the only sensible thing to do is start over." Completely alone...my rock rolled away.

"I'd like to point out that you're not alone. I'm thrilled we're friends and roomies, and I'd love to enjoy our freshman year together if you deem me worthy."

She's really good at the deep stuff and her words hit home. I know how to do Laney the daughter, Laney the ballplayer, and for a while I was pretty good at Laney and Evan, but I have no clue how to do just Laney.

"You know what, Bennett? I'm sorry. I am grateful to have you. This is all new to me and I'm not trying to be a brat. You get me an ID, I'm in."

I'm an excellent dancer, right? Every stuffed animal I own thinks so. I'd never do it at my old school, but this is my new school, my new life, so maybe I can bust a move or two.

"Laney, you're the best roommate and new BFF ever!" She claps, jumps up, and gives me a huge hug.

Yeah, I can handle this. "So, what should I wear tonight? What are you wearing?"

"Laney, why do you even ask those questions together? Imma do me, you do...jeans, heels, and maybe a halter top? Can you handle that?"

"Only if you have heels and a halter top you want to loan me."

"Of course I do!"

We're going to The K, which we've clarified is short for The Kickback. It's the most cosmopolitan thing I've ever done in my life. I am wearing a strapless bra and there's false documentation on my person. I'm picturing Pinocchio, when

Honest John leads him to the island; we're all coming home donkeys tonight, I'm sure of it.

Donned in my own MissMe jeans and Bennett's red high heels and black halter top, I'm self-conscious but as ready as I'll ever be. I put my hair in a ponytail and wear very little makeup. It's still me, and I don't look the 21 my "license" now reads, but if they kick me out, that's my flashing neon "sign" that this really is as bad of an idea as I suspect.

Bennett has gone all out—she has on a black skirt that could double as a tube top, six-inch heels, and a glittery silver tank top. Her auburn hair is down and bouncing. She looks old enough to be one of our professors with her makeup job, and the look in her eyes is scandalous—Drama Girl is on the prowl. Well good, I can shrink behind her spotlight all night.

Zach looks great in dark wash jeans and a black button up shirt and his hair is styled; he even trimmed up the goatee a bit.

I send Evan a text on the way. I wish he was with me for many reasons, but at least I know I'm safe as I glance at Zach in the driver's seat.

Laney: I love you, for all we are and all we're not right now too. If you love something, let it go. If it comes back, it's yours.

Evan: I am yours, always have been, always will be. I hate what this did to us, hate college.

Laney: Not a fan myself, but we had to grow up sometime right?

Evan: I will never love anything even half as much as I love you. We will find our way back.

Laney: I hope so.

Evan: Have a good night Laney, be safe.

Laney: Night Ev, u2

"You okay?" Zach looks at me from the corner of his

eye.

"Yeah, I'm great." It's taking every effort not to let the tears I'm holding back fall. I didn't think anything could ever come between Evan and me...and look at us now.

"Yes, you are, Laney, one of the best. Now have some fun, okay? You say ready and we're gone, girl. And keep your phone on vibrate in case we lose each other. You won't hear it, but you'll feel it." Zach seems very sure of his plan, so I relax a little.

"Let's just not lose each other," I offer weakly.

"Laney, this is going to be fun, I promise!" Bennett adds from the backseat. She really has no fear.

There's a huge dude at the door who barely even looks at my ID, but looks at me thoroughly, and just like that—we're in. I can feel the pulse of the music all through me. I smell smoke and sweat, but I can see very little—this place is dark. I shiver and slide my arm through Zach's, trusting him to lead the way. He reaches up and pats my hand, making me feel a little better.

"Bennett?!" I all but scream.

"Right here."

"Okay, don't you dare run off."

"Yes, Mom."

"Don't call me that, and stay around, B, I mean it." I don't care if I'm a pain in the ass. If she doesn't like it, she can quit making me go with her.

Visibility improves slightly the further in we get, so I take my first good look around. I'm pretty sure *Boogie Nights* 2 will be shot here. The back wall is lined with dark leather, with circular booths and tables that glow blue from underneath. The DJ is up on an elevated stage with so many different lights I can't look right at it. The dance floor is huge and obviously made to be the main attraction, and the U-shaped bar, under lit with red, sits right in the middle of it.

I can barely see the south end, it's pretty far away, but it appears to have pool tables, darts and is that skeeball?! In the far corner, tucked almost behind the DJ stage, is a staircase. I look up to see balcony seating; must be the VIP section. Are there VIPs in college? I wonder if P Diddy is up there.

Bennett pulls us over to a table on the edge of the dance floor. I scoot my stool as close to Zach as I can without sitting in his lap. We're quickly approached by a blonde in a Catholic school girl outfit—poor thing lost half of it—for our drink orders. I glance around, taking it all in, and find myself in awe.

I've seen people dance and grind, but it was G-rated compared to what some of the couples on the floor are doing now. The music is a little loud, and ew...no elbows on the table, it's sticky. But other than that, I can start to see the appeal of it. The place is alive, electric, and no doubt better than sitting in your dorm room.

The blonde brings back Zach's beer and Bennett's pink thing, and then sets a tall, thin glass in front of me. "Um, what's that?"

"It's a champagne spritzer, they're good."

"But I ordered water."

"It's on the house," she says with a shrug and walks away.

I look at Zach with confusion. "Did you order this for me?"

"Not me." He shakes his head and a quick shoulder shrug from Bennett confirms it wasn't her either.

"Guys send drinks over for pretty girls all the time, Laney, don't worry about it," Bennett explains nonchalantly, flipping her hair over her shoulder.

"She didn't say from the gentleman over there, she said on the house. Either way, I'm not drinking that, no way."

Zach offers to trade me. "No one put anything in my

beer, I assure you, plus it's free champagne." He tosses back a big gulp of the free bubbly.

"She's right, it's good. You wanna dance?"

"Um, I've never really fast danced outside of my room. I don't want to embarrass you," I mumble, blushing slightly.

"Don't worry, Laney, I'm an excellent teacher." He starts to pull me to the floor and I grab Bennett's hand and pull her with us.

Three songs in and I'm having a blast! I feel bad I wouldn't dance like this with Evan at prom, but I hated those spectators. I don't know anyone here—and they don't know me. Zach's a great dancer and he moves with me, but not in a handsy slimeball way. He dips me, and while upside down, I see Tate approaching behind Bennett.

Zach pulls me up and I turn, Tate giving me the "shh" sign as he slips right up to her backside, hands going to her hips. She turns slightly to see it's him and wraps her arms around his neck. They're cute together, really, but I thought Tate couldn't come? Oh well. I turn to Zach.

"You ready for a break?!" I yell over the music.

He nods and leads us back to our table, hand at the small of my back. Eventually Bennett and Tate make their way over for a breather.

"Tate, I thought you couldn't make it. What a nice surprise."

"Well, I got done early, so I came to find this beauty." He looks over and smiles at Bennett. "Couldn't have her here alone now, could I?"

Bennett blushes and kisses his cheek.

"Where are Sawyer and Dane?" I ask as I look around the room.

"I'm not sure," he says with a smirk. "I could text them."

"No, that's okay, just asking." I don't want him texting that I was asking about them! Can you say "mortifying"? I'm really just curious...right?

Zach and I eventually go out and dance a few more songs, play some skeeball and even darts. Now I'm ready to go; these heels are killing my feet. Zach agrees, so we go to search out Bennett. I spot her back on the dance floor with Tate and start through the mass of gyrating bodies to fetch her.

I feel it; my body tells me that he's in close proximity before I see him—so weird. All of a sudden, right in front of me, is Dane. I startle a little but manage a "hi."

"Hello, Disney, fancy meeting you here." He smiles. "Small world."

"It's actually not at all. I could show you."

What?

"May I have a dance?"

Oh yeah, he can. I look back at Zach and mouth "one song" while I hold up a finger. He nods and I turn back to Dane. "Just one."

"Well then, I better make it count." He turns and does a head thing to the DJ, who for some reason seems to take notice. "Come here," he says, holding out his hand. I place mine in his, moving into him. He pulls me tight and we dance to "I'll Be" by Edwin McCain. It feels eerily similar to prom with Evan; if he starts singing in my ear I may lose it. But no, he's a whisper in your ear guy. "Who is that guy you're with, Laney?"

"Zach Reece; he lives in our dorm."

"And what is he to you?" His hot breath caresses my ear and neck.

"A friend, a good one so far."

"And Evan?" How does he know that? Bennett!

"A better friend, the best." It hurts a little when I say it.

"And I am?"

"Interesting." I feel him shake lightly against me, laughing.

"I find you quite interesting as well, Laney." He doesn't exactly say it, more like pours it slowly in my ear.

"I'm not."

"I'll be the judge of that."

"What does that mean?" I know my voice is shaking and barely a whisper, but holding a conversation when you can barely breathe is a challenge.

"It means, Laney, that I want to get to know you better."

"Why?"

"Something tells me, has been telling me, I should."

"Okay, well, I was about to leave."

"I don't mean tonight. I'm all for you leaving here as soon as possible. Tomorrow, spend the day with me; whatever you want to do."

"I'll think about it." And I will; I'm actually considering it.

"The song's over, Laney, so I'll let you go, for now…but tomorrow," he says, lifting my hand to his mouth, placing a kiss.

And with that, I go back to Zach, who has detained Bennett, and we head home. Falling asleep, I almost send a text to Evan, but stop myself.

Leave him be, Laney.

Chapter 21

LANEY DAY

-Laney-

My phone wakes me up; a number I don't recognize. "Hello?"

"Good morning, Disney, sleep well?"

How does Dane have my number? Not that I mind he has it, but I have got to talk to Bennett about her big mouth.

"Good morning, Dane, you're up early," I mumble sleepily. Seriously, do I know a guy who sleeps in?

"I couldn't wait to get started. I don't want to waste a single minute of this day with you."

"I don't remember saying yes yet." We both know I'm going to say yes, who am I kidding?

"Ah, but you didn't say no, and I'm hopeful."

"I don't know… What would we do?"

"I told you, anything you want."

"Noooo, you were brave enough to call me, aren't you brave enough to set the agenda?" I snicker as I put his words back on him.

He chuckles. "Touché, Disney. Yes, if you say I can make the plans, I'd be happy to do so. Is there anything you can't or won't do, like any phobias I should be aware of?"

Is he kidding? What the hell is he planning? "Let's see...I would prefer not to jump off or out of anything. I get cold really easily and I'm allergic to walnuts. Other than that, I think I'm good."

He's laughing heartily now. "Oh Laney, you make me smile. Wear comfortable shoes, I'll be there within the hour."

"Well, okay then, bossy boots, I'll see you then."

When I hang up, I think of Evan. I wonder if he's spending time with other girls. Time meaning, doing stuff other than sticking his drunken face in their chest of course, 'cause I'm pretty sure Dane has better plans for today than that.

I shake off the thoughts and jump out of bed, rushing through a shower, brushing my teeth, and throwing on faded jeans, a jersey t-shirt and some red kicks. I quickly dry my hair and pull it through the back of my favorite ball cap; cute earrings and some lip gloss later, I'm set just in time for the knock at the door.

"Good morning," I say cheerfully, taking a minute to look him over.

Dark, sexy jeans that hang oh so right, a gray Henley and Doc boots, still the cross necklace and perfect hair. Looking forward to today—I am! I am!

"So, whaddaya think?" He grins with one side of his mouth and that single cocky eyebrow as he notices my perusal.

"I've seen better," I say with a shrug of my shoulder.

"I haven't." He winks...every time I see him.

"Oh, please, like I even remotely believe that. You don't

strike me as a cheesy lines guy, so don't ruin it now." I wink at him this time.

He takes my hand, guiding me down the hall. "Disney, I say almost nothing I don't really mean. I honestly don't think I've ever seen anything better."

Giddy with his sweet words, I ask, "So where are we going?"

"You'll see." He helps me into his very nice silver car. That's all I know—silver, two doors, not a truck, looks expensive. He walks around the front, which I pay way too much attention to, and climbs in the driver's seat. "You want music?"

"You know the answer to that."

"So I do, Disney." He shoots me an adorable sidelong glance and starts the car and the music.

Is that? Oh, surely not. I thought I was the only person my age who knew ELO. My dad played them on records, for God's sake! Anything could have just played, some clichéd, sound-the-same crap...but it was ELO. This little surprise is doing funny things to my head.

"Have you eaten?" he asks.

"I was in bed when you called," I titter. "No, I haven't eaten."

"Me either, shall we start with that? I don't want you hungry."

I agree that sounds fine and a few minutes later we pull up to a little café on a historic district street. I wonder how he knows of this place.

We opt to sit outside on the back deck; it has a great view of the lake. The houses around the water are spectacular. I always wonder when I see houses like that, what the heck do those people do for a living? My dad used to always tell me, "Slugger, money like that comes two ways. You're born to it or you screw somebody else out of it."

My dad is the hardest worker I know—any day, any shift; and we struggled. These houses are three stories with private sand beaches and stone steps from their lower decks to the water. I wonder if they ever stop and take it all in. Do they appreciate what they have or do they wish they had the one across the water, 'cause it has more windows?

"Do you know what you want?" His question pulls me from my thoughts.

"I have absolutely no idea." I'm not just talking about the menu and I think he knows that. "I'll just have what he's having," I tell the waitress. "So, are you going to tell me what we're doing today?"

"Nope, you'll see. Are you not big on surprises, Disney?"

"Yes and no. I love good surprises. I get ants in my pants but I don't like the lingering fear from knowing most of them don't turn out that way. I have to really trust the person to know the surprise will be good."

"I hope to make everything wonderful. If it's not, you tell me, okay, Laney? Today and always, just tell me, and I'll fix it." He smiles warmly and I see sincerity in it, warming me to the idea of more time with this guy.

Our food arrives and it smells wonderful. Blueberry stuffed strudel, and the first bite confirms it—Dane has excellent taste. "Mmmmm," escapes me despite the mouthful.

"You like?"

"Oh my God, like is far from the right word. It may be the best thing I've ever eaten."

"Yeah, I love this place. Next time we'll get the strawberry chip pancakes. You can go ahead and thank me now," he laughs as he puts a piece of heaven in his mouth.

"Thank you," I say, a bit embarrassed, looking down at the table. Of course I was going to thank him at the end of the meal.

"No, Laney." He drops his fork and reaches across for my hand with a soft chuckle. "I meant you'll be thanking me for introducing you to the pancakes."

"Oh, well, thank you for that, and this."

He kisses the back of my hand he's holding. "Thank you for joining me."

I look down, focusing on my dish rather than the rush of emotions surging through me.

"Laney, how is it possible you have no idea how captivating you are?"

Evan asked me something similar once, I remember it melted me to learn he thought that way...Evan.

"Knowing me so little, what can you possibly mean?" This is a test. If he leads with the word hot, smokin', tits, or ass, he's taking me home.

"Girls came in and out of that room all night. The only one I noticed was you. Not just that you're gorgeous, you are, but a lot of them were pretty." He glances out the window briefly before turning back to me with a serious tone to his expression. "But you, I remember you asked, 'so you live three to this room?' and your voice, I couldn't have not turned around. The more we all talked, I saw your wit, your sarcasm, and the innocent but curious sparkle in your eye...I don't know, I just found myself dying to hear what you'd say next." He takes a deep breath, like a witness would when their testimony is finally over. "Oh and then the princess pajamas; I can't remember ever seeing anything cuter in my life."

We both laugh at that. "Dane, I..."

"Don't be nervous, Laney, I just want to spend time with you. I want to get to know you." He leans over the table on his elbows, bringing his face closer to mine. "There's something great about you, the way I feel when you're in a room. I want to see if my instincts are right about you, and those tell me that any kind of time with you is worth spending."

"Okay, we'll spend time together. I'd like to get to know you, too." I offer him a tentative smile and take another bite so I don't have to talk anymore.

He leans back in his chair, folding his hands behind his head and crossing one leg over his knee. "Best news I've heard all day," he coyly replies.

MK Studios is the sign on the building we pull up to and I turn to Dane. "What is this place?"

"It's our first stop on Laney Day." His lips curve up a bit hesitant of a full smile; he's nervous.

"Breakfast was our first stop, and an excellent one at that."

"I stand corrected; this is stop two, come on." He comes around to open my door, extending his hand to me.

The receptionist greets him immediately. "Mr. Kendrick, so good to see you."

Mr. Kendrick? He's like twentyish years old.

"Thank you, Angela. I believe Paul is expecting us. This is Laney Walker."

"Of course, come on back."

Come on back? Who is expecting me for what?

Breathe, Laney, breathe. I agreed to let him make the plans, and I agreed to go with him today in the first place, so time to man up.

Paul is a fascinating man, definitely same-sex oriented, and apparently he loves me and I'm his darling. I love the way he says both incessantly. It becomes clear very quickly that I'm here for a photo shoot and I suddenly feel nauseous. Surely this isn't a normal first date—well, this isn't a date, but this is as intimidating of an event as it gets…Dane is a "go big or go home" guy apparently.

"Dane," I lean to him and whisper. "What the hell?! I can't do this! Why would I do this? If you think I'm putting on some lingerie and posing, I'm gonna run out of here…and I'll be nixing the whole 'spend time together thing,' you perv."

He rubs water from his eyes he's laughing so hard. "Oh, Disney, never quit talking, please." He catches his breath. "I already know you well enough to know lingerie would never be an option, and while I'm confident you'd look fabulous," he winks, "I wouldn't orchestrate for other people to see you in it."

Oh, Lord, good answer; I feel heated and oddly flattered.

"I want you to see how beautiful you are, accomplished perfectly with clothes on. Now go with Paul and I'll wait here."

I start to slowly drag my feet in the direction of Paul.

"And Laney!"

I turn back to look at him. The little sneak.

"Have fun."

Paul puts me in a silky, flowing dress of beautiful light green with a cream overlay. I argue with him a bit about it being a dress because I don't do dresses, but he assures me that he does this for a living and I look marvelous. "I think Mr. Dane wants you to see what he sees. Let me bring that out for you. Trust me."

I go with it; might as well make the most of the experience, this is something I'd never have thought of myself.

When Paul's crew is done, my hair is down and curled and my feet are bare with a dark red polish on my toes. My makeup is light except around my eyes, where it's heavy and smoky.

Paul pulls me to a backdrop of sheer white and places me on a dark chaise. Then he aims a fan at me from far away. This is the real deal. I feel a bit like Cleopatra or Elizabeth Taylor.

"Look up, left, at me, no smile, sultry, pout, look away, right arm back, left ankle in, arched back, shoulder down, look down and over," Paul drills out commands, jumping around me like Tigger.

I'm more than a bit overwhelmed. I ask him to stop a few times so I can calm myself, but finally he says we're done and that I did well.

Dane ambles over to me. "How was that?"

"Actually, it was really fun once I got used to it. Thank you so much."

"You're more than welcome. I'll look at the shots while you get changed. I think he got some really nice ones."

I swallow heavily. "You watched?"

"Every second. You did amazing. Did it feel good, Laney?"

If I discount away my anxiety and take it at face value, yeah, it did. "It did," I finally answer.

"Well then, stop two is a success." His cocky grin is brilliant.

When I'm changed, Paul calls me over to look at the shots on the monitor. I'm pretty sure my jaw hits the floor; I love them. I barely recognize myself and am definitely shocked at the look in my eyes he's captured.

He rolls through the pictures, Dane and I looking over his shoulder.

"That one!" Dane says suddenly. "B-dub it."

Suddenly, the picture in front of me becomes black and white. It's a close up of my face, head slightly turned, and one curl falling by my cast down eyes. Dane reaches over Paul, taps a few buttons on the keyboard, and the nearby printer comes to life. As quick as that, there are two large prints of the shot in the tray and Dane moves to put one each in a separate manila envelope.

"One for you, one for me," he says, handing me one. "You'll get a copy of all the rest later, but I had to have this one now."

Paul kisses me on each cheek and I thank him for the greatest time, promising to come back for another shoot sometime. Walking out, I stop Dane short and give him a huge hug. I can't hold it in a second longer. "Thank you again, Dane, I mean it. You'll never know how much."

He winks back at me, of course he winks, and it's enough; I'm starting to speak wink.

"So where we headed now?" The exhilaration still courses through me as I slide into his car.

He tsks. "Stop three is a surprise, too, but it's a further drive, so we have time to do a Q & A now." He looks over coyly. "If you're ready, that is. No doing a shot to pass now, so you have to answer."

"Dane, are you cowering to your own theory about the games? If you want to know something, just ask." Oh, it is so fun turning his words back on him.

"Damn, you're good. I'm not used to people actually hearing or remembering what I say simply because they choose to. I'm gonna have to up my game." He laughs. "Okay, so my first question." He pauses dramatically to think about it. "Where did you grow up?"

"About an hour from school, in Forest. You?"

"Bridgeport, Connecticut. I moved here Tate's freshman year."

"Why?"

"Tate picked a school here because it was far away. He got in, so I followed him."

"Why would you follow him if you weren't going to go to school there as well?" I'm usually not this nosy, but he's opened up the floor for questioning. Plus, I've been wondering since I met him why he hung around a school he didn't go to. In fact, I'm curious what he does all together.

"Ah ah, my turn." He dodges that one nicely. "So Disney, why Southern?"

"Easy, it's where I got a good offer; you know, softball. Evan and Kaitlyn, my other best friend, are both at the University of Georgia, but they didn't want me." I instantly wish I could take back the last part I'd just blurted out. I don't want him to think I feel sorry for myself. I was very lucky to get financial aid for my schooling and I'm grateful.

"So Dane, why not Southern?"

"I was never going to go to college." He doesn't elaborate.

Pulling teeth here. "Why not?"

"Now, Laney, with all your witty banter, surely you're able to keep up with whose turn it is." His lips curl up.

Oh, he's clever. Yes, I was firing on all pistons with no regard for turns, so I remain silent.

"How long have you been playing softball?" he asks.

"Since I was about eleven, well, on a serious level, anyway. My dad coached me my whole life until I got to high school. They wouldn't let him on the field then." I laugh at my answer. Oh, Daddy.

"I gotta tell ya, Disney, I never even thought about girls' softball, let alone appreciated it, until I met you."

"Our games haven't even started yet, what are you talking about?" I give him a quizzical glance out of the corner of my eye.

"I can tell softball's hard work and you've obviously dedicated yourself to it."

"How do you know that?"

"By your body, Laney. No way has that happened on its

own," he remarks in a deeper tone.

"Um, Dane, have you been checking me out?" I blush.

"Only when I'm breathing." He winks and gives me a sideways beam.

He'd set himself up to be able to tell me he thinks I have a nice body, and Lord help me, I appreciated the effort.

"All right, whose question?" I ask with way too much excitement.

"Mine, when we get done—we're here."

Ty's is a very nice gym and I don't even ask what we're doing here this time, working out is fine with me. I have to say, I don't think Dane's plans have or will ever be mimicked. I wouldn't have guessed today's agenda in a million years.

Here, too, it's all Mr. Kendrick this and Mr. Kendrick that, and once we're suited up in protective gear, it appears this won't be a standard workout and that we're the only two in class. A burly man named Kit explains that he's a self-defense instructor and goes through the basic moves of self-defense. He has me practice them all on him several times. It's odd how in tune to me Dane is. Self-defense class? Perfect.

Kit next wants me to spar with Dane, who's grinning ear to ear. "Take it easy on me, badass," he teases as he grins bigger, if that's possible.

I flip him off.

His eyebrows pop up. "I've never seen that move in a Disney movie." He laughs. I just roll my eyes.

We go through the scenarios and I actually do pretty well...I think. I'm a bit distracted. I mean, Evan has a great body and is a stellar athlete, but he's way across a field covered in pads. Dane is right in front of me; shirtless and sweating. It's scary hot.

The male form in motion is a beautiful thing; skin, sweat, muscles flexing…pay attention, Laney, you're gonna get knocked out. I stay off my butt, get a few blocks up and get one kick on him, which I'm pretty sure he let me do, but I'd say it's pretty good for my first performance.

"Remember, Laney, nose or groin, and then run and scream the whole way, got it?" Dane is taking this very seriously. "Let's do it again, I'm attacking you from the front."

And he does. I get the shove your nose up move in and turn to run.

"Make sure he's down before you turn your back, Laney," he reminds me as he grabs my arm.

I do the backwards elbow up to his nose that they taught me, and this time I spin and do the knee to groin motion, watching him go down before I turn to run.

"Very nice, Disney, you did very well."

I square my shoulders and chin. "Thanks."

Even Kit agrees I'm a very quick learner. Dane and I both thank him for the lesson and go to change.

Heading to the car, I'm actually bounce-skipping or something. I can't remember the last time I had this kind of adrenaline high. This has been one of the best days I've ever had and I'm euphoric.

Last stop of this exhilarating day is dinner and we agree on Mexican food.

"Okay, so it was my turn," he says as we wait for our food. "How did you like the defense class?"

"I really liked it, very cool and good to learn. Thank you." I smile.

"You're very welcome. Do you know why I took you

there?"

"Well, the shoot was so I'd feel pretty, which I did, so I'm guessing the class was so I'd feel safe?"

"In part, yes. I want you to feel in control, Laney. I see a look in your eyes sometimes, a lot like fear, and as you venture out more, I want you to have at least some control over the situation. I want that sense of confidence to emanate from you."

"Why?" It's insightful, but way forward.

"I can tell all this is new to you, Laney; college, going out, meeting new people. I want you to feel secure. Every woman should make decisions based on good sense or choice, not fear."

"How do you think you know so much about me?"

"I'm a pretty good people reader, always have been. I have to be. If I'm wrong, remember, just tell me. Either way, though, it can't hurt for you to be prepared, right?"

"No doubt, it was good to learn…but, I don't know…"

"What, tell me."

"I loved today. Everything you planned was original and creative and so fun, but both things were to make me feel something else or be someone different. It kinda makes me feel like you see all these things about me you want to fix, like I'm not okay as I am. Does that make sense?"

He looks at me thoughtfully for a bit before answering. "Yes, I can see where you'd think that." He blows a sigh up and out, ruffling his hair slightly. "I'm so sorry, Laney. Damn, talk about a backfire."

"I didn't mean to make you feel bad, Dane." I cover his hand resting on the table with mine. "I really appreciated everything today."

"I know you did, even though I was making you feel doubt the whole time. I tried to plan things to make you happy and it had the opposite effect. I'm sorry." The desolate look he now wears breaks something in me.

"Don't do that, Dane, don't shut down. Tell me what you meant, what your goal was, and let's see if I can understand where you were coming from. I bet I get it." I smile at him encouragingly. I refuse to let this day go sour.

"That, right there." He turns his hand in mine, linking over fingers together. "You're so real. The last thing I'd ever want to do is change you. I took you to the photo shoot because it's something near to my heart, capturing beauty like yours." He kisses the back of my hand. "And the class, I thought it'd be fun. You play ball, so you obviously like physical activities. And I admit I knew I'd like watching you enjoy a physical activity. So really, they were both kinda about me." He chuckles. "As of right now, I have no inventory of anything wrong with you." He winks, but it's to deflect nervousness; he thinks I won't accept his answer...

Wrong, it was a perfect answer. "See, I understand completely. Was that so hard? I mean, don't you hate it when people do that? They let a minuscule misunderstanding build and build without addressing it, and before you know it, there's a path of destruction. It's such an easy fix to just talk about things. In fact, sometimes it not only fixes things, it makes them even better!"

"Girls who talk things out calmly? Where did you come from, Laney?"

"Georgia."

"Well, Georgia is lucky to have you. Come on, you finished?"

"I am. The food was so good. Thank you, Dane."

"Thank you for always saying thank you. I like doing things with you."

I blush a bit at this. I like doing things with him, too. He's so down to earth, so easy to talk to. It's like I've known him a lot longer than I have.

It's dark when we get outside, so I suggest maybe he take

me home now, I have class early. "Dane, why weren't you ever going to go to college?"

"Ah, back to your question, huh? Okay, I'll tell you a bit, but go easy on me, Disney. I don't want to unveil all the cobwebs at once, all right?"

I nod my agreement as he holds open the car door for me, guiding me in with his hand at the small of my back.

He climbs in his side and starts the car but turns to me before we move. "I had other things waiting for me, responsibilities, so I couldn't go to college and manage those things at the same time. I couldn't let so many others down just to come out with a degree I'd never have to use. Maybe one day, if things are different, I'll go. But for right now, I made the right decision."

"Are you happy?"

This question throws him. He looks out the windshield straight ahead and it seems he's calming himself before he answers. "I think you're the first person who's stopped and asked me that. All this time, people who've known me forever, you're the only one. The answer is...sometimes. I'm happy right now."

"Why now?" My hands fidget nervously in my lap and I chew my lip, perhaps I'm digging too deep.

"Because I'm with you; I've been with you all day. The way you talk to me so openly, you make me feel alive, seen. I know you see me."

We pull up to my dorm but the last thing I want to do is get out. He turns in his seat to face me, his eyes drifting to my lips and back, unashamed. Dane's talking and I'm like a sponge, but I really do need to get inside and to bed. "You coming up to their room? We can walk up."

"Not tonight, I have to go home. But I'll walk you to the door."

When we get there, he stops and grazes my face with his

fingertips. I think he may want to kiss me, but I'm not going to let that to happen. It's way too soon for me. But he doesn't, he just takes me all in, stroking my cheek.

"See me tomorrow," he says. "I'll let you plan it."

I laugh. "You make wonderful plans. Stop, we covered that. But I have ball until six tomorrow, then probably homework. Why don't you text or call me and we'll see?"

"I can do that. Thank you for today, Disney."

"You too, Dane, I'll talk to you tomorrow." I walk inside, giving him a small wave.

In my room, Bennett and Tate are draped across her bed watching a movie. I hate to interrupt, but I really need to get some rest.

"Hey guys, sorry. I'll be asleep and out of your hair in just a minute."

"Laney, where were you all day?" Bennett asks me, slightly muffled as her face is buried in Tate's chest. God, I bet that feels nice; being held.

"Ya, Laney, where ya been?" Tate smirks.

"I was with a new friend, let me show you." I take the print Dane had made for me out of the envelope and hand it to Bennett, nervous of her reaction.

"Oh my God, Laney, you look gorgeous! You could model, seriously."

Tate looks over and smiles. "He took you to the studio, huh? You like it?"

The implication in Tate's question suddenly makes me feel foolish, as though Dane takes all his "projects" there and perhaps all of his lines about how special I am are a crock. Is this his MO and I moronically allowed myself to feel enchanted?

God, I must've looked like an idiot, modeling like some starry-eyed bimbo.

I'd call and ask him, but they're in the room and they'd hear me; further humiliation. And Dane doesn't really owe me an explanation. He's not my boyfriend; hell, that wasn't even a date. If I knew him better, I'd have a better grasp on this, on his intentions. But I don't. I don't know anyone here really. How did this wonderful day go wrong in seconds? Hadn't he just remarked how refreshing it was that I'm a girl who talks things out calmly? And yes, usually I am…but right now, I'm irrational. I knew better than to let my guard down, dammit!

"Laney, you okay over there?" Bennett asks. "You can watch the movie with us."

"No, I'm good, just tired. Don't mind me." Bennett's a good roommate, she's neat and chips in, doesn't uber get in my way, but I need my time, my sanctuary. I roll towards the wall and pop my earbuds in, but as I lie there, my anger and mortification brews and brews, so under the covers where the lovers won't see me, I text Dane…

Laney: I feel like a fool.

Dane: What are you talking about?

Laney: Photo shoot…me…I don't feel pretty anymore, I feel like a jackass.

Dane: I don't know what you're talking about. Where is this coming from?

Laney: Nvmnd, prbly overreacting. Night.

I rip out my earbuds and turn my phone completely off. Great, now I can hear them mumbling and Bennett intermittently giggling—how bad would it hurt to just pierce out my eardrums? Probably pretty bad, so I jam a pillow over my head.

Chapter 22

OUT IN THE COLD

-Laney-

I ignore Dane's calls and texts all day, and there weren't any from Evan to ignore, so tonight's practice is just what the doctor ordered; I have a lot to work through. Actually, I have a lot of "lack of" to get out—lack of boyfriend, Evan, lack of communication with best friend, Evan, lack of dignity about being Dane's puppet, lack of silence from two people going at it like rabbits in my room...yeah, college rocks. GO EAGLES!

I work out until Coach makes me stop. "Hit the showers, Walker, enough for today. I'll see you Sunday morning."

Sunday morning? Oh, just kill me now, I've forgotten all about that damn hitting clinic, and it's at UGA. What am I gonna do? Of course I'll see Kaitlyn, who I haven't talked to since she sent the picture. Actually, I wasn't talking to her much before that, either. But what if I run into Evan? What if I don't? See—since when do I question seeing Evan? And yet, here we are. AAARGH!

Finally walking into my room after a marathon day, someone yells my name behind me. Turning, I see Zach jogging down the hall to catch me.

"What's up, stranger? You just getting in?"

"Yeah, I went ham at ball practice tonight. How are you, Zach? Anything new?" I welcome the big hug he gives me.

"Nothing much, big home game this weekend, can you make it?"

"Yeah, I leave for hitting clinic early Sunday, but I can come Saturday to watch you. I'd love to see you play!"

"Great, I'll give you my parents' tickets. You don't strike me as a student section mosher." He laughs.

"Good call." I chuckle back. "I'll be there. I'll see you before then though, right?"

"Well, I sure hope so. You okay, Laney?" He rests one hand on my shoulder. "You seem off."

I am off, I'm so far off I don't know which way's up. "Yeah, I'm good, thanks, though. All I need right now is a shower. I refuse to use the team facilities." A shiver actually shakes me just from the thought. "I have a paper to finish, too; I'll see ya later, Zach."

My room is empty, thank God. I throw all my stuff down and beeline for the shower. I stay in long after I'm clean and finally get out when the water feels like ice. I change into sweats and a tank, leaving my hair wet, and climb into bed. Bennett comes in not long after.

"Hey, roomie, whatcha doing?"

"Just relaxing, getting ready to go to bed. How was your day?"

"Absolutely fabulous! I think I got the role I wanted in our play." Her green eyes sparkle and I'm so happy for her. "You'll come to the show, right, Laney?"

"Of course I will, congratulations!"

"Thank you! Tate's so proud of me; he's on his way over. I think he got me a present!"

She's so excited, I don't complain about the fact I'm in bed and would rather not have company. Nor do I want to be a third wheel spectator, so I move to go. "I'm gonna go chill at Zach's, y'all have fun." She of course tells me I don't have to leave, but I do. They need this time. Lord knows, if I had a hottie coming over to bestow "you're awesome" gifts to me, I wouldn't want an audience.

Of course Zach's not in his room, but we've reviewed this...everyone here has a life but me. What the hell do I do now? I'm in sweatpants in the middle of the hall and my keys are back in the room, along with my bed. FML.

And once again...I find myself knocking on Room 114. Tate and I really should just switch rooms, except that's not happening.

Sawyer yells "Come in!" so I ever so slightly open the door and peek around it. I like to see what I'm walking into before it sees me. "Hey, Laney, come in, girl. Whatcha doing?" He looks up from his game and I move in and shut the door.

"Which one's Tate's bed?" I ask him.

"Um, that one." He points. "Why?"

"Well, Romeo and Juliet are having private time, and I'm tired. If he's gonna take up my room, I'm taking his bed."

"Cool with me, you want a drink or something?"

"Like you'd get up from that game to get me one." I laugh. "No, Sawyer, I'm good, thanks."

I try to get comfortable enough to possibly fall asleep in Tate's bed with Sawyer in the room, basically as anti-me as it gets, when the door flies open. Ah, and just when I didn't believe in happy endings, in walk, or stumble rather, Dane and songbird bitch Whitley. She's laughing like he's the funniest guy on the planet, and of course she couldn't possibly stand without both paws clinging to him, poor girl.

Dane takes notice of me and his face goes pale as his eyes bore into mine. "What are you doing here…in my brother's bed?" He croaks out.

"Your brother's in my room and Zach's not home, so I came here and Sawyer wore me plum out."

Sawyer whips his head around to me and laughs. "Don't tease me like that! I'm trying to concentrate on world domination here." He nonchalantly turns back to his game. Liking Sawyer better and better all the time; he's so chill.

"What are you doing here, Dane? Oh, my bad, do you two need this bed?" Now why did I just say that? I'm hurt and embarrassed about the studio thing, but that's not what that was just about. Am I jealous? Yes, yes I am. Not good.

"Really?" the canary bites out.

I like the word really, it's very fitting in many a situation, but she's gotta change it up a bit. It was her signature phrase the last time I had the pleasure of an encounter with her, too. If there's one brain cell in that pretty lil' head of hers, she'll pick up on my vibes and not push me right now.

"See ya, Sawyer, thanks for letting me hang. I'm out." I jump out of the bed like it's on fire and practically run out of the room. I don't stop until I'm crashing through the lobby doors into the brisk night air. I have on no shoes, no coat…and no fucks given.

I just start jogging, sucking huge gulps of air into my lungs. The burn of it actually feels good, therapeutic even. Maybe I'll go to the campus park and sleep on a bench. Maybe I'll climb a tree, find a nice bridge; I don't even care right now.

Tears gush down my face and I refuse to wipe them. All I feel is the anger pushing me to run and run. Why am I doing this to myself? Just go back to your room, Laney…NO! Why am I here? College degrees are almost useless in today's market, not that I even know what degree I want or that it matters, since I'm having a complete nervous breakdown! Like mother, like daughter, right? I'm going crazy AND I'm running, literally.

The night temperature, which only I would think has a chill to it, wet hair, and the running barefoot thing finally win out so I'm forced to stop and sit on a picnic table. My feet aren't cut or bleeding, but they hurt. I just start to catch my breath when I see headlights slowly approaching. I really hope the panic attack taking over finishes me off before the possible murderer in the car gets out. The vehicle stops, and it's then that I realize how irresponsible I'm being.

Chest constricting, it's difficult to breathe and true fear begins to ring in my ears. No smartass comments come to mind; shit just got real. I don't do stupid stuff like this. I don't throw myself into unsafe situations. I'm head over ass in petrified shock...until I see Dane step out of the car.

"Disney, is that you?!" He's barreling towards me, hands fisted and swinging with his pace.

"No habla."

He's right in front of me now, glaring down, and it's obvious he's not happy. Well, too damn bad, neither am I.

"Laney, it's dangerous, you alone out here. What the hell are you doing?" His face is inches from mine as he screams.

"Walk away, Dane, leave me be," I say in a cold, stoic voice. "It's official, I'm just like her, and you're practically a stranger so there's still time for you to run away unscathed."

"Just like who? Laney, speak English, literally. If you're gonna spout shit off, at least make it real." He crosses his arms against his chest and it raises my defenses.

"You don't want me to be real, Dane. I don't know you like that. You don't need my sob story. Seriously, go back to your meadowlark and I'll just go home."

"Good, let's get you home. It's late and you're upset."

He moves gently now, his arms about to embrace and guide me to his car, but I push him away.

"No, Dane!" I run my hands through my wet hair. "I mean home home. I'm done. I'm going back home."

"Laney, don't be crazy, just calm down. We can fix this." He comes toward me again and this time I jump from the table and move away. I'm even more pissed now. His choice of words wasn't good, and he'd know that if he knew me—he doesn't. No matter how he'd instantly drawn me in and coaxed me out—he doesn't know me.

"That's right, I'm crazy; the whole 'rational girl who talks about things calmly' is all an act. I can't handle all of this. My first challenge and I screw it up just barely in, and now—I'm gonna run. And we aren't gonna fix anything." I'm yelling now. It's not what I do, or so I thought.

"Dammit, Laney, stop it! You don't have to prove shit to me, just talk to me, for Christ's sake. Let me take you in and we'll talk." His voice is firm but his deep brown eyes are pleading with me and I want so badly to believe he'll listen and not judge me. No, he'll use it to hurt me, just like all the other lines he's thrown me before.

"I can't go in there. My room's been taken over by two happy people who remind me my heart is bleeding every time they speak. Zach isn't home, you invaded Sawyer's room with your Barbie, and the person who knows me best in the whole wide world apparently lost my number! That or the skank he's banging, which I basically told him was okay, keeps sending me straight to his voicemail." Stop, you're scaring him with verbal vomit! My mind is reeling but I keep going. "Maybe I'll ask him when I'm at his school this weekend with the softball team I shouldn't even be on because I've sucked at it for a while now. Maybe there's time before my stalker sends me a head in a box! But, if you take me to 'the studio' again," I ramble, throwing in snarky air quotes, "cause you know, 'I'm special,' I'll feel all beautiful again and forget that I've turned into a complete whack job who gives up and runs, just like her mother! Sound fixable, Dane?"

And now he knows it all and can walk away, and quickly. I've just screamed, cried, and regurgitated onto him like a blubbering psycho. I'm officially as exposed and as vulnerable as I've ever been, and too damn numb to care. Maybe he'll tell everyone and the whole school can whisper about me, again...gotta love the limelight.

"Why are you still standing there?!" I yell. "Are you a glutton for punishment?"

All at once he moves and throws me over his shoulder, carrying me to his car.

"Put me down!" I scream, banging on his back. "If your parakeet's in that car laughing at me, I'm gonna kick her ass!"

I feel him laugh under me, but I don't see what's so funny. He throws me across the seat from his side, banging my butt against the console, and locks the doors before I can scramble out. Well, at least there's no one else in the car; a small consolation.

"Are you kidnapping me? You're crazier than I am."

He doesn't answer me, just removes his jacket and dresses me in it like a child...like I'm acting. Car finally moving, Dane just stares straight ahead and drives in the opposite direction of the dorm. The longer we ride, the more I realize I have no idea where we're going, but I refuse to break the uncomfortable silence to ask. I lean my head against the window and close my eyes, trying to sleep off this EPIC DAY.

Chapter 23

EXPOSED

-Laney-

I wake up when Dane opens my door, causing my head to fall forward. It takes a minute to get my bearings; we appear to be in a garage. Dane reaches in and picks me up, then shuts the door with his foot.

"Where are we?" I ask groggily.

"My house," he answers as he comes to an interior door. "Open that." His hands are full of me, so I lean over and do so. We walk into a kitchen, obviously made for Rachael Ray, as Dane kicks the door closed behind him. Just this room is bigger than my childhood home—well, almost—miles of beautiful dark granite and cherry wood cabinets. All the appliances are shiny stainless steel and the massive fridge could hold everything I own.

"Dane, why did you bring me here? I don't want your parents to see me like this," I sputter, looking up at him desperately from the cradle hold he still has me in.

"They're not here, no one is." He sets me down on my

feet.

"I-I need to call Bennett." I realize I don't even have my phone with me; it's back in my room...along with my shoes.

"I called Tate on the way. She knows you're safe and with me." He moves to the fridge and starts pulling things out, placing them on the large island. "Sit down, let's get you fed."

I take a seat on the large barstool at the island and put my face into my arms on the counter. "Why'd you bring me here? Won't your girlfriend be wondering why you just ditched her?"

He turns back to me and lets out an exasperated sigh. "Let's get that cleared up right now. Whitley is not, nor has she ever been, my girlfriend. And before you ask, no, I have never slept with her. You want ham or turkey?"

"Ham, please, mustard only." Wait...what? We're just gonna move right on to sandwich talk? Um no, we're not. "Sure didn't look that way tonight, Casanova, she was all over you. How'd she do on her photo shoot?" WHY, again WHY, do I care? And why do I keep opening my mouth like a jealous, insecure idiot? One minute I'm screaming at him to walk away because he doesn't even know me, the next minute I'm asking him to explain himself.

I truly don't like myself right now.

"I saw her outside the building and she walked up, shitfaced. Her friend lives in the building but didn't answer her door. I've never taken her to the studio, much like any other girl, and if you're gonna keep saying it, you could at least enlighten me why you think it." He slides my sandwich over to me, staring at me like I have two heads. "No games, Laney, remember? Tell me what it is you think you know." His eyes and tone are glacial and I feel the chill.

"When Tate saw the picture you printed me, he smirked that you had taken me to the studio," I say with venom. "I got the impression it was a regular thing." My head drops and I let my now-dry hair fall in front of my face. I want to hide from the vulnerability that consumes me.

He dips his head to meet my eyes, pushing my hair behind my ear. "Look at me, lovely." He tilts my quivering chin to him. "That's not what he meant, and I'm sorry you were made to feel bad. You're the only girl I have ever taken to a personal photo shoot. I know it's important to girls to know this kind of thing, and yes, you're the first and the only; it was special for you." He taps the end of my nose lightly with his index finger. "There, one problem solved. Now eat something."

He takes a big bite of his own sandwich and turns to get us both a bottle of water out of the fridge. Sliding mine across to me, he says, "I gotta tell ya though, Laney, for someone with a boyfriend, you sure like calling me out on my supposed female shit."

OUCH. Memo to self, be ready to take it if you're gonna dish it out with Dane.

He's obviously assumed Evan is my boyfriend based on whatever it is he and Bennett have discussed behind my back, but I've had enough humiliation tonight, so I'll let him stew on that misconception a little longer.

"You're absolutely right. It's none of my business and I'm out of line. I just...I haven't felt special since I got to college, and you made me feel that way. It hurt to think it wasn't. I'm sorry." I was wrong before, this is what a fool feels like.

"Doesn't Evan do things to make you feel special?" His voice has softened.

"Oh, God yes, all the time. That's probably why I miss it so bad."

"And now he's banging skanks? Big leap." So he'd caught every word I'd ranted earlier and was going to call me out on them one by one. Normally I'd kibosh this, but I'd put it all out there and I'll be leaving soon anyway, never to see him again, so I might as well get it off my chest.

"I don't know what he's doing. We haven't talked in a

while." I get up to put my plate by the sink; I've had all I can stomach. "I feel a lot better; can you take me back now?"

"Why don't you stay here and relax? There's plenty of room and I'll get you back in the morning." He waits for me to say something, I guess, but I don't. "You're safe here, Disney."

I'm back to Disney now, he must not be mad at me anymore.

"I don't want to impose, really, I feel better. And I'm sorry, Dane, I really am pretty low maintenance most of the time." I sigh. "I just lost it."

"I know, and you wouldn't be imposing. It's lonely in this huge house, Laney. Why do you think I'm at the dorms all the time? Come on, I'll give you a tour." He comes over and takes my hand, pulling me to a new part of the mansion.

Right out of the kitchen is a large living room with a huge stone fireplace as the focal point. The furniture is beige leather, all oversized, and the couch faces a wall completely taken up by the largest flat screen TV made, I'm sure of it.

"Well, remind me never to watch movies here." I fake a scoff. "I mean, how would I see it on that teeny tiny thing?"

He gives me a smirk but doesn't shoot back a retort.

The long hall holds several doors he doesn't open and leads to an open foyer with marble flooring. There stands the largest floating staircase I've ever seen, and to the left, a dining area hosting an enormous mahogany table with about twenty chairs. To the right is a sunken den that houses a beautiful grand piano, which makes me wonder if Dane plays.

In the corner is a set of French doors that I'm sure lead to the backyard. While it's all beautiful and immaculate, it feels cold. Sterile. I didn't see a single picture. There're no worn out recliners where dads watch the game, no throws on the couch, and no catch-all spot with papers and junk...it's not a home; the word mausoleum comes to mind.

Dane leads us up the stairs and to the left to show me a full gym, like "please fill out this application for your membership" full gym. There's at least one of any piece of equipment you could name, most of which I can't, and that's saying something, since I'm a freaking athlete. The walls are solid mirrors with speakers along the ceiling intermittently and oh, of course, a small bar in the corner…why, sure. It's the sleekest gym I've ever seen, but it would intimidate the hell out of me with all those mirrors.

"Wow," is all I can think to say.

He just laughs and pulls me out and further down the hall…to the place I'd like to be buried. It's the biggest and best home theater in the whole wide world! I can't help the gasp that escapes me; it's fabulous. There are four rows of seats, which are big and fluffy, not hard-backed and stiff, with headphones and cup holders. The screen itself is massive and oh my God, the room is the perfect temperature—I can feel my toes! The whole right wall is shelves lined with movies, and I can't decide whether to cry or get down on my knees and pay homage. I guess he sees the look in my eyes.

"I figured you'd like this. Just imagine Disney in here." He smirks at me. He read my mind. He starts to pull me by the hand to continue the tour and I dig in my heels and beg to stay in here, to which he laughs. "Come on, you can come back any time you want."

I am so holding him to that. I'm kinda in a daze now and after some twists and turns, I see a number of bedrooms that I barely register. They're all luxurious if not plain with their own bathrooms and huge tubs, but that's all I remember. Until we finally arrive in the one he tells me is his.

His room isn't representative of how I think of him at all. It's barren and bleak with lots of black, white, and gray. The only noteworthy thing about it is the biggest bed I've ever seen in my life, with large posts in dark wood, facing a fireplace. There's a balcony that he takes me out to, and from it, you can look down into his backyard paradise…which belongs on MTV. There's a waterfall, a cave, a rock slide, and an in-pool bar with a TV above it. Now, how the hell does that happen in water? And how is the water a deep sapphire blue rather than normal pool blue?

"And there you have it," I say and he laughs under his breath.

"To the left over there, you can't see right now, are basketball and tennis courts. No softball field though…yet." He bumps my shoulder with his playfully.

"Dane, this place is, well, it's overwhelming. I can't believe you l-live here," I stutter shamelessly. This is the part where I'm supposed to act all composed and unimpressed, I'm sure, but he had me at the home theater. This place is paradise and I'm flabbergasted.

"I sleep here sometimes, yeah; not a lot of living goes on here, though. It's just a lot of space." He answers me with sadness, a sorrow that reminds me I'm not the only one with issues in my life. "So you want me to show you to a room? I know you have school tomorrow, you should probably get to bed." He turns to lead me back in the house.

"Seriously, Dane, you can just take me back. I'm sure Tate's gone by now. I'll be fine. I just lost it for a minute. I'm not going postal or anything, I promise." I offer him a sheepish smile. "As embarrassed as I am, it actually felt pretty good to get it out for once."

"I get it, Laney, I promise. Everyone hits their breaking point once in a while. Don't you dare be embarrassed, okay?" He lifts my chin and catches my eyes with is. "How about this? If you're not too tired, let's grab a glass of wine and chill in the grotto; we can talk some more. Sound good?"

I know I can't fall asleep right now, and talking to Dane somehow puts me at ease. He's got this soothing effect about him, like he could solve anything that came his way effortlessly.

"Yeah, that sounds real good right about now." I take a

deep breath and feel even more of the tension leave my body.

He leads me back down the stairs and through the doors that do, in fact, lead to the backyard. Walking down the cutest little pathway, with in-ground lights and a beautiful floral border, we come to a pool house that could easily be someone's apartment.

"In that room," he says, pointing, "should be plenty of bathing suit options. Pick whatever you like, there's a bathroom to change in. I'll meet you in the pool." And with that, he turns to leave.

With a moment to myself, I stop to make sense of my thoughts. Dane is lonely, and comforting, and rich...I mean rich. So why does Tate live in a dorm? How far is this place from school? Why am I selecting from bikinis on a school night? Why is Dane so nice to me? Why do I trust a guy who keeps a bikini selection on hand for his guests?

I don't know the answer to a single one of those things, and at the moment, I don't care. The soft sounds of music drift from somewhere as I slip on the beautiful green bikini I've selected, praising myself for not being behind on lady upkeep. I try to ignore the price tag I remove, but fail; the price is obscene. I feel strange but alive as I walk out towards the pool, like I'm in an alternate universe. Laney Jo Walker doesn't do late night swims with sexy, soothing young millionaires—I am sooo out of my element right now.

Chapter 24

WINDOW

-Dane-

"There you are, I thought I was gonna have to come look for you," I say as I hand her a glass of wine and take a drink of my own. "I see you found something that fits; looks good."

I take her in from head to toe, suppressing the growl trying to escape. Laney stands shyly before me, arms wrapped low around her stomach, in a bikini. Her stance and the trepidation in her eyes floor me. How in the hell is this girl so unaware of her effect? The moonlight and slight glow from the pool give me just enough light to brazenly look my fill. She is without a doubt the sexiest girl I've ever seen.

Her dark blonde hair will no doubt look brown when she gets it wet. Her kind eyes are almost hazel in the daylight, but at night, or when she's hiding a feeling from me, they turn a deep, rich brown. Her lips are plump and she wets them when she's nervous or stalling before speaking, just a quick little dart of her tongue.

Gawking lower, I can't help but smile as I see what will

forever be my favorite part of her, one little freckle on her chest, perfectly in the middle, right above her cleavage…my new North Star. Barely covered now by green material, I see her breasts are ample and perfect. My fingertips itch to graze across them.

She knows I'm looking, her nipples harden and poke against her suit and she moves her sculpted arms higher to cover her tell. I love her modesty. Once she's mine, I know she'll never let anyone else see or touch what belongs to me. I'll bet anything she's a virgin and as caveman as it may be, it brings out every territorial feeling possible within me.

Her stomach is flat, but has a womanly curve to it, along with her hips; she has the perfect mix of athletic tone and downiness. Those legs, they seem to go on forever, and they, too, show she plays some ball. I lift my eyes to hers and twirl one finger in the air, telling her to turn around for me, and she does.

"Slowly," I grunt. Fuck me, I knew her ass was nice, clothes don't hide that, but my dick didn't go hard looking at it until now. It's high and tight, perfection. I've always been an ass man, but now I'm a Laney Man; damn, she's hot. I have to admit to myself, though, I honestly like her just as much in her princess jammies. Absolutely adorable.

I walk up to her back and place one hand softly on her shoulder, enjoying the feel of her tremble at my touch. You'll learn that touch, Laney. You and I will one day speak with no words. "Come on, Disney, let's get in. The hot tub will do you good." I breathe onto her neck and watch the goosebumps appear over her arms.

"Okay," she whispers.

Slowly, I guide her into the water, my hand at the small of her back. Her skin is like silk. I have to rein in the temptation to pummel her to the ground and ravage her. Once we're settled in the warm water, I see her visibly relax some; she's always wound so tight. She always has a guard up, her eyes always hold just a tinge of fright. Earning her trust will be my greatest accomplishment; I already know this on a molecular level.

"Dane, why are you so nice to me?" she mutters, not looking at me.

Oh, this sweet woman before me. Are people not usually nice to her? How can that possibly be? She's amazing. "I told you, Disney, there's something about you I like, a lot."

"Even after my hysterics tonight?"

She's so worried about that. I actually thought it was pretty cute. Her cheeks were all red, barefoot, wet hair, spitting mad...yeah, she's something to behold. I love that part of her anger was jealousy. Even though she may not fully understand it yet and feels guilty about it, she's jealous and I like it.

"Especially after your hysterics tonight. You let go. I liked seeing it. I knew you had a fire in you the moment I met you, and tonight it came out—I'm glad." Oh yeah, little fireball had threatened to take a bat to Whitley the first night I met her. Classic.

I could've killed Whitley for falling all over me tonight, again. That girl needs to lay off. I don't want Laney to think I'm in any way unavailable to her or that I would ever give Whitley the time of day. I'm every bit as picky as Laney is...and I pick Laney.

Laney was so upset tonight that she'd revealed a lot more than I'm guessing she normally would. Laney and Evan haven't been talking, and she'd seemed more upset that he hasn't called than at the possibility of him sleeping with other girls. In our close knit group, people talk, so I know he's not her boyfriend, yet she hadn't corrected me tonight when I referred to him as such.

There's something off about it all, but one thing I'm sure of now—I have a window. The instant, overwhelming obsession I've developed for this girl now doesn't seem so farfetched. For the first time, I can dare to let myself see the real possibility of having this girl for my own. But I have to tread lightly. I already know her well enough to know she won't pursue "us" seriously while anything with him is unsettled; she won't hurt him...it's this very character I adore. Laney's a good person, she's loyal and she's honest.

She takes a deep breath and blows it out slowly. "I told you a lot tonight; things I don't talk about, ever. I feel exposed now, vulnerable. Just when you were convinced I'm all cool anti-drama girl, I spew pretty much everything wrong in my life, all at once."

Her chuckle is insincere, like she doesn't really think this is funny and she's horrified that I might suspect she's crazy. I don't. I think she's radiant and mesmerizing and all alone for the first time, a bit scared.

"Don't. I will never use your weaknesses against you. Besides, I have plenty of other weapons in my arsenal." I wink at her to lighten the mood, but inside I know it's a monumental step—she already opened up to me so she trusts me on some level, and I her. "Would you like some more wine?" I'm not trying to get her drunk; I truly just want to see her relax. I want to hear anything she needs to unload. I want to see her smile.

"I better not; I'm not really a drinker."

"Laney, you're safe here. I'm not trying to seduce you, I promise. If one more glass would make you feel better, have one."

It only takes her a few seconds to think about it. "Okay. One more, please. It really is helping me relax."

I go get her another glass of wine, and when I return, she asks me what time it is. I know she needs her rest because of school in the morning. "Just after one, what time's your first class tomorrow?"

"I'm not going," she gushes.

"Well, while one day of missing won't ruin you, I'm more interested in why you're not going. Won't you get in trouble with your coach?"

"No, not over one absence, as long as I'm at practice; or

161

I could say I'm sick. I don't know. I don't even know if I'm staying. I was serious before. I could just say to hell with it and go home, right?"

I'm not sure if she's asking me or asking herself out loud, but I can see she's getting herself worked up again, and I definitely don't want that, nor do I want her to leave. I want her in my house, in my care. I never bring girls here and yet this girl…I'd give her a key right now if I thought she'd take it. I'd give Laney the key to a lot of things.

"Yeah, Laney, you could quit, but you don't strike me as a quitter. You could also stay and be great. It's up to you though. What do you want?"

"Maybe that's my problem. I'm not 100% on anything. You know what I mean?"

"Not yet, keep talking."

She proceeds to tell me about ball, how she's not sure if she plays for herself or her dad, how she's not sure if it really feels like a chore or she's just telling herself that. But then, the more she talks, the more her eyes sparkle and I can see she loves it. She loves coming out on top of the pitcher, she loves how she feels when she knows she's got it on point, sending it over the fence. So I tell her what I see when she speaks, and she agrees she needs to give ball just a little more time.

That means I have to take her to practice tomorrow late afternoon, but until then, she's here with me and I can't even comprehend what that does to me inside. One thing she said earlier really bothered me, though, and I have to know, the thought of this exquisite creature being unsafe makes me ill. I knew she was guarded the minute I met her, and I want to know why.

"Laney, can you tell me what you meant earlier about a stalker and a head in a box?"

Her expression completely changes to cold and hesitant. "It's nothing; I was being a drama queen when I said it."

"Explain it to me anyway." The sternness in my voice lets her know I'm serious. I'm not conceding on this.

"Just every once in a while I get a card or a note or gift from like a secret admirer. They never say anything mean or threatening, they're actually always complimentary. And the arrivals are sporadic, have been for years. Evan knows about it, but that's it. I got a card when I first started at Southern. That was the last thing."

"I'm not sure that's something to take lightly, Laney. I'm glad I know now, and I'm really glad I took you to a self-defense class." Wow—what are the odds? The anger I feel that Evan knows about it shocks me. Of course I'm glad he knows and has undoubtedly looked out for her, but why do I feel like it's now my job and I don't need his help?

"I know, I thought the same thing. You should take up gambling."

Oh, I guess I said the odds part out loud. I have to admit, as uneasy as this whole discovery makes me, I feel a small twinge of something. I read her correctly and gave her something meaningful.

"Anyway, let's talk about something else." She waves her glass in the air to dismiss the topic, and I'll let her think we're moving on, for now. I don't want to pressure her into shutting down on me, but I'm not done with the issue.

And then I go for it; I ask her to tell me more about Evan. I'm not sure I can hear her talk about him, but I have to know precisely what I'm up against.

When she talks of him, there's such love and respect in her eyes. She truly cares about this guy. She honestly shudders at the thought of hurting him; he's one lucky son of a bitch. But then a tear rolls down her face when she tells me again about not talking to him and she's afraid they even lost the friendship, and I want to hurt him now—he made her cry. I wonder if she's not in love with him, but rather simply loves him. I'm sad she's hurting, but this gives me another flash of hope.

The next thing she says makes me happy to be alive. "And then there's, well…."

"What else, Laney?"

"I barely know you, but I enjoy being around you and I'm not sure it's as innocent as I tell myself it is, or if that's okay. I almost feel guilty, like I'm doing something wrong to Evan, but I'm not really. Do you understand at all?"

I've never even close to loved anyone other than family, but God knows I like hearing her say she's feeling something about me, whatever it is.

"He's not my boyfriend," she whispers, looking down. "I should have corrected you before; I'm not a liar."

"I know you're not, Laney, and I already knew."

Her head comes up, eyes wide. "You did?"

I nod. She doesn't realize she's been honest with me all along really. I'd asked her about Evan while we danced, and she'd answered that he was her best friend before even thinking. Her omission tonight had been about self-preservation, not deceit. "How did you feel about other breakups? Was it this bad?" I ask her.

"I've never had any other breakups. Evan's the only boyfriend I've ever had, and I didn't have him very long."

I can't stop my jaw from dropping open. Where is this town she comes from that's obviously filled with the dumbest bastards on the planet? How do you not scoop up Laney? "Laney, how old are you?"

"I'll be 19 on the 23rd, why?"

I file her birthday in my mental cabinet. The 23rd of this month? That doesn't give me very long to orchestrate something spectacular, which is exactly what I plan to do. "I'm just trying to figure out how a breathtaking, funny, witty, kind 19-year-old has only had one boyfriend."

She looks down; my compliment embarrasses her and

that little tongue pops out to skim her lips. "Thank you, Dane, that's so sweet. And, well, your question...can we do that another night? I don't have any more big sharing sessions left in me tonight." She gives me a sweet smile, her eyes begging me to drop it.

It dawns on me that Laney is literally starting over. Her be-all permanent fixtures are gone. No Evan, no Dad, new ball team, co-ed dorm; she's as brave as she is beautiful. Part of her wants it, the new experiences—I can see it in her eyes. But the other part is terrified and this fierce loyalty to Evan and what she believes to be the behavior that most honors him is a constant torment for her.

She breaks my thoughts when she asks me, barely audibly, "Are you scared off yet?"

If she only knew all the demons I haven't even begun to hint at, she wouldn't even ask.

I pull her in for a hug and place a gentle kiss on her head before I know I'm doing it. I want to take care of this girl, hold her, and make everything better. I want to be the reason she laughs, smiles, gasps. What is she doing to me? "You don't scare me, Laney. You amaze me, you intrigue me." I let my lips graze her temple. "You captivate me." I land soft kiss closer to her ear. "You entice me, you excite me...but you don't scare me, and I hope I never scare you."

Her eyes grow wide, her breathing speeds...and then she deflects. "Oh, please," she scoffs, brushing off the gravity of the moment, right before the she-devil splashes me! This, of course, launches a full blown water war that keeps us laughing and touching for a while.

At around four in the morning, I wrap her in a towel and lead the way to the guest room, getting some of my clothes for her to sleep in. The thought of her in my clothes makes me feel, well, happy. I understand her so much better after all our talk tonight. She's going through a lot, dealing with many new feelings...but she'd admitted right out loud, she's 100% single.

It's been the best night of my life. Game on, Evan.

Chapter 25

BRING IT PONG

-Laney-

I manage to not drop out or run home and finally enjoyed a lunch with Zach in The Rotunda, the school cafeteria/lounge, for the first time on Friday. Bennett and I still plan to attend his game and we make plans to do something after, but not too late since I have that clinic at the ass crack of dawn on Sunday. I still haven't talked to Evan...total communication blackout. No, I haven't reached out to him either and yes, it was textbook stubborn Laney, but waiting for him to reach out just feels like something I have to do.

On Saturday, the Eagles win 34-17 and a hyped-up Zach, Bennett, and I head off campus for pizza. Tate shows up to sweep Bennett away so Zach and I opt to grab a movie and head back to his room. Drew is there when we get there, with some girl, but they head out to a frat party, an invitation we both decline immediately. While Zach takes a shower, I run back to my room to grab my phone charger.

"Laney! Come be on my team!" Bennett squeals as I walk in, my glare taking in the scene of beer pong. In our room? It's like a 4x4 space and they're spilling beer everywhere. That's not what I care about most, though—the fact that Whitley is sitting on my bed in my room watching is what has me ready to kill someone.

"Laney, you want winners? You can be my partner," Sawyer asks me as I dig through drawers. I don't dare to look up and answer him for fear I might catch Dane in my line of vision. If I do, it won't be pretty.

"No, I'm good, Saw, just grabbing my charger real quick." I keep my head down. Where is the damn thing? I'm about to give up and just get out of here. "You kick their asses though, buddy."

"Where are you going?" I don't need to look up to know who's asking.

"Back to Zach's room, we grabbed a movie." I finally look up despite myself and catch Dane's eyes staring into me.

"Go tell him to get his pretty ass in here, Laney! Y'all play me and Bennett!" Sawyer yells from the game.

Whitley snickers. "I'll play you guys, Sawyer. Dane, come on, sweetie, let's play them."

Sitting on my bed—I probably could've let it go. But dismissing me in my own room—so not gonna fly. Calling Dane "sweetie" to purposely drag him away and antagonize me— challenge accepted, girlfriend.

I give Bennett a look across the room. She tries like hell to hide her smirk; she knows what's up.

"Set it up, I'll be right back with Zach." I run down the hall like I'm on fire, adrenaline coursing through me.

I bust into the room, out of breath, and Zach looks at me quizzically, pulling on his shirt. "Where'd you go? And why are you out of breath?"

I dart my eyes away quickly while he gets the shirt completely in place. Nice abs there, Zachary. "Change of plans, big boy. You good at beer pong?"

"I'm in college and I'm good at everything." He grins. "Need you ask?"

"Zach, I'll do your laundry for a month if you help me win this game, okay? Come on." I drag him through the door.

"Well, hold up there, hot rod, do I need shoes? Keys?"

"No, nothing, you're great, just come on," I plead, pulling him even faster now.

I don't make eye contact with Dane when I walk back in my room. I do however, stare directly at Whitley. "Me and Zach versus you and 'sweetie,'" I challenge, the last word acidic. "Let's go."

Bennett snickers as she, Tate, and Sawyer settle in for a good view of the show. Bad news, Whit—I am a hollaback girl.

"You don't have to do my laundry, girl. This is gonna be fun. Let's get 'em," Zach whispers in my ear, giving me a fist bump.

"Oh, hells yeah! Kick their asses, Laney!" I love Sawyer.

Dane is trying everything he can to avoid Whitley's roaming hands. He's standing so far away from her he may as well be in another room. Zach and Sawyer start throwing out the smack talk, but when Bennett cranks up her phone for Jock Jams "Let's Get Ready to Rumble," we all burst into mad laughter.

"Ladies first," Zach says, handing me a ping pong ball.

"I'm a lady, too," Whitley pouts, "how come she gets to go first?"

"Good point, Whitley. I think you and Laney should arm wrestle to see who goes first." Bennett says it with the most serious face she can muster.

I cock an eyebrow at Whitley, telling her I am so down

169

with that plan.

"N-no, that's okay," she sputters nervously, "she can go ahead."

All the guys in the room are hanging on each and every word. What guy doesn't like good ole cat fight foreplay?

I sink my first ball and stare holes through Whitley as she downs the beer in the cup. Zach steps up and makes it. We do a chest bump and Sawyer slaps my butt. I jump a bit, almost shocked, but in a millisecond it changes to an aura of comfort. I belong here! I'm just one of the guys!

"Nice shot," Dane mumbles as he hands me the ball.

Why is he handing me back the ball? I scrunch my brows in confusion.

"Your team goes again since you both made it," he explains.

Ah.

We're down to four cups and just as I'm about to throw again, Zach grabs my arm. "Hold up, you like the cups like that?"

Again—first time I've played. "I don't know what you're asking me, Zach. I've never played."

"We can re-rack if we want. They have to rearrange the cups like we want, but we can only do it once. I like a square, or we can wait and do a straight line at three cups. Your call."

Well, obviously there's only one person to answer such a difficult question for me, I consult the expert. Sawyer's already holding up three fingers when I look to him. He knew I'd seek his infinite wisdom in all that is college party games. "Wait for three cups?" I ask him.

"Yup," he says with a nod.

"Uh, no fair," Whitley's whine is barely worse than her regular voice. "You're not in the game, Sawyer, you can't help her."

I roll my eyes and turn my head, Bennett snaring my attention. Covertly, she acts out her evil little plan. I finally figure out what the hell she's trying to tell me and shake my head no at her with a laugh. Pegging Whitley in the head with my ping pong ball is probably a bit much. Love the way your mind works though, Bennett!

"It's no big deal, Whitley, she's never played before," Dane tells her with an exasperated look on his face.

Now that all that's settled, I step up to throw and swoosh it right in the cup again. This time I look at Dane and he's beaming. I give him a smirk in return; how ya like that, mister? He winks.

"You got this," I encourage my partner.

Zach misses his shot and drops his head on my shoulder in defeat.

I giggle and pat his back. "Next time, killer."

Whitley steps up, her ball sailing over all the cups and I instinctively reach out and catch it.

"Atta girl, Lanester! Fucking drink up, Whit!" Sawyer hoots, throwing mad *Jersey Shore* fists in the air.

I turn to Zach and shrug my shoulders, causing him to laugh.

"Catch in the air means we get to pick one of our cups for them to remove," he explains. "Doesn't really matter since we have a re-rack coming, so tell her which to drink, superstar."

I randomly point to one of the cups on their end and smile over at Bennett while Whitley has to chug a lug again, putting my team at two cups left!

Dane steps up to throw and all of a sudden I feel bad. We're whipping their asses, he's noticeably uncomfortable, and I'm antagonizing the hell out of him. So I decide to throw him a bone...I raise my arms above my head and lean back, like I'm yawning and stretching at the same time. The coolness hits my tummy as my shirt rises ever so slightly and I pop back up, pulling it down in mock shyness. "Oh my, sorry about that." I bat my eyelashes at him then quickly look to Bennett for telepathic moral support.

Tate looks up at me and mouths, "You are terrible," but his smile confirms he loves watching me torture his brother. I guess Dane made his shot because Zach is drinking when I turn my attention back to the game.

I miss on my next turn, still a little flustered from my sudden brazenness, but am rewarded nonetheless when I finally dare a peek at Dane. He's staring at me, as though just waiting for when I'd look, and the light in his eyes makes me feel beautiful, brave, and silly...like tonight is okay.

The game is over in just a few more throws and as much as I don't really want to, I begrudgingly ask everyone to leave since I have an early morning. Zach gives me a big hug and makes me promise we're set partners anytime there's pong to be played and I eagerly agree while Tate and Bennett sneak away to sleep in his room so they don't keep me up. Whitley awkwardly hangs out a few minutes longer than she should before finally asking Dane to walk her out.

When they're gone, Sawyer turns me by my shoulder to face him. "He'll never just be blatantly rude to her, Laney. He can't, and he doesn't have it in him, anyway. But don't get it twisted; he's never looked at her, or anyone, like he looks at you. Try and remember that, okay?" His eyes seek mine for acceptance of what he's just revealed.

Shocked into a silent stupor, I simply nod.

"Night then, kick ass tomorrow, sweetie," he playfully throws over his shoulder on his way out.

I swat his butt at his sarcastic attempt at humor, 'cause we swat each other's butts now, right?

Just as I make my way out of the bathroom, teeth brushed and jammies donned, I hear a light knock at the door. A peephole isn't even an option, but I'm not too worried about it, probably just one of them forgot something.

He's looking at the ground when I crack open the door, but slowly his head lifts and his soulful brown eyes move to mine.

"Dane, did you forget something?"

"No, but can I come in for a sec?"

I pull the door open further to allow him entry and then close it behind him, taking a moment for a deep breath before turning to face him. His presence usually puts every sense I have on high alert, but I feel the spark of something even more intoxicating in the air right now.

He reaches out and takes one of my hands, giving it a light squeeze. "You were on fire tonight. Did you have fun?"

"I did, a lot. Did you?" Our joined hands hang between us and his thumb rubs across my wrist, so faint it's almost as though I'm imagining it.

"I did once I realized you weren't too mad." He lets out a sigh, running those long fingers through his dark hair. "I'm sorry Whitley was here, on your bed. She followed Sawyer from their room, looking for me. That's it."

"It's okay. Pretty sure I got her back." I shrug, laughing. It was way more fun to slaughter her mercilessly in pong than get catty.

"That you did, that you did." He chuckles. "You're amazing when you loosen up a bit." One eyebrow touches his hairline. "Did I see Sawyer grab your butt?" A smile tugs at the corner of his mouth, though he's fighting it.

"No!" I swat his chest with the back of my hand playfully. "There's a big difference between grabbing my butt and giving me an 'atta girl' slap."

"So you're good? We're good?" His worried brow is unnecessary so I boldly reach up a finger to smooth it.

"We're fine, Dane, I promise."

SE Hall

"Can I spend some time with you when you get back?" He runs one finger along my jawline tenderly.

Do not shiver, Laney. "Okay," I say, taking a deep breath in hopes my next words come out in a normal octave. "I'll text you."

"Good night, Disney." His voice is sultry as he leans over to kiss my cheek. "I'll be waiting."

Climbing in to bed, the glow to my cheeks and upturn of my lips can't be helped. Sleep comes easily and I wake to board the bus just hours later. If I had known what awaited me on the other end of that ride, I would have never gotten on.

Chapter 26

KEEP YOUR FRIENDS CLOSE, AND...

-Evan-

Laney will be here, on my campus, in just a little while. I don't care if I have to drive her home for missing the bus, we're going to talk. We agreed making some changes was best for our friendship—what friendship? She hasn't returned my calls or texts in way too long and I'm going to find out why today. This is unacceptable.

I pull into the parking lot right behind the bus and wait as girl after girl unloads until finally she comes into view. She's everything to me. My Laney Jo is ten feet away. She's even more beautiful than the last time I saw her, if that's possible. Her hair is pulled back in a ponytail and she's in ball gear...so sexy.

Time to figure out just what the hell is going on with her. I jump out of my truck and call, "Laney!"

She turns to look at me and a gorgeous smile lights up her face. She throws down her bags and runs into my arms. I catch her mid-jump and twirl her around, planting kisses all over her face. There she is—my girl.

I set her down on her feet, already missing the feel of her in my arms. Once she's over the initial shock of being near me again after so long, I see her smile fade and she suddenly looks angry. "Evan, why are you here? How did you know?"

"Kaitlyn doesn't hold her alcohol very well. She let it slip the other night when she was drunk at a party. I texted you right when she said it, why didn't you answer? In fact, why didn't you answer any of my texts, or my calls?" I grip her shoulders and the mere touch helps calm me immediately. "You said you were fine with our decision, Laney, but how does ignoring me protect our friendship? How does it make me feel any better to not talk to you at all?" I'm kinda rambling, and my voice could be kinder, but dammit—it hurts to be ignored by your whole world.

"Evan, what are you talking about? I haven't gotten a call or text from you in forever…NOT ONE." She pokes me in the chest and reduces me to nothing with her glare. "I thought you hated me, or had moved on, or needed time. I would never ignore you, ever, you know that."

She holds my eyes as her words linger and the look in them begins to slowly soften. Glancing over her shoulder and back to me, she sighs. "Listen, I gotta get into this clinic; we can talk more after."

The look in her eyes tells me she's not lying. She really didn't get any of my messages? What does that even mean? "Laney, do you have your phone on you?"

She hands it to me. "Why?"

"While you're in there working, I'm going to take a look and figure out what's going on, why you didn't get any of my calls or texts." I look down, taking a deep breath, not wanting to scare her with the intensity of my frustration. "That's just crazy, and it killed me."

"Oh, okay, I'll see you after then; maybe you can explain this to me." She picks up her bag, slinging it over her shoulder.

"Cause right now I'm hurt too…and a bit skeptical." She runs to join her team. Her ponytail bounces and she looks back over her shoulder at me once, gracing me with a small smile.

I could stand here, in this one spot, for the rest of my life, just waiting for her to give me that exact look again.

She'll be in there a while, so I decide to go grab something to eat and figure out this phone thing. I stop at Joe's, a mom and pop burger joint, and grab a booth in the back. I don't need anyone bothering me, so I sit with my back to the door. I've got to crack this phone and figure out exactly how my life was shattered the last few weeks.

Obvious step one, I call my phone from Laney's. I got in on my first guess, my birthday was her code. I smile at that because hers is mine and it just reminds me how we share the same brain. It also reminds me how close it really is to her birthday and I need to get her something special. Something that says "I miss you like oxygen and I'm sorry I left you. Oh, and by the way, girls wake up in my room but I swear I don't touch them and please don't leave me or I'll die." Something tells me a teddy bear and card won't cut it. I won't be able to see her on the day, but I can still let her know how much I love her.

It rings, but rather than coming up as "My Girl," or the sound of "Ho Hey" instantly lighting up my day, it comes up as just her number. So I text, same thing. What? Okay, so I call her from my phone, it doesn't ring. I text from my phone, it doesn't pop up. I scroll through her contacts, I'm in there. It's the right number and I smile when I see I'm in as "Babe." My contact picture is one her dad took of us; I'm giving her a piggy back ride out by the pond.

So the problem is my phone…I pull her up, open it, and there ya have it—the number is not her number. So when I called or texted her, it didn't go to her phone; she never got it. And she didn't call or text me, because not only was there no text to reply to or ring to answer…she thought I was ignoring her. Oh God, my poor girl thought I had just ended all communication with her. Maybe she was one of those random messages with no contact name that I deleted, thinking they were from a clingy Bulldog Babe. No way I'm opening up that can of worms by asking for clarification though. I slam my fist on the table, knocking over the salt and pepper. Too late, salt, the bad luck already hit.

Leaning my elbows on the table, head in my hands, I rub my temples. My head is throbbing and my chest is tight. I can't get a full, deep breath. Laney must've been so hurt and the thought of her hurting makes me see red. More importantly, who the fuck changed her number in my phone? The only person here that Laney and I have in common is…no way, NO! Kaitlyn is Laney's best friend! WHY would she do this? Yes, we had an awkward morning, but I thought we were cool about it.

Is what I'm about to do creepy? Yes, and I feel like an ass, but I pull up the texts between Kaitlyn and Laney. I want to see if anything in them confirms or refutes my suspicions. I'm really hoping for the latter. Laney adores Kaitlyn and this will cut her deep if true.

Oh fuck.

My whole body starts shaking and I have to swallow the burning acid that shoots up my throat. Please don't let this actually be happening. I'm so screwed. My sweet, sweet girl has seen this. A picture of me doing a tit shot off some blonde. Kaitlyn sent it the night she was "being a good friend" and got me home safely.

Laney never mentioned it. Laney would never mention it. We broke up, so she thinks I'm entitled to a motorboat with whoever I want and she'll never go back on her decision. She gave me freedom so we wouldn't fight, so she won't berate me about it.

I deserve to have my ass kicked. If I got a picture of some dude's face shoved in Laney's cleavage, I'd find him, kill him, and then check myself into an asylum. I couldn't handle it, and yet, she had. She'd drawn the image, the hurt, the betrayal inside herself and let me go on about my day.

Selflessly.

Staying on the road takes full effort as I drive back to the field to see if Laney's out yet. I had seen new contacts in her phone and she's told me about the new people she's been hanging with at school, but it hurt a little to see four new guys entered. Not nearly as bad as it hurt to think I'd become the slimiest prick she could possibly know.

I slam my truck in park and rest my forehead against the steering wheel. I just want her to come out and let me make everything better. I want to rewind and be snuggled against her, watching her movies with the smell of her hair all around me and none of this having ever happened. How do I face her? How do I look her in the eye? Do I tell her I know she knows? Do I try to explain? Would she really buy the whole "the team peer pressured me" bit? I wouldn't.

I wait a little over an hour until I see her headed my way, bag in hand. She's captivating. I swear I can see the halo above her golden locks as she ambles towards me. I bolt out of the truck as soon as I see she's crying, but I don't pull her into me right away. I don't have as much right to do that anymore.

"Coach says I can ride back with you...if you feel like driving all that way. It's getting late, so I understand if you can't. If not, I need my phone and I've gotta go right now and we can talk that way, if you figured things out with it." She sniffles and looks down, her shoulders slumping in defeat.

"Of course I'll take you. Run and tell your coach, sweetie."

She's back quickly and climbs in through my side as I settle her bag in the back.

Silently I climb in, trying to decide what I should or shouldn't say to this precious, forgiving creature beside me. After I pull us onto the main highway we'll be using for the next several hours, I finally find my voice. "Why you crying, darlin'?"

"Something's wrong, Evan, and I hate what I'm thinking. Someone sabotaged me on purpose; someone took away UGA for me." Her body tenses and she falls silent but for a second, the calm before the storm. "Someone TOOK YOU AWAY FROM ME!" she screams and breaks into full body sobbing.

I give her a minute to gather herself before I ask questions; she can barely breathe. I may be a sorry bastard, but I can't just watch her hurt from across the cab. Hesitantly, I place my hand on her thigh, hoping to fuse comfort into her.

"Laney, what are you talking about? No one took me from you; I'm right here, baby girl. I figured out the phones, we'll be able to talk now. Just calm down for me, lamb."

"Yeah, and what'd you figure out on the phones?"

"Your number had been changed in mine and I would never think to even look at that, so all the time I was texting and calling you, it was to the wrong number. And you never called me back 'cause you never got them, so you thought I was ignoring you and I thought you were ignoring me."

"And how would my number get changed in your phone, Evan?" Her head whips towards me, nostrils flared and eyes glowing.

I've never seen her so mad.

"I already know the answer, but I want to hear what you've come up with. Just tell me—cause trust me, your shocker is not even close to as big as mine." She starts shaking, crying again.

"Laney, there's only one person at school with me who knows you and would know your birthday to crack my passcode." Kaitlyn better steer clear of me.

"Say it—say her name—say out loud who did this to us!" she screams.

"Kaitlyn. It had to be, Laney, nothing else makes sense." I hate to say it, Kaitlyn's her best friend; it's got to hurt like hell.

What the fuck was that bitch up to? Sending a picture, appearing in my room, hacking my phone…why?

"It hurt so bad, Evan, to think you just took the breakup pass and ran, didn't care to even talk to me anymore." Poor angel's whole body lets out a quiver. "She couldn't have taken anything more valuable from me than you. She hit where it would hurt the worse. And then, she took more, she just had to twist the knife. I'm surprised she didn't just kill my dad, that'd have wiped me out completely." She slams her hands on my dashboard, the most gut-wrenching wail I've ever heard coming for her.

"You're scaring me, sweetie, what else are you talking about? I fixed the phones, and she'll never touch mine again…so what aren't you saying?" Please don't let her say the picture. Or maybe please let her, it might be better to just get it out in the open, cause Lord knows I'm pussing out on fessing up.

"Well, you know, I thought it was odd when my good friend and I hadn't talked in weeks, even weirder when she barely acknowledged me at clinic." Her head is snapping back and forth now, anger frothing from her. She's all kinds of worked up and I'd rather throw myself from this moving truck than hear whatever big conclusion she's leading to.

"I also found it strange when I went up to her to give her a big hug and venom dripped off her voice when she said my name and the girls around her laughed. But I gotta say…the highlight was when the freaking coach of the college of my freaking dreams, The University of Georgia, told me how sorry he was when he received my declination of his offer."

Darting my eyes from the road to her quickly, she's now slamming one fist into her other flat palm faking a huge grin in sarcasm. "He said he sure had been looking forward to having my big stick in his lineup this year!"

She's gone back to crying so hard now I find a safe spot to pull over; I have to hold her.

"Come here, baby, come here." I undo her seatbelt and pull her into my lap and hold her. I will all the love and peace I can into her, running my hands up and down her shaking arms, kissing the top of her head, whispering that it will all be okay.

"She did this, Evan! My best friend, Kaitlyn, who stood by me when my mother didn't, who helped me pick out my prom dress, who taught me how to put on makeup…she did this to me. I had the scholarship to UGA, Evan! THEY WANTED ME! I WAS GOOD ENOUGH, DAMMIT!"

I hold her as tight as I can and I literally cannot contain her thrashing.

"I could have been there with you this whole time! All this heartache, all this damage, all the misery…it was her. No one else would intercept my letter and decline for me. The only people with that kind of access to my life are you, my dad, and her. And the minute he said it, I knew what had happened with the phones, too. She screwed us, Evan, she cost us so much." Her head and body go limp against mine, exhausted.

Goddamn that bitch! How could she? WHY would she? Kaitlyn and Laney were so close; she had no reason to want to hurt Laney. It's not like Laney's spot would have cost her hers, that was on lock. And why send a picture that will only crush her best friend's feelings? Laney would never hurt Kaitlyn, so WHY? I could have had Laney at school with me this whole time; holding her, loving her, not being miserable, her not being miserable. How do I solve this? Can I solve this?

When Laney settles down a bit, I place her back in her seat gently and buckle her up. She's a bit like a zombie right now. We again set off down the road. "Laney, what do we do? Can you still come to UGA?"

"No, all the scholarships have been given out, Evan. School's started; the girls who accepted are there. It's too late. I could have been there with you!" Too tired to cry this time, she drops her chin against her chest, wrapping her arms around herself. "Tell me this isn't happening; tell me I'm having a nightmare! Why would she do this to me, to us? I guess me coming down here finally cracked her; she knew the coach would say something."

I have no idea what to say to her. I can't believe it myself. I can hardly drive; my hands are throbbing because I'm gripping the steering wheel so tightly. Laney and I were robbed of our happiness, our chance. She had her shot at playing D1 ball stolen by her best friend. Talk about keeping your friends close and your enemies closer.

Laney's eyes are closed, her head leaning against the window. I'm sure she's exhausted from all this and my heart aches for her. All this time she thought she wasn't good enough, that UGA didn't think she was good enough, but she was and now there's nothing she can do about it. She's been all alone at Southern, and I can't imagine how hard that is for her, especially when she didn't have to be there at all.

Kaitlyn will pay for this. I don't know how yet, but she will pay.

Hours later, I pull up to Laney's campus. I'm not quite sure where I'm going so I'm forced to wake her up. "Laney, baby, where's your building?"

She sleepily gets her bearings and guides me to her dorm. When we get there, neither of us move to get out of my truck. We just kinda stare blankly at one another, not sure what to do or say. The ride back was supposed to have been spent talking about why we hadn't talked and making up...but we'd never been fighting, we'd been brutally tricked. So what do we do now?

"Laney, I hate to leave you, God, especially like this, but I gotta get headed back. If I miss, I don't dress out. At least we can talk again now, right?" I try to get a small smile from her, hoping this will make her feel better, but I know it doesn't; it doesn't make me feel much better, either.

"Yeah, I guess it's good we figured that out. I've missed you, Evan. I thought I'd lost you, lost my best friend. I think a new part of me died every single day." A tear falls down her cheek as she says it.

I reach over and gently wipe it away, then pull her to me. God, she feels so good in my arms. I love her so much and my heart broke when I thought she was ignoring me. I don't ever want to let her go. Is this all worth it? College, ball, all this…all that should matter is being with Laney.

"Laney, we're going to get through this. I'll walk you to your door, sweetpea, and then you go up and get some sleep. We'll talk after I do the same and our heads are clear."

"K, promise me you're okay to drive?"

"I promise, baby girl." I lean over, cupping her face in my hands. I take in every nuance of her beauty, burning it into my brain, the image that will get me through until I see her again. I don't deserve their grace, but, as established, I'm a selfish asshat, so I kiss her lips. She tastes like my Laney, my life, my love. She deepens the kiss, sighing into my mouth, and I can actually absorb her heartache. I'm more confused now than ever, but one thing never wavers, one thing I never doubt…I am and will always be in complete and forever love with Laney.

Chapter 27

KISSABLE

-Laney-

I don't wake up until almost one in the afternoon, classes be damned today. For a brief moment, I think maybe it was all been a bad dream, that yesterday didn't happen, but too soon I realize it did. What do I do now? Nothing—there's nothing I can do.

I have no idea what would motivate Kaitlyn to do such things and I don't think I can stand talking to her to even ask why. Okay, so playing devil's advocate, maybe she thought the picture would be funny. But robbing someone of their college scholarship? That's huge! And crazy! And the phone thing? Why would Kaitlyn not want me talking to Evan? Was she trying to break my resolve or trying to block communication so I wouldn't figure out her plan?

Well duh, Laney, how blind are you? Kaitlyn wants Evan. Holy shit, that's it!

ALL. GOOD. STUFF. Really? FML.

There's only one thing I can even fathom to do at this point. I call my Dad.

"Daddy," I sob, breaking down the minute I hear his voice.

"Slugger? What's wrong?" he asks, worry heavy in his voice. "Are you okay? Are you hurt?"

"N-no, I'm not hurt." I wipe my nose with my shirt sleeve, taking a deep breath.

"Laney Jo, you're scaring me. What the hell's the matter?" he barks.

He keeps asking me to stop, slow down, start over; I'm crying so hard he can't understand a word I'm saying. I finally get it out, the scholarship and Kaitlyn saga, and he's just as shocked as I am. Maybe shocked isn't the word for it, killing mad and close to an aneurysm is more accurate.

He says he's going to make some calls and see what he can do, but I tell him not to do anything definite, making him swear he won't call her parents. We're adults now and that's how I want to deal with it. Not until he offers to try and fix it does it dawn on me...maybe I don't want to change it now. I like my coach here. I like the girls on my team all right. I like the friends I've made here, I love Bennett, I like my classes, and I don't want to see Kaitlyn every day and pretend we're on the same "team."

Even if he could fix it, which is doubtful, maybe I don't want it fixed. So he'll make some calls, but nothing for sure. Yeah, that'll work for now.

Then I tell him about Evan, in general, non-gory details. No sense in getting Evan killed to top off my problems. Dad loves Evan, and of course he'd love nothing more than the two of us to be together, so neither do I even mention Dane's name; just the confusion of my feelings about being apart from Evan, the loneliness...poor Dad, he has absolutely no idea how to talk shop with me and I didn't give him a lot of practice. It still feels good to vent it, though, and he tries his best to keep up.

"Thanks, Daddy, I feel better, I guess. I love you."

"I love you, Slugger. You're my little girl, always. If you need my help, you have it; you know that, right?"

"I know," I say, taking a calming breath. "I can handle it, Dad. I'm bound and determined to be an adult that makes you proud."

His forced chuckle is helpful. "You couldn't make me anything but, honey. Don't worry so much, okay? Just do what feels right, Laney. That's all you can do."

"10-4, Daddy. I'll be home soon, okay?"

"Sounds good, kiddo. I'm always happy to see you." My dad rocks, there's no ifs, ands, or buts about it. I adore that man and no matter what else happens, ever, I got damn lucky there.

Next I call Evan, but it goes to voicemail. "Just want to make sure you made it back safe." Pausing, I force down the frustration in my voice. I'm so sick of getting his voicemail. "I guess we have a lot to talk about; call me when you can." Hitting "end call" carries a weight I can't shrug off. I lie in my bed looking at the ceiling for long moments, fighting off the melancholy trying to consume me.

I could call Kaitlyn and ask her why the fuck she did this to me. I could call Zach to hang. I could call Bennett but I'm thinking she must be at rehearsal. So I do exactly what I knew I was going to 10 minutes ago. I text Dane.

Laney: Hey, what r u up 2?

Dane: Nothing important. You?

Laney: Just woke up lol. Had quite a day yesterday, trying to recover.

Dane: Oh yeah, good or bad?

Laney: Bad. Very. But I don't want 2 talk about that... Do you play the piano?

Dane: Um yes...random?

SE Hall

Laney: Random is good sometimes, right?

Dane: It is. You okay?

Laney: Not really, at all. Wanna do random with me today?

Dane: I'll be there soon.

I jump out of bed and run to the shower. I take extra care straightening my hair, applying light makeup and selecting my outfit. I choose jeans and a black sleeveless top with black ankle boots that I dug out of Bennett's closet. Basically, I dress unlike myself for Random Day: Laney with a dash of Bennett. I can't help that my heart flutters when I hear the knock on the door. When I open it, all moisture leaves my mouth and heads elsewhere. Dane stands before me in dark washed jeans, a tight white t-shirt, black boots and disheveled hair. He smells delicious, the light scent of cologne and freshness graces my senses from where he stands, and that half-cocked smile he wears as he peruses me is almost more than I can take. Full frontal awareness hits me—I've gone from never having a boyfriend to a full-on love triangle, head first.

"Well hello, Disney. You look like walking sin," he says, sensuality dripping from every word. Make that a love hexapolyoctagon. I'm screwed.

"Why thank you," I say with my chin held high. "Trying something random. You ready?"

"I'm ready for anything. What do you have in mind?" he asks as I close and lock my door. I really hope Bennett remembered her key.

"Well, I'm thinking I can't skip classes, so we don't have time to jet away to Fiji. So how about…we play Right Left and see where we end up?"

He gives me a curious look as he opens my door and settles me in the passenger seat of…a black SUV? Well, of course he has more than one car. I mean, who doesn't?

"You're gonna have to tell me what this is before I can

188

agree," he laughs. He hurries around to the driver's side and hops in, handing me his phone. He's going to let me pick the music, a small but very thoughtful gesture. I choose his Damien Rice playlist, skipping straight to "9 Crimes." Maybe he'll take the hint that I think of this song when I picture him at the piano. He looks over and winks at me as it starts—yep, he knows how to play it.

"Every time we come to a stop, we just choose right or left. But, in a startling new twist, we're gonna take turns saying something completely meaningless with each turn, until we end up somewhere good! Honestly, I could care less where we end up right now, I just wanna be."

"I'm game." He gives me a smile. "But I kind of wish you'd talk to me about what happened."

I give him the very condensed version, interrupting every few minutes with a "right" or "left," and so far our random facts at each tell me that he's for morning breath kissing as long as both people have it and he can also play the violin. I share that I'm the ultimate Beatles fan, but only pre-mustache Beatles, and brush my teeth about 15 times a day (totally in reaction to his morning breath comment). He doesn't ask about my time with Evan or any specifics, he just hits on the part about Kaitlyn.

"So what are you going to do?"

"I'm not going to do anything; what can I do? The chance is gone, at least for this year. The friendship's gone, so why even ask her for an explanation? There isn't one that will ever fix it. And...nothing, that's it."

"Nice try, Disney, finish what you were gonna say."

"The dorm rooms here are really nice, like way better than other colleges'. How cool is it to have our own bathrooms? You can't get that just anywhere."

"That's not what you were gonna say, either." He shoots me a one raised eyebrow look.

"Pull over then, I want you to look at me when I tell

you."

He pulls over so fast I slap him in the arm because my life just flashed before my eyes.

"Do I have your undivided attention?" I ask him with a smirk.

"Since the moment I saw you." He turns in his seat to face me and waits for me to talk, his face full of question and anticipation.

"I'm content with where I am. I don't have to have it fixed. I actually really like it here. It gets better every day. Besides, I think Sawyer would really miss me and finally go completely insane."

He chuckles at my attempt to alleviate the seriousness.

"I really like Bennett, and the girls on my team are so talented. We have a real shot at a banner year. Who cares if the games will never have a camera there, we'll still be kicking ass and taking names." I chance a peek up at him, hoping his eyes tell me what he's thinking. They're such a deep brown, almost black, and right now I can see my own reflection. His eyes mirror me in this moment. It gives me the strength to keep talking.

"And part of me hates it, hates feeling like this, and all of me is scared shitless, but I suspect my resolve has something to do with the fact that you're here, Dane. Never in my life have I instantly connected with someone, not even Evan. I made him work like a dog for my acceptance." I chuckle softly at the memory. "But I find myself wondering what you're doing all the time, and thinking about what we could do or talk about if we were together. Tell me the truth; you got anything like that going on at all?" I laugh nervously, praying that leaves some question, 'cause I can't risk him knowing I'm completely serious right before he makes me feel like a fool.

He takes a deep breath and blows it out slowly, reaching over to brush the back of his hand down my face. "I saw you last night, at the door with him. I saw you." His hand still gentle on my face, he forces me to meet his gaze. "Are you two back together?"

"No," my voice cracks.

"I won't share you, Laney. Not your lips, not your thoughts, not your body, and especially not your heart. You don't have to give it all to me just yet, but give me nothing if any of it belongs to him. Do you understand?"

"Dane, it was a long night, we were both hurting." I blink back the building tears. "He'll never not be in my life. I just don't know what that means right now." I have to be honest, with not only him, but myself. And I can't blatantly crush Evan; I won't. "If he was here with me, things wouldn't be like this. I can't lie to you. I don't know exactly what anything means right now; I'm trying to be as honest as I can. And I haven't told Evan about you, not that I've had a chance." I take a huge, cleansing breath. I feel better having put it all out there.

"Thank you for being so honest. It makes me want you even more, and I do want you, Laney...so fucking bad it scares me. Let's try this one more time—are you in a committed relationship with Evan?"

"No."

"Are you in love with him?" His hand moves down my face, his fingertips softly caressing me, and I lean into it and close my eyes. I can't look at him when I answer. I don't want him to see the scared little girl in my eyes.

"I don't know."

My own answer confuses me. I have no doubt that I love Evan, but am I in love with him? We were so perfect and the minute we changed it, things got too hard. Yes, college had everything to do with that, but why couldn't we last? Was it supposed to be Evan or was it just that Evan was always there? That's the thing that scares me most—why am I so strongly and instantly attracted to Dane? Why do I think about spending time with him? First temptation? Nope, I don't feel the pull to Zach,

Tate, Sawyer, Parker…no one else, ever. To be honest, besides Evan, Dane is the first guy I've ever considered liking in my entire life.

"You didn't say yes." His finger is now tracing my lips. He's going to kiss me, and I'm going to let him.

I blow slightly out, teasing his finger, and I hear him inhale.

"I will never kiss another man's girl…but you're not his, Laney. You're not mine…yet. But you're not his, either. So the way I see it, you're kissable."

I say nothing. I just open my eyes and look into his; if he can hear my yes in that, he can have my kiss.

"Last chance, Disney. Once I get a taste, I'm coming after you with everything I've got."

I couldn't say no right now if I wanted to. I can barely breathe. His words are so sexy; they stroke every part of me. He leans into me and I close my eyes.

"Open your eyes, Laney, look at me. Make damn sure you know it's me kissing you, and don't you ever hide from it."

I do as he says and then his lips are on mine. This isn't the kiss of a best friend, not the kiss of the boy next door who made you spit-shake on a deal and will always take care of you. This is the kiss of a madman who wants to make you scream his name up against a wall. This kiss makes it okay that I even just thought that, because it's a fact.

I can't take it. I break the contact and throw my head back, trying to catch my breath.

"Nuh-uh, not done yet, come 'ere," he growls, reaching around the back of my neck and pulling me to him. He takes my mouth again with lust, bites, and a low groan. Grabbing my face, he turns it, deepening his angle and the throbbing between my legs.

Fuck, this guy can kiss.

Dane breaks away this time, only slightly, still close enough that his breath tickles my lips… "That wasn't random, that was supposed to happen," he says, giving me another quick kiss.

After a brief silence, simply because I still haven't recovered the ability to speak, he pulls back into traffic with his right hand now interlaced with mine. He gives my hand a squeeze before he asks, "Where to?"

Seriously, I'm expected to think? "Um, right…and I hate coffee but I love coffee ice cream."

We turned until dark, never actually making it to a destination.

Chapter 28

BIRTHDAY GIRL

-Laney-

"Happy Birthday, Laney! Wake up, wake up, wake up!"

Okay, Bennett is bouncing on my bed and I fear greatly she's going to fall on me any minute.

"I'm up, I'm up!" I tell her, laughing. It must be because it's my birthday, the big 1-9. I never wake up in a good mood.

"Look on the table, birthday girl!"

I look over and see the most gorgeous bouquet of flowers waiting for me. I get up to go inspect and count 19 red roses, with lilies and baby's breath mixed in; it's breathtaking. I check the card hesitantly.

I would give anything to be there with you today. I love you, birthday girl. XO, Evan.

I can't remember the last birthday I spent without him and a silent tear trickles down my cheek.

"Who are they from?" Bennett asks from behind me.

I quickly brush away the tear before turning to answer her. "They're from Evan. Aren't they beautiful?"

"They're amazing, Laney. Are you okay?" she asks, concern etched across her face. She rubs my back. "It's not okay to be sad on your birthday, chica! I know we haven't spent much time together lately, but I have all day blocked off to ring in your 19th with cannons!"

She really is a little ray of sunshine, this girl; I'm guessing she's never screwed over a friend in her life. I silently vow to never compare her to Kaitlyn again.

"I'm good, Bennett, I just miss him, but we're gonna have a great day! I'm so glad to have you here with me. Thank you."

"Thank me tomorrow morning! You'll see…" She laughs and my phone rings.

I know it's my dad, Evan wouldn't call this early. "Hi Daddy," I answer.

"Happy Birthday, slugger! You feel any older?"

I laugh and tell him I've only been up a little while, so I'm not sure how I feel yet, then tell him about the flowers Evan sent and that Bennett apparently has a lot planned for me, although I have no idea what yet.

"Well now, I've got your presents here, kiddo, we can open 'em when you come home, okay?"

I agree that sounds great and that I love him and will see him soon. I decide while I'm at it to call Evan.

Of course, the early hour does nothing to deter the cheerfulness in Evan's voice. "Happy Birthday, munchkin, what are you doing up?"

I babble happily, describing Bennett's wake-up call, and thank him for the flowers.

"I know you're not a big flower girl, but I had to send them since I'm not there to hand you something. God, how I wish I was, Laney. I have something for you, though, when I see you."

We reminisce for a little while about all my past birthdays and what we did, both cracking up at the funny, tender memories. He doesn't mention the Kaitlyn thing and I'm glad, I refuse to talk about that today.

"Anything weird yet?" he asks quietly, perhaps afraid of the answer. On some birthdays, my admirer "strikes" with flowers, but not every year, and the 19th is good so far.

"No, nothing I woke up to."

He lets out a deep breath. "Good, good. Okay, enjoy your day, my love."

Bennett has sat back silently the entire time, but I can tell she's chomping at the bit to get going on our day.

I bask in happiness during my shower, thinking of how lucky I am. My birthday has barely started and I have a great friend ready to wow me, a dazzling arrangement on my table, and I just talked to two of the most unbelievable men on the planet— and they love me. Some things have sucked lately, but all in all, I'm pretty damn blessed…and I'm going with that.

I love the spa—who knew? I let Bennett treat me to a manicure and pedicure, my first of both. I even went with the massage and blushed through gritted teeth for a bikini wax (you only live once, right?)…but when they sit me in the chair to get my hair done, I call bullshit.

"Bennett," I lean over and whisper, "enough. Where are you getting all this money, woman? I can't let you spend this much on me." She doesn't respond, but rather shoots me a friendly sneer and texts something. My phone dings. Did she really just text me from a foot away?

Zach: I chipped in, chillax and enjoy, sweet girl.

Looking back at Bennett, I roll my eyes. "You could have just told me that, ya know." I snicker.

"Nope, he told me to do exactly that."

Laney: Well thank you very much! Will I see you today?

Zach: You will. Happy Birthday! C U soon.

I chicken out on my hair. They almost had me talked into a major change, but instead I go for a trim and some very long bangs; that's as radical as I get. After thanking all the cheerful people who have pampered us all day, we meet Zach for lunch, where I give him a big hug in thanks; he really is so sweet. After lunch, Bennett and I head to the local mall where I refuse everything she offers to buy for me. Where does this girl get all that money? Surely Zach didn't chip in that much.

Finally back in the room after the best day, I collapse on the bed. "I've had a great birthday, Bennett! Thank you so much, you're awesome!"

"Have had—Laney, you're so naïve it's precious. Girl, you ain't seen nothing yet, we're just getting started."

"What? You can't possibly have anything else planned! You've done far too much already, really."

"You're wasting time arguing with me and you're gonna want to go get ready." Her red curls bounce and she's wearing a devilish grin.

Surprisingly, I'm not the least bit apprehensive. If I'm totally honest, I can't freaking wait to see what else she has up her sleeve.

"Your hair's already done, so just shower, shave your legs and meet me back out here. I'll take care of wardrobe, your highness." She blows me a kiss and shoos me with her hand.

Oh my, what else could there be? If I have to shave my legs, it must be serious.

I get out of the shower and yell to Bennett for further instructions. She comes in and touches up my hair and does my makeup. Finally satisfied with her work, she brings in my dress for the night, one I've seen in her closet before. Frankly, it makes me nervous from the hanger.

"First things first," she says and proceeds to slide black thigh highs up my legs. Oh, dear Lord. She then hands me a black thong made out of dental floss and a matching lace, strapless, push-up bra.

"Um, Bennett, I really don't want to be arrested for prostitution on my birthday, thanks, though," I say with more seriousness than sarcasm as I shimmy the items on under my robe.

"Hush, silly, these are just the undergoodies to make you feel sexy on your special day, there's wrapping. Now lose the robe." She pulls the thin black dress over my head.

The dress is way too short, too thin, too tight, and too low cut. I can't leave the house like this, NO WAY. I try telling her this, several times, my voice in full-out panic, but she assures me that tonight will be semi-private and I look great, it's my birthday, yada, yada.

Next she adorns my wrist, ears and neck with sparkles and a princess crown on my head—now that part I like! "Oh crap, I forgot, no necklace," she says as she removes it.

I have to ask. "Is there a no necklace rule at the brothel?"

She blows a raspberry at me but doesn't answer specifically. Yup, we're headed to a brothel and they don't want girls to get their necklaces caught in the cages—I knew it!

There's a knock on our door but I don't care, I'm not leaving this bathroom, no way no how.

"Where's the birthday girl?" I hear Tate ask.

"She won't come out," Bennett whispers, like our room

is so big I can't hear her.

"Laney, are you decent? I'm coming in!"

Oh shit—that's Sawyer. "Um, no, I'm far from decent."

I see the door crack behind me and his head pops in. A flirty smile lights up his face. "Hot damn, woman, please jump out of a cake on my birthday!"

"Not helping, Sawyer."

"Laney, you look fucking amazing. Come on, shy violet, it's your birthday, strut your stuff!"

"Really? It's not too much? Or too little, I mean?" I fight the urge to bite my nails, an old habit that's hard to break.

"No way, it's perfect. It's 'I told ya there was a hot body under here' meets 'I kick ass cause it's my birthday.' I swear you look hot, now come on. I gotta find some ass now that you got me all worked up." He grabs my hand and pulls me out of the bathroom.

I walk into the living area and Tate's jaw hits the floor. Bennett jumps up and down, clapping.

"Um, Laney, one more thing?"

"Yes, Sawyer?" I'm afraid to ask.

"That's what you should wear for pajamas!"

Everyone laughs, even me; he's crude but irresistibly loveable. He really has grown on me; he's quite charming with those big blue eyes and dimples. Yes, his eyes are definitely blue, like sapphires.

"Okay, okay, let's pregame toast, people." Tate pours us each a Solo cup of champagne—only the classiest in college. "To Laney's birthday, a great night, a great year, and awakening for all!"

We all tap and down the chilled, crisp liquid. Whoo! That stuff will go to your head. I can't help but wonder where Dane is. Surely after the knee-buckling kiss he wouldn't miss my birthday?

I just can't bring myself to ask, though.

"To the chariot!" Sawyer exclaims and we all follow.

"Have fun, sweetie, it's your day and I'm right behind you," Bennett whispers as we walk down to the parking lot.

A short limo ride later we arrive at The Kickback. I don't even ask who paid for the sleek ride because I give up on that mystery; surely someone's about to drop over from all the plasma they've donated for money, and then I'll know the culprit. Oh crap, I didn't grab my ID! Oh well, I don't have to drink.

There's no line at the door and the bouncer just lets us in with not one check. We walk in to total darkness, and I'm frazzled for just a second before people jump up into beaming lights and yell "Surprise!"

First thought: I don't know this many people, who's here? I see Zach front and center, I have Bennett, Tate and Sawyer yelling behind me, hmmm. I spot Drew with a girl I don't recognize and several girls from my softball team, some with what look like dates—that was so nice of them to come. I then I realize we have this place to ourselves, how's that possible? They have to be losing a ton of revenue on this. And where is Dane?

"Are you surprised, sweetie?" Zach bear hugs me and asks with a kiss on my head.

"Oh my gosh, yes! How did you guys pull this off?"

"I'd tell you, but then I'd have to spank you. It is your birthday," he teases and I slap his arm.

Several of the girls from the team come over and greet me, a few even hand me cards; it's touching, really. Maybe this new team could be my team, my new sisterhood. Several guys are introduced to me. Some are dates, some aren't, but I keep flicking my eyes around the room, trying to spot only one guy.

Tate has jumped behind the bar and is starting to sling

drinks. I just order an "anything" when Sawyer scoots in beside me.

"So, Laney, I gotta say, I thought you were the exception, but softball girls are fucking hot!"

"Um, thank you?"

"WHO is the brunette in the red to our 3 o'clock?"

I look over his shoulder; ah, he has a good eye. The Andrews twins, Avery and Kirby, are gorgeous girls and they're a pitcher/catcher combo, which of course means they're cool as hell. Honestly though, I don't know which one we're looking at this very moment. The only difference I can find is that Avery, the pitcher, is taller, so since there's only one of them right now, I have no idea.

"It's either Avery or Kirby Andrews," I tell him with a shrug.

"Or?" It takes him a minute, and I bite back a giggle as I watch him work it through his mind. I see when it dawns on him, I have to laugh and he literally rolls his eyes up into his head and groans. "If you're teasing me, I'll beat you...are you telling me there's two of that? Like twins?"

"That's what I'm telling you." I tap the end of his nose, knowing I've just made him extremely happy.

"Oh, fuck me twice, I've died and gone to heaven. So what do you know about her, them, whatever?"

"Very little, actually," I say with a shrug. "Avery is the pitcher and she's the taller of the two. She has a 67mph fast ball, a drop curveball and a sneaky change. Kirby talks more, she's our catcher so she takes charge, she's a freakin' wall back there and she's got a cannon on her, she bats like 400..."

"Laney!" he interrupts me.

"What?"

"Seriously, woman, I need the important stats, like boyfriends? Same-sex oriented? Reputation? Views on anal?" He

SE Hall

actually said it with a straight face, not possible, and ew.

"Oh my God, Sawyer, how am I possibly friends with you?"

"'Cause I'm adorable and you love me."

He's right, he is adorable and I love him already. He's a good one; he'd have a friend's back. He's got mine, I know it.

"Okay, I'll get you an intro, but if the word 'anal' leaves your mouth, I will ball check you myself—hard. You got it?"

"Got it! All other words are acceptable, though, right?" He smirks.

I point my finger in his chest. "I mean it, mister, do not embarrass me! I barely know these girls and I have to play ball with them. Don't you dare disrespect them!"

"Ah, Laney, I'm just playing. I would never…now go hook me up, woman!"

It turns out Avery is in the red tonight. I talk with her for a few minutes, thanking her for coming.

"I'm really happy to be here, Laney. I'm looking forward to the season and your bat." She knuckle bumps me. "Maybe we can hang out sometime, get to know each other."

"That'd be great. I'll give you my number." I hope my face doesn't give away how pathetically happy I am at the idea of a new friend. "So, where's Kirby?" I glance around the room, not spotting her twin.

"Good question," she says, looking around, "not sure where could she be. There's not that many of us here."

"Um, let's ask my friend Sawyer, he knows the layout better than me. Sawyer!" I shout.

Oh yeah, he heads right over, not even attempting a blasé approach, looking more like an eager beaver trying not to trip. He's precious.

"Sawyer Beckett, my good friend, this is Avery Andrews,

202

our pitcher. She seems to have lost her twin, Kirby. Could you help her find her? You know the building better than me."

"Of course, I'd be happy to. Nice to meet you, Avery."

I almost chuckle as I watch her reaction to him; her eyes are about to pop out of her head…he is a lot to take in at once. The blush that creeps up her neck and cheeks is sweet, though, and I make a polite departure. There ya go, Sawyer, make me proud. I wink at him as I walk away.

When I hear music start, I smile; I'd know that intro anywhere. I turn to the stage and the single light illuminates him. He's sitting at the piano, half looking back at me, and he winks. "This one is for the birthday girl," he says. He plays "This Year's Love" by David Gray, his voice perhaps even more beautiful than the original.

It's the most mesmerizing thing I've ever seen or heard and when he finishes and stands, cheers go up all around but I remain frozen. I have tunnel vision straight to his eyes and can barely comply when he crooks his finger for me to join him.

My legs are wobbly as I make my way to him, limbs heavy. It seems to take forever to get to him, as though walking through sand. He mercifully meets me halfway.

"Happy Birthday, gorgeous girl," he whispers in my ear, tucking a piece of hair behind it.

"Thank you. I thought you weren't here," I answer breathlessly, shaking, unable to mentally process what the serenade did to me.

"You knew better than that." His lips are now touching my ear. "Didn't you? You think you don't know me and you shouldn't feel this, but you do feel it. Don't you, Laney?" One hand moves to the small of my back and ignites my skin through the thin fabric of my dress.

"Maybe," I barely whisper. I'm terrified of the way he makes me feel; my pull to him is animalistic.

I feel his laugh against my skin as he moves his other hand over my heart.

"No maybe to it. You feel that, Laney? Your heart beats that fast for me, for us."

I say nothing. I can't. He moves his arms around my waist to hold me up, thank God. He starts to walk backwards, pulling me with him to the center of the dance floor and as is if on cue, the DJ starts the music, "Hero" by Enrique Iglesias. Dane so gets the right song for the right moment thing, once again he's nailed it.

Others join us and I look around; Tate and Bennett are engrossed in one another and many of my teammates look to be having a great time as well. Sawyer and Zach aren't out here as far as I can tell—how a girl hasn't dragged one of those wonderful boys out by now is beyond me. Huh, so this is what it feels like, having a lot of friends and doing the public party type thing. It definitely feels strange, but a lot like magic.

Dane and I are forehead to forehead, barely swaying to the umpteenth slow song in a row, when he asks me if I've enjoyed my birthday so far. I gush to him about my wonderful day with Bennett, her and Zach's generosity and how much I am enjoying this surprise party.

My cheeks heat and eyes sting as I describe how special it made me feel and how happy I am that so many people came out. I'm hopeful there's a spot for me at Southern after all.

He watches me with a satisfied look on his face the whole time and I can see it—he's genuinely happy for me. I finally take a breath from my rambling and he beams at me. "One more song and then it's time for one of your presents."

"I thought your song was my present? And it was a wonderful one indeed." I smile up at him. It really was the most spellbinding gift I've ever received and I'll cherish it always.

He grasps my cheeks and kisses my nose, moving teasingly slow to finally land on my lips. "I'll play for you anytime,

Disney."

I wrap my arms even tighter around his neck and lay my head on his chest for "Flightless Bird" by Iron & Wine. "I love this song."

"Thought you might. Me, too."

"You know our tastes are pretty scattered. We may be the only two people our age who get it," I mumble into the sculpted plane of his neck.

"Perfect, since I was thinking we're the only two people right now anyway." He brushes his soft lips across my forehead. "You speak my language."

We enjoy the rest of the song in silence, wrapped in each other.

"Now let's go open presents," he says as he folds my hand in his and pulls me to a table. He pulls a chair out for me and once I'm settled, moves to stand behind me, leans over me, and whispers on my neck, "Close your eyes."

I glance back at him questioningly. I'm so nervous, but he winks at me and I know it's all right. I turn and do as he asked, closing my eyes.

"Lift that beautiful hair for me," he commands.

I do, as smoothly as I can despite the trembling throughout my body. I feel cool metal slip around my neck; oh my God, he got me a necklace! Instinctively, I drop my hair and my fingertips move to touch it, but I can't quite make it out.

I hear his voice, coming from in front of me now. "Open up, my brown-eyed girl."

I open my eyes and Dane is in front of me holding up a small mirror and I see it. He's placed around my neck a diamond "D" necklace. The signature Disney "D" is unmistakable. I gasp and feel the tears starting to bite; damn, this boy is good.

"Oh, Dane! I couldn't love it more; it's perfect," I say between slight sniffles, my heart about to burst. "Thank you so

SE Hall

much. You're wonderful." Before I know what I'm doing, I jump into his arms and squeeze the life out of him. The gift symbolizes what he told me before: maybe it's not about the length of time you've known someone, maybe it's about instant recognition on an unconscious level. Our souls know each other.

"Had a feeling you'd like that, Disney girl. My pleasure." He winks.

"Put her down, fool, I gotta give her my gift!"

I laugh when I hear Sawyer behind me. Back on my feet, I turn and hug him. "You got me a present, too? You didn't have to do that...but gimme it!" I laugh.

He sticks his fingers in his mouth and lets out a wolf whistle, pulling a shriek from me in shock, then waves Tate, Bennett and Zach over. "Come 'ere, y'all, time for Laney's present." Oh God, Sawyer, present, he wants an audience...if he starts stripping or dancing on my lap, I'm gonna kill him. Surely Zach or Dane will stop him short of catastrophe.

Once they're all gathered around, Sawyer disappears for a bit and comes back rolling a beautiful brown and cream Louis Vuitton suitcase! "Thank you, Sawyer! I love it!" I move to hug him, but he gently holds me off, laughing.

"Love the enthusiasm, but lemme finish, woman!" He guides me back to my chair and hands me an envelope.

I open it to find a crude, of course, but funny birthday card and a note.

Besides lugging this bag around for you all night, my gift to you is to gather all your work over the next two days, watch Dane's house, and help your coach run stations in exchange for letting you go. Now get the hell out of here. -S

Wait...what? I turn back and look at Dane, who has a sexy as hell lopsided grin going on with a gleam in his eyes. I turn back to Sawyer, who's holding out his arms to me.

"Now you hug me, sugar," he says.

206

I jump up and hug him; apparently I'm going somewhere with my new suitcase and he's in charge of taking care of all the loose ends that make it possible.

Bennett pushes through and wraps me in a hug, then pulls back and squares my shoulders, looking right into my eyes. "You light up our lives, Laney, now go light up your own. Have the most fun possible, every single second! Oh, and bring me something back!" She kisses each of my cheeks. "I love the necklace, it's perfect."

Ahhh, it clicks right then; I forgot the no necklace comment earlier, she knew what I was getting and knew my neck had to be bare. Little sneaks.

Next, Zach makes his move, pulling me into his big ole chest and kissing the top of my head. "He's a good one, let him be good to you, girl."

I still have no idea where I'm going and I'm slightly apprehensive. They're talking like I'm leaving forever, to some island where they can't communicate with me.

A panic attack is moving in fast; cue the comforting arms snaking around my waist from behind.

"Let's go, Disney, I got you. Trust me?"

I instantly nod, because I do. I trust him completely, and secretly, I cannot wait to go wherever he's taking me. I wave goodbye to as many people as I can as Dane pulls me out with one hand and my suitcase with the other. Outside the door is a different black stretch limo and a beefy man in a suit and hat opens the doors for us and takes the bag from Dane. Okay, now I've seen a lot of movies, but I guess I thought those were "prop limos," I didn't realize you could actually get a limo that looked like this on the inside. This is clearly how Dane does "limo," no comparison to the one the rest of us rode over in.

There's a TV, a small bar, wall-length bench seats that may be wider than my dorm bed, and a sound system. I know Dane lives in a big house, obviously his parents do well, but is he just allowed to spend it on whatever he wants?

And what about the rest of them? I feel sure the mob wouldn't think Bennett's flowery soul has what it takes, so I obviously haven't fallen into a crime ring. I just can't fathom having all this money to "play." Dad used to take me for burgers and bowling almost every Friday when his job was good, that was our "special splurge time" together. It kicked this limo's ass, but still…

Dane sits across from me and pours us both a glass of champagne. "Happy Birthday, Disney. I hope you had a great time and an even better time to come."

I blush. "This may be the best day and night I've ever had. By far the most extraordinary birthday ever! I feel like a princess!"

"And you have the crown, and now the necklace, to prove it." He smiles. "You are a princess. I'll always see to that."

Chapter 29

WHEN YOU WISH UPON A...

-Laney-

"So, where are we going?" I half fear the answer; I've been ready to faint all night. I don't know how many more grand gestures I can take.

"Well, about that..." He's making me skittish now and I think he can tell by my face. "It's a surprise, and I really want it to stay that way, but imagine my challenge of hiding the geography outside the windows. So, I ran through my options and I'm still undecided," he laughs. "I decided I just couldn't secretly drug you to keep you asleep."

Um, that's refreshing news and he's lucky I know he's kidding or I'd jump out the moon roof right now.

"So I thought maybe I'd blindfold you, but it's a long drive and you probably wouldn't go for that. So, what do you suggest I do?" He rubs his chin and scrunches his eyebrows.

"Okay, just winging here, but how about if I just try not to look out the windows?"

"Excellent plan, Ms. Walker, you're brilliant. So, to occupy your attention," he says, reaching behind one of the seats and bringing out my pillow from my room and a blanket, "we offer you an in-drive movie service. So get comfy and choose." He holds up the cases for several movies as I sort out my nest and remove my shoes and earrings.

I choose one and after he gets it ready, he removes his shoes, loosens his collar and joins me on my seat, sitting at the end of my pillow where I lie down. We aren't even touching, but it feels intimate and oddly familiar. I shouldn't feel this comfortable with him; it should take him as long as it's always taken everyone else to get this close. For God's sake, I'm heading off to who knows where with him in the middle of the night. I've gotten cozy in a hot tub with him. Who is this girl and why does she feel so content?

I wake to him gently stroking my hair. "Time to wake up, birthday girl." It takes me a minute to sit up and take in my surroundings. I'm still in the limo and early daylight streams through the windows.

"How long was I asleep?"

"About five hours. You did perfect, doll, we're here."

"We're where?"

"You'll see, just close your eyes for me one more time and I'll help you out, okay?"

Now how am I gonna get my shoes on and climb out of a limo with my eyes closed? I feel him slip on my shoes for me and somehow we maneuver our way out. Warm air hits me and it takes but a second for me to pick up the music. "It's A Small World." I remember him telling me that it really wasn't. What's he playing at?

"Open your eyes, Laney," he whispers in my ear, taking his hands away from my eyes.

NO WAY.

210

This can't possibly be real. I blink a few more times, trying to see if I'm really awake. I am, I'm awake, this is happening. My fingers and toes tingle, my breathing rapid with excitement. I fall back into him; his arms reach around to catch me and he laughs.

"Easy, baby, I got you."

I'm standing in front of a huge hotel, but it's what I can see behind it that lets me know where I am, what's he's giving to me—THE Castle. Dane brought me to Disney World!!!! I repeat, Dane "are you for real?" Kendrick has freakin' brought me to Disney "the most magical place on Earth" World!

I've dreamt of coming here since I was still scared of the dark; this is truly a lifetime of dreams come true. It just doesn't seem possible that he sees enough in me to go through all this trouble, but obviously he does, cause I'm standing here. This isn't about conquering the prude girl; this is an act of real-life chivalry. Walt himself would have been proud to base a prince on Dane.

"Welcome to Disney's Contemporary Resort, Ms. Walker, and Happy Birthday," a beautiful young lady at the door says to me. "Shall we get you checked in?"

As if by telepathy, Dane chuckles behind me when he realizes I can't speak, so he does it for me. "Yes, please, the birthday girl here is still a little sleepy."

I have no idea what happens next, I simply float along on my cloud, trusting Dane to lead the way. I'm finally able to comprehend that we're in our room now, and it's magnificent with lush furnishings—and one bed. My face always gives me away and doesn't fail now, as evidenced by Dane's next words.

"I wanted this room for the view, Laney." He pulls back the drapery and shows me. "They say the castle at night is something to behold, so I wanted you to have that. I have no problem with the couch; you saw how big it is."

"I won't have you sleeping on a couch after all you've done for me." I'm Disney-high, so it just pours out of my mouth.

SE Hall

"The bed is way big enough for both of us comfortably, no worries." I move to him and rise to give him a kiss on the cheek, leaving my hand grazing the edge of his face. "Dane, I don't know what I did to deserve all this, but thank you, so very much. It's—it's…well, it's simply the best thing that's ever happened to me. I don't even know how to express it to you out loud."

He rests his forehead against mine; I love it when he does that. I've come to think of it as a gentleman's intimacy, but still scorching. "So you're happy?"

Is he kidding? "Extremely. Euphorically. In fact, if I'm asleep, dreaming all this, do not wake me up. Feel free to go with your drug me plan to keep me asleep now." We laugh together.

"Then you've thanked me. I want to make you happy, Disney. It's really all I think about these days, 'how do I make her happy?'" Rubbing my nose with his, the words settle between us.

"Well, let me just say, you truly know how to accomplish a goal, and you better find something else to think about, because you will never top this."

"Is that a challenge?" He smirks, kissing my nose.

"Not at all, just a fact. If I could have hand-picked my perfect birthday, or Christmas, or last day on Earth, this would be it. Seriously, where were you when I was 10?"

"Off somewhere, waiting for you."

Corny? Hell no—mind-bending. I kiss him with everything I've got. For once, I go all-in, no thoughts of anything or anyone else on my mind. My hands glide themselves up his neck, gripping his hair, and I lean my body into his. I crave the physical connection to him, this irresistibly handsome, thoughtful man who has mentally morphed with me. I want to climb him and wrap myself around him like a monkey.

He kisses me back, groaning into my mouth, his eager hands hinting a tentative path to my ass, pulling me harder against him. All at once, he pulls back, breathing harder than me perhaps. "Baby, I'm gonna have my head examined later for what

212

I'm about to say, but if we don't stop, you're not leaving this room."

Part of me so badly wants to tell him that's okay, but only part of me; now that we've broken apart I'm able to think more clearly.

"My Disney princess has a lot to see, so let's get you fed and go hit the sites. Okay?"

I pout a little, just a little, because my little girl heart and my woman libido are still settling their argument, and I kinda feel rejected.

He leans in and sucks on my bottom lip. "Put that bottom lip away, pouty. I want you, you know I do, but I want to see you on the teacups more." He squats down slightly so he's at eye-level with me and gives me a smirk. "Go get changed, Disney. You know you're dying to meet Goofy."

I concede and hop in the shower while he orders breakfast. Bennett did a really good job packing for me, better than I'd have done, and it's only as I shift through my suitcase and run across my phone that I realize I haven't checked it in a while. There are several texts from Evan, so I shoot back a quick reply.

Laney: Had a great bday. Friends gave me a party. Miss U 2. Thnks again 4 the flowers. xo

I question the xo. Should I still put that, while on fantasy vacation with another guy? Yes. I'll always be willing to give Evan love, a hug and sweet kiss, so I decide it's okay. Is it okay someone else now calls me baby? Is it okay that I crave touching foreheads with a new guy? Is it okay that I just want to enjoy this fairytale I've entered and not examine it right now? Yes, yes, and hell yes. As I'm throwing my phone back into my bag, Dane walks in behind me.

"Everything okay?"

Turning to him, I give him my most reassuring smile. "Perfect, just gonna get dressed. Oh, and I'm planning on stealing this robe, just so you know. Look, it has the little ears on it," I show him the emblem right above my left breast.

He gives a slight snicker. "No need to resort to thievery, crazy girl, I'll buy you a robe. Breakfast is out here when you're ready. I'll eat with you before I shower, but give me a sec to count the silverware." The wink that follows is all kinds of smartass sexy.

I don my favorite sundress, which doesn't count as a dress because it's comfortable, and sandals. After a wonderful breakfast buffet, Dane gets ready and we head out to take in all that is the Magic Kingdom.

Dane laughs at me all day, I'm almost worse than the little kids running around here. I don't blatantly butt in front of them in line or knock them down or anything, but I can certainly gush over a character with the best of them. And it is okay to wear your ears all day, age is not a factor.

One thing I learn quickly, though, is to stay away from the shops, because he will buy me anything my gaze lingers on for more than ten seconds, and not only do I feel like I'm taking advantage of him, but he's spending another fortune paying the courier. Did you know you can pay them to take all your bags to a collection point so you don't have to carry your purchases around all day?

Brilliant.

This will be my favorite moment of the trip, maybe in life, no matter what else happens. There's a slide show being played on the side of the castle in time to the likes of Whitney Houston, Celine Dion and other female belters, and all the lampposts are releasing a blanket of bubbles over the crowd. The smaller kids are running around their parents, catching bubbles, the dads are trying to keep track of them as it's dusk now, but the ladies in the crowd all have the same look at their face as me— total amazement at this fairytale moment.

"I love the look on your face right now," he says hotly into my ear, his strong arms encasing my waist.

"What look is that?" I grin up at him.

"The look of love; you're in love with this moment, this place. It's how you'll look at your husband, your children; it's breathtaking."

"Dane?" I finally whisper after I don't know how long. I want to freeze this moment in time, to always feel like life is perfect, happy and carefree.

"Hmmm?" He nuzzles the side of my face and neck with his nose and the tenderness brushes my soul.

"Are you happy?" My hushed tone is all but silent; I'm amazed I got it out at all.

"More so every day," he says, pulling me to the center of a clear spot and dancing with me beneath the bubbles, in our bubble.

Chapter 30

ULTIMATUMS

-Laney-

If I thought being at college, living on ramen, getting very little sleep, and living in a cramped room sucked before, then I think it blows complete ass now. Having spent the best four days of my life wrapped in Disney and Dane in a posh hotel, eating at fancy restaurants, and enjoying room service, being back to reality carries an extra sting. I can't believe it's over already, it flew by.

Dane and I experienced all we could. We rode every ride, did the princess tour, watched the fireworks from our balcony, laid by the lagoon, had a candlelit dinner, you name it. Sleeping in the same bed every night wasn't awkward at all; we tumbled in exhausted every night and Dane was a perfect gentleman...almost annoyingly so. Those last few blazing kisses we shared on my birthday eluded all too well how hot things could be with Dane.

"The Crew," as I now refer to our group, is happy we're

back, and I brought each of them a pair of Mickey ears with their name embroidered on the back. Sawyer also got a t-shirt and ball cap for his extra efforts. So after a whirlwind birthday, I'm settling back down and things are going great.

Bennett and Tate are still going strong, and in a shocking twist, Sawyer, Zach and the twins seem to be a foursome; they're undecided on who's gonna pair off. Dane, Bennett, Tate and I have bets placed, but that's on the down low. I'm getting quite close to Avery and Kirby. They've come over to hang a few times and I'm so happy to have friends on the team. It really helps make it easier to accept that this is my team now; I can't undo Kaitlyn's treachery, but I can make the most of what I have.

I've seen Dane every day of the two weeks we've been back and I find myself looking forward to it from the moment I wake up each morning. Some days he catches me before my first class, breakfast snack warm in his hand. A few other times he's appeared to whisk me off campus for a nice lunch. Perhaps my personal favorites are the evenings he's waiting outside practice to drive thru for our dinner after a long day.

I love how lighthearted and easy things are with Dane, but I can't ignore the inkling eating at the back of the daze…I still know so little about him, he's disclosed almost nothing and I've laid my story bare. What does he do, in general, when I'm in class? How does he ask me to stay over every night, which I always decline? Are his parents ever home? I have so many questions; I want to know him better.

I need "meat" to a relationship, something worth sinking my teeth into, a foundation. Time spent together is empty if I know you no better when you leave than when you walked in. Yes, I've loosened up a bit since being at college, but blind leaps of faith will probably never be my strong point.

Talking or texting with Evan every day gnaws at my insides. I'm going home this weekend to spend some time with my dad and Evan will be there after his game. I'm not sure where we stand at this point or what he's anticipating and it's the same story with Dane. In fact, I'm not sure where I stand or what I want exactly. Have I chosen Dane over Evan? If so, how can I choose someone I know so little about over someone who shares my skin? And if Evan was here at school now, would I choose him? Does Dane want to be chosen?

At least Dane knows the Evan story. Talking openly with Evan about Dane this weekend is bound to be a shock to him. I'm planning to just go with the flow and see how things play out, which is what Bennett says I should do, but I'm not okay with stringing two hearts along, if that's what I'm doing. I'm pretty sure Dane is into me on a serious level, and I think Evan still is, but I wouldn't bet an arm on either. And my own back and forth confusion, well, I'm getting sick of myself, frankly.

Physically—I want them both, but with Dane it's definitely more primal, not to mention he's actually physically here, which is a pretty key component. Emotionally—I want them both, but obviously Evan and I go much deeper, though it's different now. Distance has not been good to us. "Absence makes the heart grow fonder" my ass. Not stitching that little pearl of wisdom on a pillow anytime soon. How about "absence makes the head dizzy and fills the heart with aching bewilderment?"

I have finally gotten some closure, which led to a marginal amount of inner peace, with the Kaitlyn scandal. I finally got up the nerve to call her about a week ago to ask for an explanation, and she was all too happy to tell me about it. I knew she'd jump at the chance to sound off; Kaitlyn doesn't have a demure or reserved bone in her body. That fog I used to live in incontestably extended beyond Evan, because I had no clue about the abhorrence Kaitlyn had been harboring.

She couldn't contain the bitterness in her cruel words as she told me she was "sick of the poor, pitiful me act" and that I didn't deserve Evan's devotion. In other breaking news, apparently I was a tease and secretly loved how Matt Davis crushed on me. While I couldn't get her to outright admit she'd orchestrated my fraudulent decline to UGA, she freely admitted how she'd "be happy to watch over Evan now that you aren't around to distract him with your bullshit act."

Seriously, psychopath? Like Evan would want you after you showed your true colors; Evan doesn't do evil. Somehow she failed to see the flaw in her plan, because now she's lost two friends and still will never have Evan. I'd be lying if I pretended it didn't and wouldn't always hurt like hell. How could she have faked a friendship that I thought was so good? She meant the world to me for so long and I was the person she hated with the fires of hell? It just doesn't seem possible that I'm able to drive a car, attend college, remember the signs in ball...and be so far off the mark with those around me. I must be completely clueless.

"You sure you don't want me to come with? I could meet your dad, get a hotel, whatever," Dane whines. No, whine isn't the right word, because whining is annoying and whatever he's doing is adorable. I know why he's worried, I told him Evan was going home, too, and ever since, he's offered to come with me at least once an hour. "Are you going to tell him about me?"

"Yes." The apprehension is about to kill me and a nauseous wave rolls through me every time I think about exactly what I'll say.

"What are you going to tell him?" He moves his arms around my waist now and rests his cheek in my hair.

"Good question, what should I tell him?" I peer up into his eyes. Not that I'd ever let Dane dictate my conversations with Evan, asking him was more of me playing a girly-fishing game, but it's still obvious it's time we had a "come to Jesus" talk. Is Kaitlyn right, am I a tease? Most girls go their whole life without meeting a man as wonderful as Evan or Dane, let alone finding themselves sandwiched in between two of them. The age old love triangle only seems cliché and trite until you actually find yourself in one, then it becomes agony.

"What do you mean, what you should you tell him? Tell

SE Hall

him you're mine now."

Whoa, come again? His? He hasn't proclaimed a commitment and I've seen Whitley's name still popping up on his phone…of course, there's the whole lavish gifts thing. "Yours, huh? That's news to me."

"Seriously, Disney." He lets go of me and steps back; I feel barren at once. "What the hell are you talking about? We spend every day together." He runs his hand across the back of his neck in frustration. "Why are you acting so aloof?" He looks devastated, which isn't my intention at all.

I move to him, wrapping my arms around him. "I just meant…I-I didn't realize you thought this was serious, or committed or whatever. I don't know. I didn't want to assume anything."

"Well, what did you think?"

"I thought we were getting to know each other. I know there's an attraction, obviously." I squeeze him harder. "I just didn't know you felt so serious about it." My mouth is getting chalky, my palms slick.

"Laney, I'm fixing to lose my shit here." He breaks away from me again, pacing like a caged animal.

"Calm down, Dane, I'm just telling you the truth. We're just talking; maybe it's good we're having this conversation."

That seems to help; he at least stills and looks at me now. "Yeah, no, you're right. Okay, so let's just talk about it." He sits down on my bed and pulls me into his lap. "Laney, I want to be with you, exclusively or whatever girlie label you want to put on it, meaning no one gets near here," he says, using his finger to tap over my heart, "but me. I want to touch you, kiss you, freely. I want you to be my girlfriend…my baby." He rolls his eyes and laughs. "I can't believe you make me outline things and sound like a 16-year-old." He apparently feels compelled to remind me he is a man; the way he kisses me now is illegal until you can at least vote.

He turns, laying me back against my comforter and rolling to lay his body along the top of mine. My body tenses with the shock of this new territory, but only for a second while the message from my body moves to my brain. "I do not want you to be anything more than long-time friends with Evan." He runs one hand through my hair, fanning it off my ear, and then leans down to nibble. "I want you to sleep," he says, pulling back to look at me. "I said *sleep*, in my home as many nights as possible." He runs his face down my neck, leaving open-mouthed, hot kisses along the way. "I want you to fall in love with me, Laney." He licks straight up my throat. "Is that clear enough for you?"

I have yet to open my eyes, but know he's looking at me, I can feel his stare.

"Baby? Look at me."

I'm burning from the V in my thighs to the flushed tops of my ears, like he struck a match. He and I, together, are so feral. "You make me crazy," I murmur. I'm hoping he didn't hear me, but his primal growl before his tongue demands entrance lets me know he did. He feels it too, our unbridled gravitation; his hard length presses against me and I counter against him, pushing downward to his up.

"Ah God, baby," he breathes, his whole body trembling under my fingers, "it's gonna be so good one day. You and me, explosive." His mouth teases along my neck, my jaw, and he lets out a big sigh. "Okay, we have to stop, I can't take it."

Part of me starts to pull him back to me, but I know he's right, we're quickly approaching the point of no return and my body is very ready but my heart and mind are not.

He moves off me to sit and I welcome the moment of reprieve to gather my senses. I sit up and smooth down my hair and clothes, still unable to look at him. I'm being way too lax with Dane way too soon. I have to take back control of this situation. I stand, going to grab a bottle of water out of the mini fridge. I stay on that side of the room as I dive back into our discussion.

"Dane, I wouldn't feel right about being with you until

221

I've talked to Evan. In fact, I've already done way too much. I don't expect you to understand, but that's what I have to do."

He stands and moves to me in a sleek, predatory gait. "Okay, you talk to him, but promise me you won't do anything with him, please. Promise me he won't get these," he runs his fingertips over my lips slowly, "or this." He brushes his nose airily down my neck, along my throat, across my shoulder. "Promise me," he hums.

"I promise," I say, my voice husky as my head falls back.

"That's my good girl."

My panties are soaked with his words, his proximity, and when he leans over and runs his tongue from my shoulder to ear, I think I'll promise him anything he asks.

I worry the whole drive home about my impending talk with Evan. This is it, do or die time. I can't do this to either of them or to myself a minute longer. If I wasn't driving, I'd be making a list right now, organizing my thoughts, so I decide I need to call someone to go over everything. I don't feel comfortable talking about it with Bennett. She dates Tate so she'd be biased to Dane and it'd put her in a very uncomfortable position. I decide to call Zach since he's so levelheaded and has proven himself to be clutch.

"Hey, Laney, what's up?"

"Driving home and driving myself crazy. I need some help sorting my thoughts and maybe some advice. You busy?"

"Nah, girl, never too busy for you. Whatcha got?"

I first make him promise that this conversation will stay between the two of us, which I already knew, but the confirmation makes me feel better. "Okay, so I'm on my way home to see Dad. Evan will be there this weekend. I need to tell him about Dane and I don't know what to say. I know Evan and

I agreed to cool off and be just friends, so technically I'm not doing anything wrong, right?"

"Technically you're not, but a technicality is just that, Laney, an excuse to clear your conscience. It doesn't seem to be working since you're calling me. Something's off or you wouldn't be feeling guilty."

"You're right, I know you're right. What will make it feel okay? Maybe it won't ever feel okay. Maybe it's not. Should I just forget about Dane? A-and—"

"Laney!" Zach interrupts my rambling. "Slow up, girl, and listen to me. You have to decide why you feel guilty about Evan. Is it because you love him or simply because you haven't told him? And here's the biggie, Laney—if Evan went to Southern, which one would you choose?"

And there it is. The million dollar question. Which one do I choose?

"I don't know and I don't know if it's because Dane is the one here or if it's actually something more. I'm not real good at this whole boyfriend thing, obviously. How do I figure it out if they're never in the same place?" I'm asking the guy currently volleying twins; I'm so screwed.

"I wish I could tell ya, sweetie, but I can't. I know you've been honest with Dane, so do the same with Evan and see what happens. That's all you can do, really, that or let them both go. Or you could always choose door number three and pick me." He laughs.

"Very funny, Zach. I'm thinking you're juggling plenty on your plate right now."

"I know, right? It's fun as hell, too, lemme tell ya. That's the thing though; we all know not one of us is emotionally invested, yet anyway. You, though, Laney, you couldn't do just for fun if you tried. You're already in deep with both of them and I'm pretty sure they're both in love with you. Somebody's gonna get hurt any way you go, Laney, so just make sure you're absolutely positive before you crush one of them."

"So you're saying to string them both along until I decide? I can't do that."

"Hell no, I'm saying be honest with Evan. Dane already knows the score, Evan deserves that, too. They're big boys; let them decide after that what they want to do. Maybe they'll walk away and tell ya to fuck off or maybe they'll fight for ya, but at least they'll both be making the decision with their eyes open. It's okay for you to be confused, Laney, that doesn't make you a bad person. Just be honest. Don't stray from that beautiful heart of yours, okay?"

"Dane made me promise not to kiss Evan this weekend. How the hell am I supposed to pull that off?" I can't help but laugh. I can't believe me, of all people, is in this situation.

"I just told ya; be honest. How about 'Hey, Evan, I promised Dane I wouldn't touch your ass until I figure all this out,' or 'Hey, Dane, there's no way I can avoid kissing Evan, I spoke too soon.' I don't know, say you have mono."

I crack up at him because neither of those would go over well and I'd have a hard time explaining to Evan how I had the kissing disease! "Is this as exhausting to you as it is me? Truth is, Zach, I'm scared. Do I really know Dane well enough to take a chance on him?"

"Don't you dare do that, Laney. Do not second guess you and Dane just for the sake of a decision. You know there's something there."

"Since when are you Dane's biggest fan?"

"I'm a Laney fan. Your pretty lil' face lights up when that kid walks in and that tells me all I need to know. He obviously makes you happy, so he and I are good."

"Thanks, Zach, for everything."

"No sweat, my pet. Now go figure your shit out and call me if you need me. I'll see ya when you get back."

Settled into the comfort of my old bedroom, I'd normally have no trouble going to sleep at this hour, but tonight sleep evades me. My skin is crawling from the inside out and I'm on edge. There's no Disney movie for this, no band-aid. I decide to call Evan, maybe do a little prep for our talk tomorrow. I can tell he's been drinking in three words.

"Hey, hot stuff."

"Hey, Ev, whatcha doing?" I know what he's doing; I can hear the party in the background. The night before a game, really?

"Just hanging out, you?"

"Nothing, I'll just talk to you later, I can tell you're busy. I'll see you when you get here."

"Don't be mad. Please, listen, I can't really hear you, let me call you back," he yells into the phone, and about ten seconds before I say okay, I hear her.

"Get off the phone, Evan, the booty call's right here."

Oh hell no—I know that voice. It's drunken and slurred, but it's Kaitlyn. Why is he in the same room with her, close enough I can hear her? She destroys me and you hang with her? Evan has never blatantly hurt or disrespected me, all these years, but this is a straight shot.

"Fuck you, Evan." I hang up.

I turn off my phone and go down some Nyquil. I'm done with this day.

Chapter 31

CONFESSIONS

-Laney-

Daddy's up at the crack of dawn, as always. I get up and amble into the kitchen to join him.

"Go sit down, Daddy; I'll get your breakfast." We eat together, talking little and I know exactly what will make me feel better. "You feel like going fishing?"

"I sure as hell do, kiddo."

It's a great day for it and soon we're out of worms. My soul feels lighter; I hope his does, too. He's been all smiles, casting and reeling with gusto all day. I love this time with my dad. He's such a companionable man. I always wonder how she couldn't find solace in him, in a life with him. I know he'd have done anything she needed.

We get home at dusk and I clean up and make us tuna casserole. My dad scarfs it down; he's obviously gone too long without someone cooking for him. He heads to bed early, so I finally turn my phone back on; no one gets to interrupt fishing or Daddy time.

I don't even open the texts from Evan, I'm still so mad I can't see straight. I text Zach to see how his game went and then I call Dane back, he'd called once last night and twice today.

"Hey, finally, where you been?"

His voice covers me like a blanket, wrapping me in repose instantly. In that very moment, I know Evan could move into my room and my skin would still tingle when I see, hear, or think of Dane. This isn't going away.

"I'm sorry, I turned off my phone 'cause I fished all day with my dad. How are you?"

"Better now that you called. I miss you, baby."

I miss him, too, surprisingly badly. I just can't say it out loud, though, so I change the subject. "Tell me about your day. What'd you do last night?" I ask, trying to concentrate on his answer. He could just keep calling me baby over and over; it makes me crazy when he says it.

He tells me The Crew hit The Kickback last night and then all went to Zach's game today, which the Eagles won. Now he was lying in his bed "missing me."

"Dane, tell me something real. Tell me something as important as everything I tell you." He has to do this, right this minute; it's vital that he instill some trust in me. The next few sentences out of his mouth are as important as anything he's ever said to me. I have to know this connection isn't one-sided and goes deeper than physical attraction.

"You name it, baby, what would you like to know?"

I could probably get "the real number" out of him right now, the one every girl wonders the minute she decides she likes a guy. That's not really what I want to know. Shoot, who am I kidding, yes I do...but I just can't ask it. "So, let me think...how about one light and one heavy question, okay?"

"Anything, ask away." He wouldn't just agree like this if he didn't know I'm testing the weight of us before I see Evan. I probably shouldn't take advantage, but I want to feel close to him emotionally right now.

"What's your middle name?" Crap, I'm off my game and jumped the gun. I wasted a coveted question on something I could easily found out elsewhere.

"Dane."

"Uh…" I know what he's saying, and want to know his first name, but I can't ask or he may count it as my second question.

He snickers. "Don't want to burn a question, huh?" Scary ESP on this boy. "Okay, I'll be nice. My name is Michael Dane Kendrick. I go by Dane, my middle name."

"I like it, Dane's a beautiful name. It suits you. Not that Michael isn't great, too."

He's amused by my long-winded response. "Thank you, baby."

The knock at the door comes and I have to let him go before my "deep" question…of course.

"Laney, please call me when you're done talking to him, okay?"

"Okay," I sigh, the dread building up inside of me.

"Seriously, Laney, no matter what time, you call me."

For a split second, the moment I see him, I forget that I'm mad at him. I forget we're miles apart now. I forget all that I've done, become, and experienced without him. He's so handsome, so familiar. He has bags under his eyes, which aren't as sparkling blue as usual, but his slight smile still affects me.

"Hey, pretty."

Look at him, my Tod, my best friend. The righter of wrongs, protector from evil, prom date, first kiss, standing before me in the flesh. Spending only a fraction of the time apart that we've spent together, I've let another slip in and divide us. How could I be so callous? How could I cast my forever aside so easily?

But it hadn't been easy, and we had mutually agreed… no…I can't keep doing this. I can't feel guilty for feeling, for living; but I can feel guilty about only being completely honest with one of them. I'm about to fix it right now.

"Hey, come on in." I scoot back to make room for him and close the door behind him.

He sits on the couch and rests his arms on his knees, head in his hands. It takes him a while to gather himself and finally look at me where I sit at the opposite end of the couch.

"Laney, I'm so sorry…for so much. I'm sorry for what Kaitlyn did and for what she said last night. That drunk bitch followed me around all night, trying to tell me she loves me, but I didn't give her the time of day, Laney, I swear. I hate her, you know I do."

I want to believe him, if just for the sake of our friendship, but part of me doesn't. "Why didn't you leave when you saw her there?"

"Why should I leave? That bitch isn't going to dictate where I go."

No, just where I go. "Sometimes you have to be the bigger person and walk away, Evan. Staying just gave her the chance to keep following you, to keep talking to you. If it really bothered you, you would've left." I cross my arms over my chest, eyebrows raised, challenging him to tell me I'm wrong.

He ponders on this a while before speaking. "You're right. I know you're right, but I was drunk and not thinking. I'm sorry, Laney, please forgive me."

"I can't be friends with you if you continue to allow her

opportunities to be around you. I think of it as a direct betrayal."
Yeah, I can hear the hypocrisy in my words, but this is different—the base of everything is true friendship, and I haven't betrayed that, and he shouldn't, either. If you blatantly screw Evan over, well then, I'm done with you and I demand the same loyalty in return.

"I agree; it won't happen again, Laney. I swear."

"Okay, then I'll forgive you." I relax my shoulders. I do believe and forgive him, but I had to make sure he knows how serious I am about my stance.

He moves close to me and puts his arms around me. I can't help it, I breathe in his scent, soak up his feel and I think of what could have been.

"Can I stay with you tonight? I miss you so much, munchkin. I love you so much, I need to hold you."

God, what do I do?

"I miss you too, Evan, all the time, but I can't do the merry-go-round thing anymore. I'm making myself crazy trying to figure out you and me or me and Dane." Oh shit, it just popped out. I didn't want to tell him like this.

"Who the fuck is Dane?" he growls, his back bowing.

"I-I told you about him. I met him at school. He's part of my group of friends. My roommate dates his brother, remember?"

"Vaguely. I don't remember you telling me anything much. Now you have to figure you and him out? What's that mean?" His face is red and his eyes narrow.

"Lower your voice, Evan, you're gonna wake up Dad!" I angry-whisper at him.

"Sorry," he says, much lower, "but tell me, Laney. Tell me about Dane, right now."

"I don't know what to say, really. First of all, he knows about you, our past, our problems with distance, how I feel about
230

you. He likes me and he wants me to be his girlfriend or whatever."

"Have you fucked him?"

Whack—I straight up slap the shit out of him. "Get out!" I whisper-scream this time.

"No. Shit, sorry, I shouldn't have said that." He runs his hand over his face, up and down, trying to scrub out the anger. "I was wrong to say that, but you don't get to just drop a bomb and throw me out. I deserve better than that, Laney. I deserve an explanation. I'm not leaving; slap me again if you want, but you're telling me everything."

"You ever talk to me like that again, Evan Mitchell Allen, and it'll be the last time you ever speak to me, you understand?" I'm so mad I might take him up on the offer to slap him again.

"Yes, I understand, and I'm sorry, Laney. That's all I do anymore is apologize to you. What happened to us?" His question comes out choked.

"Life, that's what happened to us." I'm not sure exactly what it even means, but I'm completely sure it's the right answer.

"Ain't that the truth…so tell me, please, Laney? I'm dying over here."

"No, I haven't slept with him, but you already knew that. I also haven't let him shove his face in my cleavage. You know me better than that." I quirk a brow and wait for him to make the connection. I honestly hadn't planned on ever throwing it in his face, but I'm thinking Evan threw down the gauntlet already.

His face pales and his eyes dart away from mine. Finally he whispers, "What do you want to know about it?"

"What do you want to tell me?"

At a couple spots in his story about initiation, Bulldog Babes, parties, seeing the picture on my phone, I actually think he's going to cry, but he doesn't. It's obvious I couldn't possibly make him feel any worse about himself than he already does, and that's not my goal here, anyway. At least he knows now that I know, so he can stop with the holier than thou act for the rest of our Dane conversation.

"I have kissed Dane, but that's all…well, physically anyway. He did buy me a necklace." I take a deep, deep breath. "And, well, he, uh, he sorta took me to Disney World for my birthday." 3, 2, 1…

"WHAT?!" He jumps up from the couch this time, arms flying out, chest heaving.

"Evan, again with the volume! I'm gonna quit talking if you can't keep it down." I scowl at him; this is probably way too serious a conversation to be having while my dad is asleep, but going outside is out, we'd just wake up the whole neighborhood.

"You went on a trip with a guy you barely know? Who are you, Laney? And why is this guy going all out if you've only ever kissed him?" He hisses the last part; it's not a pretty side of him. I knew he'd really flip about the trip and honestly, it was pretty out of character of me, but I just know I'm safe with Dane…just like I know I'm safe with Evan.

"Well, I don't know, Evan, maybe he sees something in me. You do wonderful things for me all the time and I don't put out for you!"

"Ah, babe." He sits back down and runs his hand down my arm. "I know you're worth it, but he doesn't. He barely knows you. I just question his motives. If he knows you're mine, he's a douche for making a play."

"Actually, he made it clear he wouldn't make a play if I was with you, and I'm not, remember? He didn't touch me on that trip, Evan. He really did it just to be nice."

"Bullshit, we didn't agree to go kissing other people! I may have done some stupid shit, but I haven't kissed anyone! And you can bet I'm not taking trips with anyone or buying them jewelry. Damn, Laney, what is this guy to you? Have I lost you?"

I can see the tears in his eyes and it splinters me. My

sweet, sweet Evan. This boy, not so long ago, represented all that was good in my life, all that I could ever want. Now I'm ripping his heart out.

"I don't know, Evan. All I know is I love you, always." I move closer and wrap one hand around his neck to stroke his hair and make him feel the weight of my words and solace. "If you were there, we'd be together, just like we planned and wanted. But you're not there, and he is and he's good to me. I like him, and yes, I'm attracted to him. He wants me, with no romantic ties to you, but I told him very clearly that I do love you and I won't hurt you."

"But you are hurting me. Nothing could hurt more, nothing." He lifts my chin, demanding I look at him. "I love you, Laney, and I'll do whatever it takes to keep you. I know you were just lonely and I don't blame you. I haven't been perfect, either, but I will be. For you, I will be."

He pulls me into his strong arms and holds on tightly. I'd be lying if I didn't admit it feels cathartically wonderful in his arms. There's nowhere in the world like Evan's embrace. It's here and only here that I find total acceptance, unconditional love, and a man's desire for only me.

"You don't even know this Dane. You know me, Laney, you know us. I won't let you mistake companionship for love. I won't let you throw us away."

Absolutely everything he just said makes sense and speaks directly to my heart. Do I want to play two guys? No. Is he right, do I only want Dane because he's there? No. Granted, he would have never gotten near me if Evan had been there, but had he, I still would've been tempted. Dane pulled me from across the room the minute I met him, undeniably. But I already knew this, thus my dizziness. My thoughts are just wicked circles these days.

"I don't know what you want me to say, Evan. I love you. I don't love him, but I like him. I wish you were there and that this never happened, but—"

He silences me with his fingers, rubbing my lips gently. "You must be drained, sweetness, you go to bed and don't worry over this nonsense. I'll fix everything, Laney." He pulls me in for a hug and a kiss on the forehead. "I'm really sorry for speaking out of line to you and you know I didn't mean it. I adore you, Laney. I always have and I always will."

He looks at me for my acceptance and I give him a weak smile. He's right; I'm absolutely exhausted, physically and emotionally. He doesn't mention staying with me again and I head to bed.

Chapter 32

CALLING CARD

-Evan-

I wait for Laney to get to her bedroom and shut the door before I grab her phone and forward his contact to mine. No cute pet name, just "Dane." No song attached. I still have a shot. I know my Laney, and if she hasn't attached a song, he hasn't cracked through her layers all the way to the center yet.

I thought about texting him from her phone and telling him "I'd" changed my mind and to leave "me" alone, but being the recent victim of phone fraud, I'm not going to sink that low. No, I'll go man to man with him all day long. When Laney finds out, she'll be pissed, but she'll get over that. She might not get over this Dane prick if I don't do something, though, and it's that thinking that propels me to proceed. Without caution.

When I'm clear of her house, I dial him, sure he'll be up waiting for her to call. "Hello?"

"Yeah, is this Dane?"

"It is. Who's this?"

"This is Evan Allen." I let that sink in for a minute.

Ya douche—you know who I am.

"What can I do for you, Evan? Where's Laney?"

"Laney's in bed. She's had a very long day, not that you need to worry about it. What you can do for me, Dane, is stay the fuck away from her. What kind of guy goes after another man's girl?"

"Evan, listen, I've heard a lot of great things about you and what you've done for Laney. So out of respect for that, I don't want to be rude, but what's between me and Laney is none of your business. I won't discuss her with you behind her back."

"Don't pull that shit with me, like you respect her and I'm betraying her. No one cares about that girl more than me. I love her more than my own life and I'm not about to walk away."

"Really? I thought you'd already done that."

Now he's taking me from pissed to drive there and kick his ass mad. I want to go real country on his ass right about now.

"Whatever, man, I had school. I didn't walk away just for the hell of it. Either way, it's none of your fucking business. I've been beside that girl for ten years, you've been there for ten minutes, so don't ever kid yourself that you know our story."

"Evan, I understand your position, I really do. I can't imagine losing a girl like Laney, it would make me crazy, too, but this is not for you and me to decide. We can't duel it out for her hand, that's hers to give."

"I haven't lost her and she gave her hand to me! If you care about her, back off! You're just confusing her and stressing her out."

"I will do whatever Laney asks me to do…Laney, not you. Have a good night."

I'm not sure what that phone call accomplished. It didn't make me feel any better and his proper ass shows no signs of backing off anytime soon. His calm rationale and confidence in what he has with Laney burns through me like acid. How is it that he's he all smug about where he stands with Laney and I'm standing here doubting everything I thought I knew about us?

I have to narrow our gap, literally. Laney Jo Walker is my future, no way I'm gonna stand back and let some tool blind her with fancy trips and gifts. There's no way he's had enough time to steal her whole heart. His time stops now.

The next morning I knock on the door nervously, not sure how I'll find Laney on the other side. If Dane told her I called him, then I'm sure to be greeted by my lil' hellcat. Luckily, she opens it with a sleepy smile. "Hey."

"Morning sunshine, how you feeling today?"

"Better, more grounded. Come on in, Dad's in front of the TV. Go keep him company, please. I'll get breakfast."

I watch her walk half-dazed to the kitchen. She's so not a morning person, but cute as hell. I can't wait until she wakes up in my arms every day. My Laney...please God, don't let anyone take her. If you give me this, I swear to wake her every morning with "good morning, beautiful" and kiss her to sleep every night. I'll keep her safe and hold her tight. I'll take care of her, I swear it.

"Hey, Mr. Walker, how are you?"

"There he is. How are you, son?" He stands and gives me a hug; he calls me son. Dane doesn't even know him. He has no idea what lure he throws for top water or his favorite NFL team. Too bad Laney's dad doesn't get the deciding vote. I'd win that shit hands down.

"I'm good, glad to be home." I give him the most sincere smile I can despite the sadness inside me. My angel is slipping away. I never thought I'd see the day. Another man's lips have touched hers. He'd shown her Disney World, like only her biggest dream come true. I've probably already lost and the thought causes a very real crushing feeling in my chest.

He asks me about school and ball. I concentrate to keep up my end of the conversation, telling him we're 2-0 in conference play. That news makes him smile and scrub my head.

Laney walks in with a breakfast tray for her dad. "You want something, Ev?"

"No thanks, lil' bit, I already ate at home. Your dad and I were just talking about school."

She looks over to me and holds my stare. Can she feel it? Does she know that I'll do anything for her? "Are you happy there, Evan?" she asks.

She wants me to say yes so that she knows I'm fine without her. No matter what, Laney would never simply disregard my feelings, but I don't want to be her pity pick. I want her to want me, like the way she did before I left her. I left her. This is all my fault.

"I'd be happier if you were there." I give a simple answer for the sake of her dad and pat the seat beside me for her to sit.

The rest of the late morning is spent watching TV and visiting with her dad and by the time we've finished lunch I still haven't found any time to talk to Laney alone. We've both got to get back on the road soon, and before I know it, I'm loading her bag for her.

She meets me on the porch on my way back in. "Evan, what do we do, ya know, about…us?" She looks anywhere but at me and I see the tears in her eyes, about to fall. "Please tell me you know, Evan, because I don't have a clue. I don't know anything anymore. "

"Look at me, Laneybear." I tilt her chin up and wipe her cheek with my thumb. "Everything is gonna be all right. You don't worry about me. I'm not going anywhere. I love you, Laney Jo, and I'm always going to love you. We're always gonna be okay, no matter what, so you don't worry." I kiss her on the forehead, breathing in the sweet smell of her. "If there's nothing

238

else in the whole world you know for sure, know that you are always the most important thing in the world to me. Just take care of you, Laney. I'll take care of everything else."

I don't press her about the Dane thing right now, leading us to her truck. I don't want to stress her out anymore, she's got to be able to drive and right now she looks like she may crumble any minute. Besides, I'll take care of that little inconvenience soon enough. I just hope I'm not underestimating him until I can get things in place.

As stoic as possible, I open the door and lift her in by the hips. No matter how badly I want to dig my fingers in, throw her against the door, and kiss her until she can't breathe, I hold it together. Giving her a smile, despite the ache in my chest seeing her watery eyes, I lean in her window and place a gentle kiss on her lips. Her brows furrow and she shifts, unnoticeable if I didn't know her like the back of my hand. "It'll all be okay soon, Laney, I promise."

Chapter 33

TIT FOR TAT

-Laney-

There was a time, not too long ago even, where I automatically assumed the worst about people. I didn't let just anyone in; and no one in easily. I very seldom gave new people a chance. College kinda takes that option away from you; dorms, classes, projects, sports—detachment poses a challenge and thank God for that! My crew is a blessing; I'd be lost without them. It's surreal how easily we all "fit" and how natural it feels when we're all in a room together. They're my crutch these days, so pizza night is a must.

I refuse to leave in my pajamas and Zach doesn't know how late he'll be, so the group text declares our room the meeting spot. Avery drew the "bring dinner" card tonight but I know Sawyer or Zach will see to it that the replacement cash finds its way to her. Bennett and I have a bit to catch up on before anyone else shows up and I'm grateful; we've been spread too thin lately for a good heart to heart.

She's excited for her big production and its approaching opening night. They're doing *A Streetcar Named Desire* and the truly fabulous Bennett has been cast as Blanche Dubois. I now understand why there are pictures of Vivian Leigh pinned around the room and bathroom. She'll be great, I know it. Bennett is a flash of secure individuality in any room. It makes me very happy to hear the elation in her voice and see the flush in her cheeks as she then sings Tate's praises; he supports her, reads lines with her, even read the play himself so he'd be able to discuss it intelligibly. That last part really does impress me; if it's not your thing, reading a play can be torture.

Speak of the hero...Tate and Sawyer walk in, sans knock, which no longer aggravates me, bearing beer and smiles.

"Ah, Gidget's home!!" Sawyer lifts me and twirls me in a giant hug; with his big old self, you're risking a rib fracture every time.

Gidget—I have got to find time to watch that movie so I know what the hell he's talking about. Bennett talked them all into watching a classic one night without me, and Sawyer hee-hawed the whole movie about how much I remind him of "the sweet lil' blonde coming of age."

"Hey, Sawyer, I missed you, too." I giggle, giddy with the realization that I did miss him. "Hey, Tate, how are you?" I volunteer a hug for him as well.

"I'm good, we all missed you." I see right then what has Bennett so enamored. His kind eyes, his reflective smile...it reminds me of his brother.

"Thanks, Tate, you too," I simper as Kirby pops her head inside the door.

"Knock knock." She peeks inside shyly.

I usher her in, Avery right behind her. They're both in red, which makes it even harder to tell them apart. I try not to gape as Sawyer moves to them and literally welcomes them at the same time, touching them both in some way. Man, I'm feeling unsure about my bet, I can't tell with any certainty at this point which one he prefers. And when Zach finally shows up and glides the threesome comfortably into a foursome, I'm even more puzzled.

I steal a glance at Bennett, who just shrugs at me and grins. Oh yeah, definitely gonna have to form an alliance with her for an impromptu game of Truth or Dare or something—the truth shall set us free! The suspense is killing me! Those are lucky twins, though; you can't make a wrong choice between Sawyer Beckett and Zach Reece.

We all fall into an amicable rhythm, grabbing our pizza and drinks, vying for a seat in the cramped space. Avery graces Sawyer's lap, but he entwines his leg with Kirby's, who's sitting beside him…killing me!

Zach comes and sits by me, seemingly unfazed by the show, and tells me how he missed me. "How'd your talk go?" he whispers.

"Confusing and nothing got resolved, but at least I told him." I shrug.

"What'd he say?"

"That he forgives me, he'd fix it, and not to worry. I honestly left more confused than when I got there. He didn't ask me back and he didn't ask me to stay away from Dane. I have no idea." I give him a questioning look. "You got any other ideas?"

He kisses the top of my head. "That's all you can do, Laney. It'll all pan out, you'll see."

I so hope he's right.

"Laney, where's Dane?" Kirby asks.

Good question, I was wondering the same thing.

"He should be here any minute," Tate offers.

"Maybe he thought we were in our room. He'll figure it out," Sawyer answers with his mouth full of pizza.

"I'll go look for him." I stand to navigate my way through everyone's legs.

I hear him before I see him, his voice lowered and heated. As I get to the end of the hall I start to feel sick, I can make out enough to know who's around the corner with him. When he jerks his head and meets my eyes, I don't venture to guess what he sees in them because even I don't know what I'm feeling right now. Quickly assessing, I've interrupted a serious, concealed conversation between him and Whitley. I flick my eyes to her and the snarky brow lift she gives me shoots fire all through me.

Taking in Dane's expression, I can actually read his mind… "Oh fuck" is exactly what he just thought.

I find my voice. "We thought maybe you went to the wrong room. I was just coming to look for you, sorry." I'm not going to cry, not even a hint of tears building. I'm not going to punch either one of them, my anger surprisingly restrained. I think of Evan's soft goodbye kiss, a direct violation of my breathy promise to Dane, and decide to simply turn and walk back to my room.

"You not find him?" Tate asks as I step inside.

"Actually, I did. He's in the hall, I'm sure he'll be in here in a sec."

Bennett gives me a concerned and confused look to which I respond with a slight "let it go" shake of my head. It's about twelve minutes, not that I was keeping track, before Dane joins us. I don't look at him but rather stare straight ahead at Bennett. She looks like a crazy cat lady glancing quickly back and forth between us, frantically trying to figure out what's just happened. You'd have to be asleep to not feel the tension in the room.

I'm trying to understand. I'm not unfamiliar with the whole obsessed fan thing, but he has to be stringing her along or something. I mean, it's all the time—she calls him, she always knows where to find him, and now she seems to be able to lure him into a secret hallway rendezvous. It pisses me off to think I'm hurting Evan for a player, but that can't be right...my instincts are screaming at me that Dane simply isn't a player and basing my decision on Evan solely off whether or not this thing with Dane is real, well, that'd make me the biggest player of all.

Evan deserves better than to be a wishy-washy girl's fallback guy. Evan deserves someone's fire, someone's all-consuming passion, and someone's love; nothing less. He should be someone's everything.

Dane makes his plate and comes to sit down by me. He says "welcome back" out loud but whispers, "I need to talk to you."

I want so badly to play it off and give him the jealous girl cold shoulder, but I just can't make myself do it. I've told Dane all along that I don't want to play games so I have to stick to that. I hitch up my big girl panties and head to the hall, indicating to him non-verbally to follow me.

He steps in the hall, clicking the door shut behind him, nervously moving towards me. "So, about Whitley...it's not what you think." He runs a hand through his sexy brown hair, messing it up just right.

"I'm not sure what I think, to be perfectly honest with you."

"What do you want me to do? I can't change my number; too many important people have it. I can't get a restraining order." He shakes his head and looks down. "What do you suggest I do? Tell me and I'll do it. I don't want to be a dick, but I can't get her to leave me alone."

"You could block her number. You could keep walking and ignore her. I refuse to believe she physically contains you."

He leans into me, teasing me with his musky scent and his hot breath. "I could tell her my woman's getting mad and is gonna kick her ass," he whispers, running his hands down my arms until he links his fingers with mine.

244

I gulp, not ready to forgive him just because he talks purty and lights up my whole body. "You just want to see a cat fight, you hornball. You're as bad as Sawyer."

"Mmmmm," he hums as his lips and nose graze my neck, "I could watch you do anything. If that happens to be a cat fight, so be it." He chuckles slightly into my skin, earning my forgiveness with the fire it shoots through me.

"Come on." I roll my eyes and pull him to the room.

The tension fizzles and I know everyone is grateful. The night turns out very fun with lots of laughter. I almost forget all about the Whitley thing…almost.

Even after our little spat about Whitley, or the teeny tiff over the night I promised to call him after talking to Evan and forgot, or less-than-happy texts due to having almost no time for him this week because of late practices…Dane has still been wonderful, greeting me with dinner and a massage every night, no matter the time.

By Thursday, fatigue is about to completely take over. He shows up at my room around eight, and after we say our goodbyes to Bennett and Tate, who are on their way to some new movie Bennett's been raving about, he settles beside me on my bed, stroking my hair gently.

"What time do you have class tomorrow?" he asks softly.

"Only one class tomorrow at three then ball at five-thirty," I reply through a yawn.

"So nothing until three? Why don't you come home with me tonight, baby? I can pamper you all night and most of tomorrow."

It sounds wonderful and new life springs into me at the thought of it, but I haven't met his parents yet; will they be there? Thinking about it, I talk about my dad all the time. Hell, I've even told him bits and pieces about my mom, who might be a Buddhist hiding in the mountains for all I know, and he's never said anything about his own parents.

"What about your parents? I don't want them to meet me as the floozy creeping in after dark."

He shakes his head. "They won't be there, baby, just us. Well, that's not entirely true. Helen, the housekeeper, will be there for a bit in the morning." He gives me a slow, lingering kiss. "But I'm hoping you sleep through her visit."

Even I, fog girl, know what he's insinuating. Am I ready?

"No, Laney, you just need your rest."

My damn telling face! He knew exactly what I was thinking and answered before I'd even answered myself.

"Um, okay, sounds good." I prop up on one elbow and kiss his cheek. "Sounds wonderful, actually. Why are you so good to me?"

He really is. He's barely gotten past first base and has no real commitment from me, Evan calls every day and he knows it and yet he continues to pamper me every chance he gets. What do I possibly give back to him to deserve all this?

"Laney, I've told you a dozen times, making you happy, doing things for you…it makes me feel whole, like nothing ever has before."

I roll on my side and scoot as close to him as possible, burying my face in his chest. He smells so good. I found out a while ago that he wears Fierce by A&F; I love it.

"You do make me happy," I mumble into his chest. "Very happy."

"Ditto, baby, now let's go before I have to carry you out asleep." He stands, putting his hand out to help me up.

"Let me pack some stuff real quick."

"No need." He shrugs, smiling at me.

"Yes need, I haven't showered and I'm not wearing this," I motion to my sports tank and Sofe shorts, "tomorrow."

"Okay, grab an outfit for tomorrow, but I've got your jammies and girly bathroom stuff covered." He winks at me with a devilish smirk.

"Oh, do tell." I start to rummage through my clothes for something to wear. "This I'm dying to hear."

"Toothbrush, check. Lady razors, check. New pajamas, check. Makeup, check. Your kind of shampoo, check. Did I forget anything?"

Every weirdo warning in my brain should be firing on all cylinders right about now, so why is my whole body flushed? "Okay...do I want to know how you know all that stuff? Am I gonna look like a clown with non-conditioned hair?" I actually don't care if I do; his effort is undeniably adorable to me.

"If it's all right, then I get the credit. If it's all wrong then blame Helen and Bennett." He laughs.

I continue grilling him on the way to his car, my arm looped through his. I can't wait to see what he's gathered...there's no way he had her get Moroccan Oil shampoo and conditioner, my fave. Through more interrogation, I discover Dane is quite the smooth operator. He's actually blushing as he admits to sending Helen to the stores with lists Bennett made him for the makeup and toiletries...oh and a picture off the internet for the pajamas he'd picked. Good Lord.

We laugh the whole drive as he describes Helen's fiasco of putting a clerk on the phone with him to list off all the scents of bubble bath and candles since he hadn't specified on those items. Bennett and I don't burn candles in our room, so that'd been all him. Adorable. It's then and there that I decide one day soon I am devising a tampon run where Dane simply has to go in for me; can't wait to see what he does with that!

When things calm, he reaches for my hand, lacing our fingers. He lifts my hand to his mouth for a kiss. A pang of familiarity shoots through me, but I give him a small smile. He sees it in my eyes, he clears his throat and lowers our hands, but leaves them connected. "About your trip home this weekend..."

"Yeah?"

"I was thinking I'd take you." He glances out of the corner of his eye at me. I'm not sure I'm ready for him to meet my dad, or if Evan's going home this weekend; we haven't talked about that at all this past week.

"I'm going all weekend, Dane. How will I get back? You don't want to stay that long, I'm sure. I'm not even sure my dad would let you sleep there, quite honestly." I bite my lip; I can't imagine how Daddy would react. I can imagine exactly how Evan would react, even scarier, but the thought of having Dane there with me is enticing.

"I'll stay there all weekend, too, as long as you want. And whatever your dad wants, I can get a hotel for the nights. Please, Laney, let me in." His thumb traces quick circles into my palm and the longing for acceptance in his voice is palpable.

I don't like ultimatums, I really don't, but I also don't like putting myself "out there" without feeling secure in reciprocation, which is why I ask faintly, "Will you do the same?"

He exhales loudly. "I'm trying, Laney, I really am. I'm just not ready for you to leave and I'm afraid you might." He looks over at me, his chocolate eyes darker than usual. I decide to lighten things up a bit. Much like me, Dane likes little games of give and take...

"Let's make a deal." I wiggle my eyebrows up and down at him. "For every fact I take from you, I'll give you something."

His hand tightens on the steering wheel, the other flexing its grip on mine. "Go on," he rumbles deeply. We've pulled into the garage now; he turns off the car and turns in his seat to me, awaiting my answer.

"When's your birthday?" I'll start slow with easy questions.

248

"February 6th."

I lean over and kiss him chastely. Pulling back, I wait for his eyes, a twinkle in mine. "How old are you, Dane?"

"Twenty-one."

I lean forward and kiss him again, this time deeply, running my tongue along his bottom lip until he opens fully to me. It's the most seductive kiss I've ever given; I moan, I bite softly, I suck his tongue. When I pull back, he grabs me around the neck, pulling me back for more.

"Uh, uh, uh," I taunt, retreating against him. "Where do you work?"

"For myself; corporation, investments, spoiled rich kid making it last."

Although vague, I'll take it. I really don't want a full portfolio right now, boring. I reach over and pull his shirt up, running my hands along his stomach and chest. His body is magnificent, tanned and toned, hard and hot to the touch. "See, was that so hard?"

"Baby, it's so hard it hurts." He lunges for me but I squeal and jump out of the car. I beat him to the interior door but stop short of opening it, still mindful enough to not just barge into his house. He moves in behind me, pressing his body into the back of mine while moving my hair to the side. He bends his head down and breathes heat on my neck. "I love it when you're playful...so fucking sexy." He swats my butt and I yelp. Running his hands down my sides, he finds mine and pulls them up, guiding them to the wall in front of me. Pushing into the back of me harder, he pushes my hands flat against the wall. "Your choice, bubble bath or hot tub?" He nibbles along my shoulder. "Just to help you relax, I swear."

"Hot tub," I moan.

"I'll get the wine and meet you there. I bought a new suit for you, it's on the bed in the pool house; wear it. Don't keep me waiting." He releases his lock on one of my wrists, reaching around me to turn the knob.

I quickly scamper through the kitchen to the patio doors; I feel better already. Oh how I wish all things in life could be this easily solved.

Much later, after I've had ample time to soak and relax, he meets me in the water, carefully balancing a bottle of wine and two glasses. I rise out of the liquid heat to help him and hear the hiss through his teeth. I look up to see what's wrong, but I can't meet his eyes because they're moving down my body, now housed in the black string bikini he'd laid out for me. Usually way too skimpy for me, I feel sexy as hell in it since I know it's for his eyes only.

"Turn around," he growls. I turn slowly. I'm 100% sure that Dane is 100% an ass man, which works out perfectly since I'm packing a badonk. "Your ass is like a work of art, baby." He sets everything down and pulls me into him, my back to his front. He rubs himself against me and I fall slightly forward, my knees suddenly weak. His arms glide around me, his hands spreading out across my stomach and hips, triggering tingles throughout my body.

"Your body drives me crazy, Laney. It's so hard to keep my hands to myself with you." He leans in to kiss along the side of my neck, my ear, my shoulder. I feel his hands move lower very slowly. "You're the sexiest thing I've ever seen. I could get lost in you."

I turn around and gaze up at him, looking for the sign, the one that tells me this is all right.

Surrounded by steam, droplets of water skating down our half-naked bodies, moonlight, and soft music in the background—how am I possibly supposed to resist? I push on his chest slightly, guiding him to sit on the ledge under the hot water.

"What do you do all day when I'm in school?" I give him a seductive look so he's clear that I'm not just asking; we're back to the reward for an answer game.

250

"Work, deal with my businesses, work out." His eyes devour me, his tongue licking slowly along his bottom lip.

I acknowledge his answer by sitting down on him, straddling his lap and pushing down on him suggestively. "When's the last time you brought a girl to this house?"

"Never, only you."

I run my tongue up his neck, tasting every inch. "Why do you have a collection of bikinis?"

"I have no idea," he strains out. "I think Helen thought I'd make friends."

I snicker at his answer and reach around and untie the bottom off my bikini top and feel him tense beneath me. "How much did you chip in on my birthday stuff?" I've suspected for a while; Bennett and Zach couldn't afford all that.

"What do you mean?"

I move to re-tie my suit, but he stops my arm.

"Not a lot, they all did the spa stuff." He sighs in relief as I bring my arms back down.

"And the club? Who paid to rent out a whole club?"

"No one," he spurts out.

I click my tongue at him and shake my head—wrong answer—moving once again to tie up and get off his lap simultaneously.

"No baby, come back." He pulls me back down on him. "I own The Kickback, Laney. No one had to pay, it's mine."

What? I wasn't expecting that, but a deal's a deal...I reach behind myself and free the knot around my neck, my top falling into the water. I don't move to cover myself, looking deeply into his eyes to gauge his reaction. His eyes enlarge and his teeth bite his bottom lip.

He hisses out, "Exquisite, baby...fucking unreal."

SE Hall

He gradually slides a hand up my slick torso and flicks his stare to my eyes, asking for permission, which I give by arching my back and pushing my bare chest forward into his hands.

"Oh, Laney," he purrs as he surrounds my breasts with his strong hands, rubbing and kneading.

A guttural sound escapes me, my nipples hardening to his touch. Instinctively, I run my hands into his hair, pulling his face into me; I want to feel his warm, wet mouth on me. His teeth catch my nipple first, biting and teasing before he widens and sucks in as much as he can. I clench between my legs, feeling the gush of moisture despite being in the water. His mouth, his tongue, his hands are so intoxicating I can't stop my hips from rocking into him, hard and downward, seeking a cure to the nagging in my core.

His wicked mouth breaks suction. "God, you're gorgeous, Laney. You like my mouth on you?"

"Mmmmm," is all I can respond. I'm so close, gyrating into him harder and faster. He's so hard beneath me, his swim trunks a flimsy barrier. I can feel every inch of him twitching for me. I'm not sure how I'm even aware, but I register "Collide" beginning to play in the background and that does it. Perfect song, perfect moment…the allure mentally pushes me right to where I need to be to continue this and I moan loudly as the tingles inside me grow stronger, using one hand to push his head into me harder. He's feasting on my chest, his hands exploring all over my body.

He kisses on my breasts, between them, then up my throat. "You are radiant," he moans against my skin.

I lean down to kiss him madly. I could so easily climb to complete ecstasy right now. I want to do something for him too, but feel hesitant. I'm not very experienced, and I don't know his history. What if he's disappointed with my amateur attempts?

"Dane, I—"

252

He covers my lips with his finger, silencing me. Just like clockwork, he speaks my deepest thoughts out loud. "Baby, what all have you done?"

I go with what I know and alleviate awkward with humor. "That sounds like a personal question. Be prepared to reward me." I raise an eyebrow and grin.

"Anything you want, just answer me," he growls.

What to say? I mean, does he want a play by play?

"Um…"

"Did he suck these?" He runs the backs of his fingers over my breasts and I nod. "Use his fingers on you?" I nod again, looking anywhere but at him. "In you?"

I shake my head back and forth this time. He'd never had to, I exploded at the newness of his mere touching, amateur and loaded to fire. Why would Dane want me replaying things with Evan in my head right now?

"Did he put his mouth on you?" His fingers slink under the water and brush along my sex through my suit.

I gasp at the contact and my mouth drops open as I realize what he means. I shake my head no.

"And that's all, just him? Just that little bit?"

"Yes, why?" This very intrusive line of questioning will never backfire on him. I may one day want to know how many girls he's been with, and how long ago, but I will never want a detailed replay of his excursions to plague my thoughts.

He pulls me back deeper into his lap and runs his fingers through my hair, pulling it back away from my face and neck. I love it when he bares my neck, it means his mouth is on its way and I crave it as much as he seems to.

"Because I want to know everything about you. I want to know exactly what only I give to you."

"Oh," I whisper. It's possessive and territorial—and

strangely hot as hell.

"I can't tell you how happy it makes me." He moves against me, igniting another firestorm within me. "How little you gave him…all that will be just mine."

Chapter 34

ALL IN

-Dane-

"Dane," she whispers in a shaky voice, avoiding looking at me, lowering herself into the water, no longer sharing my lap or her naked chest to my view. "I have to tell you something."

My stomach clenches instantly. What is she about to say and why does it scare me so much? I've been with many girls, but never have I felt that my whole world balanced on the next words out of their mouths. What has Laney done to me?

Rocked my damn world—that's what.

She's got me bringing her to my house, buying jewelry, taking trips...and now she's seducing personal information out of me that only a select few are privy to. I couldn't be happier about it. I'll give her the combo to my safe inside if she shows me anything else. She's mystical. Without even trying, she makes me want to invest myself completely. So captivating, gorgeous, kind, and driven; I simply can't get enough of her.

Knowing she's so untouched, a virgin to almost every

sexual act, makes me crazy. Makes me want to lock her away in a tower forever—my own personal flower to devour. Shit, that's a little weird. She'd run scared if she could read my thoughts right now. But damn! I've never been with a genuine girl, never stopped to have a real conversation aside from how much I could spend on them. There's never been a girl I actually cared about, let alone one who burrowed her way into my soul like Laney.

As much as I can't stand the thought of Evan, I do respect and feel for the guy. He, too, had taken his time with sweet Laney, a poor sap not unlike me, just basking in any time spent with her. Now he's suffering the effects of not having her near him at all. I can't imagine the misery. Heartbreak was evident in his voice when he'd called. I saw how he looked at her that night. I don't envy him in many ways, but in so many other ways I do.

He has her past. Her secrets. Her memories. He's still the luckiest bastard I don't know.

Terrified, I answer her. "Tell me, baby, anything." She's chewing her lip nervously and I want to be her lip more than I want my next breath.

"I'm, well, I'm a little nervous." She shifts to angle herself away from me and her precious little chin quivers just a bit, drawing a twitch from me. "I'm not ready to have sex yet, and I…"

She's the most charming thing I have ever seen. I want her, like "I'd gladly gnaw off my own arm but for the chance" want her, but there'll be no rushing. I want her to give herself to me when she's completely sure—positive she never wants anyone but me, forever.

Insane? Yes, but I've given up even trying to make sense of it. The fact is, I'm tore up crazy about Laney, starting about five minutes after I met her, and it's not going away. She's my counterpart on every level—physically, emotionally, intellectually, musically—and I know she feels it, too. She calms when I touch her. She relaxes when I whisper to her. I am now the comfort she seeks. There's nothing in the whole world I'd rather be, and for no one else. When something big or funny happens, I'm who she calls to tell all about it and Lord knows I live for each time she does, hanging on her every word.

"Baby, hear me on this." I angle my head and wait for her big beautiful brown eyes to finally meet mine. "I'm not just looking for that, Laney. I don't want you to think that's what I'm expecting every time I touch you, okay?"

"Okay." Who does she think she's kidding? She doesn't believe me.

"No, baby, it's not okay for you not to believe me or be nervous at my touch. I want to do whatever you want, nothing more and nothing less. Especially nothing less." I wink to let her know I'm almost completely kidding. "Don't hold back or give in with me, Laney. Do or don't do what feels right to you, always. I'm following your lead, baby, and I'm more than okay with whatever you decide."

Now she knows I mean it. I see the minute she accepts and trusts my words; her face is like a book.

"There's something else, too, but I don't want you to get upset if I'm honest with you." And we've officially hit her point of retreat for the night. She's now staring down into the water, putting her top back on, chewing that succulent bottom lip.

I know what she's going to say. She feels guilty about Evan; he obviously did something very right. I can only pray that she one day worries about me like she does him. "I know you worry about hurting him, baby. That heart of yours is admirable, but you're not cheating, Laney. You're not his anymore and you told him what's up."

She nods and gives me a small smile, but I know it's time to pull back. Her body language is screaming to give her more time, more space. As much as she wants to, she can't get out of her own head long enough to accept the connection between us. It will be my pleasure to help her with that. Slowly but surely, I will make her mine.

"Tell you what…" I move stealthy, closing in on her. "Let's get you to bed. I brought you here to rest, remember?" I cup her cheek, turning her face to me. Now I get a real smile, which almost makes it worth the incredible case of blue balls I'll have to suffer through.

She laughs and shakes her head, causing her golden hair to bounce off her shoulders.

"What's so funny?" I ask her with a curious raise of my brow.

"I just, I don't get it. You're amazing, Dane. Gorgeous, thoughtful, talented…why do you go out of your way to take care of me? I do nothing for you physically and I'm always worried about another guy. You have to know you could do so much better than me." She chews her bottom lip and I fist my hands, fighting the urge to dive into her. "I know, we've been through this, but you deserve to be happy. Letting me ride your lap and going to bed with nothing can't possibly make you happy."

Her gaze is down, as though ashamed, and her blush is beautiful. She's worried about my dick? Yeah, that's pretty important, but she has no clue it bothers me a million times worse to know she still loves Evan, at least in some way. She talks to him every day. She has their prom picture on her headboard! Maybe she's right, maybe I should date, see if there's someone else who would be all mine. I already know the answer, though, no one's complete attention would fulfill me even half as much as one laugh I pull from Laney. The minute I met her—I was all in.

"You want the truth or the gentleman's answer?"

"Truth."

"You know I want you. You know all this foreplay is in the hope that one day I get to lay you down and love you. I think about it at least ten times a day, every day. I'm jealous as fuck of every feeling you have for Evan. I want you to tell him once and for all you're with me and never leave my arms, my life or my bed ever again." I pause, giving her time to process. "But for now, I'll settle for watching a movie and falling asleep with you in my arms." I stroke her silky, golden hair and dip my head to look in her eyes. "Sound good?"

She thinks on my words a moment before answering. "I'd love that."

This is the first time she lets me hold her all night long. In Disney World, there'd been a gap in between us.

It seemed the size of the Grand Canyon as we faced each other and talked until we fell asleep. So precious, the first day she'd literally fallen asleep while talking about all she'd seen that day.

But tonight, well, tonight she's curled around me like a kitten and every breath she takes fans across my chest. I've been fighting sleep for hours. I want to savor every moment of this; who knows when she'll let her guard so far down again.

She's perfectly soft, curvy in all the right places, and she showed me tonight that she knows how to turn on her temptress side. When she dropped her top, I wasn't sure if my heart or my dick was going to explode first. Laney's beautiful breasts bared to me, her beautiful eyes peeking up through her wet lashes, silently asking for my acceptance will be the "go to" image in my head forever.

I need to think of something else or I'm gonna gouge her with my aching hard-on.

I just have to be patient until she comes to terms with what her heart and her body are already telling her. Her eyes can't lie though, and tonight, she almost couldn't stop herself physically. Emotionally, she still needs to feel closer to me. I want to let her in, but God, my baggage would scare away Mother Theresa. Gotta give in, though, I can't let her slip away.

So many girls have put it in my face for all I could buy them or the connections I have and here's the goddess who could have it all, wanting nothing. A laugh escapes me; the little scowl that comes across her face when she can't stop me from giving her gifts is absolutely adorable.

I refuse to think about life without her now. Holy shit...I...I...oh, surely not.

Well, I'll be damned. They say you'll know right when it hits you, out of nowhere...this girl, she's mine.

Chapter 35

DADDY'S GIRL

-Laney-

I let Dane drive me home for the weekend. How could I
say no when he wants to so badly? He goes out of his way to
make my life easier, so this is the least I can do. I made it very
clear that if Evan comes around, the two of them are on their
own; I'm not getting in the middle of any "manly" pissing
contest. That made him laugh, but frankly, it made me a little
nauseous to even imagine. Seriously though, I'm over it—I've
been honest with them both and I'm done feeling guilty with
every breath...Imma do me.

As though my thoughts had conjured him up, my phone
rings on our way there. "Talking to the Moon," by Bruno Mars
blares from my purse, the new ringtone Evan assigned himself.

"Hello?"

"Hey, princess."

"Hey, Ev." I look over at Dane and seeing his scowl, I
quickly turn back to my window. "Whatcha doing?"

"Not a damn thing worth telling." He sighs loudly.

"I'm just on my way to Dad's now. Nothing exciting here, either." I glance at Dane and give him an apologetic smile.

"About that," he says, his voice now agonized. "I can't come home this weekend. Got an away game then film, you know, football shit. I'm sorry, Laney."

"It's okay, not your fault."

"I'll see you for Thanksgiving, though, long weekend. I can't wait." He sounds so excited yet I'm chewing my nails at the reminder. Not good.

"Me either, Ev. But hey, can I call you back?"

"Yeah, babe, of course. Be safe driving, and Laney…I love you."

My eyes water, moment of truth here. Do I crush Evan and ignore it or respond and hurt Dane? "Me too, Ev. Talk to you later."

Avoiding Dane's looks that I can feel flicking between me and the road, I tuck my phone away. My hair falls forward and I leave it that way, a shield from his accusatory eyes. Great, we're on the way to introduce Dane to my father for the first time and now this giant elephant joins us.

I turn my body toward him, tucking the hair behind my ear. "Hey."

"Hey."

"Are you mad, Dane?"

He blows out a breath slowly, his hand moving across the console to embrace mine. "Not mad, Laney, just confused, as usual. Can I ask what he wanted?" He gives me a curious, hopeful glance.

"He just wanted to tell me he won't be here this weekend."

"Hmm."

The awkward silence lingers in the air, my discomfort level rising until I can no longer take it. "Are you nervous about meeting my dad?"

The corner of his mouth betrays him, revealing his amusement at my lame attempt to change the subject. "Should I be?"

"I don't think so, but I'm probably biased." I chuckle. "Honestly, he's a wonderful man. I'm sure you'll get along just fine." I give him a warm smile and squeeze his hand in reassurance.

As we pull in the driveway, I decide to ensure he meets my dad in a good mood. "Dane," I say, stopping short and turning to him in the walkway, "just don't mention that you've seen my boobies."

His eyebrows shoot to his hairline right before his expression grows feral. "Your dad would shoot me for the pictures in my head right now, you little tease." He growls and tries to grab me as I giggle and skip away to the door.

"Daddy! I'm home!" I yell, pulling Dane in by the hand just as my dad comes around the corner.

"There she is! Slugger!" He wraps me in a hug briefly before pulling back and eyeing Dane warily. "Jeff Walker." He puts his hand out. "And you might be?"

"Dane Kendrick, nice to meet you, sir," Dane answers politely, shaking my father's hand.

My dad looks back to me inquisitively, asking me for an intro or explanation of some sort without words. "Daddy, Dane is Tate's brother, Bennett's boyfriend. You know Bennett, my roommate?" I babble on nervously. "Dane here spends a lot of time with my group of friends, and graciously offered to drive me down this weekend. He knows I've been worn out lately." I give my dad the most innocent smile I can.

"Y'all come in here now; quit standing in the doorway like strangers." He moves to the side and swings his arm to goad us into moving. "Where's your bag, slugger?"

"In the car, sir, I'll go grab it for her," Dane offers and turns to go back outside.

"Grab yours, too, Dane," I call behind me, now giving my dad full-on eyelash batting and puppy dog eyes. "Dane's gonna stay in the guest bedroom, Daddy. That's okay with you, right?"

A slight growl emanates from his chest, but he recovers quickly. "I guess that'd be fine. Go ahead and get the bags, Dane," my dad yells at him. "Me and Laney're just gonna have a quick word while you're gone." As soon as Dane is out of earshot, he starts the interrogation. "Young lady, you have five minutes to convince me why I should let that boy sleep in my house, with my daughter. Start talking, missy."

"He's a great guy, Dad. He doesn't try anything, if that's what you're thinking. He brings me dinner and takes me to do fun stuff. He listens when I freak out, too. We've become really good friends, and I don't want to send him to a hotel."

Dane walks in with the bags, clearing his throat.

"Laney Jo, grab my wallet and keys and go get all of us some dinner, please. Dane can stay here with me."

Shit. I jerk my head to Dane, about to tell him he doesn't have to do this, when he winks at me and subtly nods his head.

"Okay, if you're sure," I muster. On my way back through, I reach up on my tiptoes and whisper in my dad's ear. "I'll be very angry if he's maimed or bleeding in any way when I get home, Daddy. I mean it."

"So you're a model, huh?" My dad laughs when I walk in the door.

I shoot Dane a glare as he moves to help me with the bags of food. "It was nothing, don't tease me."

"Oh, you're a pretty girl, slugger, ain't nothing wrong with that." He scrubs my head as he walks by to make his plate.

"You told him?" I hiss at Dane, who chuckles at me, taking a swig of his beer. "My dad gave you a beer? Am I in the right house?" I look around to emphasize my confusion at what I've walked back into.

"Quit fussin' and get in here and eat, Laney Jo. Come on, Dane."

"Did you drug my father?" I whisper as Dane now pulls me into the kitchen.

"You're right, he's a wonderful man. Thanks for letting me come, Laney." Dane leans over to kiss the top of my head.

My father actually gets up to grab him and Dane another beer during dinner and there's not a break in the conversation and laughter. The boys get way too much enjoyment over my father's retelling of all my major childhood incidents. I can feel my cheeks heat at some of the more telling ones, like the time I accidentally sat in the minnow bucket! It took way too long to discretely dig all those squirming suckers out of my bathing suit bottom, information Dane did not need to know.

"I'm gonna turn in, I'll see you both in the morning." Dad leans in to give me a kiss goodnight. "Guest room's all yours, Dane, nice to meet you, son."

Son?! "Night, Daddy, I love you."

"Good night, sir, thank you for having me."

"You're welcome...and quit calling me sir." He laughs, shuffling down the hall.

When I hear his door close, I snap my head to Dane. "Spill."

His face lights up in a smile, his eyes smoky as he pulls me to sit on his lap. "You worry too much, baby. Your dad adores you, just like I do, so it was easy for us to find common ground. I actually like him a lot, he's great." He runs his nose along mine, ending with a kiss upon it.

"What did you guys talk about while I was gone?"

"Well…" His hand inches up my thigh, his lips grazing my throat. "We talked about you, mostly. How wonderful you are." He moves to placing kisses along my jawline. "My vow to take care of you." His next words are mumbled through a tugging kiss on my lips. "And to always ask please before I see your boobies."

"Dane!" I pull back and shove him in the chest, sending him toppling back into the couch. His body shakes with his laughter, his happy face glowing. He's beautiful, positively mesmerizing, when he's silly. Two can play the teasing game. I take his hand and move it over one of my t-shirt clad breasts. "Do you want to see them now?" My voice drops, sultry and suggestive.

"Mmmmm," he groans.

I lean in, kissing up his throat to his ear, moving his hand harder against me. "Such a shame, you didn't say please." Jumping off his lap, giggling, I tug him up. "Come on, Dad Whisperer, I'll show you where you're sleeping."

When we head back to school on Sunday, I feel fresh as a daisy; rejuvenated. My dad had been wonderful, Dane had been fabulous. I'd gotten the house clean, two meals cooked and frozen and all of Dad's laundry done while he took Dane fishing! I'm pretty much on cloud nine now, forcing Dane to jam to my rap flava' on the drive. He laughs every time I throw my deuces or strike my gangsta pose. Positively giddy—that's what I am.

Chapter 36

WRECKAGE

-Laney-

"I need a job," I blurt out over lunch. Eating in The Rotunda with Zach and Sawyer has become a habit these days. It'd been worrying me lately that the holidays are fast approaching and I don't have one dime to buy presents for my dad or friends. We're all going to Bennett's big show the last night of school before break, followed by a celebration/Christmas party to which I am not arriving empty handed.

"Why do you need a job, Gidge?" Sawyer asks.

"Um, for money? I gotta buy for Christmas. Plus, it'd be nice to have cash sometimes, in case I need anything." My scholarship doesn't cover everything, especially the biggies, gas and food, and I'm getting older; I have to lay off my dad's wallet, which isn't deep.

"Do you have time for a job? You have class, ball, Dane…" Sawyer laughs. Jerk.

"Oh my God, Zach, do you hear him?"

Zach is engrossed in his phone, paying us no attention.

"Zach, hello?" I reach across the table and punch buttons to interrupt him.

"Sorry, what?" He finally looks up.

"Laney wants to get a job, man, keep up. You talking to Ave or Kirby?"

Ooooh, my ears perk up.

"Both, keep up," he cocks off, "you're in the message, fool."

"I forgot my phone this morning. What are they saying?"

As much as I'd love to hear exactly what they're talking about, I feel skeezy. The twins would tell me if they wanted me to know their business, so I knock the devil off my shoulder and interrupt. "Guys, focus. I need a job."

"You do realize you're dating a millionaire, right? I think you should make up a price list for sexual favors. Problem solved."

The sad part is, Sawyer is completely serious and sees nothing wrong with his idea. Even sadder, you simply cannot get mad at him about it. I'm not sure how he pulls it off, but he does.

"Sawyer Beckett, did you just call me a hooker?"

Zach scoots away, obviously scared he's about to be in the line of fire from my fists of fury.

"Hell no, woman, I was kidding...kinda. Seriously though, Dane owns like, well, lots of shit. Why don't you ask him for a job?"

I just stare at Zach, willing him to help me reason with this lovable jackass.

"Saw, she can't ask her man for a job. That's not cool. Can't you get her one on the DL?"

"Where exactly do you work, Sawyer?" I remember I've aired this question before and apparently never got an answer.

"You don't know?"

"No."

"I work for Dane. I bounce at The Kickback, or take care of whatever else he tells me to."

"So could you get me a secret job at The Kickback?"

"Laney, you're not 21. You can't work at a bar," Zach points out.

Sawyer snaps his fingers; he has a brilliant plan, goodie. "I could probably get you one at MK. You could do wardrobe or something."

MK...why does that ring a bell? Sawyer sees me stewing over it. "It's Dane's studio. You could help the photographers with the sets or costumes or whatever. Want me to check it out?"

MK—Michael Kendrick. Of course. And that's why Tate had said he took me to "the studio," cause he owns it. And I'd chewed Dane about it. My lunch is now a mouthful of crow.

"No, no don't say anything. It's okay, I'll find something." I stand to throw my lunch away and get to class. "I'll see you two later. Not a word, guys, please." I give them both a pointed look and mime locking my lips.

Zach crosses his heart and Sawyer nods, so I know my secret's safe.

"Hey, stranger!" Bennett shrieks as I walk into our room later than evening, sweaty from ball practice.

"Hey yourself, Red. How are you?" I laugh and start gathering some clean clothes, heading to the bathroom. "Come talk to me while I shower, I feel like we never talk anymore."

Bennett sits on the counter while I let the warm water

wash away the day, catching me up on her life.

"Where's Mr. Wonderful tonight?" I ask. I can't remember the last time I saw Bennett without Tate no more than five minutes away from her side.

"He's with Dane tonight, not sure what they had to do. He'll be here after, probably around 11," she says, the pout in her voice audible.

"Oh, that's right, Dane told me he'd be out. I forgot it was with Tate. So okay, you wanna go out with the girls tonight? Avery and Kirby asked me to do something, probably assuming you'd be with Tate, but you know we'd love for you to come. Until he's done, anyway." I giggle. I know I'm old news the minute he punches his timecard, which I completely understand.

"I wish I could, but you wouldn't believe how behind I am on homework. It's like I can't get anything done when Tate's in the room."

"Actually, I would believe it. I've seen it with my own eyes," I tease her. "Will you hand me a towel?" I step out and start to dry off, hearing my phone going off in the living room. "Crap, Bennett, that's Avery. Will you go grab it?"

She runs out and I can hear her talking as I come out. She's relaying back and forth for me so I can get dressed in dark jeans, my red and black 00 flag football jersey, tied in the back, and white Keds.

"Just tell her I'll meet her somewhere. Find out where, I need about 20 minutes to dry my hair and I'll be good to go."

"She said how about The Kickback?" Bennett yells over the blow dryer.

I debate internally for just a second, surprised to find I am in fact in the mood for The K, then smile, shooting her a thumbs up from under my hair. Taking a quick final look in the mirror, I decide to leave my hair down and invite Bennett one more time before I head out the door minutes later. She declines, so after stuffing my phone and ID in my pockets, I bounce into

The K all by myself! This is new for me, brave, and it feels good!

My eyes quickly find Kirby's waving hand from a table across the room and I make my way through the bearable crowd to her. "Hey, catch!"

"Look at you, Sporty Spice! I'm glad you came out!"

"Where's Avery?" I shout over the music.

"At the bar with Zach. You want something?"

My brows crinkle. Zach? Love him, but I thought this was girls' night?

"Sure." I whip the one five dollar bill I brought out of my pocket. "I'll take whatever that will buy me."

Kirby grins mischievously. "Laney, we don't have to pay for drinks. That bartender look familiar?"

I turn and look, well after the people blocking my view move, and see Sawyer behind the bar. Smiling to myself, I shake my head. We can't sit here and drink for free off Dane's dime. Not that I'd drink enough to make a dent, but still. "Just one free drink for me, something light. I'm going to run to the bathroom real quick, will you tell them?"

"I got you, girl, go."

The line for the bathroom is minimal, so I'm on my way back to the table just minutes later when my phone vibrates in my back pocket.

Evan: You're not old enough to be in a bar naughty girl.

I look around the room wildly, seeking him out.

How did he know I was here?

Laney: Where r u?

Evan: Behind u

So slow I'm almost still, I turn around and meet the bluest eyes I've ever loved. A breathtaking smile breaks across his face, drawing me in like a vacuum. I collapse into his arms, wrapping mine around his waist. Evan is here, with me, not my imagination.

"What are you doing here? How'd you know where to find me?" I rest my chin on his chest and gaze up at him.

"Your roommate told me. She's a nosy, but nice, girl." He kisses my forehead, leaving his lips on my skin.

"How are you here? What about football?"

"Off week, no game. So here I am, with my girl." His arms squeeze tighter around me. "Can we get out of here, juvenile delinquent? I'd love to be able to hear you."

Giggling, I move away, taking him by the hand to come with me to tell Kirby I'm leaving. Zach's eyes bore into me as we approach the table, but Kirby and Avery are all smiles, taking Evan in head to foot. Yeah, he's hot, I don't blame them.

"Guys, this is Evan. Evan, this is Avery, our pitcher. Kirby, her twin and our catcher. And this," I give Zach a pleading look to be nice, "is Zach Reece, one of my good friends."

"Nice to meet you, man." Evan puts out his hand and Zach shakes it.

"You too, heard a lot about you."

Evan looks down to me, smiling. "All good I hope."

"All good," Zach answers good-naturedly. I shoot him a smile in thanks.

"Nice to meet you both as well, ladies," Evan says to the twins. "How's my lil' baller here doing?" Evan pulls me tighter into his side, arm around my waist.

"She's amazing, we're lucky to have her," Kirby answers with a gleam as Zach throws his arm around the back of her chair.

I clear my throat. "Guys, I'm gonna go. I haven't seen Evan in a while and it's loud in here. I'll talk to all y'all later, okay?"

The three of them nod, but Zach's eyes are worried. I know he simply cares about me and knows what the back and forth does to me, especially since things have been going so wonderfully with Dane. Evan and I turn to head out when I hear someone yell my name. Turning to see who is beckoning me, Sawyer is already striding toward us.

"Hey, Gidge, who's this?" Sawyer's glare is intimidating and I put my hand on his chest defensively.

"Sawyer Beckett, this is Evan Allen, from home."

Sawyer's eyes soften as the name registers and he gradually reaches out a hand to Evan. "So you're Evan, the man, the myth, the legend. Nice to meet ya." Sawyer uses his free hand to slap Evan on the shoulder. "You understand, just watching out for my girl. Wasn't about to let some dude I didn't know walk out the door with her."

"No, man, it's cool. I appreciate you looking out for her," Evan answers kindly.

"Okay," I interrupt them, "we're gonna go, Saw. Thanks for having my back." I lean in and stand on my tiptoes to lay a kiss on his cheek. "I'll see you later."

He turns his face quickly to catch my ear. "I won't lie if he asks, Laney."

I meet his eyes and pull Evan towards the door. "I would never expect you to. Neither will I."

Evan wraps his arm around my waist, pulling me tight against his side as we walk to his truck. "It's so great to see you, princess." He lowers his head to kiss the top of mine.

"You too, Ev. I can't believe you're here, and you tracked me down." I nudge his shoulder teasingly with mine.

Both settled in the truck cab now, he wastes no time and leans over to me, elbows resting on the console. "Laney, baby,

I've missed you so much. Can I please have some sugar?" His voice is shaky, his eyes pained.

I can fix that pain I see, but at what cost? I know that all I have to do is tell him everything's okay and the shadows in his eyes will disappear instantly, but a pair of brown eyes plague the back of my mind, stopping me from doing so.

Heart in my throat, I push any guilt or confusion out of my thoughts and scoot towards him, my hands cupping his soft, handsome cheeks. Right now, I need to try and heal the best friend I have ever had, in some way. I look right in his crystal blue eyes so he can see what's important, that which will never change: you are the most amazing person I have ever had in my life and I cherish you.

I drop chaste kisses on his cheeks and nose, a quick peck on his lips, and lean back, giving him my warmest smile. "How long do you get to stay?"

"As long as I'm back for class on Monday, I'm all yours till then." He starts his truck, grinning over at me. "Where to?"

Uh...good question. "I guess my dorm," I say with a shrug. "Let me just text Bennett and let her know we're coming." I do just that, silently praying she gets it and intercepts Tate. Something tells me it would get real awkward real fast if he and Evan meet...in my room...before I even tell Dane about my surprise guest.

Shit—I don't even know where Dane is right now. What if he's there waiting for me? Oh God, Bennett, check your phone! The trip is way too short and we pull up in front of my dorm with still no response from Bennett. We're going in blind.

Evan parks and hurries around the front of the truck to open my door, taking my hand to help me down. "Is it okay if I go in?" he asks anxiously.

A squeeze to his hand. "It's a co-ed dorm, silly. They won't know you don't just live here."

We're about ten steps from the front door when my

roommate comes barreling towards us. I catch her just as she's about to plow into me head first, and up close, I can see she's a mess. Her body is shaking, tears rolling down her face and her lip is quivering.

"Bennett, what's wrong?!" I shake her by the shoulders but she doesn't answer. Suddenly holding her becomes a strain, she's like dead weight, and thankfully Evan reacts quickly and reaches out to grab her seconds before she would've hit the cold pavement.

"Bennett, answer me! What the hell is wrong?" I'm screaming now, scared out of my wits. My phone starts ringing, and I'm really hoping it's Tate, telling me they had a silly fight and he's on his way to get her. "Evan, you got her?" He nods, so I let go and dig out my phone.

"Hello?"

"Laney, it's Zach. Listen, Sawyer just got a call and we're headed out now. Where are you right now?"

"In front of the dorm, why?"

"I need you to get Bennett, Laney. Can you go get Bennett?" His words are staccato, like he's talking to a three year old.

"I'm here with Bennett now and she's wigging out. What's going on?" The irritation at all the mysterious hysteria is starting to show in my voice.

"It's Tate. He's been in a wreck, Laney. I need you to get Bennett and head to Mercy, okay? Can you do that?"

"Is he okay?" My voice now a whisper, I have to fight for the nerve to ask my next question. "And D-Dane? Was he— was he with him?"

Somehow I'm able to register Evan's hand taking mine. Looking up, I see he's literally carrying Bennett with one arm and leading me to the parking lot with the other. "Zach—" I struggle to find the words again. "Zach, was he with him?"

He exhales loudly. "I don't know, sweetie. I haven't heard about him, just Tate. Sounds bad, Laney, can you get there? Do I need to come get you girls?"

I glance around me aimlessly; does he need to come get us? "No, no. I'm in Evan's truck. Bennett's—" I look, Bennett's in the backseat. "We'll be there as soon as we can."

Evan takes my phone so I let my head fall against the window.

"Laney! Laney, snap out of it!"

I come to and see Evan's eyes filled with worry. I don't know how long it's been, but we seem to be at the hospital already.

"Help your friend, Laney, she needs you. Be my strong girl, come on." He guides me out of the truck, one arm never leaving me as he manages to get Bennett out as well.

"Here, man, let me help you."

I turn when I hear the voice. It's Zach. "Zach! Zach, how are they? How's Tate? Dane?" I'm shaking him, grabbing his t-shirt in my fists.

"Listen to me, Laney," he whispers in my ear, pulling me into his chest in one firm movement. "Dane is absolutely fine, he wasn't hurt. But Tate was, so pull your shit together right now, for Bennett. Do you hear me?" He jolts me, squeezing me harder. "Do you hear me?"

"Yes." I suck up my tears and runny nose. "Yes, I hear you." I pull from his grasp, turning behind me and grabbing Bennett's hand. "Bennett, I'm here." I take a final swipe at my face, drying the tears with my sleeve. "I got you, Bennett. You ready to go inside?"

Her green eyes are lifeless, dead, no recognition.

She's a zombie on her feet, in shock.

"Zach?" I reach behind me and blindly find his shirt, pulling him forward. "Lean on Zach, Bennett. He's gonna take you in and I'm gonna be right beside you." I give Zach a nod, urging him to get her moving.

Turning to find Evan, I grab his hand. "Thank you, Ev, for being here, for helping."

"Of course, princess." He hugs me. "Of course. Let's go check on your friend." He kisses my hair before we head in.

Sawyer, Kirby, and Avery are huddled together in the corner, the girls comforting Sawyer as his head hangs between his knees. I can see his huge shoulders shudder from here and find myself crying again at the sight of his pain. I run to him, dropping to my knees. I lift his head to look at me, offering him a weak smile. I had my lapse on the way over, now I've got to be strong for these wonderful people who've grown so dear to me.

"Saw, I'm here buddy. Gidget's here, Saw, it's gonna be all right."

His navy, watery eyes are rimmed in red but soften when my voice registers, and all at once I'm buried in his embrace. I murmur words of assurance to him, stroking his short hair until he finally calms enough to sit, keeping me in his lap.

"Have we heard anything?" I look to Kirby and Avery as I ask, both of them shaking their heads. "Sawyer, Kirby's gonna sit with you, okay?" I give her a look and she moves to us. "Just while I check on things, okay?"

He doesn't answer but loosens his grip on me, Kirby slipping in his lap seamlessly with my retreat.

The woman at the window can't seem to be bothered by me and I'm milliseconds away from ripping her through the damn window when Evan comes up behind me. He rubs my shoulder as he calmly asks her, "Ma'am, I know you're busy, but could you give these worried people any news on their friend? His name is Tate—" He looks to me.

"Kendrick," I growl at her.

"Tate Kendrick. He was in a car wreck and any news would be much appreciated." He flashes his signature Evan smile and her features instantly relax.

She stands and says she'll go see what she can find out, so we step back to the group and let them know.

Evan offers to go get everyone coffee from the cafeteria and I move to hold Bennett's head in my arms. It's only been a little while but it seems like eternity, and I still haven't seen Dane. Zach told me he was fine and it's the only thing keeping me in this chair right now. Bennett has yet to speak and Sawyer's a mess, so I turn to Zach beside me. "Has anyone called their parents? Where are they?"

Zach's expression is as confused as I feel as he gets up to ask Sawyer.

"Do you and Dane ever talk?"

At first I think I'm hallucinating it was so quiet, but no, Bennett did in fact just speak.

"What?" I lean closer to hear her better.

"How do you not know? Do you and Dane not talk?" She rises up out of my arms, her voice gaining volume. "Or do you only talk about you? There's bigger shit than your boy problems, Laney! How self-absorbed are you?"

I open my mouth to speak, not sure of what to say, but am beat to it.

"That's enough, Bennett!"

My head whips around, spotting Dane behind us. I leap up, almost flying, wrapping my arms around him. Slowly, his arms move around me too, his body gradually relaxing against mine. "How's Tate? How are you?" I lean back and look up at him, stroking my hands down his arms. Sawyer and Bennett have crowded around, clinging for his next words.

He blows out a deep breath. "He's in surgery now. He has some internal bleeding, they think his spleen. Lots of cracked ribs, concussion, banged up, but they're hopeful." Both hands move over his face, back through his hair, finally resting at his sides. "Thank you all for being here." His voice cracks, his cheeks hollow, and I hug him to me once again, one hand rubbing his back.

His head soon lifts from my shoulder, his face rubbing mine. "Can I get a coffee?" he asks no one in particular.

"Here ya go, man."

I don't turn around right away, but rather peer up to gauge Dane's reaction.

He moves from me, extending a hand. "I don't believe we've met. Dane Kendrick."

"Evan Allen. Sorry about your brother," Evan offers sincerely with his shake.

Dane is either completely out of it, which would be understandable, or he has the best poker face in the world. Nothing in his expression or body language changes as he meets Evan. My eyes flick nervously between the two of them, the right words evading me.

"How long will he be in surgery?" Bennett squeaks, her voice once again meek and frightened.

"I'm not sure." Dane sighs heavily, moving to slump in a chair.

Zach, always clutch, steps forward. "It's late, and it might be a while, so I'm going to take the twins home and grab some food for everyone. I'll be back later." He turns to Evan. "You're welcome to stay in my room, man; I know it's a long drive. Unless you're leaving now, Laney?"

Bennett latches onto my hand fiercely, her eyes pleading with me to stay, which I had planned to do anyway.

"No, I'm staying here," I say, squeezing Bennett's hand and smiling Dane's way. "Evan, can I talk to you?" I gesture with my head, moving us away for some privacy. "Evan, I can't leave.

These people are my friends and they need me. I'm so sorry you came all this way, I hope you understand."

He lifts my hand with his, placing a soft kiss on my knuckles. "I do understand, Laney; don't worry a thing about it. I don't really want to drive back tonight, though. Should I stay with that Zach guy?"

"Stay in my room. I'll be here, so take my bed." I grab him my key out of my purse and walk back, handing it to him. "If anything changes, I'll text you."

His expression tightens slightly and he chews the inside of his cheek before finally asking, "Laney, are you staying for Bennett or for Dane?"

"Both," I answer solemnly, honestly, without hesitation.

He nods. "Thought so."

Zach, and only Zach, turns and waves, a look of understanding on his face, as he walks out with Evan and the twins.

Chapter 37

PLAYLIST

-Laney-

Eleven days—that's how long Tate stayed in the hospital. After seven long hours of waiting, the surgeon had come out to say he'd made it through surgery like a champ. Another two hours and Dane, Bennett, and Sawyer had all taken turns going back to see him. Two hours after that, I finally got Bennett to agree to go home and bathe, eat, and change, and I dragged Sawyer with us. Dane wouldn't leave, but he did at least eat the sandwich I'd brought back.

Evan swung by the hospital on his way out of town, toting a burger, Red Bull, and clean clothes for me. I apologized profusely and he insisted he understood. The first time he got a weekend off and drove all the way to see me and look what happened; what are the odds? Oh well—Tate was fine and that's all that mattered.

Thanksgiving came and went in a blur. I'd gone home, eaten, and been back in five hours. My dad and Evan both said they understood and the visit had been a short but nice break from all the trips back and forth to the hospital, making sure

Bennett was taking care of herself, and managing ball and school. And now, here we all are, almost three weeks since that horrid night; days away from winter break. First semester of college done and so much more learned than what I'd been taught in class.

Tate's living in that big ole house with Dane while he recovers, and since Bennett's parents are going on a cruise, she'll be spending the break out there, too. She'd given her big part away to her understudy, which I know pained her to the core, but was reflective of her beautiful soul. She'd apologized over and over for her little outburst at me. I'm chalking it up to her stress level and Dane's constant evasiveness and letting it go, truly forgiving her. I do tend to worry about my own problems above all else, so I'm gonna give her this one free pass.

Sawyer and Kirby are heading out in a few days to his parent's house for a stay before meeting Zach and Avery at the twins' parents' house. I'm not sure if the couples have officially split off or drew straws, nor do I have the energy right now to ask. I have one final to finish, and then I'm driving home to give my father his Christmas present early. No, I never got a job, but mysteriously Sawyer had a week-long hunting trip and cabin paid for that he "just couldn't use," so there ya have it. My dad will be over the moon and I'll find a way to pay Sawyer back eventually.

Dane hasn't been himself since Tate's accident. The light is gone from his eyes and there's no bounce in his step. His shoulders sag and he doesn't speak unless spoken to. I'm very worried about him and downright furious with his parents. If they'd made an appearance at the hospital, it'd been in one of the brief windows of time I hadn't been there. Just thinking about it makes my blood boil, but I have got to get through this studying before I go off on a rant.

Feeling a sense of accomplishment bigger than any I've ever experienced, I turn in my final exam, knowing I nailed it, and skip to my truck. I did it! I finished my first semester of college, and with a damn fine GPA, if I do say so myself. Now I have almost a month off; no school, no ball practice…nothing but wintry, blessed goodness!

"Hey, you!" I squeal cheerfully into the phone as Dane answers.

"Hey, Laney, how are you?" His voice is dull.

"I'm good, all done with finals! How's Tate?"

He scoffs, his voice lightening a bit. "He's doing great. Bennett's fussing over him like a mother hen and I'm sitting back and laughing."

"So you're good, feeling better?" I ask hopefully.

"Yeah, I'm good."

He's not helping with this conversation, but I don't want to let him go. He's doing it again, keeping me at arm's length, and I'm in far too good of a mood to allow it. Not to mention, I've worked really hard on his Christmas present and am dying to give it to him. I've pulled off a few presents I'm really proud of for less than fifty dollars, but I'm hoping they mean a lot more to him than that because my whole heart went into them.

"So, um," I swallow down the knot in my throat, "what are your plans for tonight?"

The silence draws out, killing me slowly. "I don't have any really," he pauses, "why?"

"I thought maybe I'd come out. I could bring dinner and your Christmas presents." It's my best offer. I wish I could see his face right now, a clue to what's going on in that head of his. Gnawing my nails, I wait endlessly for him to penetrate the silence.

"Don't worry about dinner, there's plenty here. I'll text you the address. Can you GPS it?"

"Yup. I'll see you in a little while then."

"See you in a little while, Laney. Be careful."

Dane's waiting on the porch as I pull into his driveway. He's wearing a plain white t-shirt, gray sweats that hang achingly low on his narrow hips, and no shoes. He's positively mouthwatering and I don't feel a bit bad that I take my time with the view.

He stays put as I make my way to him, my hands full of presents. "Let me help you. These better not all be for me," he grumbles.

I follow him in the house, butterflies playing tag in my stomach; melancholy Dane makes me very nervous.

He sets the presents down and turns. "Let me take your coat."

I shrug it off slowly, suddenly not sure how long I'll be staying, and watch him closely as he hangs it in the hall closet. "Where are Tate and Bennett?"

"I gave him that end of the house," he motions with his head, "so we don't drive each other crazy." He fights back a smile.

I wrap my arms around my middle, needing some warmth from somewhere. Dane's usually warm brown eyes are cold, as is his whole demeanor. "Are your parents home?" I shift my eyes away from him, looking nowhere really.

He snorts. "No, Laney, no one else is here, just Tate and Bennett."

It feels a lot like a stand-off as we stand on opposite sides of the room, both refusing to be the next to speak. When I break enough to meet his eyes, he's already staring but giving nothing away. I'm not sure when exactly, or why specifically, but things have definitely changed between us. Might as well get this over with and get the hell out of here, he doesn't seem to want me here.

"So, how about you open your presents?" I walk over and pick them up, and then sit on the couch, hoping he'll follow me.

He does eventually join me, sitting miles away.

Awkwardly, I scoot closer to him and place the first present in his lap. "Open it, Dane," I say, nudging his knee with mine, "please."

Gradually he peels off the gold paper, revealing his first present. I'd gotten him three DVDs; *Toy Story*, *Monsters, Inc.*, and *The Fox and the Hound*, his professed favorites. I'd wrapped them, imagining snuggling with him and watching them all in a row, but something tells me that isn't ever going to happen now.

For the first time since I arrived, he gives me a genuine smile. "Thank you, Laney. These are great, I love them."

"You're very welcome." I wait for him to say something else, anything, but he doesn't. He gazes at me, unmoving, so I hand him the next present. "Okay, open this one."

"You didn't have to get me anything, Laney."

"I know I didn't have to. I wanted to. Now open!"

He digs into this one a little faster than the last and tries to hide his inhale. It's a CD, pictures of us decorating it. "It's our playlist, for you to listen to anytime you want," I explain. I'd downloaded every song Dane and I had shared from the first night I met him… "End of All Time," "The Cave," "This Year's Love"…all of them.

Dane scoots closer to me now, a look on his face I can't begin to interpret. "Our playlist?" he asks on a whisper, one eyebrow raised.

I nod and silently hand him the last present. He, too, remains quiet as he opens it. His hand trembles as he flips through the pages in the binder, the sheet music for every song on the CD. Obviously he knows how to play many of them, but maybe not on both the piano and guitar? And I want to hear him play every single one of them, on both instruments, time and time again, so I printed them all out.

Burning into me, the look in his eyes is now unmistakable. He sets down the binder and moves to me, cradling my face in his hands. Moving up, his fingers glide through my hair all the way to the ends and he rubs them between his fingers. Leaning in closer, he runs his nose along my neck, breathing in my scent the whole way and ending his path with a nip on my earlobe.

"I need some help here, Laney. I thought I could wait out the Evan thing, keep things casual with us, but I was wrong." He nuzzles his face into my neck. "Then I thought I could let you go." His hands slide down to grip my waist. "I was wrong again."

His words, seductively angry whispers against my flesh, inflame parts of me I didn't know existed. My breath stutters; can he feel my body react?

"So you tell me what's right, Laney, cause I can't take being wrong again."

I lean back, wanting to see his eyes. They'll tell me everything Dane won't, every secret, every avoided question, the entire unknown. They'll let me know it's okay that I don't know everything right now; what I do know is enough.

I know that my day is better if I see him in the morning before getting started. I know that I sleep better if his is the last voice I hear. My body knows the minute he walks into a room. My heart knows he needs me to give him time just as badly as I need him to give me answers. My mind knows that if I walk away now, I'll eventually be fine, but fine isn't the term I want used to describe my life.

I know if he plays a song around me it's because he wants me to listen to the words and hear what he's saying to me. I know he takes care of everyone around him anytime he can and he'd do anything possible to take care of me. And I know the feeling seeping up from my toes, tugging at me, doesn't happen every day or to everyone.

He pulls me against him, leaning to whisper in my ear. "Close your eyes." He rests his forehead on mine, his hands sneaking lower down my waist. "Do you see us now, Laney? When I close my eyes, all I see is us, perfect. What do you see, Laney?"

The words are right there, fighting to escape, caught in my throat. I picture it behind my eyelids, me and Dane, every day, no one else. Contentment washes over me first, the acceptance of choosing what I really want. Then the wave of excitement, anticipation…want. I want Dane. I want him in a way I've never wanted anyone else, not even Evan.

Like a cloud moves out from in front of the sun, the heat and light finding its way through, with clarity, I too realize—Lil' Laney will always love Evan and appreciate what we have, but it's unlike what I have with Dane. The woman I am today wants this man.

I'd known it before I walked in tonight, known it for a while, but it ends tonight. My Christmas present to myself: I'm going to put my feelings first. No more guilt, I've hurt no one on purpose; in fact, I've kept myself in constant turmoil in an attempt to avoid that very thing, but I can't fight it any longer.

"I see us," I whisper back. "I choose us." Opening my eyes, I stare at him for long seconds. A smile creeps across my face along with my realization.

He sees it, my surrender. His low growl echoes around us and he lifts me, hands gripping my ass. I wrap my legs around his waist and ram my hands into his hair, attacking his mouth with mine. Our tongues collide in harmony, perfectly stroking each other. God, I love his mouth; hungry, seeking, rough, and sinful. There's no way anyone has ever walked away from a kiss like this. His hands knead my ass while mine pull his hair. I slide my tongue along the roof of his mouth, teasing, before I pull back and nip his bottom lip, sucking on it.

Tucking my head down, I lick a torturously slow, straight

SE Hall

line from the hollow of his throat to his chin. Looking into his eyes, now filled with a hunger so deep I tremble, I purr, "Your choice: bedroom or right here."

Chapter 38

MINE

-Dane-

You don't kiss like that if you're still on the fence, right? She chooses us, me. That's what she said. She could already be driving home, but she came here. She made me those thoughtful gifts, the most wonderful I've ever received, so she must mean it. I have to be sure; I can't take the unsure footing anymore. I almost lost Tate, all I knew for sure I had...I have to know Laney is hanging on to me as tight as I am to her.

I thought things were great with us and then Evan walked in behind her. I don't want to know why he was there that night at the hospital. I don't want to know where they'd been before all hell broke loose and they got there. I will never ask and I'm hoping she never tells me. Forward—that's the only direction we're going now.

Any red-blooded male would pick bedroom and run in there like he's on fire, but I have to keep myself in check. She only gets one first time, and I only get one chance to make it perfect for her, for us, so I need to slow my roll. Here's what's gonna happen—I'm gonna put on the CD she made me, mostly because I'm dying to hear what she put on there and I can't imagine making love to Laney without music. Then I'm going to walk her into my room, a threshold no female has ever crossed, and make sure she's mine. When I'm convinced, I'm gonna make love to her all night. Then tomorrow, I'm gonna do it again.

"Are you sure?" My voice comes out huskier than I'd intended, but damn if this girl doesn't fuck with my head.

She nods, blonde curls bouncing on her shoulders, full lips swollen and wet from me—ME. Her brown eyes are always big, and beautiful, but right now they're almost green and they're half-closed, brimming with desire. Laney Jo Walker tiptoed in that dorm room a doe caught in headlights, walls of stone around her…and now she's wrapped around me, handing herself over.

Setting her down, I entwine our hands, leading her to the backyard. I need to buy some time. "Baby, let's get in the hot tub, relax. Sound good?" Looking back at her, I suppress a chuckle at the disappointment I see in her eyes. My baby is hungry for this, which fills me with a pride I can't explain. "You change and get in. I'll be right back." With a long, slow kiss, barely able to pull myself away, I move to leave her.

This is one of those neon signs flashing "love." I'm planning the romantic set-up rather than the excuse to leave afterwards. I'm thinking about where I put the candles instead of the KY.

"Umm…" She pouts, sexy and adorable.

"Go on," I say with a swat on her ass. "I won't be gone long, I promise."

I hurry back into the house, mind and body running on all cylinders, ticking off things in my head faster than I can act them out.

Shoot Tate a text. **You and Bennett are not to come out for ANYTHING. I mean it! Laney's here—ruin this and you'll be back on crutches.**

Pop CD in sound system, program to start in T-minus 10

minutes, play in bedroom/backyard only. Tate doesn't get to hear our soundtrack.

Bound up stairs and almost fall changing into swim trunks.

Grab candles, light, scatter strategically around room.

Sprint to kitchen. Open wine, spill some, who cares. Walk calmly outside with two glasses.

Breathe.

"See, that didn't take—" Words cease as I swallow my tongue. If I go blind tomorrow, I'm okay with that. "Um, baby, you forgot your suit," I tease.

"I couldn't find one." She bites her bottom lip and shrugs.

Trying to hide my gulp, I wade through the water slowly, moving to her. I hand her a glass of wine and set mine down behind me, turning back to her when the CD starts to play around us, her sweet voice echoing through the backyard.

"Hi, Dane, Merry Christmas! I know it's nothing fancy, like say, a trip to Disney World, but I hope you like it. I just thought a collaboration of us was worth having all in one place, so you could play it over and over...kinda like it does in my head. And here's to hoping I get to make you another one next year. Love, Laney."

I turn and look at her, the most beautiful blush across her face. "Well, that was kinda embarrassing," she mutters. "I didn't think I'd be with you when you heard it. While naked." She casts her gaze down, wrapping her arms around herself.

Sitting and pulling her beside me, I lift her chin by one finger. "It's the most amazing gift I've ever received, Laney. I love it."

The thank you kiss starts out gentle, but this naked miracle has other plans, climbing up on my lap and never breaking her lock on my mouth. Her arms slide around my neck, her knees spreading to grip the outside of my hips. I refuse to take her anywhere but in my bed the first time, so I stand, clutching her against me.

We're dripping wet, but I'll be damned if I'm stopping for a towel. I take the stairs two at a time, her legs gripped around my waist, and kick my bedroom door shut behind us, Laney sucking my mouth the entire trip. Her fingers muss my hair, pulling, her little moans and mews making me delirious.

"Baby," I pant into her mouth, "tell me what you want. I need the words." I walk to the bed and lay her down gently. Standing over her, my eyes raking up and down her unbelievable body, I send up a silent thank you that I'm a man, followed by a prayer to do right by her.

"Love me, Dane." Her eyes are hazy, her arms opening to me. She's so fucking gorgeous, unreal even, lying wanting in my bed. Beads of water still visible on her golden body and my chest aches with each breath I manage to take.

"I do love you, Laney. I love you more than anything." I silence myself now, though all I want to do is profess on and on what she means to me.

She pushes herself up on her elbows, her beautiful, ample breasts thrusting towards me. Her nipples are a deep pink, just like her lips, and mine itch to kiss her there. "You love me? Like love me, love me?" Her eyes water and her mouth twitches, afraid to smile until she's sure I mean it.

I move on the bed, hovering over her on my forearms but close enough to feel her warm body beneath me. "I'm not sure what kind of love you mean, baby, but if you mean do I want you to be with me forever, that I can't bear the thought of being without you as my lover, my best friend, my whole world...one day my wife, and my baby mama," I wink at her and smile, "then yes, I love you love you."

Tears roll down her cheeks now, so I shift to lie beside her, wiping them away. "Happy tears, I hope?"

Chuckling, she nods. "Yes, very happy tears. You overwhelm me, but in such a good way." She rolls on her side, burying her face in my chest. I run my hand down her side, over her hip, down to that little dent between hip and stomach, "Dane's Dent." Her breathing staggers against my chest as my hand treks to her delectable ass. I growl as I squeeze it, finest fucking ass ever; tight, round and all mine.

Timidly, she unburies her face and flicks her tongue on my nipple. Animalistic, I roar and roll her underneath me. I pin her hands above her head and roll my hips against her, making her gasp. "No more, Laney, I fucking mean it. No leaving me," hip thrust, "no hiding shit from me," hard, slow thrust, "and just me. Mine. For good." I finish with a grinding circle against her core.

She nods her head. "I promise, Dane." She raises her shaky hand to my face and strokes my cheek tenderly. "I love you, too." Pulling my face to her, she kisses me deeply and whispers on my lips, "I'm all yours now. So what are you gonna do with me?"

Finally hearing the words from her, "I love you" and "I'm all yours," the tension I've carried in my body for months vanishes. No more back and forth indecisive "oh what about Evan?" bullshit. She's mine now, she knows it, and after all this time, I can finally say I do, too. I can take the woman I love now and I get to keep her. Releasing her hands, I skim mine down her body, memorizing the feel of every inch. Her hardened nipples poke into my chest, so I take one in my mouth, teasing the other with my fingers.

"Oh God, Dane," she groans, arching her back like a wet dream.

"Like that, baby?"

"Mhmmm," she moans, so responsive. Her little hand sneaks to the drawstring of my suit, but I snatch it away. My pants absolutely cannot come off yet or the show's gonna be over before the opening credits are done. She's a virgin, and I'd die before I hurt her, so I have to make sure she's more than ready.

"Not yet." I kiss along her throat, trailing my fingertips down until they meet her bare, wet center. She lets out a little whimper at the contact, her thighs quivering against me. I suck in a breath; fuck, she's so sexy.

I tease along the edges of her until her head is thrashing side to side, gradually slipping a finger inside her. She hisses and pushes down against my hand, so I add another.

"D-Dane," she sputters.

"What, baby?" I bite a nipple gently. "Tell me."

"I need." She groans as I increase speed, adding my thumb against her hot button. "Oh, oh I need that, just like that, Dane."

I chuckle; learning sweet Laney is going to be nirvana. "Just like that?" I mock, running my other hand through her hair. I feel her tighten around my fingers, spasming from within. "That's my girl."

She wails, drawing up her knees, and comes on my hand. It's the hottest, most erotic thing I've ever seen and I can't wait much longer to be inside her. I kiss, suck, and nibble my way up her belly, paying extra attention to both breasts before taking her mouth feverishly. She runs her hands up and down my back before sliding them under my shorts, digging her fingers into my ass. She pulls my rock-hard groin against her, grinding into me. I refuse to believe all innocents are so good at this; Laney's a fucking fireball. And she has no clue she's walking sex. Good.

"Dane!" She bites my chin, forcing my attention to her face. "I need you, right now."

"Baby," I say as I drop a kiss her forehead, "you can plan our dates, tell me what to wear, run the radio," I wink, "you can even name our kids one day…after Disney characters even. But in the bedroom, the hot tub, against the wall or basically anywhere I have you naked and wet…let me lead."

My fingers find her again, thrusting two in unforgivably. "Can you do that for me, Laney? Can you trust me to take care of you?" I curl my fingers up and stroke inside her, drawing a throaty whine from her. "Hmm?"

"Yes," she pants.

"Good girl," I croon, pinching her clit and sending her off like a rocket. She writhes and twists, a vision, my vision. When she comes down, I ease off the bed to the bathroom, returning with a condom that I toss on the bed. Lowering my trunks, my eyes never leave her face.

Standing before her naked, I watch her expression go from skittish, to surprised, and finally settle on warm. She raises her gaze to mine and my heart seizes in my chest at the love and acceptance I see there.

Shifting to her hands and knees, she crawls to the edge of the bed, rising up inches from me. She traces every line of my upper body, smoothing her palms across my abs, switching back to fingertips along the grooves leading down to my groin. Her chestnut eyes peek back up at me as her little tongue slips out over her bottom lip. "You are magnificent. Thank you for waiting for me, for this." She blows out a long breath. "I love you. I didn't know what that really meant until I met you. You were made to be my other half and I yours."

I know this should be a sweet, romantic moment, but hearing her heartfelt words draw out every barbaric chemical in my body. I lift her, shifting her to the middle of the bed, and swiftly settle over her. "Gotta have you baby, gotta get inside." I kiss her manically, working her up again. "Not gonna lie, love," I say, firmly kneading her breasts, "it's probably gonna hurt a little bit, but I'll be as gentle as I can."

"I trust you," she whispers breathily. She watches intently as I roll on the condom, eyes curious and sparkling. Opening her arms to me, I move back over her, wanting to savor every second as much as needing to take care with her. "Ah," she winces and bows her back off the bed as I enter her.

"Relax for me," I growl, bracing myself, running my hands through her hair, kissing her face. Holding back for what seems like hours, her body becomes less rigid. "Ready for more?" I whisper, waiting for her eyes to say yes. Every baser instinct screams at me to thrust deep into her but I fight against it, my jaw clenched. She's so damn tight, so warm, and I will never, ever be the same. I couldn't have dreamt she'd feel this good or imagined the all-consuming feelings that would instantly enter my head, my heart…my soul. Amazing that I'm able to have profound thoughts at this moment, but even more amazing when I realize my body and mind's recognition of another person as my whole collide. Not a fuck, not a crush, not lukewarm—cosmic.

She nods jerkily, so I ease further in ever so slowly, kissing along her neck, devoted to the spot behind her ear that drives her mad. Hitting her barrier, I rock back and then break-through in one smooth stroke. She cries out, her chest heaving rapidly, her legs clinching.

"Relax through it, baby." I nuzzle her neck. "Tell me when you're okay." I resolve myself not to move until she tells me, again, no matter how badly I want to.

Blowing out a few breaths, she runs her hands down my back, picking up her head to kiss my chest. I feel her body begin to relax. "I'm ready. Love me, Dane," she says sweetly.

I rock slowly into her, lost in the sensation. Perfection; hot, mind-blowing perfection. "You feel amazing, Laney." My words are a huff. I slide my hands under her ass, tilting her up, wanting to get as deep into her heaven as possible.

"Oh, oh," she murmurs, igniting the animal in me once again. Her little sounds are my undoing and my cock hardens impossibly more with each one.

"Wrap your legs around me, baby," I command her as I lean down to pull on her pebbled nipple with my teeth. "Just like that, yeah. Oh shit, unbelievable, baby. So. Damn. Good."

Barely able to comprehend, Laney shocks me, splintering the man in me to pieces, by reaching up and bracing her hands against the headboard. She uses the leverage to push back into me, hard.

"Fuck, Laney, I'm not gonna last if you keep doing that."

"S'okay, let go, Dane," she goads in the sexiest growl I'll ever hear.

Just a few more strokes and I explode with a guttural roar. White sparks blink on the edges of my vision, but I dare not close my eyes, taking in every nuance of Laney's face, eyes, body. My orgasm draws out longer than any I've ever had and I keep thrusting slowly into her long after I'm finished, not ready to lose the connection with her quite yet.

Finally completely spent, I collapse astride her, caressing her hair and tucking my face into her neck. She smells of Laney, sweat and…me, best thing I've ever smelled in my life. "My bad, baby, I finished without you," I mumble.

Her body shakes against me with her sweet laugh. "I don't think I'm expected to, you know, um, during the first time. The pain kinda throws ya off. The warm up was stellar, though." She offers me a smile and kiss on my nose.

"We're not stopping next time until you come around me." I run my tongue along her lips. "At least twice."

Chapter 39

DIZZY

-Laney-

Hot, too hot. What? I groggily come to, overheated, odd for me since I'm always cold. Getting my bearings, the hot flash quickly becomes complete incineration. One very fine man is covering me, the heat of his body suddenly not a burden, kissing his way up my body.

"Looking to try out that morning breath theory of yours, huh?" I giggle, my voice rough with sleep.

Dane lifts his head and flashes me a dazzling smile. His sleepy eyes and messy bed-hair are irresistible and I feel my nipples tighten at the sight. He slides up me, placing kisses along my jaw, forehead and nose before finally greeting my lips softly. "Good morning, baby," he rumbles sexily.

"Good morning, yourself, did you sleep well?"

"Mmm hmm," he hums into my neck, where his tongue is toying with my sanity. "Never better."

I run my hands up his back, tracing the taut muscles

there, and shift my legs slightly so he can fall deeper into the cradle of me. I've never felt more comfortable in my own skin than I do right now, never more in sync with another person. No, never; not like I do with Dane. Being with Dane, I feel womanly, sexual, alive, and even rhythmic.

My reverie is broken by the sound of Dane's phone. He leans across me to grab it off the nightstand, laughing when he reads it.

"What's funny?" I ask.

"I forgot to tell Tate it was okay for them to come out. They're hungry and want to go in the kitchen." He types out a response and tosses the phone back down.

"You told them they couldn't come out?" I grin. "You're so bad. Thank God they at least had access to a bathroom. Speaking of which, I need to get up and shower." I push on his shoulder. "Get off me, you brute."

"Why the hurry?" He looks up at me with big eyes. "You're not leaving, are you?"

"Well, at some point today, yes. I have stuff to do before my trip home." I try to slide out from under him but he cages me in, both arms beside my head.

"Laney, are you running?" His brow crinkles and worry etches his face.

"No." I run my finger down his nose. "It's Christmas break. Of course I have to go see my dad for the holidays. Don't you have family stuff to do?"

He doesn't answer for far too long, letting his forehead fall against mine. Pain emanates from him and I brace myself for whatever it is he's working up the courage to tell me. I lightly stroke my hands through his hair, patiently waiting for him to open up to me. Finally.

"Tate's the only family I have, Laney."

No sudden gasp or line of questioning; I don't react, but

rather keep the same calming speed to my strokes of his hair. Placing kisses on his crown intermittently, I remain silent and mentally will him to continue.

"My parents aren't just never home, they're gone. Been almost three years," his voice wobbles and I wrap my arms around his neck, holding him to me.

"Go on," I whisper.

"My dad, our dad, loved to fly. He'd whisk my mom away for weekend trips, hell, sometimes even just lunch," he lightly chuckles, "all the time. One trip, they didn't come back. Mechanical failure, landing gear didn't even come down." His voice is somber now and a shudder runs through him. "So Tate's all I have now. And you." He lifts his head and looks at me hopefully. "I have you."

It's a statement, but question lurks in his eyes, laced with insecurity. "Yes, Dane, you have me." I smile weakly, still saddened to hear about his parents. Every time I asked where they were or if they'd be home, I'd been driving a dagger in his heart. I talk about my dad non-stop. I left Dane here alone on Thanksgiving. I've been an idiot and Bennett's words ring in my ears. "Dane," I cup his cheek with one hand, "I'm so sorry. I'm sorry about your parents, and I'm sorry I didn't know, or ask—"

"Laney, don't. Not your fault at all. I didn't exactly tell you the truth. I wanted to, so many times, especially knowing how you feel about your mom, but I just didn't. So I'm sorry, too."

"Don't even think about apologizing to me. You told me now, when it felt right, and that's all that matters." Wrapping myself around him once again, unable to not just hold him, love him, comfort him, I continue. "And Dane, your mom didn't leave you, she was taken. I'm sure she loved you very much. How could she not?"

"Let's just say I didn't know my mom as well as I thought I did, and maybe there are things you don't know about yours, too, Laney."

"What do you mean?" I lean back and look up at him.

He sits up and drags me on his lap, wrapping a sheet around me loosely. "My mom, not Tate's mom, was our father's second wife. When they died, I got everything. I have more money than I'll ever spend, Laney, and Tate got nothing." He looks down, as though ashamed, speaking again from that pose. "My mother couldn't accept Tate. He represented her husband's past life, the one before her. She was so jealous she took it out on Tate until he finally just quit visiting. I didn't know that's why he disappeared until he came for our father's funeral and I had to drag it out of him."

Running a slow hand down his face, he kisses my shoulder and leaves his lips there, his next words soft upon my skin. "I was sole beneficiary, to everything. So it would seem my mother talked our father into hurting him, too, even after death. I'm not sure why he even speaks to me, but I'll spend the rest of my life making it up to him."

"Look at me." I lift his head, cupping his face. "It's not your fault. You shouldn't feel guilty for their wrongs, Dane. All you can control is you, and you are a wonderful person."

He covers my hands with his own. "Tate won't take a dime; says he won't touch their hate money. So I just see to it that he benefits in clever ways." He almost smiles. "That's our secret though, baby, okay?" He raises his brow in question.

I nod and smile, his secrets are safe with me and my heart floods with admiration. Dane doesn't have a greedy bone in his body and knowing what he does to help his brother, well, it's just another reason I adore him. I'm still a little lost at how this all relates to my own mother, however.

And cue the slightly frightening Dane ESP. "So, sometimes you may think you know people, and things are actually worse. Whereas sometimes you may think the worst and don't know the real person at all." He quirks a brow at me.

What? "What?"

"Go take your shower, and brush your teeth." He laughs and kisses me. "Then I want to give you one of your Christmas presents."

The hot shower feels wonderful. I ache in the most intimate places, and think for a second about really milking out my discomfort to tease Dane. I decide to go easy on him, though, when I step out and see the casual set of pants and shelf-tank he's left on the counter for me. Silky and light pink, the new clothes glide over my body and I smile to myself, thinking about how good he is to me; but I damn near tear up when I see the two pain relievers and glass of OJ. This man—if I told people the things he does for me, they'd think I was making him up.

Steam billows out as I open the door and walk back into the bedroom, scrubbing a towel through my damp hair.

"Come here, baby," he says to me, sitting in the overstuffed chair in the corner.

"Thank you." I smile as I saunter to him, motioning to my new outfit.

"You're very welcome, beautiful. They look lovely."

I climb onto his lap and wait impatiently for...I don't know.

"Promise me you'll let me finish before you react, and that you will try to remember, no matter your initial instinct, that anything I ever do is because I love you. I want to take care of you, in every single way. I want to be the one you come to when you need or want something, when you're hurt, sad, scared...anything. Even if it's me that pisses you off, I want it to be me you scream at about it." He reaches behind the chair and pulls out a folder, not a present. "Promise me," he reiterates.

"You're scaring me," I whisper.

"Laney, you are my forever, and we can't move forward

until we clear up the past. I would never put you in a bad spot, I of course checked things out first, and feel sure this is something you need to know. I will help you every single step of the way, baby." He hands me the folder and moves his arms tightly around my waist.

I open it, hands trembling with the anticipation of the unknown. The first thing that catches my eye is a picture of my mother; I'd know her anywhere. I quickly slam the folder shut and jerk my eyes to Dane. "What is this?!"

"It's your mom, Laney. It's important that you know; I didn't just set out to find your mom, get in your business. It started as my desire to keep you safe and it led here," he grabs my hand and squeezes, his eyes full of doubt. "You told me about the stalker and it worried me, badly. You got flowers on your birthday—"

"Those were from Evan," I interrupt, agitation in my voice.

"You got another delivery, while you were out. I had Tate open the card, I admit it, and I didn't like the message. So," he lets out a shaky breath, "I did some digging. Sometimes money comes in handy, like when you're trying to track down a stalker. I only did it to keep you safe, Laney, I swear to you. I had only the best intentions."

I believe him, but I still feel somewhat violated. "You and Tate had no right to open the card," I huff.

"You're absolutely right, and for that you should probably be angry, but I'm not sorry I did."

No response jumps off my tongue, so I simply give him the "go on" big eyes.

"Your stalker is not a stalker at all." He pauses, taking both my hands in his and rubbing my wrists with his thumbs. "It's your mother. You told me the gifts and things popped up sporadically, yes?" I nod, the word mother still knocking around in my head. "I'm guessing at big moments for you; moments a mother would also think were a big deal."

Holidays, birthdays, prom, starting college…yes, contact was almost always on a milestone.

"She kept up with you, Laney. She's watched you grow up as much as possible, from afar."

Barely able to comprehend, I stand and begin to pace the room. So many questions and different emotions are flowing through me right now that I can't organize my thoughts. I concentrate on breathing in through my nose and out through my mouth and raise my hands behind my head.

"Laney, your mom, she's not evil, nor does she not love you, she's just not well. I'm not supposed to know this, but I had to find out, for you." He's moved to me now, hands bracing my shoulders. "She's schizophrenic, Laney."

"What? I mean, how?" I'm sputtering incoherently, more thinking out loud than actually asking a question.

"Your mom lives in a facility where they make sure she eats, bathes, and takes her medicine. Most days she doesn't comprehend reality, Laney. She left to protect you, to give you a normal life. But in moments of clarity, she always made sure you got something on your big moments." He pulls me into a hug, which for a moment offers comfort, but I quickly pull back, still reeling from so many conflicting emotions. "As far as I can tell, she has a cousin who visits her regularly and must have helped her with the execution. That, to me, says she loves you. When she's thinking clearly, she's thinking of you." He falls silent now and just watches me, his eyes following my path back and forth across the floor.

"Why would my dad not have told me this?" How can they just lock her up, or whatever, and not tell her family? She could have been dead for all we knew!" The dam I've built for years breaks all at once, and my body shakes with the sobs. Images of my mother, alone and afraid, tucked away in some padded room, replace all the ones I'd created to protect myself; her happy with a new family, just not wanting me.

"I'm sure your dad doesn't know. Like you, he assumes she just left. Like you, he's dealt with the pain all this time of thinking she didn't want him, either. Like I said, it took some doing for me to find her."

"I have to tell him," I say, maybe out loud, I'm not sure.

He moves behind me, wrapping his arms around me. "Baby, are you okay? Can I hold you?"

Part of me feels like I should be angry with him right now, but the feel of his arms around me washes that away this time. He's found my mom and solved the stalker mystery; he's given me back love and safety in one fell swoop. Dane takes care of me, in more ways than he sometimes even means to, and damn if that doesn't feel so right. It's that sense of having someone put you first that I choose to cling to instead of some passing anger. I'm not his cause and he's not saving me, so I don't have to feel like a bitter pity-case; he's pulling his weight as part of the team. That's what Dane and I are, equals, a team.

"You can always hold me," I murmur, turning into him and burying my tear-stained face in his chest. "Just don't open my cards anymore, nosy butt."

He swats my bottom and laughs. "I love you so much, Laney. I'm going to try my hardest not to scare you off with the intensity of it. I have a tendency to want and control everything around me, but I know if I go overboard, I'll suffocate who you are, and I wouldn't change who you are for anything in the world. So..." He hugs me tighter and leans down to brush his lips lightly against mine. "I'll work on it, I promise."

"Don't change too much," I mutter into his shirt, "I kinda like ya the way you are."

So much for getting anything done today; the sun is low in the sky when I wake up from the nap I'd fallen into. The phone call to my dad had been exhausting and highly emotional.

As Dane suspected, he really had no idea about my mother either, thinking all this time she had just left us. Obviously there'd been signs of a problem, like maybe depression, but to finally know the gravity of her condition floored us both, to say the least. I told my dad I wasn't ready to make any big decisions; there'd be no phone calls, letters or visits to see her in my immediate future. I need time to process, at my own speed, and he's very accepting of that, as had Dane.

"Whatever you want or need, Laney, that's what we'll do. If you want to go see her, we'll do that, whenever you want. I also did some looking, and found a specialist nearby that we, or you, can visit with and talk about what the diagnosis entails, if you'd like to do that. Anything that helps you, baby, I'll make it happen."

Thinking back on Dane's supportive words, knowing I can lean on him as much as I need to, my heart and mind feel lighter. I have to admit, there's also a new feeling inside me, one I have yet to come to terms with, but like, knowing my mother kept up with me, cared about me, all this time. If I choose, I can see her, talk to her...maybe even hug her.

Now that all that's settled, as much as it can be for the time being, I'm starving! I quickly freshen up just a bit and creep quietly down the stairs, unsure of where everyone in the house is right now. Skidding to a halt, I hear Bennett's laughter in the kitchen. Shit! She and Tate will know I slept here, and—

"Get in here, baby!" his voice carries around the corner.

How does he do that?

Great, now I have to try and walk in casually, like I haven't just been hiding around the corner. I hold up my head, throw my shoulders back, and glide in. Well, as close as I come to gliding. I needn't have worried; Dane's brilliant smile as I enter sets my soul at ease. I don't care what anyone else thinks; that man loves me. He holds out an arm and I walk into it, wrapping mine around his waist and snuggling into his chest.

"Hello, roomie." Bennett giggles.

I peek at her and give a finger wave as Tate chuckles beside her. "Tate!" I scurry around the island and wrap him in a hug. "You look great! How are you feeling?"

"I feel good, a little better every day," he answers with a smile.

We'd come so close to losing him, and looking at him now, knowing how much he means to Dane, it makes me shiver. I make my way back to the sanctuary of Dane's arms, silently laughing at myself. All of a sudden I am so touchy feely, and it feels so natural.

"So, what are you guys doing tonight?" Bennett asks.

Looking down at me, Dane waits for my answer. I flush a bit. "I want to sit in the hot tub," I whisper.

He turns his head so fast I'll be surprised if he doesn't feel it tomorrow. "We're going in the hot tub. You guys have a good night."

Tate smirks at his brother's polite dismissal as Dane pulls me toward the door.

This time in a bikini, I ease down into the hot water and let out a long moan.

"Are you sore?" Dane asks me sweetly, rubbing my shoulders as I lean back between his legs.

"If you mean what I think you mean, then yeah, kinda."

"I'm sorry, baby." He crooks his neck to kiss my cheek. "Thank you so much for enduring it. What you gave me," he sighs, "was amazing. There'll never be anything better, Laney, never."

A tingle runs through me and I lay my head back against him. We stay in a long, comfortable silence until the sound of his voice actually jars me from almost asleep.

"Are you okay...with everything?" He runs his hands up and down my arms, kissing my temple softly.

I turn my face to him and smile. "I actually am. It's a lot to take in, but having you, and my dad, I know I'll be fine. I just need some time to process."

He nods in understanding, giving me a gentle, comforting smile. "My strong girl, I love you."

I kiss his nose, leaving my lips there and sigh contently.

"Will you invite your dad here for Christmas?" he asks.

I look at him questioningly. Not go home for Christmas?

"He can stay here. I'll order in a big meal, anything you want." His brown eyes are pleading with me.

"Okay." The truth is I won't leave Dane alone for Christmas for anyone, not even my dad. Dane is now my first priority. It's crazy how a moment of instant clarity sneaks up on you and poof—you know exactly what you want. No doubts, no excuses, and no apologies.

"Okay?" His smile lights up his handsome features.

I giggle and nod eagerly. "We can't do, um, anything while he's here, though."

"Then he's not staying very long," he teases, sinking his teeth into my neck.

Chapter 41

GIFTED

-Laney-

Dane ordered in a wonderful, catered feast that we enjoyed with Dad, Tate, and Bennett. Everyone laughed, stuffed themselves, and had a wonderful holiday. After the meal, I forced Dane to play some holiday classics on the piano which Bennett was all too happy to sing. Dad loved his hunting trip present and he got me a new fishing pole, batting gloves, and some money. It was an ideal time and I couldn't have wished for anything better. The next afternoon, I walked my dad to his truck, nervously bouncing from one foot to the other. I'd never told my father a major lie in my life and had certainly never asked him to cover for me, but that mold had now been broken. I begged him to please pretend, if anyone happened to ask, that I was sick with the flu. He knew exactly who I meant by "anyone." I was now with Dane for good, and I just couldn't bear to break Evan's heart over the holidays, so my plan was to lay low. He'd agreed, but only when I promised to make things right as soon as possible. His hesitation had nothing to do with my choice in Dane, he seemed to really like him, but he thought the world of Evan and didn't support me dragging out any more pain than necessary.

I agree completely; hurting Evan couldn't be farther from my goal, but who rips someone's heart out over Christmas? Not to mention, I'm not going to tell him over the phone or via text, and if I try to go home to tell him, Dane will want to come…and I'm not "ganging up" on Evan. I'll tell him, alone, when it's right. Until then, I'm just gonna have to live with the self-attached title of Chicken-shit.

"You ready for bed, baby?" Dane sneaks up behind me and wraps his arms around my waist.

"Mmm hmmm," I answer, exhausted. It's been a long day and I can't think of anything in the world I want to do more than snuggle in with him. I shriek as he sweeps me up in his arms, carrying me up the stairs into his bedroom. He sets me down in the bed, gently pushing me back and tucking the covers under my chin before walking around and climbing into his side. His side. A sleepy smirk sneaks up on me when I think about the fact that I just labeled the sides of his bed.

His breathy, whispered words once he's tightened up against my back get my attention. "If you're tired, I understand. But if not, your Christmas present is under your pillow."

Well now he knew he had me at "present." My eyes pop open. "You got me a new outfit. And let's not forget you found my mother. I'd say you've met the present quota." I roll over and smile at him.

"So you don't need any more presents then? That's okay; I'll just give it to Bennett." He slinks a hand under the pillow to nab my present so I roll over, pulling him on top of me.

"Very funny, smarty-pants. You know I want that present so bad I can't see straight, but I wanted to make sure you also knew that you've already done too much."

"Baby, I could shower gifts on you every single day and never give you enough. You're my world and I love making you happy." He starts kissing my neck slowly, softly, and I forget what I was going to say. "So you'll take your present, right?"

"Of course I will, but you already knew that, you big tease." I poke him in the ribs. He rolls onto his back, taking me with him so I now sit on top of him, straddling his hips. He reaches under my pillow and does pull out the gift this time, handing it to me. Gripping my hips, his eyes glaze as he licks his bottom lip. "Open it right here, where I can stare up at you."

Fumbling, I unwrap it and gasp, my hand flying to my mouth. I shake my head and giggle. "You got us tickets to Hawaii?"

He nods and leans up to lift my shirt slightly, placing a kiss on my stomach. "Two weeks, me and you, in Kauai."

"But when? I mean, I have school soon. And you, don't you have work?"

His lips never leave my body, kissing and nipping my belly, waking up every butterfly, so his words are said into my enflamed skin. "Look at the dates on the tickets, baby. We're going during Spring Break."

Sure enough, the tickets are dated for exactly when I have almost two full weeks off. My heart beats faster and delight coats my face. He'd booked these tickets when? Before I officially chose him? I'll bet he did; a giant leap of faith in "us." He was sure we'd be together months from now. Not that he'll top Disney World, he simply never will, but he upped the stakes. He sees us as a "we," and planned this trip, his future, on that. Knowing he really is as invested in me as I plan to be in him mentally excites me, the message soon reaching the rest of my body. I toss the tickets to the side and collapse on top of him, thanking him properly.

The next morning I wake with a stretch, frowning when I realize I'm alone. A quick scan confirms Dane isn't in the bedroom or bathroom, and while I'm anxious to go find him, I also realize it's the perfect time to reach out to Evan. Dane doesn't give me much alone time and I know Evan's wondering why I'm not home for break, so I need to say something to him.

I find my phone on top of Dane's dresser and turn it on to madly scroll through all the text messages from Evan. Yup— he wants to know where I am. It takes about five attempts at a message, deleting and starting again, before I've got one my conscience can live with and I hit send.

Laney: Merry Christmas Ev! My dad came here for Xmas & that kept me busy. Now I'm sick so just gonna stay here, but I'll call you soon. Need 2 catch up on things. Hug your parents for me and have a gr8 break!

That's all I can say right now and I just hope it placates him enough where he can enjoy his time at home until I figure out a way to talk to him face to face. Who knows, maybe he's met someone, too? Surprisingly, that thought doesn't make me sick, but rather makes me smile. I do so want Evan to be happy, loved, and cherished. He's worthy of a woman looking at him the way I now look at Dane.

Dane! I flick my phone off and shove it under my pillow, and after a half-assed attempt at straightening my clothes and hair, I scamper down the stairs to search him out. My body already tingles at the thought of finding him.

"Well hello, sleepyhead." Bennett beams at me from her perch at the kitchen counter.

"Hey, B, where're the boys?"

"I don't know, some Top Secret mission, said they'd be back in an hour. I made it very clear Tate can't handle any more activity than that." She snaps her fingers. "Oh, and Dane said to tell you, and I quote, 'you looked like Heaven so I didn't want to wake you, but I'll be back soon and I love you.' So sweet, Laney, you're so lucky."

"That I am." I blush. "I'm gonna jump in the shower then. What are you gonna do?"

"I think I'll enjoy the hot tub," she teases, "since it's actually free."

312

I head upstairs with a chuckle. She's right—I do love that hot tub.

Chapter 41

CARETAKER

-Evan-

Poor Laney, sick on break. My truck can't make it to her fast enough. I'd decided to surprise her and just show up with some soup, Kleenex, medicine, and a huge stack of movies. I hate that she isn't feeling well, but my skin still tingles in anticipation of seeing her. My arms ache to wrap around her, hold her, fuse her to me. And her Christmas present? My hands shake at the thought of watching her open it.

I might as well have been driving backwards as long as it took to get here, but my frustration lifts with every step I take towards Laney's dorm. My girl is inside there, sick and needing me. I try the door, but it's locked. Growling, I glance around, my eyes desperately seeking out someone to let me in. I could call her to come down and let me in, but then she'd have to get out of bed in her bad health, let alone ruin the surprise, so I opt to mill around and pray someone will come by soon.

Thankfully, I only have to wait about ten minutes when I see him approaching. I know this guy; he was at the club and the hospital the night I was there with Laney. I remember their interactions, he's her good friend.

"Hey, man." I stick out my hand as he approaches.

"Hey, um, Evan, right?" he asks, returning my handshake.

"Yeah, and you're—"

"Sawyer Beckett."

"That's right, good to see ya. Laney's sick, so I came to surprise her, and take care of her. You mind letting me in?"

His expression is confused. He quickly recovers, but I didn't miss it. "Um…" He looks at the ground, feet shuffling. I stay silent, waiting impatiently for what he'll say next. The instinctual ache in my chest tells me I'm not going to like it. "Laney's not here, man."

Is that it? I blow out in relief. So she ran to the store, or…doctor? Now I'm worried again. "Well, where is she? She's sick, where could she be?"

Sawyer rubs the back of his neck nervously, his eyes bouncing everywhere but in my direction.

"Please tell me, man. I came a long way and I'm worried about her. Help a guy out," I implore him.

"Sit down." He motions to a bench just behind us, which I reluctantly move to and sit on. My leg is bouncing up and down while I wait for him to continue. "I think the world of Laney, she's the coolest fucking girl ever, and I don't make a habit of being friends with chicks. So I'm not looking to betray her or get up in her business exactly."

I suppress my growl and don't move to wring his neck. I'm not a fool, this guy is freaking huge, but I'm about to lose it. "Just spit it out!" I bark before easing my voice back, not wanting an ass-beating. "Sorry, I mean, what can you tell me?"

"Well," he says, scrubbing his chin, "why don't you tell me about you and Laney first? Like, y'all together or what?"

What? Why are we sitting here, virtual strangers, discussing my love life when all I want to do is make my precious girl some damn soup! "What? What kind of question is that?"

"I know you this much," he indicates a small space between his finger and thumb, "and I adore Laney and my friends. So before I get balls deep in the bullshit, I want a little info. That too much to ask?" He raises his brows, no sign of compromise evident.

"Fine," I sigh, "Laney and I have been best friends since…" I'm too distraught to do the math. "Well, since ever. Our senior year, I finally told her how I felt and got her to date me." I smile at the thought. "But a second later, we had to leave for different schools."

"That sucks," he mutters.

"Yeah, to say the least." I laugh at his simple, yet accurate, summation. "So we broke up. Easier that way, or so Laney thought." I shrug. "Anyway, things have pretty much sucked ass since then, and here I am."

"Shit, man." He leans over and runs his hands up and down his thighs. "Okay. You're a good guy. I know this because Laney cares about you and has nothing but good things to say about you. So I'm gonna help you, and her, once and for all." He stares at me, a deadly force in his eyes. "But know this. Keep your cool no matter what. You raise a hand to any friend of mine and I won't hesitate to take your ass out. Capisce?"

I nod, to what I have no idea, really, but he's my key to Laney. "Capisce."

"Come on." He stands and motions to the parking lot. "I'll drive."

Fifteen minutes into the most awkward silence and eerie car ride I've ever endured, Sawyer opens his phone. "Gotta make this call. Nothing personal," he shrugs, "loyalties and all."

WTF did he just say? I nod, completely lost, much like I've been doing since I ran into him.

"Hey, man, it's Saw. Yeah, you too." He's listening to the person on the other end now. "Listen, about that…I'm on my way to your house right now. What? Oh yeah," he laughs, "over that, dude. Saw my folks, got in, got out. Huh? Nah, she's cool, but not gonna make the cut." He laughs again, then glances over to me and quickly back to the road. "I'm gonna be at your house in less than 20, so shut the hell up and listen to me. Found Evan at the dorm when I got back and he convinced me to take him to Laney, so we're on our way."

There's a long pause on his end of the conversation. His voice when he speaks again has an angry edge. "Fuck that, man, you know better. Last goddamn thing I want is to be involved, but somebody needs to man up or something, cause this is bullshit. Everyone involved is better than this." Silence again, but I can hear a heated male voice coming through his phone. "Yeah, yeah, yeah…see ya in a bit." He closes his phone and tosses it on the dashboard.

There's tension leering in my body and this whole thing is too weird, so I speak up. "Is Laney okay? She's not," I gulp, "in danger or anything, is she?"

"Fuck no." He looks over at me, his face relaxing. "Seriously, man, she's fine. I wouldn't let anybody hurt Laney. But I don't envy you."

My hackles go up instantly. "What does that mean?" I ground out.

"It means," he starts, thinking about his next words carefully, "you wanted to see Laney, I'm taking you to Laney. Ain't never been in love, thank fuck, but I can't just do nothing. I'm just not made up like that. You do love her, right?"

"More than anything," my mouth answers on its own.

"Thought so." He sighs, drumming his fingers on the steering wheel. "We're headed to Dane's house. She's there."

My stomach rolls over and I wipe my hands down my face, hoping to squash the nausea. "Why?" I manage to ask.

Sawyer turns and gives me a dumbfounded look. "Why you think? You been away from her what, five, six months? She went on, Evan. She's fucking hot." He chuckles. "Sorry, man. But hell, she is, and cool, and real. Dane noticed. We all noticed, but those two clicked."

Clicked? Laney doesn't "click" with other guys. Laney doesn't care about guys and their pathetic come-ons. Right?

My breathing is erratic at best. I quickly roll down my window, needing some fresh air, stat. We don't speak again and soon pull up in the driveway of a mansion. Fucker.

Palms sweaty, I take two swipes before getting the door open. My steps to the door feel like they're taken with cinder blocks for shoes and despite spastic swallowing, my mouth is ashy. Sawyer reaches out to ring the doorbell as I shove my hands deep in my pockets, not wanting anyone to see them shake. The girl I recognize as Laney's roommate answers the door, her eyes widening when she realizes who I am.

"H-Hey, Sawyer...Evan?" she stutters.

"Hey, Ben, go get Laney, would ya?" Thank God Sawyer's able to speak, cause I sure as hell can't.

Despite my head, my heart bounces and my breath catches as she comes around the corner. My princess, long blonde hair damp, beautiful body clad in silky pj pants and a tank top, walks towards me with surprise in her eyes. She chews her bottom lip and looks to Sawyer first. "Thought you went to your parents' house?"

"Cut it short; Kirby got on my nerves." He shrugs and opens his arms for her hug, but she doesn't give it.

"I didn't realize you were coming." Her eyes narrow at him.

"I told Dane," he says firmly.

She nods at him before closing her eyes and sucking in a deep breath. When she opens them, she meets my gaze dead on.

"Hey, Evan," she whispers.

"Hey." I clear my throat loudly. "Surprise."

She smiles, but it falls instantly. "Evan, I—" She shudders and stops, Dane moving in behind her, wrapping his arm possessively around her waist.

My eyes move to where their bodies connect, searing, before I look back at her. The chocolate brown symbols of my existence are filled with tears, begging to spill. They tell me everything I need to know, answering every question I can't ask out loud. I shake my head, dismissing the flashing image of my happily ever after nose-diving and bursting in flames. She isn't sick. She's with Dane. With Dane. I lost. I left, and I lost.

I feel like I'm being gutted with a dull knife. I did a lot of things wrong, things I'm ashamed of, but I never gave my heart to another. My heart always waited for her and I took for granted that hers would do the same. With the last shred of strength and dignity I have left, I rip the shiny envelope from my back pocket. "Merry Christmas, princess," I muster, shoving it into her hand.

In it, my transfer slip. I walked away from UGA and a full scholarship to sit the bench for a year of ineligibility at Southern…to be with her. I can't change it now. I've been released; I'm as good as at Southern. When she opens it, will she come back to me? If she does, will it be for the right reasons? Would I ever know for sure?

"Evan, I—" her voice calls and then fades.

I don't turn back to look. I'll never know if she tried to come after me, Dane pulling her back, or if she just let me keep walking. I don't know if she's crying or sighing in relief.

Sawyer falls into step beside me and throws his arm over my shoulder. "You a drinker?"

"Not really," I mumble.

"Wanna be?"

"Fuck yes."

"Thought so," he chuckles, banging his hand on the hood. "Get in, bro, I'll find ya a cure."

I doubt it.

Look for Book Two, Evan's story, coming Fall 2013!

Here's a sneak peek!

Chapter 1

-Evan-

My phone is burning a hole in my pocket. Ninety percent of me wants to respond to Laney's text she'd sent about an hour ago, but the other ten percent, the shred that still has some dignity, is winning. I am definitely not qualified to write the manual on Plan B, Plan A being plunge head over ass into a year of ineligibility for said girl who is now with another, having blown up in my face. As much as I want an exact explanation, I simply can't bear to hear it right now.

Sawyer's a godsend, shoving beers in my hand and attracting every lady in the bar over to our table. He's doing a better job than anyone else could at distracting me, including the brunette currently perched on my right leg...Manda? Mandy? She's hot, with long, dark hair, full lips and huge tits that she's not afraid to let play peek-a-boo. She even smells decent and her hands know no boundaries, but all I can think about is the one who got away; a beautiful blonde with a quick wit, smart mouth and devastating smile.

"Dude, you need another one?" Sawyer's question drags me from my mental misery, and I'm almost sure he's asking about another beer, not another girl.

"Sure," I respond, with no feeling whatsoever. It's sadly the correct answer no matter what he was asking.

"Want me to get it, sugar?" M-whatever asks, with a syrup to her voice I just noticed and don't like.

"Two, Amy," Sawyer directs her and hands her some money.

Amy? Shit, I wasn't even close. Good thing I hadn't spoken to her even once.

"She's hot, bro." Sawyer raises his brows and motions to Amy with his head, to which I shrug noncommittally. "What is it, you need a blonde? I figured that'd be too much, but I can—"

I hold up a hand, cutting him off. "I appreciate it, man, I do," I stop and take a swig of beer, "but a parade of girls to choose from isn't gonna help me tonight. I just need to crash, wake up to a new day. You think you can take me to my truck?"

"Nah, but you can bunk with me." He throws some bills on the table and stands. "Let's go."

Connect with S.E. Hall
and discover more about Laney, Dane, and Evan!

Explore More About the Evolve Series!

Twitter: @emergeauthor
Goodreads: http://bit.ly/19xitqD

Facebook:
https://www.facebook.com/S.E.HallAuthorEmerge
Dane Facebook: https://www.facebook.com/DanefromEmerge
Evan Facebook: https://www.facebook.com/pages/Evan-Mitchell-Allen/409174755862025?directed_target_id=0
Sawyer Facebook: https://www.facebook.com/pages/Sawyer-Beckett/227467650737311

Book Trailer:
Emerge book trailer, by Lisa at Pixel Pixie:
http://www.youtube.com/watch?v=aZhNPJW_FE4

Playlists:
Emerge playlist: http://www.pinterest.com/emergeauthor/emerge-playlist/ Embrace playlist:
http://www.pinterest.com/emergeauthor/embrace-playlist/ Entangled playlist: http://www.pinterest.com/emergeauthor/entangled-playlist/

Other works by S.E. Hall—
Emerge on Amazon: http://amzn.to/18nKceN
Embrace on Amazon: http://www.amazon.com/Embrace-Evolve-Series-S-E- Hall-ebook/dp/B00FGFY86G/ref=sr_1_1?ie=UTF8&qid=1383446073&sr=8- 1&keywords=SE+Hall

Acknowledgements

To my wonderful husband who brings me snacks while I'm typing away, cleans around me, surprises me with cool pens and notebooks and makes it possible for me to be exactly who I am—I adore you Jeff. You are my better three-fourths and I am lucky you continue to pick me.

To those two fabulous little girls wandering around calling me Mom—you guys are just the best! Thank you for seeking me out and demanding my attention, always remembering to kiss me goodnight. You guys are the greatest thing I've ever done and gotten exactly right! I hope in all my distracted absence lately that I've at least shown you to go for what you want...go for it full force and be grateful for those still waiting around for you when you reach the end.

To my CP, Angela—anyone who doesn't believe in kindred spirits has yet to find their CP! This book wouldn't be what it is, or even finished, without you. Thank you so much for all the calls, jam sessions, ideas and brutally honest feedback. Can't wait to work our next books together!

All my friends and family, which I dare not name individually in fear of forgetting someone—thank you all so much! So many of you read version after version, ran over and let me read to you, made me copies, gave me pep talks, bought me "writer goodie packs" and accepted me for the bitchy author in the corner with the far off look in her eyes, not really paying attention to a word you're saying.

Last but not least, thank you to my Lue for the inspiration. Since the minute you took a breath, you saved me and I have been in awe of you ever since. Your beauty, laugh, wit and ability to light up a room never leave me short of amazed. I am so damn proud to be your mom and have to admit; I'd kill to go back and be young again, as you. World wrapped around your little finger— that's what you have. I never doubt you'll always bounce back; vibrant, playful and charming...lovely and loved.

Emerge Playlist

"Big Green Tractor"—Jason Aldean
"Amazed"—Lonestar
"Ho Hey"—The Lumineers
"End of All Time"—Stars of Track & Field
"The Cave"—Mumford and Sons
"I'll Be"—Edwin McCain "9 Crimes"—Damien Rice
"Let's Get Ready To Rumble"—Jock Jams
"This Year's Love"—David Gray
"Hero"—Enrique Iglesias
"Flightless Bird"—Iron & Wine
"Collide"—Howie Day
"Talking To The Moon"—Bruno Mars

While you're waiting for Evan's story, be sure to check out

Inevitable
by Angela Graham

After experiencing a humiliating breakup, twenty-two-year-old Cassandra Clarke is fresh out of college and living a simple solitary life without any intentions of pursuing love anytime soon.

When the estate next door sells, the last thing Cassandra expects is the unnerving attraction she feels for her sinfully handsome neighbor, Logan West, the young and charming single father with a playboy reputation.

It's through Oliver, Logan's four-year-old son, who keeps popping up in her childhood tree house, that she slowly begins to catch glimpses of the compassionate and wounded man Logan has hidden beneath his strong exterior.

Cassandra knows it's wrong and that she's heading for another heartbreak.

Logan will never be able to give her what she wants...love